W9-CIL-396

Dear Reader,

Spending the past year living with proper British headmistress Lady Emma Wells-Finch and Texas golf pro Kenny Traveler has been an adventure. Please believe me when I tell you that—each morning as I sat down to write—I *never* knew what these two would be up to! All I could do was hang on for the ride. I found Emma and Kenny funny, vulnerable, and completely maddening!

Many of you will notice the reappearance of Dallie Beaudine and Francesca Day Beaudine from my 1989 novel *Fancy Pants*. Getting reacquainted with these old lovers was a special joy, even though Dallie and Francesca make Kenny and Lady Emma's lives so much more difficult!

I hope these characters who've become so dear to me bring you pleasure. Happy reading!

Susan Elizabeth Phillips

SUSAN ELIZABETH PHILLIPS

Lady Be Good

AVON BOOKS ◆ NEW YORK

To Carrie Feron, my guardian angel

This is a work of fiction. Names, characters, places, and incidents either are the product of the author's imagination or are used fictitiously. Any resemblance to actual events, locales, organizations, or persons, living or dead, is entirely coincidental and beyond the intent of either the author or the publisher.

AVON BOOKS, INC.
1350 Avenue of the Americas
New York, New York 10019

Copyright © 1999 by Susan Elizabeth Phillips
Back jacket author photo by Sigrid Estrada
Published by arrangement with the author
Visit our website at **http://www.AvonBooks.com**
ISBN: 0-7394-0031-2

Printed in the U.S.A.

Acknowledgments

The community of those of us who write women's fiction and romance is a tightly knit one. We support each other as well as our dynamic industry. As testimony, here are the special writers who helped guide me through this book and to whom I owe my gratitude.

Jill Barnett, always there for me. Stella Cameron, my prime consultant on "Brit speak." Kristin Hannah, the best "title brainstormer" in the business. Jayne Ann Krentz, simply put—a goddess. Jill Marie Landis, who attended a very special race with me and said, "You have to write about this." Cathie Linz and Lindsay Longford, my frequent touching stones and stimulating companions on "Dinner Nights Out." Elizabeth Lowell, who is—I swear—a living encyclopedia. Meryl Sawyer, always generous and supportive to both me and our entire genre. Thank you all!

In addition, I continue to be proud to be part of the great romance tradition at Avon Books. Special thanks to Carrie Feron and everyone else at this wonderful publishing house who get my books on the shelves.

Once again, my husband, Bill, has served as my literary golf consultant and personal golf coach. He succeeds admirably at one of those jobs.

Thanks to Steve Axelrod, and to my readers who write me such lovely letters. My special gratitude to all the booksellers who've called my novels to the attention of their customers. Your personal touch is deeply appreciated.

Susan Elizabeth Phillips
c/o Avon Books, Inc.
1350 Avenue of the Americas
New York, New York 10019

Chapter 1

Kenny Traveler was lazy. That explained why he'd fallen asleep in TWA's Ambassador Club at Dallas–Fort Worth Airport instead of promptly meeting British Airways Flight 2193 at the gate. Pure laziness, plus the fact that he didn't want to meet Flight 2193.

Unfortunately, the entrance of a noisy pair of businessmen awakened him. He took his time stretching, then yawned for a while. A nice-looking woman in a short gray suit smiled at him, and he smiled back. He glanced at his watch and saw he was half an hour late. He yawned again. Stretched.

"Excuse me," the woman said. "I'm sorry to bother you, but . . . you look so familiar. Aren't you—"

"Yes, ma'am, I am." He tilted his Stetson and gave her a grin that still had a little yawn clinging to the edges. "And I'm flattered you recognize me outside the rodeo ring. Most people don't."

She looked confused. "Rodeo? I'm sorry. I thought you were . . . You look so much like Kenny Traveler, the pro golfer."

"Golfer? Me? Oh, no, ma'am. I'm way too young to play an old man's game like golf. I like real sports."

"But—"

"Rodeo. Now that's a real sport. Football, too, and basketball." He slowly unfolded all six feet two inches of himself from the chair. "When it comes to tennis, though, that's when things start getting iffy. And golf isn't something a real man wants to get too close to."

The gray suit hadn't been born yesterday, and she smiled. "Still, I seem to remember watching you win the AT&T and the Buick Invitational on TV this winter. I swear I thought Tiger was going to break into tears during that last round at Torrey Pines." Her smile faded. "I still can't believe that Commissioner Beau—"

"I'd appreciate it, ma'am, if you didn't speak the name of the Antichrist in front of me."

"Sorry. How long do you think your suspension'll last?"

Kenny glanced down at his gold Rolex. "I guess that might depend on how long it takes me to get to British Airways?"

"Pardon?"

"Real nice talkin' to you, ma'am." He tipped his Stetson and ambled from the lounge.

One of his unhappy ex-girlfriends had pointed out that Kenny's *amble* was really the closest thing he had to a full-out run. But Kenny'd never seen much point in wasting energy anyplace but on the golf course. He liked to take things slow and easy, although lately that had been tough.

He ambled past the newsstand, refusing to look at the newspapers that were carrying the story of his recent suspension by acting PGA Commissioner Dallas Fremont Beaudine, a suspension that was taking place in the middle of the hottest winning streak in the history of professional golf and was going to keep him from playing in the Masters less than two weeks away.

"Hey, Kenny."

He nodded toward a businessman who had that overeager expression people frequently wore when they spotted his semi-famous face. He could tell the man was from the north because he said his name allproper instead of pronouncing it "Kinny" like God's people did.

He kicked up his amble half a notch just in case the businessman took it in his head to relive Kenny's triumphant final round at Bay Hill last month. A big-haired, tight-jeaned woman gave him the twice-over, but she didn't look like a PGA fan, so Kenny figured it was his good looks had attracted her.

A former girlfriend had said that, if Hollywood ever made a movie of Kenny's life, the only star pretty enough to play him on the screen was Pierce Brosnan. That had sent Kenny right through the roof. Not because she'd called him pretty, which he could sort of understand, but her casting choice. He'd told her right then that the only way he'd ever let Pierce Brosnan play him was if they rumpled Pierce up first, got rid of that prissy foreign accent, then fed him enough chicken-fried steak so he didn't look like the first storm out of West Texas would blow him over. But most of all, they'd have to teach old Pierce exactly how God intended for a man to swing a golf club.

All the walking was making him tired.

He stopped to rest at a cart selling nuts and candy, bought himself some Jelly Bellys, flirted just enough with the Mexican cutie working there to convince her to pull out the banana-flavored ones. Although he liked his Jelly Bellys mixed up, he didn't like the banana, but, since it took too much effort to pull them out himself, he generally tried to talk someone else into doing it. If that didn't work, he just ate 'em.

The British Airways gate was deserted, so he leaned against one of the support columns, pulled a handful of Jelly Bellys from the bag, and tilted them into his mouth while he thought about things, mainly how much he wanted to wring the neck of a certain Francesca Serritella Day Beaudine, celebrity wife of the Antichrist acting PGA commissioner, and a woman who was supposed to be his friend.

"Just do this one small favor for me, Kenny," she'd said. "If you'll take care of Emma for the next two weeks, I guarantee I'll talk Dallie into cutting the length of your suspension. You'll miss the Masters, but—"

"Now, how are you gonna do that?" he'd inquired.

"Never question my methods when it comes to dealing with my husband."

He didn't. Everybody knew that Francesa didn't have to do much more than look at Dallie Beaudine to melt him down, even though they'd been married for twelve years.

A high-pitched child's squeal, followed by a cheerful British voice, distracted him.

"Do let go of your sister's hair, Reggie, or I shall be quite cross with you. And there's no need to carry on so, Penny. If you hadn't licked him, he wouldn't have hit you."

He turned around, then grinned as he saw a woman barreling around the corner with two young children in tow. The first thing he noticed was her hat, a perky little straw number with a turned-up brim and a cluster of cherries bobbing at the center. She wore a gauzy green skirt printed with roses and a loose-fitting rose-colored top that matched a pair of trim little flats.

In one hand she clutched a young boy, along with a purse the size of Montana. In the other hand, she held a mean-faced little girl, an umbrella that was printed with more flowers, and a raspberry-red tote bag bulging with newspapers, books, and another colorful umbrella. Her light brown hair curled this way and that from beneath the brim of her hat, and whatever makeup she'd started out the day with had long ago worn off.

Which was probably a good thing, Kenny decided, because even without lipstick, she had about the sexiest mouth he'd ever seen. It was wide, with a plump bottom lip, and a top lip that held a distinct bow at the center. Despite her frivolous clothing, her jaw was firm. But her cheeks were baby doll round, the bones fine. Her nose was a little narrow, but not narrow enough to make him lose interest, because she also had an amazing pair of thick-lashed golden brown eyes.

He mentally redressed her in a tight top, short skirt, and a pair of stiletto heels, then added black fishnet stockings for good measure. He'd never paid for sex in his life, but he decided he'd be more than happy to throw a little extra cash her way if she ever decided she needed to earn something on the side to pay for her kids' orthodontics work.

To his surprise, she looked over at him. "Mr. Traveler?"

Fantasy was one thing, reality another, and as he gazed from her to the noisy kids, he got a sinking sensation in his stomach. The fact that she seemed to be expecting him indicated this could only be Lady Emma Wells-Finch, the woman Kenny had agreed to baby-sit for the next two weeks. But Francesca hadn't mentioned anything about kids.

He realized too late that he'd automatically nodded in response to her question instead of heading right out of DFW and straight for his Caddy. Except he couldn't do that because, more than anything, he needed to get back on the tour.

"Splendid!" She beamed. At the same time, she charged forward, skirts whirling, dragging the children and umbrellas, while her newspapers and magazines waved in the breeze and her butterscotch hair flew.

Just looking at her made him tired.

She let go of the little girl, grabbed Kenny's hand, and began to pump it. For a small woman, she had a lot of pump. "Delighted to meet you, Mr. Traveler." The cherries bobbed on her perky straw hat. "Emma Wells-Finch."

The little boy drew back his sneaker and, before Kenny could move, kicked him hard in the shin. "I don't like you!"

Kenny glared at the kid, thought about smacking him, then considered smacking Francesca instead, right after he gave her his opinion of low-down blackmailers.

Lady Emma turned to the kid, but instead of whalin' him like he deserved, she frowned. "Reggie, dear, take your finger out of your nose. It's most unattractive, isn't it? And apologize to Mr. Traveler."

The kid wiped his finger on Kenny's jeans.

Kenny was just getting ready to slam-dunk the little brat when a harried-looking woman came rushing up. "Thank you, Emma dear, for watching them for me. Reggie, Penelope, were you good for Miss Wells-Finch?"

"Perfect angels," Lady Emma replied, her tone so sincere that Kenny choked on the sour apple Jelly Belly that had been lurking in the corner of his mouth.

Lady Emma ended up pounding him on the back. Unfortunately, she pounded like she pumped hands, and he swore to God he felt a rib crack. When he got his breath back, the Children of the Damned had disappeared, along with their mother.

"Well . . ." Lady Emma smiled at him. "Here we are."

Kenny felt dizzy. Part of it might have been his busted rib, but most of it was trying to get his mind to make the connection between all that upper crust British cheer and a face that should have a streetlight shining down on it.

While Kenny was recovering, Emma made an assessment of her own. As the headmistress of St. Gertrude's School for Girls for the past two years, in addition to having been a teacher there, as well as a St. Gert's student from the time she was six, she had grown accustomed to sizing people up quickly. It only took her a moment to conclude that this All-American cowboy was exactly what she needed—a man with more good looks than character.

Crisp black hair curled from beneath the brim of a biscuit-colored Stetson that looked so at home on his head it might have been permanently attached. His navy T-shirt, printed with a Cadillac logo, displayed a more than respectable chest, and faded jeans molded to narrow hips and legs that were both lean and muscular. She noted the hand-tooled cowboy boots. They were nicely broken in, but she wasn't surprised to see that they didn't seem to have come close to a load of manure. He had a thin blade of a nose, strong cheekbones, a well-formed mouth, and straight white teeth. And his eyes. The color of wild hyacinths and marsh violets. Outrageous for a man to have eyes like that.

Her cursory inspection also told her everything she needed to know about his character. She saw indolence in his slouching posture, arrogance in the angle of his head, and the flicker of something unmistakably carnal in those half-lidded marsh violet eyes.

She repressed a small shiver. "Let's be off, then, Mr. Traveler. You're a bit late, aren't you? I do hope no one has taken my luggage." She extended her carry-all for him to take, but she hit his chest instead. The *Times* fell out, along with the new biography of Sam Houston she'd been reading, and one of the chocolate bars her hips didn't need, but which she enjoyed nonetheless.

She bent to pick everything up just as he took a step forward. Her straw brim bumped his knee, and her hat flew off to join the pile on the floor.

She set it back over her unruly curls. "Sorry." She wasn't normally clumsy, but she'd been so distracted by her troubles lately that her best friend, Penelope Briggs, told her she was in imminent danger of turning into one of those "dotty, dear things" so beloved by British mystery writers.

The idea of becoming a "dotty, dear thing" when she was barely thirty depressed her unbearably, so she didn't let herself think about it. Besides, if everything went according to plan, that worry would disappear.

He didn't help collect her possessions, nor did he offer to take her carry-all when she was done, but how much initiative could one expect from a man who had been born so physically blessed?

"Let's be off, then." She pointed the proper direction with her rolled umbrella.

She had nearly reached the end of the gate area before she realized he wasn't following her. She turned to see what was wrong.

He was staring at her extended brolly. It was a perfectly ordinary brolly, and she couldn't imagine why he seemed so mesmerized by it. Maybe he was more slow-witted than she'd originally thought.

"You . . . uh . . . always point the direction like that?" he asked.

She glanced down at her floral brolly and wondered what on earth he was talking about. "We need to go to luggage claim," she explained patiently, jiggling the handle just a bit for emphasis.

"I know that."

"Well, then?"

He developed a slightly dazed look. "Never mind."

Once he began to move, she set off. Her gauzy skirt swirled around her legs, and a lock of hair blew across her cheek. She probably should have taken a few minutes to tidy up a bit before she'd got off the plane, but she'd been so busy entertaining the children who were seated across from her that she hadn't thought of it.

"Mr. Traveler, it occurs to me . . ." She realized she was talking to herself.

She stopped, looked back, and spotted him gazing into the window of a souvenir shop. She stood patiently tapping her foot while she waited for him to join her.

He continued to stare into the window.

With a sigh, she marched back to join him. "Is something wrong?"

"Wrong?"

"We need to get my luggage."

He looked up. "I was thinking I might like a new key chain."

"You wish to buy one *now*?"

"Maybe."

She waited.

He sidled six inches to the left to get a better view.

"Mr. Traveler, I really think we should carry on."

"See, I've got this Gucci key chain a friend of mine gave me a couple years ago. But I don't much like things with other people's initials on them."

"You received this key chain a few *years* ago?"

"Yes, ma'am."

She remembered a sermon she'd once heard about the way God sometimes compensated human beings who were born handicapped in one area by richly endowing them in another. Someone who was born with exceptional good looks, for example, might be dull-witted. A pang of compassion struck her, along with a sense of relief. His denseness would make the next two weeks so much easier. "Very well. I'll wait."

He continued to study the display.

Her arms were beginning to ache from the combined weight of her carry-ons. She finally extended her carry-all. "Would you mind taking this for me?"

He regarded it doubtfully. "It looks heavy."

"Yes. It is."

He nodded vaguely, then returned his attention to the window.

She switched the carry-all to her other arm. Finally, she couldn't stand it any longer. "Would you like some help?"

"Oh, I can pay for it myself."

"That's not what I meant. Would you like some help making your selection?"

"Now, see, that's what got me into trouble in the first place. I let somebody else choose my key chain."

Her shoulders had begun to scream in protest. "Mr. Traveler, we really have to be going now, don't we? Perhaps you could do this some other time?"

"I s'pose I could, but the selection might not be as good."

Her patience frayed. "Very well, then! Get the one with the cowboy on it."

"Yeah? You like that one?"

She forced her jaw to unclench. "I *adore* it."

"The cowboy it is." Looking pleased, he walked into the shop, paused on the way to admire a display of tea towels, then took forever to chat with the attractive young woman behind the counter. Finally, he emerged with a small package, which he immediately deposited in her cramped fingers. "Here you go."

"What's this?"

He looked exasperated. "The key chain. You said you liked the cowboy."

"The key chain was for you!"

"Now, why would I want a key chain with a cowboy on it when I've got a perfectly good Gucci in my pocket?"

He took off down the corridor, and she could have sworn she heard him whistling "Hail Britannia."

Twenty minutes later, they were standing in the parking garage while Emma stared at his car in dismay. It was a large American luxury automobile, a late-model champagne-colored Cadillac Eldorado. "I can't possibly afford this."

He unlocked the trunk with a flick of his wrist. "Beg pardon?"

Emma did an excellent job managing St. Gert's finances, but a poor one managing her own. Since the old buildings were expensive to maintain, there was never enough money, and when the school desperately needed a new copying machine or piece of laboratory equipment, Emma had developed the habit of dipping into her own pockets. As a result, she was operating on a tight budget.

She couldn't quite hide her embarrassment. "I'm afraid there's been some mistake, Mr. Traveler. I have a limited budget. When I told Francesca I could only afford to pay my driver fifty dollars a day, she indicated that would cover your services. But it can't possibly be enough for the use of a car like this."

"Fifty dollars a day?"

She wanted to believe her head was pounding from jet lag, but she'd always been a good traveler, and she suspected her headache came from frustration. Communicating with this gorgeous fool was more difficult than dealing with her slowest students. Not only did he move like a snail, but he didn't seem to understand any of her instructions. Even after the incident with the key chain, it had taken her forever to get him to baggage claim.

"This is quite embarrassing. I thought Francesca would have discussed all this with you. You're expecting more than fifty dollars, aren't you?"

He lifted her two heavy suitcases into the boot with surprisingly little effort, considering that, only moments earlier, he'd acted as if carrying those same bags out to his car posed a major threat to his skeletal system. Once again, her eyes strayed to the well-developed muscles his T-shirt didn't quite conceal. Wouldn't a person actually have to expend energy to build muscles like that?

"I guess it depends on what all besides driving that fifty dollars is supposed to cover." He took her carry-all and tossed it next to her suitcase. Then he regarded her handbag. "I'm surprised the airlines didn't make you check that thing. Do you want it in the trunk, too?"

"No, thank you." Her headache had traveled from her temples to the back of her neck. "Perhaps we should return to the terminal where we can sit down and discuss all this."

"Too far to walk." He crossed his arms and leaned against the trunk.

As she considered how much to tell him, she gazed at the cheery April sunshine outside the parking garage and thought what a contrast it provided to her dismal thoughts. "I taught history before I became headmistress at St. Gert's, and—"

"Head Mistress?"

"Yes, and—"

"You really go around calling yourself that? A Head Mistress?"

"It's what I do."

He looked vastly amused. "For proper people, you British sure do have some racy job titles."

If another American had twitted her about this, she would have laughed, but there was something about his manner that made her get as starchy as Helen Pruitt, the chemistry teacher. "Be that as it may . . ." She paused as the stuffy phrase echoed in her ears. She even *sounded* like Helen Pruitt. "I've spent the past year working on a paper about Lady Sarah Thornton, an Englishwoman who traveled through Texas during the 1870s. She also happened to be a St. Gert's girl. The paper's nearly done, but I need access to several of the libraries here to finish it, and since I have a break between the spring and summer terms, this seemed like a good time for the trip. Francesca recommended you as my guide, and she indicated that fifty dollars a day would pay for your services."

"Services?"

"As my guide," she repeated. "My driver."

"Uh-huh. Well, I'm glad to hear that's all you've got in mind, 'cause when you said *services,* I thought you might have meant something else, in which case fifty dollars wouldn't nearly cover it."

He still looked amused, although she didn't understand why. "There'll be quite a bit of driving. In addition to Dallas, I need to visit the library at the University of Texas, and—"

"Driving? That's all you want."

It wasn't nearly all she wanted, but now wasn't the time to mention that she would also need him to introduce her to the seamier side of Texas life. "It *is* a large state."

"No. I meant no other services."

"What other services do you offer?"

He grinned. "Tell you what. I'll start you out with the basic package, and then we can talk about add-ons later."

With her limited funds, she wasn't comfortable with uncertainty. "I always think it's better to clear up things right from the beginning, don't you agree?"

"We're clear enough for now." He moved toward the passenger side of the car and opened the door for her to slide inside. "You're paying me fifty dollars a day to drive you around for two weeks."

"I have a list."

"I'll just bet you do. Watch your skirt there." He slammed the door, then got in on the other side. "You could save money, you know, by buying a couple of road maps and driving yourself." He shut his door and slid the key in the ignition. The spacious interior of the car smelled like gracious living, and the image of the Duke of Beddington sprang into her mind. She pushed it away. "I don't drive," she said.

"Everybody over the age of fourteen drives." With the barest glance over his shoulder, he backed out of the parking space, then headed toward the exit. "How long have you known Francesca?" He swung out onto the roadway.

She peeled her eyes from the Cadillac's speedometer, which, from her vantage point, seemed to be climbing at an alarming rate. She forced herself to pretend that it registered kilometers.

"I met her several years ago when her production company chose the grounds at St. Gert's—they're quite lovely—to film an interview she was doing for *Francesa Today* with several British actors. We enjoyed each other's company, and we've kept in touch ever since. I'd planned to visit her while I was here, but she and her husband have temporarily moved to Florida."

Planes flew to Florida, too, Kenny thought. He was beginning to suspect Francesca knew exactly what a pain in the butt Lady Emma could be and that's why she'd deliberately dumped her on him.

"About your expenses . . ." Lady Emma looked worried as she regarded his Caddy. "This is such a large car. The cost of petrol alone must be prohibitive."

A small crease formed in her forehead, and she began to chew on her bottom lip. He wished she wouldn't do that. It was the damnedest thing. She'd annoyed the hell out of him from the moment she'd first opened her mouth, and he swore to God the next time she pointed at something with her umbrella, he was going to break it over his knee. But seeing that moist two-hundred-dollar-an-hour mouth working away made him wonder how he was going to survive these next two weeks.

In bed.

The idea popped right into his head and stuck there. He smiled. This was exactly the kind of thinking that had made him a champion on three continents. The best way to avoid killing her was to get her naked as soon as possible. Preferably in the next couple of days.

Moving in on her that fast would be a definite challenge, but Kenny didn't have anything better to do, so he figured he was up to it. He thought of the fifty dollars a day she was supposed to be paying him, then remembered the three million he'd be picking up in commercial endorsements this year and smiled to himself. It was the first time he'd smiled about money since his crooked business manager had landed Kenny in the scandal that had led to his suspension from the pro tour.

His smile turned into a frown as he imagined Francesca's amused reaction when Lady Emma had offered her fifty-dollar fee, and her even greater amusement when she'd decided not to pass that particular tidbit on to Kenny. It never ceased to amaze him that a stony-hearted, steel-eyed bastard like Dallie Beaudine couldn't control his wife better. The only woman who'd ever gotten the best of Kenny had been his crazy mother. But having her nearly ruin his life had taught him lessons he'd never forgotten, and he'd made sure no woman held the upper hand since.

He glanced over at Lady Emma with her butterscotch curls, baby-doll cheeks, floppy pink roses, and bouncing cherries. He'd been maneuvering women all his adult life, and he'd never yet let one of them forget her proper place.

Right underneath him.

Chapter 2

"This isn't a hotel." Emma had dozed off, but now she was wide awake. Through the windows of the Cadillac, she saw they'd driven into a small court in an affluent residential area.

She hadn't meant to fall asleep, especially when she'd waited so long to get her first glimpse of Texas, but he'd ignored all her polite hints about his driving, and she'd been forced to close her eyes. Jet lag had taken care of the rest.

At home, she avoided cars as much as possible, walking or riding her bicycle instead, much to the amusement of her students. But she'd been ten when she'd been involved in the terrible automobile accident that had killed her father. Although it had left her with nothing more serious than a broken arm, she hadn't been comfortable in a car since. She was ashamed of her phobia, not only because of the inconvenience it caused her, but because she didn't like weakness in herself.

"Since you seem interested in saving money," he said, "I thought you might want to stay here instead of at the hotel."

The residential court was enclosed by expensive-looking stucco maisonettes, what the Americans referred to as townhouses, all of them topped with roofs of rounded green tile. Flowers bloomed everywhere, and a gardener was tending a bougainvillea that grew along a small dividing wall. "But this looks like a private residence," she protested as he turned into a driveway.

"A friend of mine owns the place." He pressed a button and the garage opened. "He's out of town right now. You can take the room next to mine."

"Yours? You're staying here, too?"

"Didn't I just say so?"

"But—"

"You don't want free lodging, fine by me." He threw the car into reverse. " 'Course, this could save you a hundred bucks a night, but if that's what you want, I'll take you right to the hotel." He began to back out.

"No! I don't know. I'm not sure—"

He stopped the car so it hung halfway out of the garage and regarded her patiently.

She wasn't accustomed to being indecisive, especially when she didn't know why she was protesting. It made no difference if he was staying here, too. Hadn't she come on this trip for the precise purpose of losing her good name? Her stomach felt queasy at the thought, but she'd made her decision and she wouldn't let St. Gert's down.

"Made up your mind yet?"

"Yes. I'm sure this will be fine."

He slid back into the garage. "There's a real nice hot tub on the patio."

"Hot tub?"

"Don't they have those in England?"

"Yes, but . . ."

He stopped the car and got out. She followed.

The garage had a few boxes stacked at one end, along with what seemed to be a free-standing wine cellar. Through the glass doors, she saw that it was well-stocked.

He headed toward the door that led into the house. She stopped him. "Mr. Traveler?"

He turned.

"My suitcases?"

He gave a weary, put-upon sigh, then moved to the trunk, unlocked it, and looked inside. "You know, hauling around stuff like this isn't good for a person with back trouble."

"Do you have back trouble?"

"Not *now,* I don't, which is exactly my point."

She suppressed a smile. He was infuriating, but amusing. To teach him a lesson, she marched toward the trunk and pulled out the heavy suitcases herself. "*I'll* carry them."

Instead of being shamed, he seemed pleased. "I'll get the door."

With a sigh of exasperation, she lugged the suitcases inside. They stepped into a small kitchen with a limestone floor, granite counters, and cupboards with etched glass fronts. The late afternoon sun coming in through a skylight revealed an assortment of high-tech appliances.

"This is lovely." She set her suitcases down and moved through the kitchen into a living room decorated in white, blue, and various shades of green. Several leafy plants grew near a pair of glass doors that opened onto a small, secluded patio surrounded by a vine-covered wooden privacy fence. A spacious, octagonal-shaped hot tub sat at one end.

He tossed his Stetson on the back of a chair, dropped his keys on a bronze and glass console, then pushed a button on a sleek answering machine. A woman's Texas drawl filled the room.

"Kinny, it's Torie. Call me back right this minute, you sonovabitch, or I swear to God I'll phone the Antichrist and tell him you been stalkin' little Catholic schoolgirls. And, in case you forgot, there's a set of your Pings locked away in the trunk of my Beemer, right along with that Big Bertha you won the Colonial with. I mean it, Kinny, I'm gonna break every one of them if you're not on this phone by three o'clock this afternoon."

He yawned. Emma glanced at an elegant clock on the console. It was four o'clock.

"She sounds quite cross."

"Torie? That's just the way she talks."

Emma couldn't help probing. "She's your wife, is she?"

"I've never been married."

"Ah." She waited.

He collapsed on the couch as if he'd just run a marathon.

"Your fiancée, perhaps? Or a girlfriend?"

"Torie's my sister. Unfortunately."

Despite herself, she was growing increasingly curious about this gorgeous, lazy Texan. "I didn't quite understand some of her references. Big Bertha? Pinks?"

"Pings. Golf clubs."

"Ah, so you're a golfer. That explains your connection with Francesca. Several members of my faculty play golf."

"You don't say."

"I bicycle for exercise."

"Uh-huh."

"I'm a great believer in the importance of exercise."

"I'm a great believer in the importance of beer. You want one?"

"No, thank you. I—" She stopped herself. "Yes, as a matter of fact. I'd adore a beer."

"Good." He rose from the couch. "You can have the bedroom at the end of the hall upstairs. I'll meet you in the hot tub with a couple of cold ones as soon as you take your clothes off."

Before she could reply, he'd disappeared. She frowned. For a man who moved slowly, he seemed to cover a lot of territory in a remarkably short period of time.

Kenny leaned back in the hot tub that sat in the shade of his small, private patio. It was a luxury model, and, contrary to its name, came complete with a customized cooling system that kept the water comfortably chilly during the hot Texas summer. Now, however, with the late afternoon temperature hovering just below seventy degrees, the warmer water felt good.

He'd had the hot tub installed right after he'd bought this place, one of three residences he owned, including a ranch outside Wynette, Texas, and a beach house on Hilton Head, although he'd just put the beach house up for sale to help bail him out of the legal and financial mess his ex-business manager Howard "Slezoid" Slattery had left him in.

He heard the phone ring, but he ignored it because he figured it was Torie calling again. As he moved one knee closer to a water jet, he thought about the fact that Lady Emma didn't know who he was. He supposed that should bruise his ego, but instead he was glad he hadn't been stuck with someone who wanted to rehash the details of the scandal.

The door leading from the house swung open, and Lady Emma came out. He grinned. She was covered up from here to there with another straw hat, sunglasses, and a filmy pink robe that had white flowers splashed all over it. Lady Emma sure did like her flowers.

He took a sip of beer, then tipped the mouth of the bottle toward her. "You naked underneath that?"

Those golden brown eyes flashed thirteen different kinds of surprise. "Certainly not."

"Can't get in the hot tub with your clothes on. My friend has a rule about that."

Amusement flickered in her eyes. "Your friend doesn't have to find out, does he?" Then her fingers stalled on the sash at her waist. "Are you naked?"

He took a sip of beer and regarded her innocently. "Now, see, that's one of those things an American lady would know without asking."

She hesitated, then unfastened her robe and let it drop.

He about choked. Right there, in the bubbling water, his groin shot to full attention.

It wasn't her bathing suit that did it. She had on a conservative white one-piece with a couple stems of iris running up the front. No, it was the body inside. This was one lady who sure didn't believe in running to the bathroom after a good meal and sticking her finger down her throat like some of his former girlfriends. Lady Emma had herself a woman's body, with nice curvy hips and real curvy breasts. When a man was in bed with her, he wouldn't have to do a sight check to make sure he was touching the right things.

Her skin was milky white and flawless. Her legs were a little short, but nicely shaped. And smoothly shaven. He was relieved to see that, because, with foreign women, you could never be too sure. He'd had a nasty surprise three years ago with a famous French film actress.

Despite Lady Emma's curves, he noticed that everything was trim. Although she wasn't a hardbody, the only parts of her that wiggled were the parts that were supposed to. Must be all that bicycling.

She'd put some lipstick on, but it was a light rosy color instead of hooker red, which was a good thing, because that mouth in red lipstick would have been more than he could handle. Lady Emma was one of life's great jokes, he decided. Putting that face and body on a woman with the personality of a four-star general had to have given the Almighty a few chuckles.

He picked up the beer he had waiting for her—not that he believed for a moment she'd drink it—and held it out. She marched toward him and his aggravation returned. She looked like she was getting ready to liberate China instead of relax in a hot tub. This woman didn't know the first thing about taking it easy.

She settled into the water on the farthest side of the tub from him. Pretty soon, only her shoulders and a pair of thin white straps were visible above the bubbles.

"We're in the shade here," he pointed out. "You might consider taking off your hat—that is, if you're not too self-conscious about your . . . you know."

"What?"

He lowered his voice. "Your bald spot."

"I don't have a bald spot!"

He feigned a look of empathy. "Baldness is nothing to be ashamed of, Lady Emma, although, I'll admit, it's more acceptable on a man than a woman."

"I'm not bald! Why would you think such a thing?"

"Every time I see you, there's a hat glued to your head. It's a natural assumption."

"I like hats."

"I guess they can be quite a friend to people with hair loss."

"I don't have—" She rolled her eyes, then tossed her hat aside. "You have a peculiar sense of humor, Mr. Traveler."

He gazed at a fluffy corona of butterscotch curls. They were so soft and pretty that, for a moment, he forgot what a pain in the butt she was. The moment passed when she spoke.

"We need to discuss our agenda for tomorrow."

"No, we don't. You gonna drink that beer or just hold it? And my name's Kenny. Anything else makes me sound like a schoolteacher— no offense."

"All right, Kenny. And please, just call me Emma. I never use my title. Technically it's not a title, but what's called an honorific." She tilted the longneck to her lips, took a healthy swig, then set the bottle on the edge of the hot tub without so much as a shudder.

"Now, see, I don't understand you not using it," he said. "Having a title has got to be the only good thing about being British."

She smiled. "It's not quite so bad as that."

"How'd you get it?"

"My father was the fifth Earl of Woodbourne."

He thought that over for a moment. "Seems like an earl's daughter— and stop me if I'm getting too personal here—but I'm surprised a member of royalty has to worry so much about counting her shillings."

"I'm not royalty. And a large portion of the British aristocracy lives in genteel poverty. My parents were no exception. Both of them were anthropologists."

"Were?"

"My father died when I was a child. And then when I was eighteen, Mum died on a dig in Nepal. She wasn't happy unless the nearest telephone was a hundred miles away, so there was no way to summon help when her appendix ruptured."

"You must have grown up in some pretty isolated places."

"No. I grew up at St. Gert's. Mum left me there so she could work."

Lady Emma didn't sound bitter about it, but Kenny couldn't think too highly of a woman who'd left her kid an orphan so she could spend her time running all over the world. On the other hand, if his mother had spent more time running around and less time coddling him, his childhood would have been a lot easier.

Come give Mommy a kiss, baby doll. My beautiful baby. Mommy loves you best. Don't ever forget that.

"Any brothers or sisters?" he asked.

"Just me." She settled deeper into the hot tub. "I'm anxious to start in on my research tomorrow, and I'd also enjoy a little sightseeing, but before we do any of that, I need to visit a shop where I can buy some new clothes. And would you happen to know the name of a tattoo parlor?"

He choked and sent a spray of beer right up his nose. "What!"

She pushed her sunglasses to the top of her head and regarded him earnestly. "My first choice would be a pansy. But I'm afraid the color might make it look like a bruise, which wouldn't do at all. There are so many flowers I love—poppies, morning glories, sunflowers—but they're all so large. A rose would be safe, but they're a bit of a tattoo cliché, don't you think?" She sighed and returned her sunglasses to her nose. "Normally I make decisions easily, but this one is giving me trouble. Do you have any suggestions?"

For the first time in his life, the power of speech deserted him. The experience was so disconcerting that he slid under the water and stayed there for a while to collect his thoughts. Not long enough, though. Before he'd halfway run out of breath, she started thumping him on the top of his head. It annoyed the hell out of him, and he was scowling when he came up. "You want to get a tattoo?"

She had the nerve to smile. "I hadn't realized there'd be this much of a language barrier in the States. And the next time you're going to dunk your head like that, you might warn me. I presumed you were drowning."

He could feel his blood pressure rising, which made it rise even more. "It doesn't have anything to do with a language barrier! It has to do with the fact that somebody like you has no business getting a tattoo!"

For the first time since he'd met her, she grew completely still. For a moment she did nothing, then one hand emerged from the bubbles and slowly removed her sunglasses. She set them on the side of the hot tub next to her beer bottle and gazed at him with those honey-brown eyes. "What exactly do you mean? Somebody like me?"

He could see he'd riled her, but, for the life of him, he couldn't understand why. "Somebody respectable, for one thing. And conservative."

She rose from the water, and the expression on her face told him he'd just been sent to the principal, and she was it. "I'll have you know, Mr. Traveler, that I am the *least* conservative person you've ever met!"

He started to laugh, then got distracted by the water trickling down those firm white thighs. "You don't say," he managed.

"I am—I am . . . *completely* disreputable! Just look at me! I'm in a hot tub with a man I didn't even know until a few hours ago!"

"You aren't naked," he couldn't help but point out.

She got rosy in the face, and the next thing he knew, she sank down in the water and started to tug. Right there in front of him, with nothing but bubbles hiding that milky white body, she stripped off her bathing suit. He watched her whip it out of the water and fling it from the hot tub. It landed on the pebbled concrete with a soft plop.

"There! Don't you *ever* say I'm conservative again!"

He grinned. This was like taking candy from a baby.

As Emma watched those white teeth flash in his tanned face, she knew she'd done it. She had a dreadful temper, but she'd worked hard to control it, and it hadn't gotten the best of her for years.

She fumbled for her beer and took a deep swallow as she tried to recover, but the fact that she was stark naked made it difficult. She was accustomed to dealing with rebellious students, unreasonable parents, demanding faculty members, and an overworked maintenance staff. How had she let one man upset her so easily?

As she tried to muster her dignity, she grew conscious of the slide of water over her skin. An unbridled streak of sensuality reared its silky head. She fiercely repressed it as she set the bottle back down and spoke more sharply than necessary. "Now that we have that settled, I'd like you to have the name of a clean tattoo parlor for me by tomorrow afternoon."

He regarded her with the bland expression of the mentally impaired. Physically, however, there was nothing wrong with him. Sunlight flickered across shoulders that were strong and powerful. Without his Stetson, she could see that his blue-black hair was thick and a bit curly, like a dark archangel's. If a Renaissance sculptor had ever gotten the urge to chisel a Texas cowboy into the frieze of a cathedral, Kenny Traveler would have been his man.

"Search services are extra," he said.

"What do you mean? Extra what?"

"Money. That fifty dollars a day you're paying me doesn't cover search services."

"You consider finding a tattoo parlor a search service?"

"Yes, ma'am, I do."

She'd known his fee was too good to be true. "Exactly what does the fifty dollars cover?"

"Driving, mainly. As I said, finding tattoo parlors is extra. I also don't do hair and manicures."

"I didn't ask you to—"

"Massage is included in the fifty. But, 'course, you know that."

"Mas—"

"Suitcase hauling only once a day. Any more than that'll cost you an extra *thousand* bucks. Pointing out the sights is included in the base fee, but if I have to do any Spanish translation for you, I'll need to charge you by the hour. As for sex, that's an additional fifty dollars. Does that seem fair?"

She stared at him and wondered if she'd somehow gotten water in her ears.

He shook his head. "No, you're right. It's the off season, so I need to discount. Tell you what. Let's make it thirty for sex, and that'll cover the whole night, not just one time, you understand. A budget traveler like yourself will have to agree you won't find a better rate than that."

Slowly her tongue came unglued from the roof of her mouth. "Sex?"

"The whole night for thirty dollars." He propped his elbows on the deck. "Lately I been thinkin' about how unfair that is. A woman can charge hundreds of dollars for an entire night, but a man—Hell, it's discrimination, is what it is. I swear, lately I been thinkin' about filing a complaint with the EEOC."

She couldn't take her eyes from him. She was both repulsed and strangely fascinated. "Women *pay* to have sex with you?"

He regarded her as if she were the slow-witted one. "You hired an *escort* service."

"I thought I hired a driver."

"And a guide. An *escort*. It's the same thing. Didn't Francesca explain to you about drivers and escort services?"

"Apparently not," she managed.

He shook his head. "I'm going to have to talk to her about this. She should have taken into consideration the fact that you don't understand how things work over here. Now I've been put in an awkward position. I don't like discussing money with my clients. What I mainly like to talk about is pleasure."

The way he lingered over that last word—his Texas drawl stroking it with slow molasses—sent a shiver up her spine.

Suddenly, without any conscious direction, her mind began to race. Sex for hire? Had she just been given the answer to all her troubles? Her stomach clenched. No. It was unthinkable. Impossible.

But why? She only had two weeks to escape the net the despicable Hugh Holroyd had woven so tightly around both her and St. Gert's, and this would be far more scandalous than a tattoo.

She considered the possibility that Francesca had chosen Kenny Traveler as her guide for just this reason. Francesca didn't know about Holroyd's plans, but she did know something else—how much Emma regretted her limited experience with men.

One afternoon several months ago, they'd shared tea at Emma's cottage on the grounds at St. Gert's, and Francesca's openness regarding her own painful passage into maturity had allowed Emma to reveal something of her own past. Francesa already knew how much Emma loved St. Gert's, which was the only home she'd ever known. At the same time, being raised in a girl's school had restricted her contacts with men.

Even when she'd gone to the university, things hadn't improved much. Her mother's death had left her virtually penniless, so she'd been forced to work hard. Between her job and her studies, there'd been little time left over for a social life, and most of the men she found attractive were intimidated by her. They seemed to prefer a softer sort of female, one who was milder-mannered and less inclined to take charge.

She knew it would have been more sensible for her to have accepted a teaching position in London after she'd graduated, but St. Gert's was her home, and the old place drew her back. Unfortunately, the pool of eligible men in the small town of Lower Tilbey was limited, and she seemed to inspire their respect rather than their passion.

She had just begun to resign herself to a single, childless existence when she'd hired Jeremy Fox to fill the vacancy her appointment as headmistress had left in the history department. Within a few months, she'd fallen in love with him. Jeremy was kind, good-humored, and attractive in the scholarly, rumpled fashion that had always appealed to her. Unfortunately, he was also her subordinate, but they had so many interests in common that a friendship had formed anyway.

She'd let herself be satisfied with their comfortable companionship until a drizzly day last November when she'd spent several hours with a homesick six-year-old curled in her lap. The gloomy weather combined with her upcoming thirtieth birthday and the feel of the little girl's head tucked under her chin had overcome both her common sense and her professionalism. She'd gone to Jeremy's rooms that evening and, as subtly as possible, indicated that her feelings for him went beyond friendship.

One look at his appalled expression told her she'd made a terrible mistake. He'd been suffocatingly kind as he let her know that he wasn't attracted to her in any way other than as a friend. *"You're so strong, Emma. Such a leader."*

She'd known it wasn't a compliment, and a short time later, she'd been forced to smile through his wedding to a pretty, twenty-one year-old shop girl who didn't know the Magna Carta from the Maginot Line.

Emma remembered Francesca's sympathetic expression when she'd told her about Jeremy. "So, you're still a virgin," Francesca had said succinctly.

Emma had been embarrassed. "Well, I've dated certainly. And there were several times when I . . ." She gave it up. "Yes. Quite right. Embarrassing, isn't it?"

"Not at all. You're just discriminating."

But despite Francesca's kind words, Emma felt like a freak. Still, hiring a man for sex would never have occurred to her if it weren't for Hugh Holroyd, Duke of Beddington. After weeks of agonizing over how to save her school, could the solution be so simple? And so difficult?

She needed to know more. "Your sexual services . . ." She cleared her throat. "What exactly do they involve?"

His beer bottle stalled halfway to his lips, and the smile that had been hanging there faded. He stared at her for a long moment, then opened his mouth to speak. Shut it. Opened it again. Took a swig of beer.

She watched the muscles in his throat work as he swallowed. He was obviously surprised, and she could almost read his thoughts. He'd believed she was too conservative to hire him for sex, and he regretted having reduced his price so quickly.

He set his beer on the deck. "Uh . . . anything the customer wants."

Her mind whirled with possibilities, and she had to force her thoughts into line. She couldn't consider this emotionally; she had to approach it logically, and there were practicalities to consider.

"What about diseases?" Making eye contact with him was impossible, so she pretended to study the bubbles.

For a moment she thought he wasn't going to answer, but he did, although his voice sounded as if some beer might have gone down the wrong pipe. "I practice one hundred percent safe sex."

"There's no such thing."

"Ninety-five percent. It's like Torie always says: 'To live is to risk.' But I'm sure not carrying any fatal diseases, if that's what you want to know. How about you?"

"Me?" She lifted her head. "No. Absolutely not." Once again, she dropped her gaze. Through the bubbles, she glimpsed skin and wondered how much of her he could see. "This is purely commerce? Handled professionally?"

"I, uh, offer a money back guarantee."

"And the—the customer would dictate how the . . . encounter would go?"

He seemed to be thinking that over. "The customer dictates the parameters. I dictate the particulars. For example, if the lady has any particular fetishes—"

"Oh, no. None." Her only fetish was the desire to make love with a man who loved her, and that was something Kenny Traveler couldn't provide. Just sex.

"—or if, for example, the customer said something like, 'Kenny, honey, I want you to handcuff me—' "

Her head shot up.

"—then I'd go along with that because it's a parameter, but the order of events after those handcuffs get snapped on is pretty much up to me."

"I—I see." She could feel bright red patches burning in her cheeks. Was she really considering doing this? Letting Kenny Traveler take her virginity would certainly be a lot more effective than getting a tattoo. He was the perfect man for the job—physically irresistible, but so foreign to her concept of a soul mate that she wouldn't have to deal with any emotional scars afterward. She could get it over with and then forget it.

"I should tell you that I won't wear female underwear or use a whip. The ladies do enjoy a little light bondage, of course, so there's no problem with that. I mean, I'd be pretty much out of business without those handcuffs I was talking about, so I'm more than happy to oblige."

"You handcuff women?" She was shocked. Not that it happened, but that the practice was so widespread. "Oh, no."

"Now, don't get too judgmental. I didn't think I'd like it either until the first time I snapped those suckers around a pair of—Well, I'm not saying any more. If that's not to your particular tastes, then we'll just try something else."

She drew a deep breath. She didn't need a flashing neon arrow pointing the way to realize this could be the answer both to her own freedom and to saving St. Gert's. So why did she feel like crying?

She mustered her courage. She'd known when she started this trip that her life would never be the same again. Without giving herself any more time to think about it, she nodded. "All right, then. Yes. That sounds satisfactory."

He blinked. "It does?"

"Tonight would be fine."

"Tonight?"

She finally managed to look at him. "Do you have another engagement?"

"Oh, no. Tonight's just fine with me."

She was relieved. If she had too long to dwell on what was going to happen, she'd go mad. She forced herself to focus on the practical. "Do you take traveler's checks?"

His regular customers obviously were more worldly than she because her inquiry made him grin. She regarded him coolly until he pulled in the corners of his mouth. "Yes, ma'am. Plus American Express and Visa. I can even handle Diners Club, although it wouldn't be my first choice."

"I have traveler's checks."

"Then we don't have a problem, do we?"

"No. No, we don't."

More than anything, she wanted to get out of the hot tub and hide away in her room upstairs, but she was stark naked and trapped. Her stomach felt queasy and her mouth was dry. She closed her eyes and sank farther down into the water.

From the other side of the hot tub, Kenny watched Lady Emma's shoulders disappearing into the bubbles. She licked her lips nervously, and, as the pink tip of her tongue swept along the crease of her mouth, he felt as if he were going to explode. He couldn't believe this. When he'd started talking about fees, he'd just been messing around, having a little fun. Not for a moment had he thought she'd believe him. But she was one serious woman.

Here he'd given himself a couple of days to seduce her, and it hadn't taken much more than twenty minutes. He'd always been good with women, but this was a record.

As he gazed at the water swirling around the base of her neck, he felt a moment's hesitation. Then he remembered how bossy and controlling she was, his least favorite kind of woman, and his hesitation disappeared. Lady Emma wasn't any dewy-eyed virgin, and she knew exactly what she was doing.

He could just imagine what her lovers were like, probably a bunch of old guys with names like Rupert and Nigel. They let her make all the calls, didn't give her any trouble, and didn't give her any thrills, either. But she was on vacation now, where there was no one around to tattle, and she had a hankering to get laid by someone who still had his own teeth. He was happy to oblige.

Her lids opened and she met his eyes. "I want to keep a light on."

He certainly didn't have a problem with that. "All right."

"No cigarettes."

"I don't smoke."

"Brandy, I think. Or perhaps some sherry."

"Uh-huh."

"And music. Classical would be best. Baroque, I believe."

Damn. She was giving him a list, and he had to put a stop to it before she got right down to the color of the sheets. "No music. Keeps me from concentrating on all those nice erogenous zones."

"Oh." She swallowed. "All right, then. No music." She looked down at the water. "I probably should tell you I'm ticklish."

"Forewarned is forearmed."

"And I'm a bit claustrophobic, so the position might be important to dis—"

"Excuse me for interrupting here, but let me point out that I *am* a trained professional."

"Oh . . . yes." She bit that lip again. "One more thing. After it's over, Mr. Traveler, we won't discuss it."

With a sigh of satisfaction, he sank back into the water. "Lady Emma, you just turned into every man's fantasy."

Chapter 3

Emma had bought sex. She still couldn't believe what she'd done. After a lifetime of propriety, she had turned her back on everything she believed in.

"You can look now," he said.

She felt like a fool. As soon as he'd begun lifting himself out of the tub, she'd dipped her head like a skittish old maid. Why couldn't she have been blasé and sophisticated about it? He certainly wasn't self-conscious about his body. And it was only natural for her to want to see it. Quite badly.

Now she did and her mouth went dry. He'd wrapped a towel around his hips, and the knot fell low, inches below his navel. Trickles of water slithered like tiny fingers down his chest and along the flat plane of his abdomen. He had a beautiful body, and she had hired it for the night.

"Cold?"

She looked up. "Pardon?"

"You shivered."

"Oh . . . yes, I am getting a bit chilly. Would you mind fetching me a towel, then?" She narrowed her eyes. "That is, if there's no extra charge."

He gave her the devastating grin he'd undoubtedly been using to demolish women since the cradle. He was absolutely unprincipled. But that made him perfect for what she needed.

The moment he disappeared through the glass doors, she hurried from the hot tub and pulled on her robe. "Never mind," she called out to him as soon as she'd fetched her bathing suit and stepped inside.

She rushed upstairs, gathered her toiletries, and carried them into the bathroom. Tonight she would take a giant step toward her freedom and the safety of St. Gert's.

Kenny conned Lady Emma into fixing dinner as soon as she came downstairs from her nap. All he needed to do was mention that eating in would save her money, but the truth was, he didn't want her to be around other people right now. It might bring her to her senses.

For once she wasn't giving orders as she pulled out some chicken cutlets from the freezer, then began fixing a salad, while he made a big deal out of scrubbing a couple of potatoes and putting them in the oven.

She sure wasn't dressed for sex. Not that there was anything wrong with her clothes. She wore a nice pair of beige slacks with a waist-length yellow cotton sweater that had a couple pearl buttons at the neck and a little band of crocheted lace at the bottom. The outfit was fresh and crisp-looking, and it fit her well without being revealing. But he sort of missed the flowers.

He could see Lady Emma was nervous being around him, and he didn't have the energy to work her out of it more than once this evening, so he decided to give her some breathing room while the potatoes were baking. He excused himself and slipped into his study, where he made a few phone calls, none of them to Torie. Mainly, he nosed around his contacts with the press.

Between his legendary golf swing, an eighteen-month hot streak, and the fact that he gave good interviews, Kenny had won the public's attention, but he'd never quite been able to capture its adoration. People liked athletes who'd overcome adversity—especially poverty or chronic disease—but with Kenny Traveler, there was a sense that things had come too easily. Still, the sport had treated him well, and Kenny hadn't been complaining.

Then a visit from the FBI a month ago had turned his world upside down. He'd learned that Howard Slattery, his longtime business manager, had been funneling big chunks of Kenny's money into an illegal drug operation with ties to Mexico, Colombia, and, eventually, Houston. The revelation had knocked Kenny's feet right out from under him. Even during his wildest days, he'd never had anything to do with drugs, and the knowledge that his money was contributing to other people's misery had been just about more than he could handle.

Slattery was arrested trying to flee the country, and all of Kenny's financial records became public property. Although the investigation wasn't closed, it was generally recognized by both the federal government and the public that Kenny'd had no knowledge of what was going on. Still, the entire incident had reflected badly on the PGA and made acting commissioner Dallas Beaudine see thirteen different shades of red.

"This is the last straw, Kenny! You've been coasting for as long as I've known you, phoning in your personal life, ignoring business, not working hard at anything but golf. Well, this time your laziness has cast a big shadow over the PGA, and that's going to cost you. I'm suspending you from the tour for two weeks."

"You can't do that, you son of a bitch! I'll miss the Masters! And I didn't do anything wrong! You don't have any grounds!"

"I've got grounds, all right. Gross stupidity! Maybe a little time off the tour will give you a chance to get your head in order and figure out there's more to life than hitting a golf ball."

As if Kenny could suddenly get to the bottom of what had eluded him for thirty-three years. He pressed his fingers to the bridge of his nose, hearing his mother's voice this time instead of the commissioner's.

"How dare you accuse my sweet Kenny of beating up that little brat of yours! You're just jealous because my Kenny's so much smarter than the other kids in this godforsaken town!"

He shook off the old, unwelcome memory from his childhood and turned his thoughts back to his current problem. Two days after Dallie had suspended him, Kenny'd gotten into a public fight with Sturgis Randall, an overpaid, substance-abusing, lecherous asshole of a network golf announcer, who never failed to use phrases like "born with a silver spoon in his mouth," "playboy champion," and "charmed life" when he was describing Kenny and his career.

Never apologize, never explain, was Kenny's motto. He couldn't stand it when jocks started whining to the press about how misunderstood they were, so he made it a policy never to defend himself to reporters. Instead, he let his golf clubs do the talking, and he figured people could either take it or leave it. Which didn't mean that he was averse to throwing a punch at some jerk who forgot his manners. Even so, he wouldn't have hit Sturgis if the other man hadn't thrown the first punch.

That was all Kenny had needed. But just as Sturgis was beginning to understand the full extent of his mistake, Jilly Bradford, cable television's most visible female reporter and Kenny's former girlfriend, had appeared out of nowhere, and Kenny's fist had accidentally connected with her shoulder. A network cameraman had caught the entire event on tape, including shots of Jilly crying pathetically afterward and a bloodied Sturgis Randall comforting her.

Even then, Kenny might have escaped the ensuing scandal if Jilly had been fair about it. She knew it was an accident, but ever since their love affair had run its natural course, she'd been publicly vocal about her unhappiness with Kenny. Because of that, everybody thought it was a domestic dispute, and now Kenny not only looked like a man who was too stupid to take care of his money, but also like a slug who got his kicks beating up women.

If he'd thought Dallie had been upset with him before his fight with Randall, that was nothing compared to the way he reacted after Kenny's second brush with scandal.

"You're still the same no-good spoiled rich kid who was born with more natural talent than you deserve and a screwed-up set of priorities. Well, as far as I'm concerned, it's long past time you grew up. As of now, your suspension is indefinite. And I'm warning you . . . if you want to be reinstated before you're too old for the senior tour, you'd better keep that nose of yours squeaky clean."

Kenny refused to defend himself. He didn't see the point. Dallie knew Sturgis Randall was an asshole, just as he knew Kenny would never deliberately hit a woman, but that didn't seem to make any difference, and now Kenny understood what it felt like to be betrayed by the man who meant as much to him as anyone on earth.

Hardly a day had passed since his suspension that he didn't curse the fact that he'd been born and raised in Wynette, Texas, Dallie Beaudine's hometown, along with cursing the fact that Dallie had taken an interest in him when he'd been a snot-nosed kid hot-rodding around town in the brand-new red Porsche his mother had given him for his sixteenth birthday. Except, when Kenny was thinking rationally, he knew that Dallie's intervention had saved his life.

Growing up with a crazy mother who'd suffocated him with her obsessive love, along with a distant father who hadn't cared enough to intercede, had put Kenny on the path toward the worst kind of trouble. He'd been a bully, hell bent on cutting a wide swath of destruction through the town of Wynette. Only Dallie Beaudine had been standing in the way. That was what hurt most of all. Because Dallie knew him better than anybody on earth, he understood what nobody else did— that golf was the only thing that mattered in Kenny Traveler's sorry, spoiled life.

As he hung up from an unfruitful call with one of his contacts at *USA Today*, he heard Lady Emma moving around in the kitchen, and a small corner of his depression lifted. It looked like his sex drive hadn't disappeared after all.

Even before his suspension, he'd started worrying about himself. He'd always had an active sex life, but he hadn't felt any urge to play the field since he'd gotten rid of Jilly. Instead, he'd been plagued with a general feeling that a man winning so many golf tournaments should be a lot happier with his life. But now Lady Emma had appeared, and, in a matter of hours, his body had come awake.

Despite her umbrella and order-giving, she was exactly the distraction he needed, especially now, when the top pros in the world were heading for the Masters at Augusta while he sat home at the whim of a man who was supposed to be his friend. And he didn't have to worry about Emma stirring up another public scandal—the last thing his career could stand—when he dumped her. There was no way a conservative soul like her would let on that she'd used her summer vacation to satisfy her hankering to hop in bed with a stranger.

Besides, she amused the hell out of him, which was strange, since he generally couldn't abide domineering women. But Lady Emma was so absolutely clueless that being around her was pretty much like standing in the exact middle of a perfect private joke.

Then there was that mouth . . . and her energy. . . . He smiled as he thought about having all that enthusiasm squirming naked underneath him.

Now he intended to use her to keep himself from thinking about Augusta, Dallie Beaudine, and a life that seemed increasingly pointless. Yes, sir, Lady Emma was just what he needed.

Emma dropped the potato peeler for the third time. It was a sleekly designed state-of-the-art German instrument. She bit her lip and returned her attention to the carrots. In a few more hours it would be over.

"How are those potatoes doing?"

She dropped the peeler for the fourth time and spun around.

He grinned as he sauntered toward her.

She took in the tan slacks he'd changed into while she'd been trying to nap, along with a black polo shirt bearing an American Express logo. Those neutral colors combined with his dark hair and tanned skin made a breathtaking contrast to his violet eyes.

He opened the oven door, picked up a paring knife, and poked at the potatoes. "These are about done. You got that chicken ready?"

"Chicken?" She'd forgotten about the chicken.

He straightened and nodded toward the carrots she'd just peeled. "If Bugs Bunny happens to drop by for dinner, he's going to be one happy rabbit."

She blinked and looked down. Instead of peeling just a few, she'd peeled an entire package. Enough for a dozen salads.

He gave her a knowing grin, then combined a couple of lazy stretches with retrieving a bowl and pan from separate cupboards. Somehow a

canister of flour appeared, along with a stick of butter. With a slow flick
of his hand, he dredged the chicken and set it sizzling in the pan. "You
watch those while I get us some wine."

She stared at the chicken. Her pulses were jumping, and her stomach
felt as if it had dropped to her toes. For a moment the extent of what
she was losing overcame her—a decade worth of daydreams about a
comfortable, scholarly husband with leather elbow patches on his jacket
and ink stains on his fingers. Other women might fantasize about taming
some dashing scoundrel with thick black hair, a magnificent body, and
violet eyes, but that had never been what she'd wanted.

Kenny returned from the garage with a bottle and lowered the heat
on the chicken, which was starting to smoke. "Lady Emma, you got to
relax or you're gonna expire before we get half near the bedroom."

"I am relaxed! Perfectly relaxed!" She took a deep breath as she
realized how foolish that sounded when it was obvious she was as tight
as the cork in that wine bottle he was carrying. "Please call me Emma.
I never use my title."

"Uh-huh. If you're so relaxed, how's come you jump every time I
look at you?"

"I don't jump!" She swallowed as she watched his hands turn the
corkscrew, taking all the time in the world. She thought about those
lazy hands taking their time with her, then reminded herself there was
no ink stain on his thumb, no pencil callus on even one of those long,
lean fingers.

"All right, then. I'm putting you to the test." He tugged out the cork,
pulled several exquisite crystal wine goblets from a cupboard above the
stove, and poured. "Here's what I'm gonna do. Just to make a point,
mind you. I'm gonna touch one of your body parts, and while I'm doing
it, you've got to stay perfectly still. If you jump, then you lose and I
win."

"You're going to touch me?"

"The body part of my choice."

"Oh, I don't think that's a good idea."

"It's an excellent idea." He handed her a glass of wine. Their fingers
brushed, and she jumped.

"You lose." Triumph gleamed in his eyes.

"That's not fair!"

"Why not?"

"Because . . . when you said body part . . . well, naturally I thought—"
He lifted an eyebrow at her. "You thought what, Lady Emma?"

"Just Emma! I thought—Oh, never mind!" She snatched up a cucumber. "You're right. I *am* a bit nervous. But that's only natural. I've

never . . . never done anything like this." She gazed down at the cucumber she was squeezing, realized what it was, and dropped it like one of the potatoes baking in the oven.

He chuckled. "You've never bought a man for the night?"   "Oh, dear . . . must you say it like that?"

"I was doing my best to put it politely." He flipped the chicken. "Now, why don't you finish up that salad so we can eat?"

She forced herself to concentrate, and, after a few more missteps, they were seated at a glass-topped dining room table supported by a pair of sleek black marble pedestals. The place settings seemed to have materialized out of nowhere: white linen mats with matching napkins, china banded in navy and gold, heavy sterling with swirling handles. Her companion certainly knew how to pick his friends. She'd met a few of Kenny's counterparts in England, and she hadn't liked them—handsome penniless men who bartered charm for their friends' hospitality.

The idea of eating made her nauseated, so she took a sip of wine. It was lovely—fragrant and obviously expensive. He began to eat, and she noticed that nervousness hadn't interfered with his appetite. She took a nibble of baked potato. It stuck in her throat.

He seemed perfectly comfortable with the silence, but she wasn't. Maybe some conversation would relax her. "Your friend has exquisite taste."

He gazed around at the luxurious dining room as though he were seeing it for the first time. "I suppose. Some sports posters'd be nice, though. A couple of La-Z-Boys in the living room. And a big-screen TV to watch ESPN while we're eating."

His cheerful denseness annoyed her, although he probably wasn't a bad sort, just too lazy to make anything of himself. Maybe no one had ever taken the time to suggest a better way. "Have you ever had second thoughts about your method of earning a living?" she asked.

"Not really." He dug into his chicken. "Escort service suits me just fine."

She succumbed to her natural instinct to help others build character. "But doesn't it ever present a problem for you when someone asks what you do for a living, and you have to say that you're an escort?"

"Problem?"

"People must know that's a—well, forgive me if I'm being too blunt, but a glorified term for a . . . well . . . a gigolo."

"Gigolo!"

She hadn't intended to be rude, and she began to frame an apology, only to have him grin. "Gigolo. I like that."

"It's a pejorative term," she felt duty-bound to point out.

"Maybe in that socialist state you live in, but here in the land of the free, home of the brave, people have respect for a man who's willing to make it his life's work to service lonely ladies."

"I am not lonely!"

"Or ones who are sexually frustrated."

She opened her mouth to deny it, only to shut it again. Let him think what he wanted. Besides, she *was* sexually frustrated, even if that wasn't her motivation for using his services. She fumbled for her wine glass.

He slipped his knife into a second piece of chicken, and she noticed he had excellent table manners. Regardless of the task, he performed it with a combination of lazy grace and minimal motion.

Too often in her life she'd set her own wishes aside out of deference to others, but tonight she wasn't going to do that, and she steeled herself for what needed to be settled. "This evening . . . during our . . . our interaction . . . I want to make certain you understand that I can call a halt to the proceedings at any time."

"Oh, that's no problem at all."

"Good."

"Because I guarantee you're not going to want to call a halt to a single proceeding. Unless, of course, you happen to be a lesbian. Although, even then—"

"I'm *not* a lesbian."

He had the gall to look disappointed.

She plunged on. "I simply think it would be better if we established certain ground rules."

He sighed.

"I am, after all, the customer, and as a customer—"

"You gonna eat that baked potato or just poke at it?"

She dug her fork into her potato. "I'm merely pointing out—"

"Upstairs."

"What?"

"Go on upstairs." He pushed back from the table and rose. "I can see I'm not going to be able to enjoy my meal until we get our business over with."

She gazed at his empty plate.

He gestured toward her wine glass. "You can take that with you, if you want. Or—Here, let me carry it. I know how much you like having other people haul things around for you."

"I can carry my own wine glass." She snatched it away from him. "It's my suitcase that—" Before she could finish her thought, she was somehow on her feet and being steered toward the stairs.

His hand settled warm against the curve of her back. "We'll use my

room. The bed's bigger, and I like having lots of room to maneuver.''
They reached the top of the stairs. "Dang, I forgot the tire chains.''

Her fingers nearly snapped the stem of the wineglass. *"What?"*

He rolled his eyes. "I'm just kidding. You're taking this way too
seriously.''

There was no response she could think of that wouldn't make her
look even more agitated, so she held her tongue.

He steered her through the door, flipped on a light switch, then
dimmed it to a golden glow. Like everything else in the house, this
room was furnished elegantly. Eggshell white set off shades of deep
navy and forest green. All the furnishings seemed to be pieces of art—
the sleekly designed bureau, a towering armoire finished in silverleaf,
an art deco bed with a silverleaf headboard.

She gazed at the bed and thought, *That's where it's going to happen.*
There, beneath a headboard designed for a museum, with a man she
was paying to do the job, she would finally lose her virginity. It suddenly seemed like the saddest thing that had ever happened to her.

"I—I need to use the w.c.''

"You go right ahead.'' He removed the wine glass from her hand.
"There's a black silk robe hanging on the back of the door. Why don't
you slip your clothes off and put that on before you come back out?''

Just like a doctor's office, she thought.

"Or . . . I can undress you.'' His hand reached toward the small pearl
fastening at the neck of her sweater.

She fled into the bathroom.

As the door slammed shut, Kenny smiled to himself. Lady Emma
might be all tied up in knots, but he was having one heck of a good
time. "That robe feels real good against bare skin,'' he called out.

Nothing but silence from the other side of the door.

He'd already noticed that Lady Emma liked his chest, so he pulled
his shirt over his head and tossed it aside. After he'd rid himself of his
shoes and socks—but not his pants, because he wanted to build the
anticipation—he opened the armoire to get to his stereo system and
pulled out a Michael Bolton CD. He didn't care much for Michael
Bolton himself, but it was good make-out music, and, despite what he'd
said earlier, he could perform just fine with music playing. As a romantic ballad filled the room, he decided the best part of making out
with her would be the fact that she couldn't kiss and give orders at the
same time.

Thinking about that mouth sent heat shooting right through him. It
was funny that Lady Emma didn't seem to have a clue what kind of

ammunition the Good Lord had armed her with. Her lovers must have kept that secret to themselves.

He sank back into one of the room's comfortable chairs to finish her wine. It was a real nice 1995 white burgundy. He sipped it leisurely as he stared at the door, willing it to open.

It didn't, and he finally realized he was going to have to go in after her.

He also realized the waiting was having a dangerous effect on his libido. Instead of calming him down, he was hotter than his short game at last year's Western Open. If he didn't get himself under control, he wouldn't be worth a plugged nickel, let alone the thirty dollars she thought she was paying him. And it was all because of that mouth, not to mention the curvy little body that he hadn't gotten to see nearly enough of.

He set her glass on the carpet and made his way to the bathroom door, which he rapped once with his knuckles, then eased open.

"Lady Emma?"

She stood frozen in the middle of the bathroom floor, dressed in his black silk robe with her clothes folded in a neat pile on the counter. *Oh, man.*

His robe clung like hot water to every one of her curves. As he watched, two luscious buds appeared, disturbing the smooth curl of silk over her breasts. Right there, he nearly lost it.

Then he noticed that her hands were clutching the robe at her side, and he saw how truly nervous she was. As he took in her tousled butterscotch curls and those fearful warm-brandy eyes, what was left of his honor reared its unwelcome head, and he was ashamed of himself. "You know, Lady Emma, you don't have to do this if you don't want to."

Her little chin shot up, her shoulders levered back, and those full lips set in a stubborn line. "Nonsense."

She pushed past him into the bedroom, nearly knocking him over as she swept by, and his sympathy changed to irritation. She had a way about her that riled him right down to his toes.

He followed her into the bedroom.

Her fingers clutched the sash of her robe. "You may proceed."

He'd proceed, all right. He'd proceed to drive her right out of her bossy little mind.

He unfastened his leather belt, and her eyes locked on the buckle as if she were watching a bomb getting ready to detonate. He let it hang open instead of pulling it from the loops. "Before we go any farther, I need to get the shape of you in my mind." He tucked his thumb in the waistband, right above the zipper, and wandered over to her. Then he made a big show out of closing his eyes and setting his hands on her shoulders.

She jumped, but he was expecting that, and he didn't let it stop him. Instead, he simply allowed his hands to stay there until he felt the barest easing in her muscles. Then he slid his palms along her arms.

After that, he began going where he wanted. Over the slope of her back. Along her ribs. Lingering on the outer curve of her hips.

She stood there as he stroked her through the silk. The brave little soldier. Until he got to her breasts. They slipped into his hands, warm and full and round. She caught her breath as he caressed them. Made a soft, breathy sigh. Her arms came up, and her palms settled on his bare chest in a way that rattled his senses.

He opened his eyes and gazed down to see that her lids had dropped. A faint pucker of concentration had formed at the bridge of her nose. He brushed his thumbs lightly across her nipples. They were hard as flower buds. She gasped, and her lips parted.

Those swollen, pouty lips.

They blurred before his eyes as he ducked his head and claimed them.

It was like kissing warm rose petals. She smelled like roses, too, and it passed through his mind that this balls-to-the-wall female had the softest, sweetest mouth he'd ever kissed.

She kept it primly shut, even as her body sagged against his. He slid the tip of his tongue over her bottom lip, then along the crease. She didn't have an ounce of stubbornness left, and she opened to let him in.

He liked his French kisses slow, but thorough. Lots of women couldn't get the hang of that, but Lady Emma was smart, and she didn't have any trouble. She let him take all the time he wanted, while her tongue moved gently against his and the blood roared through his body.

Her breasts settled deeper into his hands, and he realized he'd been so involved with her mouth that he'd forgotten to attend to them. That was a first for him.

He gently squeezed. She twisted against him and her mouth opened wider. Once again, he rubbed her nipples. They grew even tighter, and he wanted so badly to slide his tongue over them, but he still hadn't gotten enough of their kiss.

And maybe she hadn't either because now he felt the tip of her tongue slip into his mouth, and despite all that bullcrap bragging he'd been doing about what a stud he was, he thought he was going to explode right there.

With a moan, he pulled her backward on the bed, but the change of venue didn't provide nearly the distraction he needed to get himself back under control. He had to see more, and, as they sank into the mattress, he eased back a few inches.

She was breathing hard, and her breath stirred his hair like a warm spring breeze. "Would you—could you take your clothes off now?"

It was a whispered entreaty, not a command, and his hand moved to the fastener on his slacks. He opened it, but he was so hard that he ended up fumbling with the zipper like a teenager, and then he got distracted by the rapid rise and fall of her chest. He couldn't hold back a moment longer.

Hooking one edge of the black silk robe with his finger, he pushed it away from her breast. The fabric caught on her nipple, then fell aside, leaving her breast exposed to him, a round of pale, blue-veined marble tipped with a puckered apricot bud, all of it framed in a V of black silk. He bent down to taste.

Emma felt his mouth touch her nipple, and the breath left her body. His lips closed warmly around her. The tip of his tongue brushed back and forth. She felt as if her body were going to fly away, and she curled her fingers into the bed's silky comforter to keep herself anchored.

He began to suckle her.

Her body shivered with fire and ice. Tears clouded her eyes. She wanted him to do this forever. She would die if he stopped. He was no longer a beautiful wastrel who'd hired himself out for the night. Instead, he was her first lover. Slow and gentle. Infinitely precious.

Her limbs melted into the bed. She felt the lightest scrape of his thumbnail through the silk that covered her other nipple, and her body turned back into fire.

"I can't . . . I can't stand this." She choked out the words.

In response, he suckled deeper. Took her other nipple between his fingers and squeezed. . . .

It was the sweetest pain she'd ever felt. Tears spilled over her lids and dripped onto the pillow. On the brink of orgasm, she opened her legs and willed his hand to go there. Just a brush. The merest touch. That's all she needed.

He squeezed again, and she gave a small sob.

His head came up, and he frowned as he spotted her tears. "Am I hurting you?"

She was incapable of responding. Instead, she lay there like a wanton, her breast exposed, its nipple wet and puckered, her legs splayed under the rumpled silk.

She saw that his pants were unzipped, and he was fully erect, but a straining pair of silky black boxers kept her from seeing the imposing column beneath. She tried to gather enough air so she could ask him not to stop, beg him to touch her again, plead with him to strip off those slacks and burn his black briefs.

He moved to the edge of the bed and shoved his hand through his hair. "What do you say we slow things down here a little?" His voice sounded hoarse, as if he were pushing the words through the narrowest of openings.

"No!" She shot up into a sitting position.

He stared at her.

She licked her lips. Wiped her tears on the sleeve of the robe. Gulped in air. Left the robe open over her breast.

"No." She tucked her legs beneath her. "It's—it's quite all right."

"I got a little carried away there."

"Actually, you didn't. I mean, you did, but . . . I wasn't . . . that is, I liked what you were . . ."

Good heavens, she was babbling. She looked away to collect her thoughts and realized music was playing. She drew a breath and took in the details of the room. A wallet sat on the dresser next to a pile of change. Socks lay on the floor. Behind them, the mirrored door of a walk-in closet was partially opened.

She pulled in another breath.

There were several books on the bedside table, including a volume of Texas history and a biography of Theodore Roosevelt. A few golf magazines. The one on top had a picture on the cover of someone familiar. Someone she recognized.

Odd. Who would she know—

She looked more closely and felt all the blood drain from her head.

Chapter 4

Emma didn't remember picking up the magazine, but it was in her hands, so she must have. As she stared down at it, the words on the cover swam before her eyes.

PGA BAD BOY KENNY TRAVELER
TALKS ABOUT HIS GAME,
TOUR POLITICS, AND HIS MILLIONS

"Uh . . . Emma?"

She dragged her legs over the side of the bed farthest from him and, with her free hand, clutched the robe together.

The photograph was an action shot, with Kenny in the middle of his golf swing, body turned, club angled back. PGA BAD BOY KENNY TRAVELER . . .

Fingers of rage uncurled inside her. She hadn't thought anything could be more painful than the humiliation she'd suffered when she'd shared her feelings with Jeremy Fox, but this was a dozen times worse. She was the stupidest, the most naive woman on earth. He wasn't a professional escort! He was a millionaire athlete who'd seduced her.

She flung down the magazine, vaulted from the side of the bed, and blindly made her way to the bathroom to reclaim her clothes.

"Don't you think we should talk about this?" he said from behind her.

She hurried past him, clothing stuffed in her arms, and headed for her bedroom.

"Lady Emma?"

She shot inside, twisted the lock, and began pulling on her underwear.

He tapped at the bedroom door. "I know that magazine cover must be piquing your curiosity, so why don't we finish our bottle of wine while I answer all your questions?"

She ignored his blather, threw her clothes in one suitcase, and snapped the latches on the other. Then she gathered them up along with her carry-all and purse and marched through the door.

He was standing on the other side. Although his pants were zipped, he hadn't bothered with a shirt. Hatred, spurred on by self-disgust, rushed through her. She pushed past him and hurried down the stairs as fast as her awkward burden would allow.

"Emma!"

A terrible drumming echoed inside her head. She reached the front door and fumbled for the knob.

"Emma, it's dark. You can't go out there." He came up behind her and grasped her arm.

She tore it free and slammed the corner of one suitcase into his crotch. He let out an *oof* of pain and staggered backward.

She dashed outside.

The humid night air enveloped her. She had no idea where she was, and she didn't care. She only knew she had to get away.

She nursed her anger until it drove out her need to weep. He hadn't been dense or dull-witted or any of the other things she'd thought about him. He'd simply been manipulating her for a night's amusement, and she'd fallen for it.

The heavy suitcases dragged at her arms as she made her way to the end of the court, but she didn't feel their weight. What if she hadn't seen the magazine? What if she'd gone through with it before she discovered who he was? It didn't bear contemplating, so she distracted herself by gazing down the street that intersected the court. She needed to get to a phone and call a taxi, but she saw only expensive homes, some with luxury cars parked in the drive. No one was walking about, and, other than the hiss of underground sprinkling systems, everything was quiet.

She listened harder and thought she detected the faint sound of traffic far in the distance. The suitcases banged against her legs as she turned toward the noise. She kept walking until she had to set the bags down to rest her arms, and that was when she heard the purr of a luxury car coming from behind her.

She snatched up the suitcases and dragged them on. From the corner of her eye, she saw a familiar champagne-colored Cadillac. The driver's window slid down. "Don't you think you're overreacting just a little bit?"

Her cheeks burned. She looked straight ahead and didn't slow her pace even though her shoulders had begun to throb.

"There isn't a hotel within ten miles of here. And, in case you haven't noticed, there aren't any taxis passing by, either."

She kept walking.

"God, I hate sulky women."

"*Sulky!*" She whirled on him. "Leave me alone! Or haven't you had enough amusement for the night?"

He pulled ahead of her, angled his car so that it blocked the street, then stopped and got out, leaving the motor running and the warning bell dinging. With his shirt hanging open and his bare feet stuffed into loafers, he approached her.

She felt a flicker of satisfaction as she saw that he wasn't standing completely straight, along with a shiver of panic. Although she didn't physically fear him, she had only the most fragile hold on her composure, and she had to escape.

Waddling slightly from the weight of her luggage, she hurried to the far side of the street. He closed the distance between them and manhandled both suitcases away from her.

"Give those back."

Ignoring her, he grabbed her carry-all and purse, then took everything to the car. He opened the rear door and tossed it all into the back seat as if it weighed no more than a handful of beach pebbles.

"You owe me a thousand bucks for that."

She bit her lip, blinked her eyes, and began walking.

He dropped his hands to his hips. "Tell me how far you think you're going to get without your passport, your money, and your clothes. Not to mention those umbrellas."

She had clearly been wronged, but instead of apologizing, he was making things worse. She tried to review her options, but they were so limited as to be nonexistent. Her steps slowed. "Drive me to a hotel at once," she finally managed.

"Gladly."

She hesitated, but she had little choice, and she forced herself to walk to the car. He opened the passenger door for her. Without looking at him, she slid inside, then tried to make herself invisible by staring out the window. Her lips felt swollen, and she remembered the feel of those deep, insincere kisses.

"Just go ahead and let me have it. I know you're dying to get it off your chest." Earlier he'd driven like a demon, but now the car crawled down the street.

She said nothing.

"All right, I was having a little fun with you, pretending I was in the flesh trade. But I didn't expect you to take me seriously. And then, when you did . . . Well, I'm only human, and before you condemn me for being a man, I suggest you take a long, hard look at yourself in the mirror. Then imagine what you would have done if you were me, and you were faced with somebody who looked like you."

How cruel of him to mock her because she wasn't beautiful. She could no longer hold back her words. "I wouldn't have lied! I would never have humiliated another human being as you did."

"Humiliated?" He sounded genuinely insulted, but then she remembered what a good actor he was. He pulled out through a set of gates onto a busier street. "Humiliation played no part in it. What I was doing had to do with opportunity—I'll admit that—but mainly it had to do with lust."

"Please, Mr. Traveler. I wasn't born yesterday. This had nothing to do with lust. You're a rich, good-looking professional athlete. I'm certain you can have any woman you want. You don't have to settle for an aging schoolteacher."

"I guess I know lust when I feel it! And you've got to admit you made it easy for me. Although why you think you'd have to pay a man is beyond me."

"Yes, I made it easy for you. Painfully easy."

He stopped at a flashing red light and looked over at her. "Look, Emma, I didn't mean to hurt your feelings. It's true I got carried away. But you were hell bent on having a fling with a stranger, and I guess I couldn't see the harm."

"You lied to me about everything. You're a famous professional golfer, not an escort. And according to that magazine cover, you're a multimillionaire." Realization struck her. "That wasn't your friend's house at all. It's yours, isn't it? Everything you told me was a lie."

"You aggravated me." He pulled away from the light.

"Me! I didn't do anything."

"That's a bald-faced lie. You started bossing me around the minute you laid eyes on me, making out lists, giving orders, and poking me with that umbrella."

"I never poked you with my umbrella."

"It felt like it."

"I apologize," she said icily.

"Good. I apologize, too, so now we're even."

"Not even close."

For the first time, she thought of Francesca's part in this. But as she recalled their conversation, she couldn't remember Francesca ever telling her that Kenny was a professional escort. Instead, she'd described him as a friend. Still, somehow Emma had gotten the idea that he did this professionally, and she distinctly remembered asking Francesca if seventy-five dollars a day would be enough to cover his fee.

Only now did she remember the way Francesca had laughed. "Tell him I said he'd work for fifty." Her friend could have had no idea how her small joke would backfire.

She no longer had the energy to fight with him. "This isn't going to work for either of us, Mr. Traveler. It's obvious you don't like me, and I certainly don't like—"

"That's not exactly true. When you aren't pointing that umbrella and telling me what to do, you're fairly enjoyable to be around." He swung out onto a four-lane highway. "At least you're not boring, which is more than I can say for most of the people I meet."

"How flattering. The fact is we can never recover from the bad start we've had. First thing in the morning, I'll call Francesca and ask her to recommend someone else to help me. We don't need to see each other again."

The car slowed. "Call Francesca?"

"I'll tell her we have a personality conflict. She'll understand."

"I—uh . . . I'd just as soon we leave Francesca out of this."

"I can't do that. She insisted I call her after I got in to report on my trip."

"I'll just bet she did," he muttered, then glanced over at her. "I'll tell you what. I'll give you a hundred dollars a day if you'll let me stay on as your travel guide. I'll do all the driving, take you wherever you want. All you have to do is enjoy the scenery and keep telling Francesca loud and clear that everything's fine between us."

The lazy fool had vanished. In his place was a determined stranger with a hard jaw and intense eyes. It took only a moment for the pieces to fall into place.

"Francesca's got some hold over you, doesn't she? That's why you agreed to do this in the first place."

"You might say." He pulled off the highway onto a service road, then swung into the parking lot of a luxurious-looking hotel.

"What is it?"

"I think both of us have had enough high drama for tonight."

"Tell me."

"A hundred dollars a day. Do you agree?"

Mesmerized, she stared at him. All trace of humor had vanished from his expression, and his perpetually smiling mouth had flatlined. This was a man accustomed to getting what he wanted.

She saw now that she'd underestimated him from the moment they'd met, and she wondered how many other people had done the same thing. It was a mistake she wouldn't repeat.

"Two hundred," she found herself saying, just to punish him. "Plus expenses." One part of her wondered if she'd lost her mind, but the other part of her had gone weak with relief. Whether he realized it or not, he had just handed her the power she needed to control him for the next two weeks. From this moment on, Emma owned Kenny Traveler, and after what he'd done to her tonight, she didn't have any qualms about using him to get what she needed.

The grim set of his features as he pulled beneath the hotel's porte cochere told her it hadn't taken him long to figure out that the balance of power had just shifted. Tension clipped away the soft edges of his Texas drawl. "I'll get you a room. And I want your word that you'll be down in the lobby waiting for me at nine o'clock tomorrow morning."

"Oh, I'll be there." Her new confidence must have been reflected in her eyes because his own narrowed, and, right then, she made up her mind to find out exactly what hold Francesca had over him.

Ten minutes later the bellman escorted her to a lavish suite on the hotel's concierge floor. For a moment she almost felt guilty, but the emotion quickly vanished. She knew a bribe when she saw one, and Kenny Traveler was trying to buy her off. It wouldn't work, but perhaps he didn't have to know that just yet.

The next morning, the ringing of the phone awakened her. She pushed her hair from her eyes and glanced at the clock as she reached for the receiver—6:18.

"Hello."

"Hold, please, for His Grace, the Duke of Beddington."

She sank back into the pillows. She'd wondered how long it would take him to find her. As she waited, the events of last night swept over her, and she was almost glad when a too-familiar voice interrupted.

"Emma, my darling gel. Where have you been? You've put me through my paces finding you."

She recoiled from the nasal tones of Hugh Weldon Holroyd, the eleventh Duke of Beddington, and a man who resembled Henry VIII in more ways than his appearance. He also happened to own the land on which St. Gert's was built, as well as becoming the school's primary benefactor when his mother, the dowager duchess, had died eight months ago.

"Good morning, Your Grace."

"Now, none of that, my dear. You're to address me as Hugh, although only in private, you understand." He paused for a moment, and she envisioned him stuffing a crumpet through those fleshy lips. Not that Hugh would actually stuff anything. Even as he consumed vast quantities of food, his manners were impeccable. He'd once demolished an entire tray of her tea sandwiches without dropping so much as a single crumb. The appearance of propriety was as important to him as his title.

"Emma, Emma, we seem to have had a slight miscommunication. You were to ring me yesterday when you got in. I must tell you that it's been quite difficult tracking you down."

"I'm sorry," she lied. "I was so exhausted it slipped my mind."

"Perfectly understandable. I do hope you had a sound sleep."

"Yes, quite." His amiability didn't fool her. She'd already learned that the Duke of Beddington was a man who'd do anything to get what he wanted. She thought of his two dead wives and shuddered. Not that there had been anything suspicious about either death—one had lost her life in childbirth, the other had been caught in an avalanche during a ski holiday in the Alps. But between his physical resemblance to Henry VIII, the deaths of his wives, and the two young daughters he'd tucked away at a school far more prestigious than St. Gert's, he made her skin crawl.

"You'd told me you hired a driver, but you didn't mention he was one of the most famous professional golfers in the world. I know how naive you are, my dear, so I'm certain it hasn't occurred to you that this arrangement won't do at all."

She experienced a small stab of satisfaction. "Please don't concern yourself, Your Grace. My friend Francesa recommended him." She didn't bother asking him how he'd learned that Kenny was escorting her, since Hugh Holroyd wasn't a man to leave anything to chance. From the moment she'd announced the trip, she'd known he would hire someone to keep track of her.

"I'm sure you didn't stop to consider how this would look. I know you enjoy Francesca's company, but she's in television, my dear, which makes her barely respectable. And as the future Duchess of Beddington, you need to think about such things."

She curled her fingers tighter around the phone cord. "Oh, I'm certain it won't be a problem. I only have two weeks to finish my research, and I needed someone reliable. Mr. Traveler is very familiar with the area."

"Darling, that's not the point. We'll be announcing our engagement as soon as you return, and it's not at all the thing for you to be spending so much time with another man, even though he's only your escort."

They weren't going to be announcing their engagement, but he didn't know that yet. Just as he didn't know she was going to do everything in her power to protect St. Gert's from his blackmail. "I'm in Texas, Your Grace. None of your circle of acquaintances will ever know."

"You forget that I have business interests all over the world. As a matter of fact, I have to go to New York just when you'll be on your way home. I'd hoped to meet you in London as soon as you returned, but I'm afraid we'll have to postpone that. Actually, my dear, the more I think about this, the more I believe that you need to come home right away. From the very beginning, this trip has displeased me."

"I appreciate your concern, but I'm afraid that's impossible. I know you don't want me to continue as headmistress after the engagement is announced."

"Quite right. It would be most inappropriate."

Only in the seventeenth century, you awful man!

"Then you see why I must stay. I've promised the editors of the *New Historian* I'll have my paper finished for them by the first of May, and I'm sure you agree that I can't go back on my word." She paused for dramatic effect. "Only think how it would look if the future Duchess of Beddington didn't meet an obligation."

She knew she'd made her point when she heard the fretful note in his voice. "Still, I don't fancy having you escorted by a man who's so notorious. I know I sound like a doting husband, my dear, but I couldn't forgive myself if I let the slightest breath of scandal attach itself to your name."

"It won't, Your Grace." She narrowed her eyes at her blatant lie. If all went well, she would create a scandal just large enough to put an end to any idea of an engagement and, at the same time, ensure that St. Gert's would remained a safe, comfortable haven for another generation of girls.

When she finally hung up, she was shaking, and she flung herself out of bed. Dealing with two horrible men in less than twenty-four hours was far worse than dealing with a classroom of unruly students. At least she hadn't been forced to work with Hugh until recently. Up to the time of her death, the dowager duchess had been Emma's only contact with the family, although she'd known Hugh by reputation for years because of his well-publicized talents for making huge profits by investing in cutting-edge technology. But despite his facility with high finance and modern technology, he was an old-style aristocrat, a man so puffed up with pride over his illustrious family name that adding to his consequence had become even more important to him than making money.

His two marriages had produced only female children, and, like Henry

VIII, he was obsessed with the need for a male heir. Unless he had a son, his ancient title would go to a long-haired nephew who was a drummer for a rock and roll band. It was unthinkable, and only months after his second wife's death, he'd set his staff on a search to find his next wife. She had to be well-born—that went without saying. And solid, without a hint of scandal. No flashy Sarah Fergusons to bring his name into disrepute. He would also prefer a virgin.

She could just imagine the reaction his staff must have had to that. Later she'd learned that the only women they'd been able to come up with who fit his criteria were thirteen years old.

It was Hugh's sister who thought of Emma and suggested that Hugh, instead of herself, represent the family at St. Gert's annual Founder's Day festivities. As Emma had served him tea in her office that first afternoon, he'd reprimanded her for taking a phone call from an anxious parent in the middle of their conversation and frowned at the glitter-encrusted necklace she was wearing, a handmade birthday present from one of the seven-year-olds. She couldn't abide him.

He reappeared the next week and the week after that. She made up excuses to avoid him, but one afternoon he caught her in his office and, with a great deal of haughtiness, informed her that he'd decided she would make him a suitable wife. Their engagement would be announced as soon as she resigned her position as headmistress.

Emma was flabbergasted. She had to resist the urge to check her desk calendar to see if she'd inadvertently time-traveled back to the Regency. "Your Grace, I have no intention of marrying you. We barely know each other. The whole idea is ridiculous."

Her bluntness was a mistake. He narrowed his eyes, puffed himself up, and told her the matter was settled.

"It's not settled at all!"

"You're a titled virgin of the proper age with an exemplary reputation and an unassuming appearance," he replied. "There's nothing left to discuss."

Hearing herself reduced to such a boring description stung, and she made the fatal mistake of losing her temper. "I'm not a virgin! I've slept with dozens of men. Sailors, lorry drivers, the school handyman just last week!"

"Don't be infantile. I know that you've never had a serious relationship with a man. If you aren't a virgin, the experience happened so long ago as to be insignificant." With an expression of disdain, he'd moved toward the door of her office. "Our discussion is over, Emma. If you aren't intelligent enough to understand the honor I'm doing you, you certainly aren't intelligent enough to run St. Gertrude's, and you'll be dismissed.''

His threat stunned her, and it was a moment before she recovered. "What difference would that make? If I do as you ask, I'll lose my position anyway.''

The door shut, and she felt as if the familiar room were spinning around her. His threat made her heartsick. She slumped down in her chair and tried to absorb this violent, absurd disruption to her well-ordered life.

When Hugh's sister called the next day to fix a date for the engagement announcement, Emma told her there would be no wedding.

A week passed, and she heard nothing. She was just beginning to dismiss the bizarre incident when she saw a surveying crew moving across the school grounds. Heart pounding, she rushed to question them and was informed that they were acting on the orders of the Duke of Beddington.

He answered her call so promptly she suspected he'd been waiting for it.

"Your Grace, tell me at once what's happening. Why did you send surveyors here?''

"Didn't I tell you? It must have slipped my mind. I'm contemplating selling the property to a developer.'' He paused to let the words sink in. "He'd be tearing down the buildings to put up some very expensive homes.''

It took her only a moment to realize he was subjecting her to the most blatant sort of blackmail. The school was the only real home she'd ever had, but her emotional attachment wasn't all of it. Over the protests of Hugh's mother, she'd arranged to have a group of bright, ambitious scholarship students admitted. What would happen to them when they were sent back to schools far inferior to St. Gert's? She remembered how unsteady her voice had been as she'd asked him, "And if I were to marry you, what would happen to the school?''

"Why, my dear, I could hardly sell off a place so dear to the heart of the Duchess of Beddington, now, could I?''

That was when she decided that he was more than a little mad.

She sat up for two nights before she came up with her plan. The next day she reached him at his office. "I'm sorry I was so difficult, Your Grace. It was the shock. Of course I'll be thrilled to accept your offer . . . that is, if you haven't reconsidered marrying someone so far beneath you.'' She waited hopefully.

"Reconsidered? Of course not.''

Hardly able to conceal her distress, she'd told him that the engagement could be announced just as soon as she completed her professional obligations, which included making a trip to the States between the winter and spring terms so she could finish working on a research paper she'd begun for the *New Historian.*

She was telling the truth about the paper, but what she didn't tell him was that it wouldn't take her more than a few days to complete her research. The rest of the time she would use for something more important.

Losing her good name.

Her plan was hardly foolproof, but it was the best she could come up with. She had to alarm Beddington just enough so he'd withdraw his offer, but not enough to make him suspect that she was deliberately manipulating him. If that happened, he was vindictive enough to destroy the school for revenge.

Unfortunately, she could think of no plan that would allow her to continue her career at St. Gert's. There was no possibility of him allowing anyone with a spotted reputation to stay on there, but she'd find a new position somewhere. St. Gert's had taken care of her when she was most vulnerable, and now she would do the same.

Chapter 5

As Emma walked into the hotel lobby toward Kenny, she saw that the hard-eyed stranger who'd brought her to the hotel the night before had disappeared and the affable loafer had taken his place. This time, however, she wasn't fooled.

For a moment she forgot what a scoundrel he was and simply enjoyed the sight. He'd left his Stetson behind, and his crisp dark hair gleamed in the light coming through the atrium. He wore a faded University of Texas T-shirt, tan shorts, and brown work boots with an inch of snowy white sock visible at the top. Her sanity returned as the corner of his mouth kicked up.

"Mornin', Lady Emma. Glad to see you brought your umbrella. It's sure to rain sometime this year."

She glanced down at her floral brolly as if she couldn't imagine how it had gotten there, then regarded him with a cheery smile and deliberately jabbed it toward the door. "Let's be off, then."

She had the satisfaction of seeing his eyes narrow. "Breakfast first. Then business."

"I've already eaten."

He gazed down at her with those lazy violet eyes, then used his slow drawl to whip her into line. "Now, Lady Emma, don't tell me you've forgotten whose payroll you're on."

She should have expected this.

"I'm going to have some blueberry pancakes this morning." His fingers wrapped around her upper arm. "How about you?"

She considered mentioning her pleasant conversation with Francesca less than half an hour ago and the fact that she could call her good friend back at any moment, but then she hesitated. It would be wise to reserve her Francesca ammunition for bigger battles. Whether or not she ate a second breakfast this morning wasn't that important.

As they settled at a booth in the coffee shop, she thought about what she'd nearly done with this man yesterday and wondered if jet lag had deprived her of her common sense. What had she hoped to accomplish by jumping into Kenny Traveler's bed less than twelve hours after she'd arrived in this country? If she intended to sleep with someone, she should at least have made certain that Hugh had his watchdogs in place. Her impulsiveness was uncharacteristic, and it made her uneasy.

"Just tea for me," she said as the waitress approached to take their orders.

Kenny beamed his approval at her. "Good choice. But add some blueberry pancakes to her order, along with a side of bacon, and I believe I'll have the same for myself, except forget the tea and bring coffee instead."

He was deliberately provoking her, but she simply smiled. "Change the blueberry pancakes to toast, if you would. And substitute a bowl of strawberries for the bacon."

The harried waitress poured his coffee, then rushed off before either of them could further complicate the order.

They had work to do, and Emma had witnessed enough of his nonsense. She took only a moment to enjoy a display of fresh flowers near the door before getting to the point. "Did you find a tattoo parlor?"

"You are not getting a tattoo. The whole idea's ridiculous."

"I am getting a tattoo. And I'm doing it today. This isn't negotiable." She doubted a tattoo alone would put a stop to her engagement, but it should make Hugh begin to question his judgment. She looked around the coffee shop, wondering if any of the men hunkered down behind their newspapers had been hired to watch her. No one looked suspicious, but she didn't for a moment believe that Hugh would allow her these two weeks unobserved. The fact that he'd found her so easily this morning proved that.

"How are you going to face all those little girls you headmistress over with a tattoo?" Kenny inquired.

She wouldn't be facing those little girls, but she wasn't going to tell him that. "It'll help them relate better to me."

"If that's all you want, why not go all the way and get your tongue pierced? Or dye your hair purple?"

She'd thought about getting pierced, but she'd worried about infection, and dying her hair some outrageous color would be too obvious. A very small tattoo was as far as she dared to go. Hugh needed to believe he'd misjudged her character, not that she was deliberately manipulating him, or he'd bulldoze St. Gert's. The waitress arrived with her tea, then disappeared.

"And just where do you plan to put that tattoo?"

"My upper arm." Once this was over, she'd have to keep it covered for the rest of her life.

"Ladies don't put tattoos on their upper arms. They put them on an ankle or the back of a shoulder or, if they really want to be discreet—and this is what I'd recommend in your case if I were going to make a recommendation, which I'm not—a *breast*."

Her cup froze halfway to her lips. That single word brought it all back. The feel of the silk sliding away from her skin, the warmth of his mouth, the pull of his lips on her nipple.

He knew exactly what he was doing, of course.

"Would you, now?" She forced the cup the rest of the way to her mouth, sipped, then set it back down. "Well, I'm certain you should know."

"You're still pissed about last night, aren't you?"

"Miffed, Mr. Traveler. Headmistresses are never pissed."

He grinned, then regarded her with boyish earnestness. "Fill in the holes in my logic here, will you? The way I see it, you're a very nice unmarried lady who'd like a little sexual variety in her life. Perfectly natural. But back home in England, you have a reputation to maintain, so you sure can't do any experimentation there. In the great state of Texas, though, nobody's going to be any the wiser. Now, what I want to know is this: What difference does it make whether I happen to be a professional gigolo or a professional golfer? I've got all the necessary equipment, and I'm happy to let you use it."

"You're far too generous with your toys, but the fact is . . . I wouldn't let you touch me again if you were the last man on earth." The moment she'd spoken the words a red alert sounded in her brain. This lazy fool, who wasn't a fool at all, made his living by competing, and, unless she was mistaken, she could see the light of challenge beginning to gleam in his eyes.

"Well, we'll just have to see about that, now, won't we, Lady Emma?"

Thankfully, the waitress appeared at that moment with their food. Emma ate most of her strawberries, but wasn't able to manage more than a few bites of toast. Kenny finished his pancakes, then dug into her leftovers.

"That's not sanitary," she pointed out.

"We already swapped germs last night, so I'm not too worried about it."

She wasn't going to let him make her uncomfortable by thinking about those slow, deep kisses. "It's a wonder you aren't fat, with the way you eat."

"I burn a lot of energy during the day."

"Doing *what*?"

"Loafing's hard work."

She had to suppress a smile, and that bothered her. She wouldn't let herself be won over this easily by his counterfeit charm. "If you won't help me find a tattoo parlor, I'll simply consult the telephone directory and find one myself. In the meantime, I need to do some shopping."

"I thought this was supposed to be a research trip." He signaled the waitress for the check.

"It is, but research won't take up all my time. I do want to spend a few hours this afternoon at the Dallas Historical Society. I've made arrangements to check some of their papers. I also have a bit of work to do in Austin at the University of Texas library and in San Antonio."

"So tell me more about this lady you're researching."

"Lady Sarah Thornton? I'm doing a paper on her for the *New Historian*. Although I'm not in the classroom anymore, I like to stay involved. Lady Sarah was an extraordinary woman, a member of the aristocracy, but quite independent for her time, and insatiably curious. She traveled alone through this region in 1872."

"She managed the trip by herself, did she?" he said pointedly.

"Lady Sarah was more courageous than I am. Her account is fascinating because she saw Texas both through the eyes of a foreigner and a woman. She was in Dallas the day the first train arrived on the Houston & Texas Central. Her description of the buffalo barbecue they held to celebrate is very lively."

He tossed some bills on the table and rose. "Seems strange a lady in 1872 would have had the nerve to travel through Texas all by herself, but a modern-day, independent woman like yourself is such a pansy."

"Lady Sarah didn't have to deal with cars," she pointed out as she followed him. Lady Sarah also didn't need to make a duke uneasy by openly traveling with a good-looking man.

As they walked back into the lobby, she handed him two dollars. "To cover my tea. You made me order the rest, so you can pay for it."

"Keep your two dollars."

"No need to be surly." She tucked the bills back into her purse and, just to antagonize him, pointed her brolly toward the door. "This way."

He snatched it from her hand and pitched it at the doorman. "Burn this for me, will you?"

"Deliver it to my room, please," she told the doorman. "Ms. Wells-Finch. Number 820."

She was headed for the parking lot before she realized Kenny wasn't with her and she had no idea where he'd put his car.

She looked back and saw him moving like a snail on sleeping pills out from beneath the porte cochere. She tapped the toe of her sandal.

He greeted a pair of businessmen, then stopped to admire some tile work.

She sighed and looked around for his car. Somehow she wasn't surprised to spot it parked in a handicapped spot. She waited impatiently for him to approach.

Finally, he unlocked the door. "You sure you have to do your shopping today?" he asked as she slipped inside and fastened her seat belt.

"Yes. Someplace trendy, but inexpensive."

"Then you're out of luck because I don't know the first thing about bargain shopping. Just buy what you want and put it on my charge." They turned back out onto the highway.

"I will not!"

"Why get picky now? You didn't object to that one hundred dollars a day you're forcing me to pay to keep your mouth shut."

"*Two* hundred dollars a day. And that's blackmail money, so it's different, isn't it?" She regarded him smugly.

His gaze swept over the outfit she'd chosen for today: a short denim skirt in persimmon with a cream-colored top tucked into it. The top had a garden scene printed on it, complete with a pair of bluebirds. "Nice shirt."

"Thank you. My fifth form students gave it to me at the end of the term."

As they rode along the freeway, she finally had a chance to take in the sights of this state she knew only from history books. The collections of strip malls, billboards, and fast food restaurants held little interest to her, but the sheer size of it took her breath away. She couldn't imagine anything more different from Lower Tilbey or from St. Gert's aged red brick buildings, tidy lawns, and ancient trees. What must Lady Sarah Thornton have thought when she saw such a vast stretch of land and sky?

She leaned forward as Kenny began to pull into another handicapped space. "Absolutely not."

"I wasn't going to park here," he said with an air of injured innocence. "Shopping with a lady isn't my favorite activity, so I'm just dropping you off while I hit some balls at the practice range. I'll pick you up in three hours."

"Gracious, I know exactly what I want, and it won't take me nearly that long." She whipped his keys from the ignition. "Come along, then."

He snatched his keys back, but he came with her, although he grumbled the entire way into the mall. "You'd better not take more than half an hour. I mean it, Lady Emma. After half an hour, me and my Caddy are taking off whether you're with us or not."

"Uhm." She studied the shop windows and, almost immediately, saw what she wanted. She gestured toward a rounded concrete bench. "Wait right here. I won't be a moment."

"You are the damnedest, most order-giving female it's ever been my misfortune to meet up with! Do you think I can just sit in the middle of a major American shopping mall without starting a near riot?"

"Whatever are you talking about?"

"I'm a semi-famous person, that's what."

As if to prove his words, two young women carrying pink Victoria's Secret shopping bags came charging toward him. "Kinny!"

He glared at her. "Now see what you've done?"

"I won't be long. I promise."

She wasn't, but by the time she'd returned, he had a small crowd gathered around him, and he seemed to be holding an impromptu golf clinic.

"After you get to the top, make sure you start down nice and smooth. You want to build up that speed as you go through. . . ."

She caught his eye, but, for all his former protesting, he appeared to be enjoying himself and didn't seem in any hurry to get away. She ducked into an accessory place and added a few pieces of inexpensive costume jewelry to her purchases before he finally broke away from his admirers and led her back to the car.

"Now the tattoo," she said when they were once again on the road.

"You're really serious about this, aren't you?"

"Absolutely."

He thought for a few minutes. "All right, if you're dead set, I'll help you. But it's going to take me a little time to find a place where you can be sure they're using clean needles."

"Needles?"

"How do you think they put those tattoos on?"

"Yes, of course. I mean . . . I know they use needles. It was just the way you said the word."

"It's going to hurt, Queen Elizabeth. So if you can't take the pain, maybe you'd better rethink this."

"It won't be that painful."

His snort wasn't encouraging.

"You're just trying to unnerve me."

"Well, excuse me for being a compassionate and caring human being."

"*Ha!*"

"All right. You win. I'll look into the whole thing after I drop you off to do your research."

For once he was thinking efficiently. "Excellent idea."

They headed for the State Fair Park, where the Dallas Historical Society was located in an impressive, T-shaped pavilion called the Hall of State. She slipped out of his car in the parking lot after agreeing to meet at three o'clock.

Although she had intended to head immediately for the offices of the Historical Society, she discovered there was too much she wanted to see first, and she took her time studying the giant murals that ran around the four-story interior of the Great Hall of Texas, depicting the state's history from 1528 into the twentieth century. When she finally arrived at the Historical Society offices, she was greeted warmly, and she spent the next few hours cross-checking the notes she'd taken from Lady Sarah's journal with other sources from the time period. She was so absorbed in her research that she lost track of time and didn't arrive at the spot where she was supposed to meet Kenny until three-fifteen.

The Cadillac was waiting, along with its irate driver. "You're late. I hate that!"

"Really, Kenny, you have no right to complain. How was I supposed to know you'd be prompt today after you were so late yesterday?"

"Yesterday was different."

"Because you were the one who was late instead of me."

"Something like that."

"You're impossible. Did you find the tattoo parlor?"

"Even better. I found a lady who does tattoos in her home."

"Really? And you think she's reliable?"

"Pillar of the community. You're not going to get anyone more reliable. Only thing is, she's got a busy schedule, and she can't take you till ten o'clock tonight. I had to practically beg for that."

She hoped Hugh's detectives would be around. "That'll be fine." Her stomach rumbled. "I could use a bit of lunch."

"I know just the place."

Twenty minutes later they drove through the stone gates of a country club that screamed exclusivity. The tree-shrouded lane ended in a pillared Greek Revival–style building. After Kenny parked, she got out and headed for the front entrance. Once again, it took her a while before she realized he wasn't following. She turned.

He stood watching her, his hands splayed on his hips. "Do you know where you're going?"

She glanced around. "Not really."

"Then why are you leading?"

"I don't know. I always do."

"Well, stop. I don't like it."

Neither had Jeremy Fox. But she wasn't the kind of woman to be a follower. She'd been on her own most of her life, and she'd learned very early that she could either lead the way or get trampled.

He jerked his thumb toward a smaller building. "We're going over there."

"Sorry." She felt foolish as she followed him along a walk that led to a door topped with ornately carved gold wooden letters indicating it was the pro shop. The men inside greeted him as if he were visiting royalty.

"Hey, Kinny! How's it goin'?"

"Haven't seen you in a few days."

"Did you hear Charlie made an eagle on seven yesterday? Got so excited his heart kicked up, and he couldn't finish the round."

Kenny returned their greetings, said he hadn't heard about Charlie, then led Emma toward a glass-walled grill room that connected to one end. "Hope you don't mind eating alone." He gestured toward the hostess. "Take care of her, will you, Maryann? I'm gonna hit some balls."

"Sure 'nough, Kenny. Did you know everybody on the staff signed a petition to the Antichrist to get you back on tour?"

"Well, now, I appreciate that. You be sure and tell 'em all thanks for me."

He disappeared, and Maryann settled Emma at a window table. "You can watch him from here. And, honey, won't it be a glorious sight to behold? Nobody hits long irons like Kenny Traveler."

Emma gave her a look that she hoped was friendly but reserved. She had no interest in watching Kenny Traveler hit long irons.

Until she saw him.

Although he still wore his tan shorts, he'd traded in his work boots for a pair of golf shoes, and the University of Texas T-shirt had been replaced by a dark brown golf shirt with another logo, although she was too far away to see which one. His muscles were fluid and graceful as he hit one shot after another. The balls flew off the tee, soaring so far that she couldn't see them land. She wasn't surprised by his grace, but the display of power coming from a man so fundamentally lazy left her feeling light-headed.

He was a complete mystery to her. She had the feeling that dark waters lurked beneath that lackadaisical exterior, but she had no idea how deep they ran or how far they flowed. She thought of what he'd said in the car earlier when he'd made it evident that he still wanted to go to bed with her. *"What difference does it make whether I happen to be a professional gigolo or a professional golfer? I've got all the necessary equipment, and I'm happy to let you use it."*

But it did make a difference. She could somehow have respected herself if she'd bought his services, but she couldn't respect herself if she became a groupie for a rich, professional athlete to regard with secret contempt.

All day she'd tried to avoid thinking about last night, but as she ate her grilled chicken sandwich and watched him hit one ball after another, his strength made her grow warm and restless. She forced herself to think logically. A tattoo and a change of wardrobe weren't going to be enough to completely discourage Hugh Holroyd, merely give him second thoughts. She'd known all along she'd have to do something more dramatic. Take a lover? The idea had been nibbling away at her for some time. But not Kenny Traveler. After what had happened last night, that would now be immoral. She couldn't exactly explain why; she only knew it was true. She needed to find someone else.

The thought depressed her so much she lost her appetite. Kenny Traveler wasn't honest or trustworthy, but he certainly was sexy, and, despite her aversion to rogues, she wanted it to be with him.

She took a glum poke at her tuna sandwich, then signaled the waitress for a cup of tea she didn't want. Anything to draw her attention away from the tantalizing figure on the driving range.

Kenny dropped her off at the hotel before he went back to his condo to change into what he called his "tattoo parlor clothes." At seven-thirty, she headed down to the lobby to wait for him. When she arrived, she looked around for someone who might be a detective, but all she saw were businessmen and tourists.

Kenny came in through the revolving door. He wore a pair of navy slacks and a white polo shirt with a Dean Witter logo. She wondered if he owned any clothes that didn't have a product endorsement on them.

As he caught sight of her, he froze. "What in Sam Hill did you do to yourself?"

"Who's the Antichrist?"

"We're not talking about that now; we're talking about the fact that

I dropped off Mary Poppins and I came back to find Madonna." His gaze took in her new outfit, purchased at one of the mall's inexpensive teen boutiques. The sleeveless black T-dress was perilously short and closely fitted, with a zip-neck. Unzipped. Or at least unzipped far enough to be noted in a memo to London.

"Really? You think I look like Madonna?"

"You don't look anything like Madonna." He lowered his voice to a growl that only she could hear. "What you look like is a nympho-maniac Mary Poppins. There wasn't a single thing wrong with those clothes you had on today, and I want you to change right back into them."

"Gracious, Kenny, you sound like an outraged father."

His scowl grew more pronounced. "You're happy about this, aren't you? You're happy to be walking around without leaving anything to the imagination."

"It's not that bad, is it?" Perhaps she'd gone too far. If a playboy like Kenny Traveler thought she was dressed too obviously, maybe she needed to be more subtle. She tugged the zipper all the way up. "There."

He continued to regard her critically. "You've got makeup on."

"I've had makeup on all day."

"Not as much as you have on now."

"It's tastefully applied, and don't try to tell me it's not."

"That's not the point."

"Then what is the point?"

He opened his mouth to speak, then shook his head. "I don't know. All I know is—between what happened last night and your tattoo ob-session and now this—I'm getting a real bad feeling. It's one thing to want a little freedom on your summer vacation; it's another to change into a different person. Suppose you tell me exactly what's going on in that head of yours."

"Not a thing."

He drew her off to the side, keeping his voice low. "Look, Emma. Let's speak frankly here. You have an itch you want scratched—per-fectly understandable—but you can't let just anybody scratch it. Dressed like that, you're pretty much putting yourself on the auction block."

"Nonsense. You're going to be with me all evening, aren't you? How can anything happen?" She headed for the lobby doors.

"That's not the point," he said, coming up behind her. "Go change your clothes, then I'll take you to a great Mexican restaurant for din-ner."

"Are you afraid that being seen with a fast-looking woman is going to ruin your reputation?"

"This is about you, not me."

"I think I've made my point." She smiled to show there were no hard feelings and headed for the parking lot. On her way, she began clipping three tiny sets of fake-pierced hoops behind the silver studs in her earlobes.

He came after her. "I'm not taking any responsibility for this. Next time you chat with Francesca, you make it real clear that I did everything I could to talk some sense into you."

She waited until he was backing out of the handicapped spot. "Who's the Antichrist?"

"A person who's name I won't speak." He changed the subject. "How did your visit to the Historical Society go? Did you find out anything new about Lady Sarah?"

"More confirmation that she was an astute observer. Her account of the railroad celebration agrees with all the other sources, but she gives much more detail."

He asked about the methods she used for her research, and she found herself talking all the way to the restaurant. When she saw where they were, she was embarrassed. "Sorry. Sometimes my enthusiasm runs away from me."

"I don't mind," he replied, as they headed toward the front door. "I like history. And I like it when people enjoy their work. Too many poor slobs spend their lives doing things they hate." He held the door open for her. "I'll bet you were a good teacher before the fleshmongers got hold of you and turned you into a Head Mistress."

She smiled. "I love the classroom. But being headmistress has its compensations."

"All those furs and diamond bracelets."

"St. Gert's is a wonderful old place, but she needed to be modernized. I've loved the challenge."

"She?"

"It's hard to explain. The school has this wonderful personality, like a cozy old grandmother. St. Gert's is very special."

He regarded her curiously, then the hostess came up to them, greeted him by name, and led them to their table.

Chapter 6

The restaurant had been built in a rambling old house with creaky floors and small rooms painted in earth tones. Accompanied by the delicious scents of spicy food, they made their way to one of the rear rooms. Some of the diners called out greetings to Kenny, while others stood to get a better view. This, combined with what had happened earlier at the mall, made Emma realize exactly how big a celebrity Kenny Traveler was. The knowledge made her uneasy. What terrible thing had he done to make him vulnerable to Francesca's blackmail?

The hostess showed them to a back corner table covered in a dark green cloth slashed with awning stripes of orange and red. The walls in this room were rough brown stucco decorated with turn-of-the-century Mexican advertising posters.

A waiter appeared with a basket of chips and salsa. Kenny sent him back for the spicier version, then ordered a Dos Equis for himself and an extra large margarita for her.

"Just a large will do."

"Extra large," Kenny said to the waiter, who nodded and disappeared, obviously eager to please the restaurant's celebrity client.

"Why do you keep changing my orders? I don't want to drink that much."

"You keep forgetting about those needles. In a couple of hours you're going to be getting that tattoo you're so dead set on, and, from what I hear, it's going to hurt like hell. I seriously recommend you undertake the process semi-drunk."

Emma definitely didn't like needles, and she decided he had a point. She began to study the menu, then set it aside. What was the use? He'd order for her anyway.

She was right. The waiter arrived with their drinks, and Kenny dictated an order so large and complex, she had no idea what she'd be eating. When the waiter finally disappeared, she repeated the question he kept ducking. "Are you ready to tell me who the Antichrist is?"

"Are we back to that again?"

"Male or female?"

He sighed. "Male."

"You've known him long?"

"Way too long."

"Is he connected with your business life or your personal life?"

"You might say."

She thought about asking if he was bigger than a bread box. "Just tell me!"

He hesitated, then shrugged. "Your good friend's husband, that's who."

"Dallie?"

He winced. "Don't say it! I can't stand hearing that name."

"Even I know he's a famous golfer, but—"

"Just about the most famous golfer in the world. He's won all the majors at one time or another and more regular tour events than anybody can count. Next year he turns fifty, and he'll start tearing apart the senior tour."

"But I thought Francesca mentioned that he was the president of some kind of professional golfing organization."

"Only temporarily. He had to have shoulder surgery not long ago, and he agreed to take on the job of acting PGA commissioner while he recovered. The organization wanted to take its time finding the right person to fill the position permanently, and he was one of the few people everybody *mistakenly* trusted to hold the position until then. He didn't much want to do it, but certain people persuaded him." He frowned.

"You being one of them?"

"The stupidest thing I've ever done, considering the fact that the job gives him more ways to abuse power than a South American dictator, and he's used every one of them against me."

"That's hard to believe. Francesca makes Dallie sound like the kindest, most amiable man."

"He's a bloodthirsty, power-loving, manipulative, arrogant son of a bitch, is what he is. Now, can we talk about something else? I haven't had anything to eat since breakfast, but you've just about made me lose my appetite."

"The waitress at the country club today said something about signing a petition to get you back on the tour. Does that mean you're not actively playing at the moment?''

"I've been suspended indefinitely," he said tightly. Those violet eyes turned hard as flint.

"By Dal—By Francesca's husband.''

He gave a short nod.

"Why?''

"Stuff happens, that's all.''

When he made no effort to elaborate, she regarded him more closely. "How do I fit into this?''

The arrival of the appetizers gave him an excuse to ignore her. He busied himself with the stuffed jalapeños while she sipped her frozen margarita. A few grains of salt caught on her bottom lip. She flicked them away with the tip of her tongue. "All I have to do is ask Francesca.''

He stared at her bottom lip so long that she was afraid something was wrong. She blotted it with her napkin.

He blinked his eyes. "Francesca has a lot of influence with her husband.''

"And?''

"She's going to use it to get me back on the tour.''

"I see.'' Now she did see. "But only if you agreed to help me.''

"That's about the size of it.''

There was something missing. Why would Francesca care so much about having Kenny escort her? It made no sense. "What could she have been thinking of? She must have known we'd be oil and water.''

"All her years on that talk show have done something sadistic to her brain. She likes putting unlikely people together, then watching them kill each other so she can feast on the remains.''

That didn't sound like Francesca. There were definitely a few missing pieces here, but she was unlikely to find out what they were from Kenny.

He gazed at her with displeasure. "You going to eat or just keep licking your lip like that?''

"Licking my lip?''

"I'm not one to cast stones, since I have my own share of bad habits, but you need to leave that bottom lip of yours alone. You're always nibbling at it or licking it or something. It's distracting.''

"You know, Kenny, I'm getting more than a little annoyed with your criticism.''

"Uh-huh.'' He slid the tortilla chip he'd just loaded up into her mouth.

The salsa was hot and, by the time she'd gotten her breath back, the rest of their food had arrived. While they ate, Kenny entertained her with local lore, and she soon found herself laughing at his stories. He could be a charming companion when he set his mind to it, or perhaps it was simply the glow of her colossal-sized margarita because she found herself enveloped in a fuzzy-headed blur.

She excused herself to go to the loo, and, when she returned, another margarita was waiting for her. This one had a slightly different taste, but was equally delicious. Remembering the needles, she gave herself permission to indulge. Multicolored rainbows began dancing on the stucco walls.

Finally, Kenny pushed away the last bits of his cinnamon-dusted fried ice cream and paid the bill, even though she'd told him the meal was her treat. "It's getting close to ten," he said. "We'd better be on our way. That is if you're still intent on doing this."

"Oh, yes." Her voice was a little loud, and she attempted to lower it. "I haven't changed my mind." She stood, and the room began to spin.

"Steady, now." He took her arm and guided her through the restaurant. On their way to the door, he returned the greetings of the fans who wanted to catch his attention.

She expected the fresh air to revive her, but it didn't, and as the lights of the parking lot spun around her, she tried to make herself care that she'd had far too much to drink. "Kenny, you never told me what you did to get suspended from the tour."

"That's because you wouldn't like the answer."

She wanted to spread her arms, embrace the night, embrace him. "Tonight there's nothing I wouldn't like."

"All right then . . . among other things, I punched a woman."

It was the last thing she remembered.

Emma heard water running and realized the second form students had turned the hose on again outside her cottage. They liked to fill her birdbath, but they didn't always remember to turn off the spigot. She frowned and tried to shape the words to remind them, but couldn't manage.

The water stopped running. She settled deeper into her comfortable bed.

"Emma?"

She peeled her eyelids open just enough to see a white ceiling. Too white a ceiling to belong in her dear cottage. And where was the petal-shaped crack over her bed?

"Emma?"

She forced her eyelids the rest of the way open and saw Kenny coming across the carpet toward the bed. What was Kenny doing in her cottage?

He had a towel tucked around his hips, another draped over his shoulders. His hair was wet and mussed.

The world slipped back into place, and she realized she was in his condo. In his bed.

She groaned.

"Rise and shine, Queen Elizabeth."

"What am I doing here?" she croaked.

"I've got a fresh pot of coffee downstairs that I think might appeal to you. You definitely can't hold your liquor."

"Please . . ." she managed, as she took in the rumpled bed. "Tell me I don't owe you thirty dollars."

"Honey, after what happened last night, I owe you."

She moaned and buried her face in the pillow.

He chuckled. "You are one wildcat between the sheets, I'll tell you that."

She forced herself to look at him, then sagged back into the pillows as she took in the diabolic gleam in his eyes. "Save your energy. Nothing happened."

"What makes you think that?"

"You're still standing."

Another chuckle.

Considering her impaired physical condition, she thought that was a fairly cheeky response, but she felt too dreary to take much satisfaction from it. She eased herself into a sitting position and saw she was wearing a University of Texas T-shirt, her bra, and her underpants. Right now she wouldn't let herself think about how she'd gotten out of her clothes.

"Do you want me to turn the shower on for you?"

She stumbled toward the bathroom door. "I'll turn it on for myself. You may fetch my coffee."

"Yes, Your Ladyship."

She shut the bathroom door, peeled his T-shirt over her head, let her bra drop, and turned toward the sink.

That was when she screamed.

On the other side of the door, Kenny grinned, then listened as Emma's scream changed into something close to a sob. His grin grew broader, only to fade into a scowl as he heard feet pounding on the stairs. "Shit."

The bedroom door shot open, and a gorgeous brunette with inky black hair and a model's body burst in. "Jeeze, Kenny, did you kill one this time?"

Emma flew out from the bathroom, a large towel wrapped around her body, her eyes the size of a fairly decent water hazard. *"What did you do to me!"*

"Emma, I'd like you to meet my baby sister, Torie. Torie, this is Lady Emma Wells-Finch."

As Emma tried to get her mouth to work, Kenny noticed that Torie was outfitted, as usual, in Nieman Marcus's best, one of those simple little dresses that cost more than the national debt, along with an expensive pair of Italian sandals. A couple of divot-sized diamond studs flashed at her ears, a wedding gift from her last ex-husband.

Her hair was as dark as his and jaw-length, except around her face where it was cut shorter. At twenty-eight, she was tall, lean, green-eyed, and gorgeous. She was also a pain in the ass. Still, he loved her, and he might be the only person in the world who understood how much unhappiness lurked beneath her good ol' girl bluster.

"Don't you ever use a doorbell?" he grumbled.

"Why should I when I have a perfectly good key?" She regarded Emma with interest. "Honey, that is one *hell* of a tattoo you got there."

Ignoring her, Emma charged toward him, tears glistening in her eyes. "How could you have let this happen?"

He studied the red, white, and blue Lone Star flag that now flew across a good portion of her upper left arm along with a curling banner beneath it that read *Kenny*.

"Wasn't much I could do about it. You know how you are when you've got your mind set on something."

"I was drunk."

"You can say that again."

"At least it's not ordinary," Torie said in an attempt to be kind.

Emma stared at her as Torie extended her hand. "Nice to meet you, Lady Emma. In case you missed the introduction, I'm Torie Traveler. I had a couple of other last names, but I recently got rid of them and went back to the basics. Don't be offended when I tell you that you have terrible taste in men." She dropped Emma's hand and turned on Kenny. "You could have returned at least one of my phone calls, you sonovabitch."

"Why? You'll just tell me I have to go to Wynette, and I don't want to go to Wynette right now."

"Fine. You can ignore me until the wedding, then."

"You and Phillip Morris tying the knot?" he asked.

"His name is Phillip Morrison, and you know very well that's not the wedding I'm talking about."

"Things between you and Phillip didn't work out, I take it."

"He wanted me to stop cussing and give him ten strokes." She plopped one graceful hand on her hip. "I swear I couldn't go through the rest of my life watching that golf swing of his without providing some semi-obscene commentary."

"You broke up with him because you didn't like his swing?"

"That and the fact that he named his cock."

"Lots of men do that."

"Yeah, but do they call it Barbie?"

Kenny sighed. "You're making this up."

"I wish I was."

Emma couldn't stand it any longer, and she whirled on him. "How did I get this tattoo!"

"You were dead set on it."

"A flower! I wanted a small flower!"

"Not last night you didn't. And, honey, you should be thanking me instead of yelling because you also ordered up the Union Jack for your other arm. When I put my foot down about that, we had a rip-snortin' fight. I finally had to carry you out of the tattoo parlor kicking and screaming. I was afraid to take you back to the hotel, which is why you ended up here."

Emma sagged down on the side of the bed. "But I only had two margaritas. How could I lose my memory on two drinks?"

"Each one of them packed a pretty good wallop. And you don't seem to tolerate alcohol too well."

She buried her head in her hands. "Nothing's gone right since the moment I met you."

"Which should pretty much give you a clue how the rest of your relationship's gonna progress," Torie said, heading toward the mirror to check her hair. "Kenny has a not-so-secret aversion to intimacy brought on by an unhealthy early relationship with our late, unlamented mother."

"Will you shut up!"

Torie fluffed her bangs. "He bounces back and forth between bimbos, because they're safe, and real women with actual brains, because that's the type he naturally prefers. But the key word here is *bounce*. He's pretty much the Bermuda Triangle when it comes to committed relationships. Count yourself lucky if you figure that out early on."

"Will you get the hell out of here!" He spoke before Emma had a chance to clarify their relationship.

"Not till you promise to come back to Wynette. Daddy's planning to hold the wedding while you're on suspension so he can make sure you'll be there."

"You just said you and Phillip broke up."

"You know exactly what I'm talking about! My wedding to that dweeb Dexter O'Conner."

"When are you going to figure out that they can't have a wedding without your cooperation?" He whipped the towel from around his neck and tossed it aside.

"That's easy to say, but Daddy's putting a lot of pressure on me. He's given me thirty days to get Dexter's ring on my finger or he's canceling my charge cards. Then how am I going to pay my feed bill?"

"He's bluffing." Kenny headed into his walk-in closet.

"Not this time." Her voice grew small and discouraged. "Maybe I should just marry Dexter." She gave a self-deprecating laugh. "That and getting divorced are about the only things I do really well."

"Stop feeling sorry for yourself."

"Do you think I'd even consider it if I wasn't desperate?" she retorted angrily. "Those emus are getting bigger all the time, and it costs a fortune to feed them. Daddy's been complaining about it for a while, but he hasn't threatened to cut me off until now."

"If you'd sent those birds to that great big emu pasture in the sky like I told you, this wouldn't have happened."

"I couldn't do that, and you know it!

Emma was temporarily distracted from her own misery. "Emus?"

"They look exactly like ostriches that have been dipped in chimney soot," Kenny explained. "The most butt-ugly bird you've ever seen."

"They are not!" Torie protested. Then she shrugged. "All right. Maybe they aren't too attractive, but they're sweet."

"And therein lies the problem," Kenny drawled. "My sister, the genius entrepreneur, got sucked into the emu craze a few years back when people started hearing about how they could make a fortune raising the birds because they didn't take up much land and there was going to be a huge market for emu products."

"I needed to be self-supporting so I could get out of my marriage," Torie interrupted. "And their oil has exceptional healing properties. It's used to treat injuries in the NFL. Plus, emu meat has more protein, half the calories, and less fat than beef, but it tastes exactly the same."

"How would you know, since you've never eaten a bite of emu in your life?"

"Someday."

He snorted. "Unfortunately, the emu market has been slow to materialize. Not that it would have made much difference to my sister because the few times she's had a chance to sell one or two of her birds for meat, she's refused to do it."

She turned to Emma. "Whenever I thought about having them slaughtered, my face broke out. I tried to sell breeding pairs, but nobody's buying these days."

"Now she's stuck with feeding a growing herd of emus nobody wants."

"It's sort of an existentialist nightmare." She gave a deep sigh, then the corner of her mouth quirked. "On the other hand, life always has its bright side, and at least I don't have a tattoo of the Lone Star on my arm."

Emma glanced down at the horrific tattoo and shuddered. She would have to wear long sleeves for the rest of her life.

Her muzzy head, the trauma of the tattoo, and the sheer force of Torie's invasion into Kenny's bedroom had kept her from processing the real content of their conversation, but now she began to absorb it. "Are you saying your father is trying to force you into marrying someone you dislike?"

"Or give up the charge card that's been paying off my feed bill, not to mention a few other minor necessities like decent clothes and gas money. My daddy and Dexter's father have me trapped. They can't come up with any other way to arrange a merger than for Dexter and me to . . . merge."

"Merger?"

Kenny came out of his closet, still bare-chested, zipping up a pair of chinos. "Our father owns TCS, Traveler Computer Systems. It's located in Wynette. Dexter's father owns Com National, his fiercest competitor. Their main plant's in Austin, but he built a smaller research and development facility in Wynette just to get under my father's skin. The two companies have been duking it out since the seventies, pretty much using whatever slimeball trick either man could come up with to stay on top of the other. Unfortunately, they got so preoccupied hating each other's guts that they stopped paying attention to all the young companies nipping at their heels. Now both TCS and Com National are in trouble, and the only way they can survive is to merge. If that happens, they'll be pretty much invincible."

Emma shook her head. "I still don't understand what this has to do with Torie. Companies merge all the time without people getting married to accomplish it, especially when their fathers hate each other."

"Not these two companies," he said, bringing a light blue denim shirt from the closet. "The men have pulled too many shady deals on each other—not just business stuff, personal as well. Now neither of them trusts the other, but they both want the merger.''

''So they're making me the sacrificial lamb to hold the whole thing together.'' Torie extracted a pack of cigarettes from her purse, only to have Kenny snatch them away and pitch them in the wastebasket.

Emma felt disoriented. Was there an epidemic of marriage-by-blackmail going on in the Western world? How had it happened that she'd managed to meet another woman in a similar situation? It seemed too bizarre to be coincidental, and the image of Francesca Serritella Day Beaudine came into her mind. But that made no sense. Francesca might know about Torie's dilemma, but she didn't know about Emma's own.

She needed to be alone so she could think, and she rose from the side of the bed. ''If you'll excuse me, I'm going to shower, and then I need to get back to the hotel.''

Half an hour later she emerged from the bedroom and headed downstairs dressed in the short dress she'd worn last night, with Kenny's T-shirt pulled on top to hide the awful tattoo. The thought of living the rest of her life with a Lone Star flag on her arm was bad enough, but having the word *Kenny* permanently etched into her skin was unbearable.

Kenny and Torie sat at the kitchen counter sipping coffee and eating donuts. Torie pointed a blue-green fingernail toward the open carton. ''You want a donut, Emma? There's a cream-filled here that your lover boy hasn't gotten his mitts on yet.''

''He's not my lover boy, and I think coffee is all I can handle at the moment.''

''If he's not your lover boy, why were you naked in his bedroom?''

''That was an accident. We're not sleeping together. He's my driver.''

''Your driver? Kenny, what's goin' on?''

He explained, although, in Emma's opinion, he placed unnecessarily negative emphasis on her leadership skills.

When he was done, Torie said, ''So you're really a lady?''

''Yes, but I don't use my title.''

''I sure as hell'd use *my* title if I had one.''

''That's what *I* said.'' Kenny shot Emma an I-told-you-so look.

Emma gave up.

''Wynette's not that far from Austin, Lady Emma.'' Torie uncoiled from the stool as gracefully as a lynx and headed to the sink to rinse off her sticky fingers. ''And it's a real nice town. As long as you're in Texas, why not see how the natives live instead of just hitting the tourist spots? Kenny can take you back and forth to the UT library whenever you want, and San Antonio's not that far either. What do you say? As a gesture of feminist solidarity, will you help me get him back to his hometown?''

"She doesn't have any say in this," Kenny responded, clearly irritated.

Emma thought about it. Despite what she was telling everyone, her primary purpose in coming to Texas wasn't to do research. As long as she had access to the libraries she needed, she could finish that up in a few days. Far more important was the task of casting a shadow over her character, and she could do that just as easily in Wynette as anywhere else. Besides, being in the presence of a woman as outrageous as Torie Traveler was bound to upset Hugh. And it might be easier for Beddington's detective force to keep track of her in a small town. She had to admit the idea of having her base in Wynette was more appealing than moving from one impersonal big city hotel to another. "All right. Yes, I suppose that would work."

"No," Kenny said. "Absolutely not."

"Just think about our stepmama," Torie said to him. "She'll wet her pants having a real, live member of the British aristocracy in town."

"The best reason of all to stay away," he retorted.

Torie's expression grew cagey. "Do I have to remind you about a certain Christmas morning during our childhood when our mother showered you with a couple thousand dollars' worth of presents, but never got around to buying me anything?"

Emma straightened. What was this?

Kenny shot his sister an exasperated look. "I've spent the last seventeen years trying to make up for our dysfunctional childhood, and you're not putting me through any more guilt trips."

"Or maybe I should bring up the time I bought that great big Minnie Mouse cookie with my allowance money. It had those cute little stickyup ears and a bow across the top. Remember the fit you kicked up because you wanted it, and how she slapped me across the face when I refused to give it to you? You stood right in front of me and ate the whole thing while I watched."

He winced. "Torie, everybody in the world knows that she was crazy and I was a spoiled brat!"

"I remember there were a couple bites of that hair bow left over—"

"Torie . . ." His voice sounded a warning note.

"But instead of giving them to me, you threw them in the—"

"All right! You win, damn it! But this is against my better judgment."

For a moment Torie appeared almost fragile. Then she curled one arm around his neck and pressed her lips to his cheek. "Thanks, bubba. I owe you one."

"You owe me more than one," he sighed. "But I'll still never catch up."

Chapter 7

"*Surely your sister exaggerated,*" Emma said. "*Your mother couldn't* really have permitted such a thing."

Kenny pointed toward the passing landscape through the Cadillac's window. "Look at those bluebonnets over there. And that red's Indian paintbrush. Isn't this just about the prettiest view you've ever seen?"

He obviously didn't want to talk about his childhood, and, once again, Emma let herself be distracted by the beauty of the Texas Hill Country. They were west of Austin now, not far from Wynette, on a two-lane highway that offered breathtaking vistas of rugged hills slashed with limestone and expansive valleys carpeted with fields of wildflowers, some stretching nearly as far as the eye could see. Since they'd left, she'd spotted her first Texas longhorn cattle, glimpsed several deer, and watched a bird Kenny identified as a red-tailed hawk circle a ribbon of crystal-clear river that sparkled in the sun. Now, however, she forced her attention away from the view to once again concentrate on piecing together the story behind what she'd heard this morning. Even though it was none of her business, she couldn't seem to help herself. She simply had to know more about him.

"Tell me about your childhood, Kenny. I'm only inquiring as an educator, you understand. I'm fascinated by the effect upbringing has on adult behavior."

"Believe me, if I'd let my upbringing affect me, I'd be locked up in a penitentiary somewhere."

"Was it really that bad?"

"Unfortunately, yes. You know those old teen movies where there's always this nasty rich kid who tortures the poor but valiant hero?"

"Yes."

"Well, I was that nasty rich kid."

"I don't believe it. You're immature and annoying, but you're not cruel."

He raised one eyebrow at her.

"Please tell me." She unwrapped a package of cheese and crackers she'd hurriedly purchased when he'd stopped for petrol and it became apparent that he had no interest in lunch.

He shrugged. "Everybody in Wynette knows how I was raised, so I guess you'll hear about it as soon as you hit town." He slipped into the left lane, passing a pickup. "My mother was beautiful, born rich, and not exactly known for her brains."

Emma immediately thought of Torie, then decided that wasn't fair. She suspected that Torie Traveler was extremely intelligent, but hid it just as her brother did.

"My father grew up poor," Kenny said, "but he was smart and hardworking. I guess it was a case of opposites attracting. They married quick, then found out they basically hated each other's guts. Neither of them would consider a divorce. My father won't ever admit he's failed at anything, and Mother said she couldn't live through the disgrace."

"Rather old-fashioned."

"My mother spent her life on that thin edge between neurosis and psychosis, with psychosis winning out as she got older. She was a classic narcissist married to a man who ignored her, so, as soon as I was born, she made me the center of her life. Whatever I wanted, she gave me, even if I shouldn't have had it. She never said no, not about anything. And because of that, I was supposed to worship her."

"Did you?"

"Of course not. I paid her back with bad behavior, and the more she indulged me, the more I pushed her. Then, whenever something did go wrong in my life, I blamed her for it. I was just about the most unpleasant child you can imagine."

No wonder, she thought, feeling a stab of pity for the boy he'd been, as well as reluctant admiration for his honesty. "Where was your father while all this was going on?"

"Building his company. I guess he did his best when he was around. He made sure he pointed out all my faults and practiced some harsh discipline, but he wasn't at home enough to be effective. I was such a repulsive little cuss I can't blame him for not hanging around more."

But he did blame him. Emma heard it in his voice. What a confusing upbringing it must have been to have one overly indulgent parent while the other only criticized. "From what I heard earlier," she said carefully, "I gather your mother didn't feel the same way about Torie that she felt about you."

"That's what I really blame her for. I was four when Torie was born, and, like any four-year-old, I didn't cater to having a stranger in the house. But instead of protecting Torie, Mother abandoned her to baby-sitters. Nothing was going to upset her perfect little Kenny, you understand. Certainly not another female in the household."

"Your poor sister."

He nodded. "Luckily, my father fell in love with Torie the moment he set eyes on her. When he was home, he kept her right by him, gave her all his attention, and made sure the baby-sitters reported directly to him. But he wasn't home enough, and she's still got a lot of scars."

Torie wasn't the only one with scars. His father's favoritism of his daughter must have been just as damaging as his mother's over-indulgence. "Where's your mother now?"

"She died from a brain aneurysm just before I turned seventeen."

"And you were left with your father."

"One other person had shown up in my life by then, and, for some reason I can't imagine, he took an interest in me. He taught me everything I know about golf, and, at the same time, he made sure I learned the hard rules of life. Man, was he tough. But he gave me a chance."

Interesting that it was someone other than his father who'd seen his potential. "Who was he?"

Kenny didn't seem to have heard. "One lesson he taught me early on was how to treat my sister." He laughed. "He'd call her up right before we headed out for the golf course, and he wouldn't let me tee off unless she told him I'd been behaving with her. Can you imagine? A seventeen-year-old boy held hostage by his twelve-year-old sister." He laughed again. "Fortunately, Torie doesn't have much bloodlust, and after the first few months she lost her appetite for revenge. Not too long after that we discovered we liked each other. We've been just about each other's best friend ever since."

"What about you and your father?"

"Oh, we got ourselves straightened out a long time ago." He spoke too casually. "Once I started to win some golf tournaments, he realized I wasn't completely worthless. Now he sets up his whole schedule so he can watch me play."

So that was how Kenny had earned his father's approval. By winning golf tournaments.

While she was pondering the fact that child abuse came in many forms, the cell phone rang. Kenny answered, gave her a puzzled look, then handed it over. "Some guy who says he's a duke."

Emma set down the cheese and crackers she hadn't gotten around to eating before she pressed the phone to her ear. "Good afternoon, Your Grace."

"It's not afternoon here, my dear," that unpleasantly familiar voice responded. "It's late, and I should be in bed, but I've been too worried about you to sleep. Where have you been? I was told you didn't return to your hotel last night."

So, his watchdogs were in place. "Last night?"

"I know you were there, of course—where else could you have been?—but I wish you would have called."

"But—"

"Why did you check out of the hotel? I thought you were going to stay in Dallas."

She found it unsettling that he didn't even consider that she might have been out carousing all night. It occurred to her that he had an unfortunate habit of believing what he wanted to believe.

"Kenny and I are on our way to Wynette. It's his hometown. As for last night—"

"Wynette? That sounds familiar. Why on earth are you going there?"

"Kenny has some personal business to take care of. I said I'd accompany him."

"I see. And where will you be staying?"

She'd planned to stay at a hotel, but now she realized she couldn't afford that type of conservative behavior. "I'll be staying at Kenny's ranch, of course."

Kenny swerved.

She clutched the dashboard as Hugh began to sputter. "Impossible! He's an unmarried man, and you can't stay there by yourself."

"I'm so sorry to upset you, but it's necessary to my research. It's very important for me to . . . fully experience the Wild West." There! she thought. Let him make what he would out of that.

"I'm gonna give you some Wild West," Kenny muttered.

She slipped her hand over the mouthpiece and shushed him.

"Emma, my dear, apparently it hasn't occurred to you that you're being a bit careless in your behavior. Even in a foreign country, you need to be more circumspect."

She drummed her fingers on her lap as he began to lecture her about propriety, his family name, and her reputation.

"You're staying in a hotel," Kenny said when she was finally able to hang up. "Not at my ranch. Now suppose you tell me who that was and what he wanted."

Even though he'd just shared some painful details of his private life, she wasn't anxious to do the same. "It was Hugh Holroyd, Duke of Beddington. He owns St. Gert's. Do you think you could slow down a bit?"

"How did he get my cell phone number?"

"I have no idea. He's quite an influential man, and he has a way of unearthing things. Look! More wildflowers!"

"I think it's time you tell me exactly what's going on here." He spoke in those deadly, humorless tones she was growing to dread.

"Pardon?"

"I'm starting to get a funny feeling right behind my knees. It's the same feeling I sometimes get just before I miss a four-footer."

Without warning, he angled the car off the road into a small graveled area that held three picnic tables, one of which was occupied by a family with two young boys. He got out of the car, but she decided to stay where she was.

He opened her door and gave her a look that promised he'd pull her out if she didn't get out on her own. She grabbed her umbrella at the last second to annoy him, then did her best to poke him in the head as she popped it open. "The sun is beastly."

"Not nearly as beastly as my temper." He snatched away the umbrella, pushed it shut, and threw it back in the car. With the family of picnickers watching curiously, he steered her past the last table toward a gnarled tree on the perimeter of the picnic grounds that afforded them a small measure of privacy. Releasing her arm, he drilled her with eyes that reminded her far more of surgical lasers than marsh violets. "Start at the beginning."

"The beginning of what?" she said carefully.

"Cut the crap. My instincts have been telling me all along there was something strange about this whole situation, but I made the mistake of not paying attention. Now, I'm going to spell it out for you. I have a suspension hanging over my head, my career's in jeopardy, and that means I can't afford to head blind into someone else's problems. You tell me exactly what's going on."

She'd never thought of herself as fainthearted, but he looked entirely too formidable. "I don't know what you mean."

"Let me remind you that you're standing in the middle of a foreign country with a man who recently got suspended for drug dealing along with smacking a woman."

Before Torie had left, she'd told Emma what had happened with Kenny's business manager. "You weren't suspended for drug dealing, and I don't believe you about the woman."

"Honey, I've got the video."

"Really, Kenny, this isn't any of your business."

"Bull! My career's on the line, and I'm not risking that for anything. What's your relationship with this guy?"

"I told you. The Duke of Beddington owns St. Gert's. He's also the school's principal benefactor."

"And?"

As she studied the grim set of his mouth, she felt a pang of nostalgia for the good-looking fool she'd originally taken Kenny to be. "And, nothing."

He stared at her for a long moment. "I guess I misjudged you. I figured you had some guts, but you don't even have enough courage to be honest."

That stung. "This has nothing to do with you!"

He didn't reply, merely studied her, and she could have sworn she saw disappointment in his expression. It made her feel like a coward. But she hated the idea of revealing the intimate details of her life, especially when those details would make her seem pathetic in his eyes.

"You're being absolutely beastly about this," she said.

He waited.

He was right. She was being cowardly, and everything would be much easier if she simply told him. After that, she'd be able to accomplish what she had to without trying to hide it from him. If only the truth weren't so embarrassing.

The two young boys at the next picnic table began chasing each other. She envied them their freedom. "All right, I'll tell you," she said reluctantly. "But you have to agree to let me stay at your ranch."

"We'll talk about that after I hear your story."

"No. You have to promise me first."

"I'm not promising anything until I hear what you have to say." He crossed his arms and leaned back against the trunk of a hackberry tree.

She mustered her courage by reminding herself that she hadn't done anything wrong, and she certainly didn't need Kenny Traveler's good opinion, but somehow that didn't make her feel any better. "The Duke of Beddington is a very powerful man in England," she began hesitantly. "An old family. He seems to have a genius for investing in new technology, and he's quite rich. Unfortunately, he's also a bit mad. He's . . ." She pleated her shorts with her fingers. "Well, he wants to marry me."

He watched her carefully. "Seems to me most women would be flattered at the idea of marrying a duke."

"Believe me, there's nothing personal about his offer. He has two girls from his former marriages, and he needs a male heir. The woman has to be wellborn and have a spotless reputation. God forbid that the family name should be soiled by a commoner with a normal sex life." She realized the implications of what she'd said and went on hastily, "I know it sounds like something out of the seventeenth century, but he's deadly serious. I refused him, of course, but he paid no attention."

She went on, telling him about her panic when Hugh threatened to sell the school and the plan she'd conceived out of desperation. "I had to agree, Kenny. I can't let him close St. Gert's. But I can't marry him, either."

Warming to her topic, she described her plan to scandalize Bedding-ton just enough so that he would call off the engagement. When she was finally finished, Kenny stared at her for a moment, then walked over to the nearest picnic table and slumped down on the bench. "When you mentioned you haven't had a normal sex life, exactly what did you mean?"

She couldn't believe that was the only thing he'd picked up on. "Is that all you can say after everything I've told you?"

"First things first."

The two young boys who'd been chasing each other darted into the trees. "I never said I hadn't had a normal sex life."

"You implied it. Now, exactly what kind of abnormality are we talking about here?"

"Nothing! We're not talking about anything."

"You're not a secret dominatrix, are you?"

"Don't be ridiculous!"

"You already said you're not a lesbian, and I'm prone to believe you. Foot fetish?"

"No!"

"A masochist?"

"Don't be absurd."

"Sadist?"

"This is rubbish."

His eyes narrowed. "You tell me right this second you're not a pe-dophile."

"Oh, for God's sake, I'm a *virgin*!"

Silence.

Her cheeks grew hot. "Go on, then! Laugh! I know you want to."

"Let me get my breath back first." His eyes drifted to her breasts. "How does anybody get to be your age and stay a virgin?"

"It just happened, that's all. I didn't intend for it to turn out this way." She shot her chin a bit higher. "I was busy, and I'm not good with men."

"That's because you're too damned bossy."

"I didn't ask for your opinion." A shout from the larger of the two boys distracted her. She watched him wrestle the younger one to the ground, bringing the other child's head perilously close to the sharp corner of the concrete slab that held one of the picnic tables. "Careful, boys! If you want to wrestle, do it over there."

The brothers stopped what they were doing and stared at her. So did their parents. Kenny rolled his eyes. "Would you mind your own business?"

She turned her back on him. "I knew you'd be difficult about this. That's why I didn't want to tell you."

He came around in front of her. "Of course I'm being difficult. You climbed into bed with me two nights ago without once mentioning that particular piece of information."

"It wasn't relevant."

"It sure as hell was relevant to me."

"Why? What possible difference could it make?"

"A big difference. You were using me!"

She stared at him, feeling both anger and the beginnings of a perverse sort of amusement. "As I remember, it was the other way around. Do you always try to turn the tables like this when you know you're in the wrong?"

He scowled.

"Do you have any idea how pathetic you are?" she said.

"Me?" His eyebrows shot up. "You're the one who's never been laid."

"Life is about a lot more than sex."

"Yeah, well, you don't play golf, either." He stalked off toward the car, looking far more upset than he had any right to be.

She marched after him. "You are the most selfish, self-centered, person I've ever known. I've just told you how my life's falling apart, and all you can think about is how it affects you."

"You're damn straight." He turned to confront her. "You listen to me, Emma. The only way I get back on the tour is to keep what's left of my reputation so clean that it squeaks. Now, near as I can gather, that puts the two of us at cross purposes, because you seem hell bent on destroying yours."

"I don't have a choice."

"You sure do. The answer to your problem is as clear as the nose on your face." He jabbed his finger toward his car. "Get on that phone right this minute and tell that pussy duke you have no intention of marrying him!"

"Didn't you hear anything I said? If I don't go along with this, he'll sell St. Gert's."

"That's not your problem. You can get another job." He unlocked the door and climbed in.

She raced around to the other side and jimmied the handle until he finally unlocked it. "You don't know what you're saying." She climbed inside. "St. Gert's is special. I've started a new program for scholarship students. If the school closes, they'll be abandoned. And St. Gert's is my home. The only one I've ever had."

"It's just a pile of old bricks."

"Not to me. Oh, why am I even bothering? I knew you wouldn't understand."

"What I don't understand is how you've let this whole thing get so complicated."

"Beddington isn't stupid. If my behavior is too blatant, he'll see right through what I'm trying to do and get rid of St. Gert's just to punish me for defying him. I have to be subtle, make him believe he's misjudged my character at the same time I pretend to go along with him."

He scowled and jabbed his keys into the ignition. "Well, I'm not sleeping with you, if that's what you've got on your mind."

"I don't want to sleep with you!"

For some maddening reason, that seemed to calm him down. His hands went slack on the key, and his eyes made a lazy journey along the buttons of her blouse. "You sure did want to the other night, Queen Elizabeth."

She hoped he didn't notice the gooseflesh that broke out on her skin. To compensate, she sat up straighter in the seat. "That was when I thought you were honorable."

"Honorable?" His exasperation returned. "I told you I was a *gigolo.*"

"At least you were open about it."

"I was *lying* through my teeth."

"Yes, well, I didn't know that at the time." She sniffed. "And if I make up my mind to sleep with someone in the next two weeks, it won't be you."

"You aren't sleeping with anybody in the next two weeks. As long as Francesca's looking over my shoulder, you're going back home in exactly the same pristine condition as the day you arrived. When you lose your virginity, Lady Emma, you're damn well going to do it on somebody else's watch."

She began to respond, only to have the words slip away as his eyes locked on her mouth. Slowly his expression changed. She watched his lips part ever so slightly and his eyes darken. She felt light-headed. After all her talk about not wanting to sleep with him, she was the one lying through her teeth because everything about him stimulated her— his extravagant good looks, lanky body, Texas drawl, even his peculiar sense of humor. She hated herself for it, but some part of her wished she hadn't discovered that magazine cover until after they'd made love.

He jerked his eyes away from her. "That's it! You're staying at a hotel!"

"I am not!" She couldn't stay at a hotel. It was exactly what Beddington expected from her. "I didn't want to mention this, but I'm afraid you're forcing me to remind you that I can call Francesca at any time."

"You leave Francesca out of this."

"You keep forgetting that I'm desperate. And I'm certain Francesca will be very upset when she hears how you got me drunk, then dragged me to that horrible tattoo parlor where I was disfigured for life."

"Can't you see that I'm doing this for your own good? Don't you realize that putting the two of us together under one roof is just plain stupid?"

"I know we've argued a lot, but if we both try a bit harder to be polite—"

"I'm not talking about us arguing."

"Then what?"

He gave a deep sigh. "For a smart lady, you sure are dumb."

She regarded him more closely. Could he possibly be attracted to her? She drew herself up sharply. This was no time to indulge in fantasy. Besides, he was a playboy, and she was very nearly a dotty, dear thing.

"All right," he said. "You win this round. You can stay at my ranch, but I'm charging you two hundred dollars a day rent."

That would wipe out her profit. "One hundred dollars."

"Two *fifty*."

"All right," she said hastily. "Two hundred."

They drove for the next few miles in silence, but even the glorious scenery couldn't lift her spirits. She didn't want to dwell on her own troubles, so she made herself think of other things. Before long, her thoughts drifted back to Torie Traveler. "Don't you find the similarity between my odd situation and your sister's a bit too coincidental?"

"It's not coincidental at all. A certain English busybody's got her nose in where it doesn't belong. And this time we're not talking about you."

"But Francesca knows nothing about my situation with Hugh."

"Francesca knows everything. That's how she's been able to keep her television show on the air for so many years. She's pretty much like God, except sexy."

"I'm going to call her tonight and ask."

He adjusted the sun visor. "You can ask all you want, but if Francesca doesn't feel like telling, you won't learn a thing."

"Do you really think she has some plan behind throwing us together?"

"You bet I do."

"But what could it be?"

"Sadism. You live with the Antichrist long enough, you turn mean."

In the luxurious bedroom of a rented home in Palm Beach, Florida, an elegantly beautiful forty-four-year-old Englishwoman with chestnut hair and a heart-shaped face curled deeper into the pale peach sheets and gave a sigh of contentment as she gazed at the indentation in the pillow next to her. Time had only improved her husband's lovemaking techniques.

The shower went on in the connecting bathroom, and she gave a soft laugh as she wondered how Emma and Kenny were doing. Putting the two of them together had been decidedly wicked, but irresistible—Francesca Serritella Day Beaudine's own sentimental journey. Although it wasn't exactly a case of history repeating itself, since Emma bore no resemblance to the spoiled little rich girl Francesca had been when Dallie Beaudine had picked her up on that Louisiana back road twenty-three years ago.

From the moment Francesca had met Emma, she'd felt a kinship with her. Beneath her friend's deep intelligence and innate goodness, she'd glimpsed her loneliness.

Then there was Kenny Traveler . . . her darling, unhappy Kenny. . . . Francesca's eyes drifted shut, and she recalled another too-handsome Texas golf pro who'd endangered his game by spending too much time fighting demons he wouldn't let anyone else glimpse.

Still, Emma and Kenny? What could she have been thinking of? If it hadn't been for Torie's situation, she would never have thought to connect them in her mind.

Francesca's sources were impeccable, and she'd learned about Beddington's peculiar search for a bride almost as soon as it had begun, but she'd been stunned when she'd learned he'd latched on to Emma. Right away, she'd been struck by the similarities between Emma's situation and Torie's. That had made her think about Kenny, and then the most incredible image of Kenny and Emma together had taken shape in her mind. It was ridiculous, of course, to believe two such unlikely people could help each other. Still, stranger things had happened.

The water stopped running in the bathroom. She stretched lazily, even though she had a thousand things to do. First she needed to call her best friend, Holly Grace Beaudine Jaffe, who also happened to be Dallie's first wife, and was now the mother of four boys—five if Francesca counted Holly Grace's husband Gerry. Then she needed to get to work. Putting on a monthly television special didn't happen by accident, and she had a long list of calls to make, beginning with her producer in New York.

The bathroom door opened, and she forgot all about her calls as her husband's deep drawl drifted across the room.

"Come here, Fancy Pants."

Kenny's ranch sat in a valley just south of Wynette. He turned off the main highway onto a narrower road, then headed down a lane marked by a pair of rough limestone pillars topped with a rustic wrought-iron arch.

"My property starts here." Emma heard the subtle note of pride in Kenny's voice.

They drove through the entrance, past a peach orchard just beginning to come into bloom, and across a wide wooden bridge that spanned a stretch of shallow, crystal-clear river. "That's the Pedernales. It floods during big storms and covers the bridge, but I still love having it in my front yard."

And that's exactly where it was, Emma realized—in his front yard. Kenny's ranch house sat at the top of a gently sloping bit of lawn shaded here and there with live oaks. The house itself was a graceful rambling structure built of creamy white limestone with smoky blue shutters and trim. Twin limestone chimneys rose from the expansive tin roof she'd already seen on so many buildings in the area, and a galloping horse weather vane turned lazily in the April breeze. Big wooden rockers sat on the front porch, extending a silent invitation to rest awhile and gaze down at the meandering path of the Pedernales. Off to one side, she glimpsed a windmill, a limestone stable, and a white fence surrounding a picturesque pasture where horses grazed.

"You have horses!" she exclaimed as he pulled up to the side of the house.

"Only two. Shadow and China. They're quarterhorses."

She could see his affection for the animals in his smile, and she tried to take it all in. "Gracious, Kenny, you have so much. Horses, that beautiful condo in Dallas, this wonderful ranch. . . ."

"Yeah. Not bad for a kid who was born with a silver spoon in his mouth, is it?"

She was startled to hear a faint tinge of bitterness in his voice, and she tilted her head to look at him. "Did that silver spoon make all this magically appear by itself?"

"I guess I worked for it," he said begrudgingly. "If you call what I do for a living work." His expression indicated he didn't quite believe it.

Emma found it curious that he wasn't more impressed with all that he'd accomplished. "I call it work. I'm sure no one handed you those championships just for your good looks. You also seem to endorse a number of companies."

"I am pretty good-lookin'." He shot her a smug smile, then pulled her suitcases out of the car without being asked. Both acts distracted her, which was probably what he intended as he moved ahead of her to the front porch.

Just as he got there, the door shot open and a young man in his late twenties flew out. He had a slight build, curly carrot-colored hair, rather prominent eyes, and a huge smile.

"Kenneth! Let me take that before you throw your back out. Whatever *can* you be thinking of?" He snatched the suitcase away. "You're too bad not letting me know you were coming. I barely had a chance to get the house ready. If Torie hadn't called to warn me, I don't know what I'd have done."

"Sorry. It was a last-minute decision." Kenny followed the young man into the cool, quiet foyer, which was painted in wide, muted stripes of vanilla and beige. "Patrick, this is Lady Emma. She's going to be staying here for a while. *Unfortunately.* Put her as far away from me as you can manage. Emma, this is Patrick. My housekeeper."

Emma regarded the young man curiously. Really. Kenny knew the most extraordinary people.

"*Lady* Emma?" Patrick exclaimed. "Please, God, tell me you're the real thing and not another stripper."

The man was so winning, it was impossible not to smile. "I'm real, but please, just call me Emma."

Patrick pressed one hand to the front of a neon green silk shirt. "Oh, God. Your accent's fabulous."

She couldn't resist a little probing, and she glanced over at Kenny, who was leafing through a pile of mail he'd taken from a small wooden chest that also held a majolica vase spilling over with spring flowers. "*Another* stripper?"

"Don't look at me," he said. "Torie's the one who brought her here."

Patrick's eyes gleamed. "Your stepmother is going to have a public orgasm when she meets Lady Emma."

"Do you *mind*?" Kenny growled.

"My, my. Someone's out of sorts, isn't he? I should think a very nice Clos du Roy 1990 Fronsac will take care of that." He picked up her suitcase. "Come along, Lady Emma, I'll show you to your room while Kenneth puts his happy face back on."

"Just Emma," she said with a sigh.

Kenny smiled without looking up from the mail.

As she followed Patrick toward the stairs, she gazed off at the living room to the right where the walls were covered in the same faux-painted vanilla and beige stripes as the hallway. Wing chairs, a cozy, overstuffed couch, and well-worn Oriental rugs gave the room a comfortable, lived-in look.

Patrick noticed her interest in the decor. "Do you want to see the rest of the downstairs?"

"I'd quite like that."

"The kitchen is the best. Kenneth absolutely lives there when he's home." He set down her luggage, then led her back along the hallway into an enormous country kitchen that stretched in a spacious L across the rear of the house. She blinked in surprise. "It's lovely."

"Thank you. I designed it."

The walls and ceiling were painted a bright, cheery yellow, while the floor with its large terra-cotta tiles added even more warmth. An informal seating area, positioned in front of the fireplace, held a couch with a floral design in shades of yellow, coral, and emerald, along with several comfortable chairs. Two separate sets of French doors, one of which opened out onto a sun porch, sent light splashing over the array of colorful abstract canvases that graced the walls.

The eating area held a bay window and an elegant Regency dining table, which was surrounded by a comfortable hodgepodge of Chippendale, Louis XVI, and Early American chairs covered with unmatched, but coordinating, fabrics. The polished tabletop reflected another spray of flowers, this one arranged in an earthenware pitcher.

"Everything's so beautiful."

"It was risky, but Kenneth needs cozy roots." Patrick made a small, fluttering gesture.

Emma didn't mean to stare, but Patrick's presence had definitely taken her aback.

He brushed his hand over the top of the table. "You're wondering what someone like me is doing here, aren't you?"

"Wondering?" She was dying of curiosity, but much too polite to make any inquiries on her own.

"Small Texas towns aren't terribly kind to a gay man."

"No, I don't imagine so."

A flicker of unhappiness crossed his face, then disappeared. "I'll show you to your room."

Chapter 8

Emma ate by herself that night. After announcing that Kenny had gone off to practice, Patrick served her a delicious pasta salad, along with fresh green beans drizzled with olive oil and garlic, a crusty French roll, and a thick wedge of blueberry tart for dessert. She ate on the sun porch, which was furnished in shiny black rattan covered in a crisp green and white awning stripe. More flowers overflowed from a collection of rustic vases sitting on antique tables. Behind the house, a grove of pecans grew, while a patio and swimming pool sat off to one side, and the white-fenced pasture where the horses grazed stretched in the distance. Earlier she had taken a walk along the river to enjoy the wildflowers.

Despite the peaceful atmosphere and the scented air blowing in through the screen door, she felt restless. Why hadn't Kenny returned? Even though she'd told him she'd stay out of his way, she wished he didn't find her presence so unpleasant.

Patrick refused her offer to help with cleanup, so she spread out her research notes and worked for a while as it grew dark. Bugs, attracted by the lights on the porch, slammed into the screen, while crickets sawed away. She heard the quiet hum of the dishwasher, the call of a night bird. The peacefulness reminded her of St. Gert's after the girls were asleep.

Her spirits dipped lower. At this rate, she would return to England with her reputation more intact than ever. She saw Patrick crossing the lawn toward the small apartment he'd told her he maintained above the garage. Impulsively, she called out, "Do you have Torie's number posted somewhere?"

"There's a list on the side of the refrigerator."

A few moments later, she had Kenny's sister on the phone.

"No, I don't have any plans," Torie said after Emma explained what she wanted. "But I don't think Wynette's bars will exactly suit your taste."

"What's the fun of going on holiday if I don't try new things?"

"Well, all right. If you're sure about this, I'll pick you up in half an hour."

Emma dressed in the pair of dungarees she'd bought the day before along with a stretchy white bubble-knit just short enough to reveal a thin band of skin at her waist and just tight enough to emphasize her breasts. Although the short sleeves hid most of the Lone Star tattoo, they revealed the banner bearing Kenny's name. Humiliating, but necessary, she decided, and vowed not to look in the mirror. She only hoped Beddington's henchman was bright enough to bring along a camera.

Torie picked her up in a dark blue BMW, which she drove at an alarming rate of speed. Emma closed her eyes and clutched the armrest.

"You look nervous."

"I'm not good in cars."

"That makes life hard, especially in Texas." Torie slowed down.

"It rather does everywhere."

Now that they weren't moving so fast, Emma took a moment to study her companion. Torie wore a turquoise body suit with fitted black jeans that displayed a pair of endlessly long legs. A concho belt glimmered at her waist, and Mexican silver earrings swayed from her lobes. She looked rich, lovely, and wild. Not for an instant would Beddington ever have considered making Torie Traveler his wife.

Torie glanced in the rearview mirror. "You really should learn to drive."

"Uhmm . . ."

"Really. I could teach you."

"That's lovely of you, but I don't think so."

"The devil's got quite a grip on you, doesn't he?"

"I suppose so."

"I guess I know what that's like."

Emma heard sadness in her voice, and something told her that a marriage to Dexter O'Conner wasn't all that bothered Torie. Her breezy manner and spoiled, rich-girl demeanor camouflaged a great deal of pain.

"Are you getting along all right with Patrick?" she asked. "He's pretty protective of Kenny, and he can be funny about people."

"He was very helpful," Emma replied.

Torie laughed. "It drives Daddy crazy having an openly gay man living at the ranch with his only son. But everybody knows Patrick's the best housekeeper in the county, and, if you ask me, the day Kenny rescued him was lucky for both of them.''

"How did he rescue him?''

"Patrick was driving around taking photographs for this coffee table book he wants to do on out-of-the way roadhouses. Stopped at a place near the limestone quarry and ran into a bunch of rednecks who decided to prove their masculinity by beating the crap out of him. Four against one. Kenny came along just in time. He can't stand stuff like that. It about drives him crazy.''

"What did he do?''

"Let's just say that Kenny doesn't lose his temper too often, but when he does, it's a wondrous sight. He ended up taking Patrick back to his house to recover, and he got up the next morning just in time to see a pan of homemade cinnamon rolls coming out of the oven. Kenny took one whiff and hired Patrick on the spot. There's been a ton of gossip about it, not to mention all the trouble Kenny got into with the PGA when the roadhouse fight made the papers.''

"He did the right thing.''

"I think so. Still, he got criticized. I swear, if you listen to the locals, the only thing Kenny can do right is win tournaments.''

"People don't like him? That surprises me.''

"Oh, no. They love him. Everybody knows he's done more good for this community than all the rest of us put together. He's built a community center and provided the seed money for the new library—a whole bunch of things like that. And he lends his name to every good cause that comes along. But giving Kenny a hard time has been this town's favorite leisure activity for so long that nobody thinks twice about it.''

"How so?''

"People have long memories, and they're still holding a few grudges from his misbegotten childhood. Nobody yet has broken his record for the most suspensions from high school. And the retired police chief can tell you stories that'd make your hair stand on end. Seems everybody has a grudge. Judy Weber won't let him forget that he copied off her arithmetic quiz in fourth grade, then convinced the substitute that she was the one cheating. He stole a Hank Aaron baseball card from Bob Frazier in sixth grade, then tore it up. He took kids' lunch money, broke their toys, dumped girlfriends right and left, and pretty much cut a wide path of destruction wherever he went until Dallie Beaudine finally took him in hand after Mother died.''

So Dallie Beaudine was the mysterious person Kenny had referred to earlier that day. Obviously Kenny's relationship with Francesca's husband was far more complex than she'd guessed. "Still, he's apparently been a model citizen since his late teens. It seems that people should let bygones be bygones."

"Kenny doesn't mind getting teased. And he might be a model citizen, but he sure has some big character flaws. In case you haven't noticed, he's lazy."

"I did notice," Emma said dryly. "Still, laziness isn't a major crime."

"Sometimes it is with him. He just—I don't know. It's hard to explain. He just doesn't care about anything but golf. That's how his bloodsucker business manager siphoned off so much of his money. Kenny never bothered to check up on him."

Emma remembered the matter-of-fact way he'd described the child he'd been, without displaying a morsel of sympathy for the circumstances that had led to his misbehavior. While she didn't believe that adults should use a dysfunctional childhood as an excuse for not getting on with their lives, she'd also seen a great deal of parental incompetence in her career and she didn't think anyone should continue to do penance for it. Yet that seemed to be what Kenny was doing.

"He distances himself from everything but golf," Torie went on. "Especially women. He's treated every girlfriend he's had like a queen—buys her expensive presents, sends her flowers—but the minute she starts getting her hopes up that the relationship's permanent, he vanishes."

Emma realized Torie was issuing a subtle warning, but she said nothing.

Torie continued, "Everybody in the world wants to be Kenny's best friend, but I'm the only one he lets get halfway close. I never knew a man so determined to hold himself apart from other people. I guess he's afraid if he starts caring too much about anybody, they'll manipulate him like our mother did. Manhood didn't come easy to Kenny, and he's sure not going to let anything threaten it."

"It's ironic that someone with so much natural charm is fundamentally a loner."

"He's the friendliest man in the world, until somebody either pisses him off or tries to get inside his head. Then he uses that charm to isolate himself. Or he acts dumb. About drives me crazy when he does that, since he's the smartest man I know. My brother goes through books like most people go through potato chips."

Torie fell silent. Emma considered simply telling Kenny's sister that she had no intention of getting personally involved with her brother, but she didn't want to make herself look foolish.

"It's strange," Torie said. "Unlike Kenny, my second ex-husband had a picture-perfect childhood, but he turned into an immoral slimeball. You just never know with people."

"How long have you been divorced?"

"A year, but we were separated for a while before that. Tommy was a womanizer. Daddy warned me not to marry him, but I wouldn't listen." A deeply unhappy expression crossed her face. "Maybe if I'd been able to have a baby, Tommy would have settled down, but it didn't happen."

"I doubt that a baby would have kept him faithful."

"I know you're right. Still, it's hard being a two-time loser." She pushed a hand through her hair. "My first husband was a college romance gone bad. He drank, and when he drank, he'd go on these crying jags, then he'd bust up our apartment. It didn't last a year." She reached for the radio. "Daddy says I can't be trusted when it comes to men, which is why he wants me to marry Dexter. But I don't—" She looked into the rearview mirror, and her hand stalled on the radio buttons as she frowned. "That sonovabitch has been tailing me ever since we left Kenny's ranch. I swear he was parked there waiting for me."

"Really!" Emma twisted around to look and saw a dark green Taurus. "Do you think he's following us?"

"Could be."

Emma's mouth went dry. Beddington's watchdog was on the job.

Wynette, Texas, was a charming old town with a shady square at its center and a prosperous, downtown shopping area that hadn't been forced out of business by a mall. Since Kenny had bypassed Wynette when he'd driven to his ranch, this was Emma's first chance to see the town, and Torie took her on a tour that ended up at a honky-tonk called the Roustabout. A green Taurus stayed with them all the way.

As they went inside, Emma kept trying to look over her shoulder to see who might follow them.

"This is where everybody in town hangs out," Torie said. "It's been here for years."

Unlike the cozy pubs in Lower Tilbey, the Roustabout was a vast, open room, with a square wooden bar in the middle. Emma saw two pool tables, a row of video games, and a small dance floor with a jukebox blaring out country music. Although it was a weeknight, most of the tables were occupied, as were the booths that ran along one wall.

Once again, Emma glanced over her shoulder, and this time she saw a beefy man in a floral sport shirt coming through the door. The skin on the back of her neck prickled as he began to stare at her, and her heart beat faster. Was he Hugh's spy? Was he the man who'd been driving the green Taurus?

Torie moved ahead of her toward the bar, lifted one hand to her mouth, then let out a shrill whistle. "Listen up, y'all."

Although the jukebox continued to play, the conversation died as everyone regarded her with interest.

"This is Lady Emma," Torie announced. "Kenny's showing her around for a few days. She's from England. She also happens to be a real, live aristocrat, despite that tattoo on her arm. Lady Emma, say a few words to these rednecks, so they'll know you're for real."

"I'm delighted to meet all of you," Emma said self-consciously. She tried to hunch her shoulders just enough for her sleeve to drop lower, but it didn't move, and several people's eyes lingered on her tattoo. Even so, her British accent seemed to impress them.

Torie took Emma's arm and turned her to the bar. "Joey, give me a glass of Chardonnay, will you? What would you like, Lady Emma?"

"Gin and tonic, please." Emma didn't like gin and tonic—not like she liked margaritas—but she wanted everyone to see her drinking. At the same time, she had a permanent reminder emblazoned on her upper arm of her need to stay sober, so she made up her mind to dump the drink and substitute water as soon as she got the chance. No one would be the wiser.

The bartender served their drinks, and a number of the bar's patrons came up for personal introductions, which Torie provided. One man suggested she lock away her valuables before Kenny stole them, and a woman said not ever to let him turn a jump rope for her because he'd trip her sure as anything. Both comments were greeted with knowing chuckles from the crowd.

Eventually, Torie led her toward a table in one corner where a young male who looked to be in his early twenties sat by himself sipping a beer. As they approached, Emma wondered if there was something in the Wynette water supply that produced such good-looking people. First Kenny, then Torie, and now this young man. He had crisp auburn hair and strong features that included high cheekbones and a square, solid jaw. His shoulders were broad, his body slim but hard-muscled.

"Hey, Ted. How you doin'?" Torie took a seat at the table without waiting for an invitation, then gestured toward the empty chair on the other side for Emma.

"Can't complain. How about you?"

"Same old. Same old. This is Lady Emma."

As Emma nodded, the man named Ted glanced at her tattoo, then gave her a lazy, meandering smile that made her wish she were ten years younger. "Ma'am."

"He's only twenty-two," Torie said, as if she were reading Emma's mind. "Isn't that a major crime for us older women?"

Ted smiled and ducked his head to study his beer bottle.

"You seen Kenny?" Torie asked.

"He was here a minute ago."

The fact that Kenny had gone out on the town without inviting her was annoying. Apparently she was going to have to drop Francesca's name again to remind him who was in charge.

As if she'd conjured him, Kenny came ambling across the room. He had a beer bottle in one hand and a golf club swinging loosely from the other. He tossed it to the bartender, who tucked it away.

His eyes narrowed ever so slightly as he saw Emma, then he looked at Ted. "The next lesson in the alley's on you. Randy Ames keeps wanting me to fix his slice, but he won't do a thing I tell him. Maybe you'll have more luck."

"Are you a golfer, too?" Emma asked Ted, deliberately ignoring Kenny as he took the chair next to her.

"I've been known to play a little." Although Ted phrased his sentences like a Texan, he didn't have any drawl. Curious.

Kenny snorted. "Ted here was the top amateur in the state three years running. Second best golfer UT's ever had play for them."

"There's some debate about that." Torie shot her brother a sly look. "Ted did manage to win three NCAA individual titles, instead of somebody I could mention who only won two. Plus, Ted also managed to graduate, something else a certain person I could mention seems to have neglected."

"College is hard." Kenny scratched his chest. "And the debate over who's the best is resolved as far as I'm concerned." He regarded Ted smugly. "Only one of us had the guts to turn pro."

Ted smiled his shy smile.

Torie turned to Emma. "See, Ted's this egghead genius, so all his life he's been torn between golf and nerd stuff. Around here people consider him sort of a genetic freak. Even his own parents."

Instead of taking offense, Ted nodded. "That's so."

"He's just finished his bachelor's and master's degrees at the same time." Kenny's pride was visible, and Emma could see there was something special about the relationship between these two men. "Playing varsity golf slowed down his academic career or he'd have finished up a lot earlier."

"Didn't see any need to hurry."

"Exactly what I told you," Kenny said with satisfaction.

Emma pretended to sip from her drink as the three of them chatted with the ease of people who'd known each other for a long time. It was Torie who introduced the subject of Kenny's suspension. "It's so unfair," she said. "Anybody who knows Kenny knows he wouldn't hit a woman on purpose. He'll drive 'em crazy and screw around on 'em, but he won't hit them."

Kenny looked aggravated. "That's not why I was originally suspended, and I never screwed around on a woman I cared about in my life, at least not since I was sixteen." He glanced over at Ted. "I swear, somebody needs to swat her."

"Don't look at me. I'm scared of her."

Torie leaned over and kissed Ted's cheek. "If you were just a couple years older, sonny boy, I'd show you the time of your life."

"I doubt I'd survive it."

"You ask me," Kenny said, "the Antichrist is going through some kind of midlife crisis. Sonovabitch turns fifty this year. I think it's twisted his mind."

Ted tilted his chair back and stretched out his legs. "He's just pissed off at you is all."

"Abuse of power," Kenny grumbled. "Thinks he's the damned President of the United States."

Ted smiled.

"I'm serious," Kenny went on. "Everybody who belongs to the PGA expects the commissioner to be fair. Even though he only has the job temporarily, he should at least pretend to be impartial."

At that moment, Emma spotted the man in the floral shirt who'd followed them into the bar and realized he was watching her quite closely from across the room. A rush of excitement went through her. He really was Beddington's watchdog!

She knew she had to make the most of the moment, but all she could think to do was grab her gin and tonic and take a healthy slug. As a scandalous act, it was fairly pathetic, but she couldn't think of anything else. And then another idea occurred to her, although she didn't want to do it. Still, she wanted to be married to Hugh even less.

Steeling herself, she rose out of her chair, looped her arm around Kenny's neck, and planted herself in his lap.

He lifted an eyebrow. "Have I missed something?"

She curled her mouth into what she hoped was a seductive smile and tried to speak without moving her lips. "Kiss me at once."

"No," he said indignantly.

"Why not?"

"Because I don't like your attitude."

She had been a bit bossy, but that was only because she was nervous. "I apologize."

His eyes settled on her mouth. "Okay, I'll kiss you."

The burly man turned away, and she immediately ejected from Kenny's lap.

He frowned at her as she grabbed for her gin and tonic. "Are you drunk again?"

"Certainly not."

"Good. Because Wynette doesn't have even a halfway decent tattoo parlor."

The burly man had moved over near the jukebox, but he was still watching her. He was balding, with straw-colored hair and prominent jowls. Thinking hard, she looked over at Ted. "Would you mind very much dancing with me?" Beddington definitely wouldn't like her dancing with anyone, let alone an obviously younger man.

"I wouldn't mind at all," Ted replied.

"He's a terrible dancer," Torie said. "You want somebody good, you get out on the floor with Kenny."

Ted looked injured. "She asked *me* to dance, not John Travolta here."

Torie shrugged. "It's your feet, Lady Emma."

Although Emma didn't look at Kenny, she sensed his eyes on her as she got up from the table. Ted took her hand and led her toward the floor, where a ballad was playing. As they began to dance, she experienced the unusual sensation of being led around a dance floor by a sexy young man. *Very* young, she reminded herself.

And very sexy.

He smiled down at her and asked how she liked Texas.

She smiled back and said she loved it. He wanted to know if she'd enjoyed the ride in from Dallas and what she thought of the United States. They chatted easily.

The song ended, and a fast tune began to play. The crowd reshuffled and started performing a line dance. "Maybe I'd better sit this one out."

"I'll show you the steps," Ted said. "Torie's right. I'm not much of a dancer, but this one's pretty easy." He led her to the side, and she caught on quickly as he demonstrated.

As soon as they were back on the dance floor, she spotted Kenny and Torie dancing together. With their gleaming dark hair and easy grace, they moved like mirror images of each other. Kenny laughed at something one of the women passing by said to him. Torie flirted with an older man wearing a cowboy hat. They looked beautiful, rich, and a little jaded. Emma thought of Gatsby and Daisy Buchanan transplanted to a Texas honky-tonk.

The music slowed. Emma turned to go back to the table only to have Ted tug on her hand. "One more, Lady Emma. I like dancing with you. I always appreciate it when the lady leads."

She laughed and slid back into his arms. It was nice being with someone who enjoyed her company. But they'd barely begun to dance before Kenny tapped Ted on the shoulder. "I'm taking over, little boy, so you go on back to the table and let Torie fight with you."

"I don't want to fight with Torie," Ted said mildly. "I'm enjoying myself with Lady Emma."

"And I'm real sure she's enjoying herself with you, but right now, I'm suggesting you move aside."

Emma felt a prickle of alarm as Ted gave Kenny a long hard assessment that suddenly made him look much older than his twenty-two years. "You and I are overdue for a reckoning."

"Just name the time."

"Seven o'clock tomorrow morning."

"You're on."

Emma held up her hands. "Stop this at once!"

Kenny frowned. "Stop what?"

"Threatening each other! You're acting like children."

"We're not threatening. We're playing golf."

"*I'll* be playing golf," Ted said. "It remains to be seen what John Travolta here'll be doing." He gave Emma a slow smile and walked away.

As Emma watched him disappear, she actually felt weak-kneed for a moment. If Ted was this bone-melting at twenty-two, what would he be like in another ten years?

Kenny took her in his arms, and she got weak-kneed all over again. Her instinctive attraction to him irritated her.

"You just put your eyeballs right back in your head, Lady Emma."

"Excuse me?"

"Don't play dumb. I know exactly what you're doing. You're mentally screening candidates to put an end to your you-know-what. Your virginity," he added, in case she'd missed the point. "And my little pal there just moved to the top of your list."

"Don't be ridiculous. He's much too young." She couldn't resist adding, "But very sexy."

"Yeah, well, take if from me . . . your friend Francesca won't like it too much if you try to seduce her baby boy."

She stumbled. "Her baby boy?"

He led her back into the dance steps. "Not to mention what the Antichrist might have to say about it. He has a lot of pride in that son of his."

"He's their son?" She blinked her eyes. "Oh, my . . . she always refers to him as Teddy. I never thought . . ."

"Theodore Day Beaudine. The only child of Francesca and you-know-who."

"I got the impression that her son was much younger, still a child. I never thought . . ."

"Well, start thinking now, Mrs. Robinson, because he's definitely not a child, and he's off-limits to you."

"I wasn't really planning to seduce him. He's young enough to have been one of my students. How could you think such an awful thing?"

"Do I have to remind you of a certain unfortunate incident two nights ago?"

"That was different. I intended to *pay* you."

He chuckled, then moved his hand on her back. She felt his finger slide along the small band of skin between her top and the waistband of her jeans. She couldn't tell if it was accidental or not, and she gave an involuntary shiver.

His voice deepened a notch. "Until this minute, it never occurred to me that you might be so desperate for sex you'd actually prey on one of our town's innocent children."

"He's hardly—"

"I may have to abandon my principles and go to bed with you after all."

She stumbled again, and he lifted one dark eyebrow. "Although, to be honest about it, I don't know if I'm up to all the work involved in having sex with a you-know-what. Still, I guess there comes a time in every man's life when he has to sacrifice himself for the greater good of the community."

She deliberately stepped on his foot. "Sorry."

"You did that on purpose!"

"I most certainly did not."

For a moment he said nothing, then he gave a long, put-upon sigh. At the same time, he slipped his thumb beneath the hem of her top. "All right, you win. I'll let you mess around with me."

Even though she knew he was teasing, she felt this funny quiver in her middle. Then she thought about picking up a beer pitcher from one of the tables and pouring it over his head. How had so much arrogance gotten packaged in one man? "Thanks, but I couldn't put you to the trouble."

He drew her closer so her breasts snuggled against his chest. "Not much trouble. I'll just lie there and let you do all the work. You'd probably like that best anyway."

Before she could come up with a response, he stopped dancing. "Uh-oh. Just when you think it's safe to go back in the water . . ."

Emma looked up and spotted a rather disheveled man in his early thirties wearing chinos, a rumpled blue oxford cloth shirt, and wire-rimmed glasses approach the table where Torie sat with Ted. Ted immediately rose and held out his hand, obviously pleased.

Torie, however, wasn't. Her spine straightened, and she shot him a look of pure venom.

"That's Dexter O'Conner," Kenny said. "The heir to Com National, Torie's intended, and the biggest nerd in Wynette, Texas. Most of the time Ted's the only person in the entire county who has any idea what he's talking about."

Dexter O'Conner reminded her of Jeremy Fox. They both had that same pleasantly untidy look, although this man was taller and thinner. His bony scholar's face was a bit long, but still attractive. He had a wide, intelligent brow, well-spaced eyes, and shaggy brown hair. It didn't take Emma more than a few seconds to realize that Dexter O'Conner was exactly the kind of man who had always appealed to her.

Kenny let her go. "We'd better get over there before Torie takes too big a bite out of him and lets the poor sonovabitch bleed to death." He approached the table like the masked avenger. "What the hell are you doing here, O'Conner?"

"Dex came here to meet *me*," Ted said. "You and Torie are the damned interlopers, so go away. Lady Emma, you can stay."

She smiled at him. "Thank you."

Ted introduced her, and Dexter O'Conner acknowledged her presence with a brief, level-eyed survey, then a courteous nod. There was something about his manner that made her warm to him. He pulled off his wire-rims, revealing a very nice pair of gray eyes, and extracted a handkerchief from his pocket to polish them.

"As a matter of fact, I'd like Victoria and Kenny to stay, too. As long as we're all here, I think it would behoove us to reach some sort of understanding."

"You hear that, Kenny? *Behoove*. He talks like he's inhaled a damned dictionary. And, I swear to God, Dexter, the next time you call me Victoria, I'm going to body slam you."

"I doubt that would be possible." He slipped his glasses back on. "I'm quite a bit bigger."

Torie slumped forward and caught her forehead in her hands. "Jesus . . . you are such a dork."

"He's a smart dork," Ted pointed out. "And unlike you, Dex has actually *earned* his share of the family money."

"Shut up, you little putz." Torie reached for her cigarettes only to have Dex take them from her hands.

"I really don't like seeing you smoking, Victoria."

"That does it!" With a growl, she sprang to her feet and lunged for his throat.

Kenny caught her around the waist just before she struck. "Settle down, now. You know how you hate it when you get blood on your clothes." He shot Dexter a warning glare as Torie struggled in his arms. "You'd better get out of here, Dex. I don't know how much longer I can hold her."

"I see no reason to leave," Dex said. "I have something to discuss with her. You're welcome to listen."

As Torie's growls of outrage grew louder, Ted rose. "You're right, Kenny. Somebody needs to swat her. I'll take her away till she cools down." He sighed. "Even though I don't want to." He grabbed Torie by the waist, just under Kenny's arm, and yanked. "Let's go play Foosball. And this time, let me win!"

Torie shot Dexter a venomous look as Ted dragged her away.

Emma observed Dexter with interest. She'd known Texas would be fascinating, but she hadn't expected to find herself thrown into the middle of such an absorbing drama. This was like a rerun of *Dallas*, except with much nicer people. Well, nicer except for Kenny Traveler.

Just then, she spotted the burly man watching them and felt a thrill of anticipation. Beddington would hate having her involved in this kind of public scene.

Kenny took a seat. "I'd advise you not to hang out in any dark alleys, Dex. She doesn't fight like a girl."

"As I'm sure both of her ex-husbands discovered." Dexter settled in the chair Torie had abandoned. "I'm not afraid of your sister, Kenny. I thought you'd realize that. She, of course, is terrified of me."

Kenny grinned and shook his head. "Whatever you want to believe."

Dex looked resigned. "I should have expected this." He turned to Emma. "How long have you known Victoria, Lady Emma?"

"Just Emma. I only met her this morning."

"I suppose that's too little time for you to have any influence with her. It's unfortunate. You seem quite level-headed."

Kenny shot out his hand. "Now, Lady Emma, level-headed isn't the same as being conservative, so keep your clothes on."

"I had no intention of taking them off."

Dex studied her more closely.

"Why don't you just leave Torie alone?" Kenny said.

"It's not that simple. Remember that our fathers are involved."

"If you had any balls, Dex, you'd tell both of them to go to hell instead of letting them torture Torie like this."

He gave Kenny a long, inscrutable look. "I suppose I shouldn't be surprised at your reaction." With a shrug, he rose. "I'll talk with Ted later. It's been very nice meeting you, Emma. I look forward to seeing you again soon." He nodded at Kenny and, without so much as a glance toward the Foosball game, headed for the door of the Roustabout.

"Coldhearted sonovabitch."

"I found him very pleasant," Emma said.

"It figures you'd like him. He's just your type."

"Quite."

"Is that a gleam of speculation I see in your eye?"

When she didn't reply, he frowned. "First you're after a little boy. Now you've got Dex sighted through the crosshairs. Nobody could ever say you're particular."

She wasn't going to let him bait her. "Desperate women can't be particular."

"I guess I'd better dance with you, then." He spoke just begrudgingly enough to let her know he was doing her a favor.

"Oh, no." She gave him a pleasant smile. "It would require far too much effort on your part."

That made him so mad his teeth started to itch. Damn, but there was something about this woman that rubbed him wrong. He'd wanted to get away from her tonight, but then she'd shown up here. The worst thing was that part of him had been glad to see her, which was why he hadn't behaved too well, because he didn't want to be glad to see the virgin head mistress.

She made no secret of the fact that she disapproved of him, and he didn't like the notion that he was nothing more than a sexual convenience, even though he felt the same way about her. Or at least he thought he did.

He wasn't used to being confused about a woman, and his thoughts returned to the person who'd put him in this position in the first place. If it weren't for Francesca, he might be able to talk Emma into a discreet fling. The two of them could use each other, then forget about it. But Dallie's wife had more ways of finding out other people's private business than anybody he knew, and she'd never forgive him if she thought he'd taken advantage of her friend. It also wouldn't be the slightest use telling her that Lady Emma had started the whole thing when she'd tried to buy his body.

He felt claustrophobic, as if he were being forced into a small, windowless room with no exit. Lady Emma was too bossy, too difficult, one of those women who could run right over the top of a man, beating on him with her demands until he'd been flattened like a cartoon coyote. Frustrated, he pulled her to her feet and led her, none too gently, back to the dance floor, where it didn't take more than a few seconds for his temper to bubble up again.

"Stop trying to lead!"

"Then move faster."

"It's a ballad."

"That doesn't mean you have to fall asleep."

"I'm not falling asleep! I swear . . ." But whatever he'd been about to swear slipped from his mind as her hair brushed the bottom of his chin.

For a moment he could have sworn he smelled violets, which was very peculiar, since he had no idea what violets smelled like, except somehow he knew they smelled just like Lady Emma.

Chapter 9

Even though she knew she should put her time to better use working on her research paper, Emma luxuriated in her leisure the next morning. She visited Kenny's horses, took another long walk along the river, then changed into her bathing suit, fetched her straw hat, and accompanied Patrick to the pool. They sat beneath a French market umbrella at one of the rectangular tables around the water and shared a glass of peach-flavored iced tea along with still-warm slices of a dark, spicy sweet bread drizzled with icing. As they ate, Patrick filled her in on some of the local lore and told her a little about his book of photographs before he excused himself to develop film in the basement darkroom.

Emma moved to one of the chaises that sat in the shade and opened up her notes from Lady Sarah's journal. The day was warm, and she wanted to discard her cover-up, but she was afraid Patrick would come back, and she didn't like the idea of him seeing her tattoo. It was one thing to show it off when she thought she was being watched, but quite another to expose people to it privately. She was thankful for her caution when she looked up to see an attractive blonde coming toward the pool with a baby in her arms.

The woman was a few years younger than Emma and a bit plump, but not unpleasantly so. Everything about her reeked of money, from the diamond tennis bracelet that glimmered on one tan wrist to her linen tunic and shorts. She had sleek, jaw-length blond hair and flawless skin enhanced with little more than some tawny lip gloss.

The woman beamed at her. "Lady Emma, it's such an honor to have you in Wynette. I'm Shelby, of course." Mystified, Emma set aside her notes and rose from the chaise. As she shook the woman's outstretched hand, the baby squealed and reached for his mother's hair. "This is

Peter.'' Her smile faded and her words developed a bite. ''The forgotten child.''

''How do you do? Hello, Peter.''

He gave her a shy, droolly smile set off by four small teeth, then buried his face in his mother's neck. The baby was adorable, and Emma felt a pang of envy. He had curly dark hair, a button nose, and beautiful eyes with sooty black lashes. His eyes were an unusual shade of blue, so deep they were nearly violet.

Something uncomfortable prickled at the back of her neck.

The woman took a seat at the umbrella table and shifted the baby onto her knees. ''I thought Kenny might be here, but I should have known he'd do his best to avoid us.''

''He's, uh, playing golf this morning.'' Emma sat next to her. ''How old is Peter?''

''Nine months, and he's still nursing. He's a bruiser. Twenty-two pounds and thirty inches at his last checkup.'' She automatically pushed Emma's empty iced tea glass out of the baby's reach. ''Kenny's been in town since yesterday, but he hasn't made the slightest attempt to come to the house, and I can't forgive him for that. Ignoring his own flesh and blood.''

Emma's stomach wrenched. *His own flesh and blood.* She took in the little boy's dark hair and violet eyes. Kenny must have looked exactly the same. She felt dizzy. His baby.

Even as she thought it, she struggled for another explanation, but those bright violet eyes were so unusual that the resemblance couldn't be coincidental, and this woman would hardly be so upset if she were a distant relative. The possibility that Kenny had fathered a child, then walked away, made her feel sick.

''I'm sorry,'' she managed. ''I didn't quite get your name.''

''Hello, Shelby.''

She turned to see Kenny approaching. He wore a pair of coral swim trunks and had a yellow towel draped around his neck.

At the sound of Kenny's voice, the baby's legs stiffened, then began to pump with excitement. Ignoring Shelby, Kenny tossed aside his towel, then scooped up the little boy and brought him to his face. ''Hey, buddy, how you doin'? I was coming to see you this afternoon.''

The woman gave a short snort.

Saliva bubbles dripped from Peter's bottom lip as he grabbed Kenny's hair and kicked his chubby bare feet.

They looked so much alike that Emma could only stare. At the same time, the sick feeling in her stomach wasn't going away. How could he have deserted such a beautiful child? Then again, why should she be surprised? This was a man who always seemed to take the easy way out.

"You want to swim, Petie boy?" Kenny asked.

"Don't get his overalls wet," Shelby said. "I just bought them at Baby Gap yesterday."

Kenny unfastened the straps and slipped off the overalls. "I think we'll keep that cloth diaper on, just in case you forget to act like a gentleman." He dropped the overalls on the table and tucked the baby in the crook of his arm as he looked down at Emma. "You want to come in with us?"

Her neck felt so stiff she could barely manage to shake her head.

"Come on, Petie. It's just us guys, then."

As Kenny carried the baby into the water, Emma tried to think what she could say to Shelby. She heard a faint sniffle.

"Damn him."

She looked across the table and saw Shelby's eyes fill with tears as she watched Kenny and the baby in the water.

Emma's heart went out to her. The diamond jewelry and expensive clothing showed that Kenny had been generous with his financial support, but that meant nothing if he'd abandoned his responsibility. She was filled with a crushing, irrational sense of disappointment. Despite every signpost along the way, she'd expected better of him.

Emma reached across the table and laid a sympathetic hand on her arm. "I'm so sorry."

The woman sniffed and gave a self-conscious laugh. "I guess I shouldn't take it so hard. I must still have a little postpartum depression, what with not losing all my weight and all. But when I look at the two of them together . . ." Her face twisted and a big tear ran down her cheek. "He won't take responsibility! And Peter is his own flesh and blood."

Emma could feel her heart hardening against him. Logically, she knew her reaction was extreme—they'd only been acquainted for a few days—but emotionally she couldn't help it. "He's despicable," she said, speaking to herself as much as Shelby.

Shelby looked a bit startled by Emma's reaction, then gratified. "I guess it takes an outsider to see things clearly. Everyone in Wynette just shrugs it off. They say, well, that's just the way Kenny is, and then they start telling stories about how he threw a stone through somebody's window or stood up his prom date. Since he wins golf tournaments now, he doesn't have to follow the same rules of decency as everyone else."

Once again, her eyes filled with tears. "I just love that little baby so much and—" She fumbled in the pocket of her tunic top for a tissue.

"I'm sorry, Lady Emma. I don't usually get like this, and I really wanted to make a good impression on you. But it's nice to have some sympathy for a change." She stood, blew her nose, then picked up Kenny's discarded towel and walked to the edge of the pool. "Bring him here, Kenny. We have to go."

"We just got in. He's having a good time. Aren't you, Petie boy?"

The baby gave a squeak of delight and slapped the water with his hands.

"He needs his nap, and I want him now!"

Kenny frowned and brought the baby to the edge of the pool. "Jeez, Shelby. What's wrong with you?"

"*You're* what's wrong with me! Come here, Petie." She leaned down and snatched the baby from Kenny, then wrapped him in the towel Kenny had brought from the house. As she walked over to pick up the overalls and her purse, she gave Emma a wobbly smile and something Emma was very much afraid might be a small curtsy. "Thank you, Lady Emma. This has meant a lot to me."

Emma nodded, and Shelby walked away without so much as a glance at Kenny.

Emma heard a faint splash and turned to see that Kenny had dived under the water. Long moments later, he emerged at the far end of the pool and begin to swim laps. One after the other. Slow, lazy laps. The laps of a man with nothing better to do. No honest work. No responsibilities. No children he'd abandoned.

He flipped to his back, poked along, and as she watched, her anger singed away at all the soft, forgiving places inside her. She'd dedicated her life to being a champion for children, and this man represented everything she detested. Her stomach coiled in self-disgust as she remembered how close she'd come to letting herself be seduced by him.

He emerged from the pool, looked for his towel, then apparently remembered Shelby had left with it wrapped around his illegitimate son, so he sluiced the water from his skin with his palms. As she watched those long, languid strokes, nausea propelled her to her feet. Dimly, she understood that this wasn't her fight, but she couldn't reason away the avalanche of angry emotion that was churning inside her. Anger and the awful, suffocating *disappointment* that he wasn't who she thought. It pushed her forward, toward the side of the pool.

He looked up at her. Smiled his lazy smile.

She didn't plan to do it. Didn't even feel it coming. But the next thing she knew, her arm was swinging through the air, and her hand had connected with his jaw.

From some distant, red-hazed place, she watched his head jerk and saw beads of water fly. A stain spread across his jaw where she'd hit him. Her stomach cramped.

"*What the hell's wrong with you?*" He cursed, then stared at her with eyes that had gone as deep and dark as a bruise.

Her legs felt as if they'd turned to water. She should never have struck him. Never. This wasn't her concern, and she'd had no right to appoint herself his executioner.

His eyes blazed. "I'd throw you in that pool right now, except you've got your suit on, so what would be the point?"

His anger recharged her. "You're despicable."

A muscle jumped in his injured jaw, and at his side, his fist clenched. "Aw, hell . . ." Without warning, he scooped her up and threw her out into the deep end of the pool.

She came up, sputtering and furious, only to see him stalking toward the house, walking away from her as he'd walked away from that beautiful baby. "What kind of man are you?" she cried. "What kind of man abandons his own child!"

He froze in his tracks. Slowly turned. "What did you say?"

Her hat floated up next to her. She snatched it as she treaded water. "Being a man means more than planting sperm and then writing a big check. It means—"

"Planting sp—"

Her anger rekindled. She plunged through the water toward the side of the pool, the weight of her sodden cover-up making her movements awkward. She lost her hat as she reached the ladder, but she was on a mission now, and she didn't care. "He's a beautiful baby! How could you—"

"You're an *idiot*!"

He stood in the center of the back lawn with the sun striking flash fires in his wet hair. His legs were braced, beads of water gleamed on his skin, and he looked as if he were getting ready to murder her. "That beautiful baby boy is my *brother!*"

Everything inside her went still. His brother? *Oh, my . . .* She *was* an idiot. "Kenny!"

But he was already stalking away.

She hauled herself from the water and regarded his retreating back with dismay. What had happened to her? She'd never been a person who rushed to judgment. At St. Gert's she listened to every side of a dispute before taking action, but she hadn't been willing to do that with him. She owed him an apology, and she could only hope he'd have the good grace to accept it.

Motivated by a combination of cowardice and dread, she showered and changed first. Then, hoping he'd had a chance to cool down, she set out to look for him only to discover that he'd left the house. Shadow was missing from the paddock, and she glimpsed a man on horseback riding away from the ranch.

Patrick came up from the darkroom and invited her to go into town with him while he shopped for groceries. She accepted the invitation, thinking she might find some sort of gift for Kenny by way of apology. But by the time they'd reached the town limits, she'd realized that no bottle of men's cologne or expensive book would make up for the insult.

When they returned to the house, Shadow was once again in the paddock, but there was still no sign of Kenny. "He's probably in the exercise room," Patrick said when she asked.

"He exercises?"

"After a fashion."

She followed Patrick's directions to a room at the far end of the second floor. The door was partially ajar. As she pushed it open, she realized her palms were clammy, and she wiped them on her shorts.

Kenny was working out on some sort of rowing machine, or at least moving it back and forth a bit. He looked up as she walked in and scowled at her. "What do you want?"

"I want to apologize."

"It won't do you any good." He slowly unfolded from the rowing machine and nudged a cordless phone out of the way with his foot.

"Kenny, I'm sorry. Really."

He ignored her, dropping to the carpeted floor instead and beginning a set of push-ups. His form was excellent—she'd give him that—but he didn't seem to be putting much effort into it.

"I had no right sticking my nose into something that was none of my business."

He kept his eyes on the floor as he continued his push-ups. "That's what you're apologizing for? Sticking your nose into my business?"

"And slapping you." She advanced farther into the room. "Oh, Kenny, I'm so sorry about that. I've never hit anyone in my life. Never!"

He said nothing, merely continued with his lazy push-ups, taking his time, just as he'd swum his laps. She thought she detected a faint whiff of male heat coming from his body, or at least male warmth, but she didn't see any sweat.

The sight of his body in nothing but a pair of navy athletic shorts was distracting her, and she brought her attention back. "I don't know what came over me. I got so upset, so disappointed in you. It was like some sort of temporary madness."

He set his jaw and didn't look up at her. "It's not the slap I can't forgive."

"But—"

"Just get out of here, will you? I don't even want to look at you right now."

She tried to think of something she could say to make it all up, but there was nothing. "All right. Yes. I understand." She backed toward the door, feeling ashamed and miserable. "I really am sorry."

His push-ups grew a bit more rapid. "You're sorry for the wrong thing, but you don't even understand that. Now get the hell out of here! And if you want to call up Francesca and tell her I just cussed you out, you go right ahead."

"I wouldn't do that." She turned toward the door, then turned back, needing to know. "If you can forgive me for hitting you, then tell me, what is it you can't forgive?"

"I don't believe you have to ask." The push-ups continued. Muscles bunching without any apparent effort. Not a drop of sweat.

"Apparently I do."

"How about the fact that a woman I consider my friend thinks I'm the type of slimeball who'd abandon his kid?"

"We only met three days ago," she couldn't help but point out. "I don't really know you that well."

He shot her a sideways look that managed to combine outrage and incredulity. "You damn well know me well enough to understand that much about me!" His breathing had picked up, but she got the feeling it was from anger, not the exercise.

"But Kenny, your stepmother is so young. She can't even be thirty. It never occurred to me—"

"I don't want to hear any more! I mean it, Emma, get out of here. I promised Shelby I'd bring you to the house tonight for dinner, so I'm going to do it, but believe me, I don't want to. As far as I'm concerned, our friendship is over."

Until that moment she hadn't actually known they had a friendship, but now that she realized she'd lost it, she felt strangely bereft.

Chapter 10

Kenny was scrupulously polite that evening as he drove to his family's home, but he didn't tease her, try to manipulate her, or even criticize. Clearly she had offended his sense of honor. But how could she have known that honor was important to a man who, only three nights earlier, had led her to believe he was a gigolo?

As they pulled through a set of ornate gates into the Traveler estate, she wished she hadn't agreed to accompany him tonight, but she was frustrated. She had apologized, and there was nothing more she could do.

As she focused on her surroundings, she realized his family home was actually an estate with a long drive winding through carefully landscaped grounds. A Moorish-looking structure came into view, built of rose-colored stucco with a crenellated rooftop. They drew nearer, and she saw that the house had several wings, along with arched windows and a tiled roof. An enormous mosaic fountain near the entrance made it look as if the entire place had come out of the Arabian nights instead of the Texas Hill Country.

"My mother wanted something out of the ordinary," Kenny said politely as he parked the car. She waited for a wisecrack about sultans or harems, but he said nothing else.

As she got out the car, the evening chill penetrated the bright yellow rayon crepe dress she'd chosen to wear that evening. It was splashed with crimson poppies and had three-quarter sleeves to cover her tattoo. Beddington would have approved of her outfit, she thought glumly, but she simply couldn't stomach the idea of offending Kenny's family by showing up in her trendier apparel. Besides, the duke's watchdog could hardly follow her into a private setting. Her spirits dipped lower as she realized she hadn't done anything all day to ruin her reputation.

They walked toward carved double doors banded in hammered brass. The house was impressive and exotic, but not very homey, and she couldn't help but compare it with Kenny's comfortable ranch. What had it been like for him to grow up here as his mother's little sultan and his father's disappointment?

He held the door open for her, and she stepped into a tiled hallway that was decorated like an English country house, although not nearly as worn around the edges. In contrast to the foyer's Moorish architecture, a highly polished Hepplewhite table held a pair of Dresden figurines while an old English landscape painting covered much of the side wall. The juxtaposition was a bit disconcerting but not unattractive.

Torie came down the stairs. She was dressed in a chartreuse tank dress with a black T-shirt. "Welcome to Marrakesh-on-Avon, Lady Emma." She gave Kenny a swift kiss on the cheek. "Hey, bubba. The Munsters are waiting for us on the terrace. We're dining al fresco."

"Lucky us."

She followed Kenny and Torie through a high-ceilinged living room decorated in eighteenth century furniture and chintz, along with an array of silver-framed photographs and hunting prints. A pair of Moorish doors with mosaic inlays opened onto a pleasantly shaded terrace paved in a herringbone pattern of pink brick edged with navy and rose tiles. Banquettes with curving arms had been built into the stucco walls and were cushioned with colorful paisley pillows. A large tiled table with a brass lantern at its center had been set for dinner. At one end of the terrace a very American-looking play yard held a dark-haired baby who grabbed the mesh sides and began squealing and pumping his legs as he saw Kenny.

"Hey, there, son!"

Emma didn't need an introduction to identify the man who shot to his feet as Kenny's father. He was a burlier version of his son, still handsome, but with coarser features and thick hair grizzled with gray. His too-hearty greeting and overly eager smile signaled a man who was unsure of himself. As he stepped forward to embrace his son, Emma sensed Kenny's nearly invisible withdrawal. Although he permitted the embrace, he gave nothing back.

Emma saw right then that Kenny had not forgiven his father for the years of childhood neglect. She also sensed that his father very much wanted that forgiveness.

Kenny disengaged himself as soon as he could and headed for the play yard, where he scooped the baby into his arms. "How are you doing, little brother?"

Was it Emma's imagination, or did he place unnecessary emphasis on that last word?

Peter let out a squeal of delight. At the same time Shelby came through the doors. She wore white leggings and an oversized lime-green V-neck cotton cardigan. She looked like Mr. Traveler's daughter instead of his wife.

"Lady Emma, it's such an honor having you with us this evening. I don't know if Kenny told you, but I'm crazy about everything that has to do with England. I have a whole collection of books about Princess Di if you'd like to see them. Did anybody introduce you to my husband Warren?"

He gave her a warm smile. "Lady Emma. It's nice to meet you."

"Just Emma is fine. Thank you both for inviting me."

"It's our honor," Shelby gushed, then gestured toward one of the banquettes. "Tell me how you're enjoying your trip. Both Warren and I love London, don't we, Warren? Do you live near the city?"

Emma explained that she lived several hours away by car in Warwickshire, then answered Shelby's questions about her trip. Before long, Shelby was regaling her with stories of backpacking in England after she'd graduated from college and a research project she'd once done on D. H. Lawrence. As she spoke, Torie stood off to one side, sipping a glass of wine and watching Kenny and Peter with a deeply unhappy expression on her face. Warren, in the meantime, seemed content to sip his bourbon and let his wife do the talking.

Shelby, who looked plump, blond, and merely pretty in this family of dark-haired demigods, glared at Torie as she lit up. "Put that out. You know I don't like it when you smoke around Peter."

"We're outside. I'm not even near him."

"No, you never are, are you?" Hurt clouded Shelby's eyes, and Emma remembered what Torie had said earlier about not being able to have a child. Had that caused the sadness that lurked just beneath her outrageousness?

"Warren, Lady Emma doesn't have a drink," Shelby said.

"What would you like?"

"A soft drink would be fine."

Warren wandered over to a bar set into one end of the terrace and addressed his son in an overly hearty manner. "Kenny, what about you? I've got one of those sissy red wines you like."

"I'll get it later." Kenny didn't even bother to look at his father. Instead, he propped Peter on his shoulders, holding his arms to keep him steady, and took his little brother over for a closer view of a squirrel that had climbed into the branches of an olive tree.

Torie folded her fashion model's body into one of the banquettes and crossed her legs. "So what do you think of Mother Shelby, Lady Emma?" She splayed her fingers through her dark hair and propped one elbow on a paisley pillow. "I know you're dying of curiosity, but too polite to ask. Shelby's twenty-seven, exactly thirty-one years younger than our daddy and a year younger than me. Doesn't that just about turn your stomach?"

"Torie, can't you at least wait until Petie's in bed?" Kenny said.

She ignored him. "Daddy knocked her up about a year and a half ago, and they had to get married."

Warren looked amused, but Shelby had stiffened. "You'll have to excuse Torie's rudeness, Lady Emma. She's very threatened by my relationship with her father."

"Revolted is more like it," Torie snapped.

"That's enough, girls." Warren spoke mildly, as if he'd grown so used to their bickering that it didn't bother him all that much. He sipped his drink and looked at Emma. "Shelby was Torie's little sister in their college sorority. They've been best friends for years, although you wouldn't know it now. They even shared an apartment between one of Torie's marriages."

"I was only married twice," she retorted. "Don't make it sound as if there were a dozen. Besides, the first marriage barely lasted six months, so it didn't count."

"You made me buy that awful pink and lavender maid-of-honor dress," Shelby said, "so it definitely counted."

Torie blew a thin stream of smoke. "Yeah, well, all of us know that Kenny had you out of that dress by midnight, so it couldn't have been too awful."

Emma sat up a little straighter. Tonight's episode of *Dallas* had taken an unexpected turn. It occurred to her that just being associated with the Traveler family might be enough for Beddington to call into question her character.

Kenny sighed. "I didn't have her out of the dress, and you know it." He kissed Peter on top of his head and swung him back into his play yard. "Do we have to do this every time we get together?"

"Leave 'em alone," Warren said. "It's part of their ritual."

Torie gave a dry laugh. "Wouldn't it have been funny if Kenny'd knocked you up, too, Mother Shelby? One of those corny father-son bonding activities."

"That's disgusting even for you," Kenny said. "Now settle down, Torie. I mean it. Shelby and I had one date. We kissed each other at the door, and that was it."

"Did you use your tongue?"

"I don't remember," he growled.

"I remember." Shelby shot Torie a superior look. "And I'm not telling."

Kenny headed for the bar.

Warren Traveler chuckled. "Home sweet home. Right, son?"

"Whatever."

The Rolex on Warren's wrist gleamed as he took a sip from his drink. "I hear you and Ted Beaudine went at it today. Word is you beat him by three strokes."

"He shot two under. We both had a decent round."

"I swear, when I get my hands on that sonovabitch Beaudine . . . If I was you, I'd have my lawyers all over this."

Emma realized he wasn't talking about Ted Beaudine, but his father, Dallie.

"I'm handling it," Kenny said.

"It's the week before the damn Masters! Every top player in the world is heading for Augusta except Kenny Traveler. You can't let Beaudine get away with this. All you have to do is call Crosley. He's the best lawyer in the state, and he told me—"

"I asked you to stay out of it, all right?" Emma heard the edge of steel in Kenny's voice and watched Warren's almost invisible withdrawal.

Torie made a languid movement on the banquette. "I'm half starving to death. If we're not eating soon, I swear I'm gonna order a pizza."

As if on cue, a maid appeared with a large tray holding individual salads. Shelby rose and directed them to their places. As Kenny moved toward the table, Peter let out a wail and gazed piteously at him, then extended his arms to be picked up.

"Leave him alone," Warren said. "You'll spoil him."

"That's what big brothers are for, right, Petie?" Ignoring his father, Kenny walked over to the playpen and lifted Peter out.

Shelby frowned at her husband. "You can't spoil a baby by picking him up, Warren. I keep telling you that. I'm not like your first wife, and Peter's not going to end up useless and lazy like Kenny, so stop worrying. Besides, all my books say that, if you don't meet their needs when they're little, you'll pay the price when they're older."

He regarded her with a mild irritation that didn't mask his fondness for this too-young wife. "I guess I might know a little more about raising kids than you."

"Like you did such a wonderful job," she retorted.

"She's got you there, old man." Kenny threw his father a faintly mocking look as he tucked Peter under his arm.

The maid had set out five bone china plates holding salads that combined Bibb lettuce, avocado slices, and wedges of ripe pear with a crumbling of Gorgonzola. Shelby took Peter from Kenny and tried to set him in his high chair, but he started to fuss, so Kenny took him back, then scraped off the Gorgonzola to give the baby a piece of pear. As he began to eat his salad, Kenny seemed oblivious to the mushy bits of fruit that were dripping on his slacks.

Shelby questioned Emma about any contacts, no matter how remote, she might have had with the royals, then Torie cut in with a story about a European trip she and Shelby had taken several years ago. The two of them began trading stories and, for a little while, they seemed to forget they'd become enemies.

The salads were replaced with an entrée of herb-crusted lamb and roasted potatoes. Kenny and his father began discussing some new computer softwear being developed by TCS, and Emma noticed that Warren acted as though Kenny couldn't understand the technology, even though Kenny didn't appear to have any trouble.

When Warren introduced Dexter O'Conner's name to the discussion, Torie immediately reacted. "Could we talk about something else, please?"

Shelby leaned across Emma to wipe Peter's chin. "I don't know why you dislike Dex so much, Torie. Nobody else does."

"I do," Kenny said.

Torie shot him a grateful look.

Warren tossed down the dinner roll he'd just buttered. He might be insecure when it came to his son, but not with his daughter, and Emma saw the strength of will that had made him such a successful businessman. "It doesn't matter whether she dislikes him or not. The first two times she got married for herself, and this time she's going to do it for the family. Unlike her last two husbands, Dex doesn't happen to be a scumbag. He's one of the brightest new minds in the business, and TCS is going to take advantage of it."

"I'm not marrying Dexter O'Conner just so you can get your hands on the next microchip wonderboy."

"Then you'd better be ready to support that emu farm yourself, Princess, because I'm not doing it much longer."

The evenness in his tone told Emma he wasn't bluffing, and she suspected Torie realized it, too. Although Warren obviously loved his daughter, he had apparently decided enough was enough. Emma's and Torie's circumstances were too much alike for her not to sympathize.

But she also wondered if Warren might not be doing his daughter a favor by making her stand on her own feet.

Torie apparently decided to retreat. She took a sip of wine and turned to Emma. "So, are you and Kenny going to Austin tomorrow?"

Emma carefully avoided looking at Kenny. "I'm not certain."

Torie regarded her curiously. "Something wrong?"

"What do you mean?"

"Both of you have been acting funny all night. Too polite, like one of you is really pissed off at the other, except I'm not sure which one."

"Me," Kenny said.

Torie's fork paused in midair. "What'd she do?"

"I won't embarrass her by talking about it." He pushed his dinner plate out of Peter's reach.

"Well, that's no fun. Tell us what happened, Lady Emma."

"A misunderstanding on my part, that's all."

"Must have been a big misunderstanding," Shelby said. "Kenny doesn't hardly ever get mad."

"Oh, really?" Emma stabbed at her lamb, and her sense of being ill-used overcame her British reserve. "He's been angry with me since the moment we met."

Kenny glared at her. "I have not!"

"You certainly have." Everyone was staring, but injustice bubbled inside her to the point where she didn't care. "You've complained about everything. You don't like carrying my luggage or the way I hold my brolly or the fact that I walk fast. You say I'm too conservative, and you tell me I'm too bossy. You refuse to accept my apology for a very natural misunderstanding. You don't even like the way I dance!"

"You *lead*!"

"And who made the rule that only men can do that?"

The others were watching intently, except for Peter, who blew a pear-flecked spit bubble. Mortified by her outburst, she set down her fork and tried to regain her dignity. "I simply misinterpreted Shelby's visit this afternoon. As a result, I became upset with Kenny, and now he's upset with me."

Everyone continued to regard her with interest except Kenny, whose brow had furrowed. "When she says she got upset, what she really means is that she slapped me."

"Oh, my God!" Torie's mouth dropped.

"You didn't!" Shelby's eyes widened.

Kenny glowered at Emma. "The slap wasn't the important part, and you know it."

"Tell us why you did it," Torie said. "I'm sorry, Kenny, but I'll bet she had a good reason."

"Thanks a lot for the vote of confidence." Kenny shot her a disgusted look.

"Well . . ." Emma's inherent sense of breeding fought against her need to defend herself. Then she remembered that none of these people seemed to have any compunction about airing their dirty linen in front of her. When in America, do as the Americans. "What Shelby told me led me to believe that . . ." She could feel herself faltering, and she sat a bit straighter in her seat so she could deliver the truth bang-on. "I mistakenly assumed Peter was Kenny's child and that Kenny had abandoned him."

Torie's wine glass stalled in midair. "Uh-oh."

Shelby looked shocked, and even Warren seemed taken aback. "No man in the Traveler family would ever do anything like that, not even Kenny."

It occurred to Emma that the Travelers had a peculiar moral code. Apparently it was acceptable for Kenny to pretend he was a gigolo, for Torie to go through two husbands and live off her father's money, for Warren to get a woman thirty-one years his junior pregnant, but it wasn't acceptable for her to experience a very natural misunderstanding.

"Shelby called Peter a forgotten child," she pointed out with some asperity. "She told me Kenny had abandoned his responsibility to his own flesh and blood. And Peter looks like a miniature version of Kenny, doesn't he? What else was I to think?"

Torie glanced over at Kenny and shrugged. "Put like that, I guess it's a natural conclusion for somebody who doesn't know you too well."

Kenny would have none of it. "She knows me plenty well."

"Actually, I don't," Emma pointed out. "We only met three days ago, and, technically, you're my employee."

That brought Warren's eyebrows to the center of his forehead, but Kenny merely snorted.

Shelby had been silent, but suddenly it was as if someone had lit a fire under her. "Peter looks *exactly* like your baby pictures. You're two peas in a pod, and that's what makes this whole situation so ugly. You only have one brother on the face of this earth, Kenny Traveler, and you've turned your back on him."

Kenny rescued a table knife from Peter's reach. "I haven't turned my back on him."

But Shelby was off and running. "You're lazy and irresponsible. You don't go to church, you roam all over the country, you refuse to date any of the nice girls I've found for you, you hand your money over to drug runners, and you don't show one single sign of settling down. If that isn't turning your back on your responsibility to your baby brother, I don't know what is."

Emma wasn't following this, but, as she tried to sort it out, Shelby's voice grew choked. "Your father is fifty-eight years old! He doesn't eat right. He doesn't get enough exercise. He's a heart attack waiting to happen, and he could die any minute! That leaves Peter and me. And if something should happen to me, my baby boy would be alone." Her face crumpled. "I know all of you think I'm being silly about this, but that's because none of you know what it's like to be a mother."

Torie shoved herself back from the table and headed for the bar.

Shelby went on. "I never knew I could love anybody like I love Peter, and I just can't stand thinking about my baby all alone in the world."

"He wouldn't be alone," Kenny said with such exaggerated patience that Emma suspected he'd been over this ground before. "In the first place, the chances that both of you will die before he's grown are min-uscule—"

"Don't tell me that. It happens all the time!"

"—and I told you I'd be his guardian."

"What kind of guardian would you be for a little boy? I can't sleep at night worrying about it. You live all over the place, you currently have no job! You get into fights and mess around with bitchy women." She shot Emma a quick, apologetic glance. "I didn't mean you."

"Thank you." Emma realized no one had mentioned the possibility of Torie becoming Peter's guardian. Why was that?

Shelby looked over at her husband. "You agree with me, don't you, Warren?"

"I'm not ready to climb into the grave yet, but I have to say that it's hard to see Kenny as anybody's guardian."

Emma's spine stiffened, and even though this was none of her business, she couldn't keep silent. "Kenny would make a fine guardian."

They all stared at her.

She blinked her eyes, not quite certain what had come over her, but knowing she had to speak. "It's obvious he cares about Peter, and Peter adores him. Shelby, I sympathize with your concern, but as an educator, I believe I can safely tell you it's misplaced. One only has to see Kenny and Peter together to understand that you couldn't find a better protector for your son."

Everyone looked over at Peter, who was busy gumming away on Kenny's thumb.

Shelby's eyebrows drew together. "Just this afternoon you thought Kenny had abandoned him. Haven't you changed your mind awfully fast?"

Emma replied simply. "I know him better now."

For the first time since their blowup, Kenny regarded her with something other than chilly courtesy. The beginnings of a smile caught the corners of his mouth, but whatever response he might have made was lost as Shelby leaned forward.

"But Peter'll need a mother's influence, too. And what if Kenny marries someone awful, like that bitch Jilly Bradford?"

Torie returned from the bar, a wine glass in her hand. "I don't know why you ever asked her out, Kenny. The only thing she had to recommend her was an eleven handicap. Plus a D cup."

"She had other things," Kenny said defensively. "Unlike your and Shelby's friends, her IQ was in three digits."

"That's not fair," Shelby said. "You dated my sophomore roommate, Kathy Timms, and I distinctly remember she was Phi Beta Kappa. Or was it Phi Mu?"

"It was Phi Mu." Torie sat on the banquette. "But I know you went out with Brandy Carter's big sister, and Brandy took a three-hundred-level math class her senior year. Don't you remember, Shel? She was always complaining about it."

"Are you sure it was math?" Shelby said. "It might have been that class on family life and sexuality where she had to make up a weekly budget."

Kenny rolled his eyes. "I know you won't believe this, Lady Emma, but both Shelby and Torie have college degrees."

Torie grinned and turned to her brother. "You dated Debbie Barto for a while."

"It was her older cousin Maggie," Shelby interjected.

"Well, blood's thicker than water, and Debbie was real smart." Torie's eyes glittered. "Remember, Shel? No matter what food you named, she knew exactly how many calories it had."

Kenny sighed. "I swear, this conversation proves exactly why the rest of the world makes fun of Texas women. I can only apologize, Lady Emma. All our yellow roses aren't this lamebrained."

"It's quite all right," Emma replied, "although I'm afraid some of what they're saying is getting lost in the translation."

"Consider yourself fortunate."

Torie leaned back and lifted an eyebrow at her brother. "Go ahead

---

and scoff. But I'll bet you don't have the slightest idea how many calories are in a Life Saver."

"Can't say as I do."

She shot him a triumphant look. "Then I suggest you keep your opinions on the intelligence of Texas women to yourself."

Chapter 11

It wasn't quite nine o'clock, and the lights were still on inside the drug-store when Kenny swung into a diagonal parking space near the front door. "I'll just be a minute. I broke a lace on my favorite pair of golf shoes, and I need a replacement."

"I'll go in with you. I want to buy some film."

Though their earlier tension had faded, he'd made no real attempt at conversation since they'd left his family's home. She'd already apologized, and she had no intention of groveling. The next move was up to him.

She went inside as he held the door open for her. He immediately headed toward the back of the store to find the shoelaces, and she walked over to the film display. For nine o'clock, the store was busy. She was just getting ready to make her choice when she caught sight of the burly man who'd followed her into the Roustabout entering the drugstore. For a moment his gaze locked on her, then he looked away.

Her pulse quickened, and she immediately regretted her conservative yellow dress. Then it occurred to her that she might not have to write off this day after all, but she had to act quickly. What scandalous thing could she do in a drugstore?

Her watchdog was pretending to study a display of sunblock. Without giving herself time to think, she grabbed one of the small shopping carts and flew down the first aisle, her gaze darting left to right. She grabbed a book, tossed it in the cart, and careened around a corner. Her eyes automatically skimmed the shelves of shampoo. She spotted a plastic bottle and threw it in. With no time to ponder, she headed down another aisle and added to her purchases. She didn't try to make rational decisions; she simply needed to act.

More aisles, more items, until the bottom of her shopping cart was strewn with purchases. The burly man glanced over at her as she came around the front. Then he wandered toward the cashier. She needed to get there first so he could take a good look at what she'd bought, and she nearly overturned the cart in her rush to cut in front of him.

She was slightly breathless as she came to a stop before the cashier, who was a blank-faced teenage girl with dark brown lipstick. She sensed the watchdog coming up behind her and began unloading her purchases. She took her time to make certain each item was positioned so he could clearly see it. The cashier began to scan, then paused as she realized what she was scanning. She gazed curiously at Emma.

Although it was difficult, Emma kept her composure. "Would you add a pack of Camel cigarettes, please?" She pulled a tabloid off the rack with a picture of Elvis kissing Princess Diana. "And this."

The cashier turned to get the cigarettes, and Emma risked a sideways glance at the burly man. He was staring at her purchases.

Her hands were shaking as she reached into her wallet for her credit card. Had her luck finally changed? Surely this would be enough to convince Beddington he'd made a terrible mistake.

The cashier bagged up everything, and Emma stepped aside to wait for Kenny. The burly man bought a bottle of sunblock and left the store. She saw him pause outside, then cross the street, and she would bet everything she owned that he'd be lurking in his car when they came out.

Kenny approached the register and paid for his laces. "Sorry it took me so long. They had to go in the back to get the right length." He spotted the bulging plastic bag she was carrying. "That's a lot of film."

"There were a few other things I needed." She looped the handles together so he couldn't see inside, then drew the bag closer to her body. Her studied her for a moment, then moved toward the door.

When they left the store, she glanced around for a dark green Taurus, but there were a number of cars parked along the street, and she couldn't search for it without being obvious. Still, she knew he was there, which meant another golden opportunity lay before her. Her heart raced.

Now!

Turning quickly, she threw herself at Kenny. He was taken by surprise, and he stumbled backward only to bang into the brick wall that separated the drugstore from a dry cleaner's. Ignoring his grunt of pain, she smeared her body against his. Her bag of purchases whacked his thigh as she wound her free arm around his neck and kissed him as hard as she could.

His words were muffled as his lips moved beneath hers. "What 'n th' hell 're you doing?"

"Kiss'ng you." She kept her mouth smeared to his as she spoke and moved her body. "Put your arm 'round me."

"Why're you wiglin' like that?"

"I'm slith'ring."

"You're *what*?" He started to draw his head back, but she dug her fingers into his hair to hold him in place. Their teeth banged. "Pretend you're kiss'ng me."

"More orders, E'ma?"

She could feel his jaw tense and knew her habit of taking charge had set him off again. Why hadn't she been less direct? He was getting ready to push her aside, but he couldn't do that—not when everything was going so well. She wouldn't let him.

She softened her mouth, parted her lips, and gave him everything she had.

The seconds passed. *Oh, my . . .* He was really the most intelligent man. It didn't take more than a moment for him to see things her way.

His hands settled warm against her back and his own mouth softened in response, then opened. . . .

His tongue moved, eased inside, and she forgot all about burly men and giving orders. Instead the world cracked open and swallowed her.

The knowledge that she'd been starved crashed over her as she feasted on his kiss. She wanted his mouth everywhere—at her breasts, her waist, between her legs. Yes, there! She wanted all of him loving her, filling her. She wanted to feel his weight holding her down, experience the resistance of bare skin rubbing together.

They were making noises—earthy, crude. He was hard against her, ready to penetrate, and she wanted him so badly she nearly sobbed her relief when his hand curled around her bottom.

He turned her without breaking the kiss so that she was against the brick, and his body shielded her from the street. His hand slipped under her dress to the outside of her thigh. She wore sandals and no stockings—those blessed bare legs!

His strong fingers curled around her inner thigh. She parted her legs and invited him to that place where he belonged. His hand went there, cupped her, rubbed—

A car horn blared.

Kenny whipped his hand from under her skirt and jumped back. She sagged against the brick. They both gasped for breath.

He thrust his fingers through his hair. "*Shit*."

The sight of his angry face defeated her. How could he look like that after what they'd just been through?

He grabbed her elbow and began dragging her toward the car, their beautiful kiss lying in ruins around them. "Don't you *ever* do anything like that again!"

She had to launch a counterattack, but she was too depleted to muster the right words. He pushed her inside the car and was still steaming as he got in himself.

"We almost *did* it! Right there in the middle of the busiest street in Wynette, Texas!" The Caddy shot out of its parking space. "Another few seconds, your skirt would have been up around your waist and my pants would have been unzipped, and don't you try to deny it. Damn it, Emma! I told you yesterday that I wasn't going to let anything keep me from getting back on the tour, but apparently you weren't listening. Or maybe you forgot that this happens to be the commissioner's home-town and everybody knows him."

She said nothing.

He shot out onto the highway. "By tomorrow morning he'll have heard every detail—how I was groping his wife's dear, *virginal* friend right in the middle of Main Street. In case you're missing the point here, this wasn't the best way for me to establish my reputation as an athlete with a solid moral character!"

"Please stop yelling at me." Perhaps the fact that she'd spoken softly instead of yelling in return made him glance over at her.

He frowned, sighed. "All right. I know this isn't all your fault. I could have pushed myself away. I should have. But, damn it, Emma, I'm a man, and that mouth of yours—"

"I've heard more than enough about how bossy I am. If my leader-ship skills threaten your masculinity, then you'll simply have to deal with it."

He looked startled. "I wasn't talking about your leadership skills; I was talking about your—Never mind. The thing is, if I'd known I was this irresistible to you, we could have taken care of it in private."

He *was* irresistible to her, but in all the wrong ways. "This didn't have anything to do with you being irresistible. It had to do with your being handy. The man Beddington hired was watching me, and I had to do something scandalous."

"Someone really is following you?"

"I told you it would happen. Last night he showed up at the Roust-about."

"What does he look like?"

"A large man with a very round head and thinning hair that's sort of straw-colored. He might drive a dark green Taurus. Do you know him?''

He stared at her for a very long time. "I might."

"Kenny, I only have ten days left before I have to go back to England."

"I'm well aware of that fact." The headlights from an approaching car slashed his face. "So I was being used back there?"

"It was necessary," she said stiffly. And then, to reclaim her pride, "You were the only man around."

He gave her a long look, then slid his hand lower on the steering wheel. "Don't even think about trying something like that with Dexter or Ted Beaudine, do you hear me? I mean it, Emma. Those men are off-limits. *All* men are off-limits."

"The story of my life," she muttered.

"What does that mean?"

"Not a thing." She could have bitten her tongue, and she quickly changed the subject. "I enjoyed watching Peter tonight. He didn't want to be with anyone but you all evening."

"Except his mother when chow time came around." He slowed as the road that led to his ranch came into view. "I want you to know that I appreciate what you said to Shelby tonight, not to mention the way you put up with everybody. I've decided to forgive you for what happened this afternoon."

"Hooray," she said dryly.

He turned down the drive, then glanced over at her. "You're gonna play hardball?"

"I believe so."

"I guess I overreacted a little. I should have taken your do-gooder impulses into account when you slapped me. You hurt my feelings, is all."

"Well, I certainly know how that feels," she said pointedly.

He swung the car into the garage, which opened off the side of the house. "If you're trying to suggest that I hurt your feelings, forget it. Both of us know that's impossible because you don't care one bit about my good opinion."

"That's true," she replied, just to irritate him.

But it didn't work because he grinned and grabbed the plastic sack from her lap. "I'll carry that inside for you."

"No, I—" But he'd already taken it away, and she had to hurry after him into the kitchen.

The light Patrick had left on threw a soft glow over the furniture in the family area, as well as the colorful canvases on the walls, but she was too intent on getting her sack back to appreciate the decorating. As Kenny walked toward the dining room table, she saw to her dismay that the handles she'd looped together had somehow come unfastened.

He dropped the sack on the tabletop so that it fell to the side, dumping out some of its contents. "Now, what do we have here?"

She shot forward, but he'd already picked up the first item that had spilled out.

"Hemorrhoid cream? That's a little more than I wanted to know about you, Lady Emma."

"It's not—I don't actually have—Give that back to me!"

Ignoring her, he reached into the bag and pulled out a paperback book. "*Talking Back to Prozac*. You be sure to let me know exactly what to say."

"No!" She sprang forward as his hand closed around a plastic bottle. "Give me—"

He held it just out of her reach and studied the label. "Now, who would have imagined a member of the British aristocracy would have a problem with head lice?"

"It's seasonal," she managed.

He pushed aside the Camels, the tabloid, and an early pregnancy test kit to pick up a series of small boxes. "Sheik Lubricated, Trojan Ribbed, Ramses Extra, Class Act Ultra Thins. I guess I know who to borrow from if I ever run out." He pushed away a package of clothesline. "I'm not even going to ask about that."

Only one item remained in the bag. Maybe he hadn't noticed it. Maybe he wouldn't—

"Now, what do we have here?" He scooped it out and held it up. "Vaginal moisturizer." His eyebrows shot together. "What in the *hell* is *this* for?"

Her face flamed. "Well, I don't know. . . . I would imagine it's for—"

"Now, *this* is where I draw the line! It's bad enough everybody in town's going to be thinkin' I'm sleeping with a depressed, lice-ridden, hemorrhoidal foreigner who likes to be tied up and might be pregnant, although—since she's just about cornered the market on condoms—I don't know how that could have happened. But I will *not*—you listen to me, Emma!—I absolutely will *not* have anybody thinkin' a woman of mine needs a *vaginal moisturizer*, do you hear me?"

"It was—" She swallowed and tried to speak calmly. "It was an impulse buy."

He snorted.

"I told you Hugh's man was following me. He came in the drugstore, so I scrambled to buy all this."

"He was in the drugstore?"

"He saw everything!" Her enthusiasm bubbled to the surface. "I think this just might do it! Especially with what happened between us outside the drugstore. I know you weren't happy about that, but I'll explain to Francesca the next time we talk. Beddington's going to be appalled when he hears, and, by this time tomorrow, the engagement has to be over."

"This is what your grand plan has come down to? Convincing the duke the two of us are having an affair."

"It didn't start out that way. Honestly. But I need to work with what I have."

"And I guess that's me." Kenny transferred the vaginal moisturizer from one hand to the other and looked thoughtful. "Emma, you're making this way too complicated. Just call him up and tell him you're not marrying him. It isn't right the way you're letting him push you around."

"I can't do that. If I make him angry, he'll close St. Gert's. I have to be subtle."

"Subtle?" He shook his head. "You sure do bring new meaning to that old song about being true to your school."

"It's not just a school. It's my—"

"I know. It's your home. And excuse me for pointing out that's more than a little pathetic, although, after what you saw tonight of my family at dinner, I guess I don't have much room to talk."

She hesitated. "Peter really is adorable."

He smiled. "I have a couple of irons already cut down for him, just waiting till he's old enough to hit a ball around."

"I'm sure he'll love that. Especially if you're with him."

Silence fell between them. It was night and the house was quiet. Her gaze dipped to his mouth, and she remembered the kiss they'd shared. She wondered if he remembered.

"I'm going for a swim," he said abruptly. "I'll see you tomorrow."

He began to walk away, then seemed to remember what he was holding and turned back to put the tube of vaginal moisturizer in her hands. "You'd better hold on to this just in case you completely lose your mind and decide to seduce Dexter O'Conner."

Before she could reply, he disappeared.

Torie stood by herself on the patio smoking her last cigarette of the night. She kept telling herself she was going to quit, and this time she'd do it. As soon as her life settled down.

A light flickered on above her in Peter's room. Shelby had gone in to check on him.

Torie's heart shriveled with envy. Peter was so dear, so perfect. She loved him with all her heart, yet she could barely stand to look at him. Only once had Shelby broached the subject of Torie being his guardian, and that had been right after he was born. Torie had made certain it never came up again.

The door that led into the house opened. She looked up, expecting to see her father, but Dexter O'Conner emerged instead.

"What in the hell are you doing here?"

"Your father let me in. I was invited for dinner, but I had a business meeting, and I couldn't get away."

Shelby hadn't told her that Dexter was invited. One more betrayal.

He pushed his hands into his pockets and gazed up at the sky. She caught a whiff of his cologne. It smelled crisp and clean as the air. "What a beautiful night."

Something like awe resonated in his voice, as if the clear, starlit night was magical instead of something rather ordinary. She had to force herself not to look up to see what she'd missed. Instead, she crossed her arms over her chest and glared at him. "I'm getting sick of this, Dexter. There are laws against stalking."

"I'm hardly stalking you, Victoria. I didn't know you were going to be at the Roustabout last night. And tonight I had an invitation."

"Let me be a little clearer. I don't like you, and I don't ever want to talk to you again."

"In point of fact, we're not well-acquainted enough for you to dislike me. You know, if you could stop being so frightened by this situation, our entire problem-solving process would be a lot easier."

"Frightened? Of a dweeb like you? Don't flatter yourself."

"If you weren't frightened, you'd be anxious to talk to me so we could get this sorted out."

He was right, but she would never admit it. "There isn't anything to sort out. I don't want to marry you! I can't make it any plainer."

He looked up at the sky, then tilted his head as if he wanted to star-gaze from a different angle. She couldn't help but notice the clean, strong lines of his profile. He had a broad forehead, a well-shaped nose, and a mouth that was rather alarmingly sensual. The surprise of his mouth, combined with his composure in the face of her turbulent emotions, infuriated her.

"You know what I think? I think you cooked this whole thing up yourself. You want me, but you know I'd never look twice at a nerd like you, so you came up with this whole scheme, then convinced your father to go along with it."

He looked mildly startled. "Is that what you believe?"

"You're damned right I do."

"Fascinating."

As he wandered over to the banquette, she found herself studying the shoulders beneath that rumpled oxford shirt. They weren't overly broad, but they were solid-looking.

He turned back, and she had the weird feeling that he could read her mind. "In fact, this was *your* father's idea."

"Yeah, right," she scoffed.

He pushed his hands in his pockets, stretching his slacks over a very firm abdomen. "Contrary to what you seem to think, it really hasn't been all that difficult for me to find female companionship." He walked over to sit on the banquette and stretch out his legs. "As for my father . . ." For a moment, she thought she saw amusement in his eyes, but that was impossible since he had no sense of humor. "To be frank, he's not all that fond of you. But he does want the merger, and your father made it very clear this was the only way he'd agree to it."

She sucked in her breath. "You're lying! Do you really think I'll believe this was my father's idea?"

Again, the glimmer in his eyes that, on anyone else, could only have been amusement. "Apparently he's desperate to get rid of you."

She wanted to go for his throat, just as she'd done last night, but she felt too frozen to move. How could he even suggest her father was behind this? It was *his* father! It had to be.

"If you and your brother had been willing to talk with me last night," he said quietly, "I could have explained all this."

Her heart was beating so hard she wanted to press her hands to her chest to keep her skin from splitting. "Daddy would never have proposed something so horrible on his own. I don't know why you're lying. All I have to do is ask him."

"I hope you do. You'll find out that Warren is the one who's doing the blackmailing, and I'm the ransom. If Dad wants the merger, he has to turn me over."

"Ransom!" Sparks shimmered behind her eyelids. "Listen here, you bozo! Marrying me would be the highlight of your sorry life!"

He looked thoughtful. "That's highly debatable. It's true that you're quite beautiful, but you're also a very difficult woman."

Torie tried to absorb the fact that Dexter O'Conner, the biggest nerd in Wynette, Texas, might not want her. "I am not!"

"You're a two-time loser at marriage," he said slowly. "You have an unstable family background. You cuss like a man. I'm sure you could beat me at whatever sport you put your mind to. And you smoke, which I detest, even though I understand it's a sign of how little regard you have for yourself." He paused, and his voice grew strangely gentle. "You also don't seem to be able to have children."

She felt as if she'd been struck. "You prick." Her voice sounded tight and forced. "Who told you that?"

He stood and walked toward her, stopping several feet away. "Wynette's a small town."

"Get out of here."

"I'm not trying to hurt you." He spoke with a gentleness that sounded too much like pity. "But I don't play games, and it's only right that I tell you I'd very much like to have children."

A sting of tears prickled behind her eyes, but she refused to let them form. "Then it's a good thing you're not marrying me because I'm as barren as the Sahara, you son of a bitch!"

"That's not what your father told me. He said there's no medical reason why you can't conceive. Shelby believes it's simply a case of your body waiting for the right man to come along. Improbable, but then who's to say?"

She barely pushed the words through the constriction in her throat. "They discussed this with you?"

"It came up."

She felt so betrayed she couldn't speak. Shelby had once been her best friend. As for her father . . . for years, he had been the only safe harbor in her life. And then Shelby had seduced him and pushed Torie into the background. Now her father wanted Torie removed from his daily existence so he could concentrate on his new family. Ironic that Kenny, the evil tormentor of her childhood, had become the only dependable person in her life.

Pride kicked in, and she lifted her head. "For someone who's so repulsed by the idea of marrying me, you certainly seemed to have asked a lot of questions."

"I didn't say I was repulsed. I happen to be strongly attracted to you."

His words were a small Band-Aid over her open wounds, enough for her to curl her lip and scoff. "Like that's a news flash."

He smiled. "It's the strangest thing. I'm not a violent man, but ever since Ted made that remark yesterday about somebody needing to swat you, I keep having this recurring image of you turned bottom-up over my lap."

A rush of heat shot through Torie's bloodstream. She didn't like it one bit, so she sneered, "Am I wearing clothes?"

He seemed to be thinking it over. "A full skirt tossed over your head. Panties draped around one ankle."

The heat inside her jumped ten degrees, and she realized the biggest nerd in Wynette, Texas, had just turned her on. She felt disoriented. She was supposed to be the outrageous one. At the same time, she couldn't let him know that he'd outmaneuvered her. "What's it going to be, Dex? Do you want to marry me or not?"

"I'm not certain. Probably not. On the other hand, there is that attraction. Still, I resent being manipulated this way by your father."

"Finally, we agree on something."

"Yes, well, I could have told you that at the beginning if you hadn't decided to approach this situation emotionally instead of logically."

"All right, Mr. Logic, what's your solution?"

"It's really very simple. That's what I was trying to tell you last night. We need to spend time with each other. Neither of us can convince your father to back off if we haven't even made the effort to see if we can get along."

"How can we get along? We don't have a single thing in common."

"Are you forgetting the sexual attraction?"

"*You're* the one with the sexual attraction! I think you're a dweeb."

He lifted his hand and stared down at it. "It's the most incredible thing—my palm is actually itching. I never imagined I would have the urge to spank a woman."

Again, that little thrill of excitement. Maybe Dex wasn't quite as boring as she'd thought. "Yeah, well, it'd take you and the entire Dallas Cowboys' defensive line to pull it off."

"I'm stronger than I look, Victoria."

"Will you stop calling me that!"

"Will you stop smoking cigarettes?"

"No!"

"Very well . . . Victoria."

Something inside her snapped, and she lunged for him. She couldn't help it. He was so smug, so superior and condescending that she wanted to bash his face in, but she'd settle for hurling him into the stucco wall.

Unfortunately, as the heels of her hands slammed against his chest and he didn't move, she realized it wasn't going to be that easy. He caught her wrists. She gazed up into gray eyes flecked with green and experienced the uneasy sensation that he was peering through all her carefully erected defenses. The idea paralyzed her.

She recovered only as she realized he was going to kiss her. Lots of men had wanted to do exactly that, so she wasn't surprised. What surprised her was how much she wanted him to go through with it.

Her eyelids drifted shut. Their bodies fit together. She felt his lean, hard chest pressing against her breasts. His lips brushed her cheek. She tilted her mouth toward his.

"I can't wait to kiss you," he whispered. "But I want it to be perfect. We'll finish this as soon as you don't taste like cigarettes."

Her eyes shot open.

He kissed the end of her nose, then set her aside as if she were a dear, but annoying, child. "I've given you my opinion of how we should go about this. Now it's up to you."

After one last glance at the night sky, he left her alone.

Chapter 12

Emma was fuming by the time she'd finished breakfast. Once again, Kenny had left to practice before they'd made plans for the day. Her research schedule was falling sadly behind. He kept forgetting that he was supposed to be working for *her*.

The phone rang twice, and a moment later Patrick called down from the second floor, "It's for you, and I think I'm going to faint. The man says he's a duke!"

Finally! Beddington had heard about last night, and he was calling to break off the engagement! She flew across the kitchen, took a deep breath, and picked up the wall phone that hung near the counter. "Good morning, Your Grace."

"Emma, my dear, I've heard some distressing news."

Her muscles tensed with anticipation. This was it, then. Within minutes, she'd be free of him, and, if luck was with her, St. Gert's would still be safe.

"Word has reached me that you were seen purchasing a tabloid newspaper. A small point, I admit, but still troubling. I had no idea you read garbage like that."

She frowned. Buying a tabloid had been her least scandalous activity. What about the rest?

She waited for him to mention the other purchases she'd made or comment on the fact that she'd misbehaved at the Roustabout. What about the fact that she'd kissed Kenny in front of the drugstore?

"If you must read those awful rags, would you at least get someone else to buy them for you?"

She held her breath and waited for him to comment on the pregnancy kit, the condoms, the *lice* shampoo!

"I nearly forgot. My sister asked me to tell you that she's found a gown for you to wear to the engagement party. She'll have it waiting when you get back."

She sank down on one of the chintz-covered barstools at the counter, trying to think what to say. "Are—are you having me followed?"

"Followed? Of course not. I simply have my sources."

"And that's all your sources told you? That I bought a tabloid newspaper?"

"I can't think why you'd be interested in such drivel. Still, if that's your worst sin, I'm sure I can live with it. Anne, my second wife, was fond of the tabloids." There was a pause as he turned away from the receiver to speak with one of his aides. "I have to go, Emma; I have another call waiting. And from now on, please try to remember that whatever you do reflects on me."

He broke the connection before she could reply.

The blueberry muffin she'd enjoyed for breakfast clotted in her stomach as she sat on the stool, receiver in her hand, telephone cord twisted around her fingers. How could he know about the tabloid, but not the rest of it? She tried to sort out her thoughts, but nothing made sense.

Patrick came into the kitchen, eager to hear the details of Emma's connection with a duke. She gave him a highly abridged version, and he was just beginning to press for more information when Torie entered from the front hallway. "Hey, Lady Emma. Let's get hoppin'."

She wore white jeans along with a light blue T-shirt, and her fashionably untidy hair tumbled from a bright yellow banana clip at the crown of her head. She was also working away at a piece of gum.

"Where are we going?"

"Driving lesson." Torie spit her gum into the trash and immediately pulled another stick out of her pocket.

"I don't have any desire to learn how to drive."

"I know, but you're going to anyway." She plopped the fresh piece in her mouth.

"Really, Torie—"

"Haul ass, Your Ladyship. My royal chariot's waiting. Or are you chicken?"

"Of course I'm chicken! Why do you think I've gone all these years without learning to drive?"

"All you have to do is steer up and down Kenny's driveway. You can steer, can't you?"

"Probably, but there's no point."

"There's always a point to spitting in the devil's eye." Torie's familiar green eyes held a challenge.

Patrick took Emma's arm and drew her off the stool. "Do what she says, Lady Emma. Life's too short to spend it bogged down by phobias."

Emma could fight one of them, but not both, without looking completely spineless. "All right," she said reluctantly. "Up and down the drive. But that's all."

It wasn't all, of course. After half an hour in the drive, Torie somehow managed to bully her into pulling out onto the road by promising that hardly anyone ever used it.

Emma found herself with wet palms and a damp T-shirt, driving a car with the steering on the wrong side. As her fingers gripped the wheel, she fought the memory of that terrifying day when she'd been ten and she'd watched a bright yellow lorry come barreling toward the car.

She crept too close to the center line and jerked the wheel.

"Relax," Torie said. "You're fingers are going to start cramping up."

"Stop cracking your gum!"

"Damn, you're cranky. By the way, in this country we drive on the right side of the road instead of the left."

"Oh, God!" Emma wrenched the wheel to the right, but didn't straighten in time to keep the tires from biting into the gravel on the shoulder. Finally, she managed to maneuver the car into the proper lane. "You should have told me at once! I think I'm going to faint."

"Take deep breaths."

"I can't believe you talked me into doing this! Oh, Lord, Torie, there's a car coming up behind us!"

"As long as you don't slam on the brakes, you've got nothing to worry about."

"Why are you *doing* this to me?"

"I decided to stop smoking, and I need a distraction. Making somebody else miserable seemed like a good idea." Torie's voice grew belligerent. "And I'm giving up cigarettes for myself, not for anybody else. So if anybody says anything to you about the fact that I'm not smoking, you tell him to mind his own gee dee business!"

"I can't do this much longer. I want to stop."

"There's a diner in town. We'll stop there."

"Town! I can't!"

"Now that you've got your tendency to drive on the wrong side of the road straightened out, you're doing just fine."

"I don't—I don't have a license."

"I'm good friends with most of the cops around here. Don't worry about it."

"I'm not worried. I'm terrified!"

"We're both still alive, so that should count for something."

Somehow she made it into town and managed to pull into a large space next to the diner. She turned off the ignition and leaned back against the seat in relief.

Torie grinned. "Proud of yourself?"

Emma scowled at her.

"Come on, admit it. You've done something you didn't think you could do."

Now that her heart rate was beginning to return to normal, maybe she did feel a little proud. Being unable to drive limited her life in so many ways. Not that she could drive now. "I'll admit I'm happy we're still alive," she said begrudgingly.

Torie laughed. "Come on. I'll buy you coffee to celebrate."

Inside Jimmy's Diner a model train chugged along a track that ran just below the ceiling. Chrome chairs sat around tables covered in black-and-white-checked oilcloth, and two ceiling fans spun overhead. A blackboard near the entrance listed the day's lunch special: chicken-fried pork chops, stewed okra, along with a carrot and "raisen" salad. Emma was uncomfortable with the idea of a young child coming in and seeing that, so she requested a piece of chalk from the woman at the register and corrected the spelling.

Torie hooted and hugged her.

They sat at a table that held A-1 Steak Sauce and Tabasco, along with the more usual condiments. On the wall next to them hung a painting of a rooster and a red lantern. As the model train passed over their heads, she saw that each car was painted with the sign of a local business.

While Torie sipped the coffee the waitress brought and Emma waited for her tea, she thought back to her conversation with Beddington. Why hadn't the burly man told him everything he'd seen? What kind of incompetent spy had Hugh hired?

"Good morning, ladies."

Dexter O'Conner approached the table. This morning he wore a yellow oxford shirt instead of blue. He looked pleasantly rumpled, a bit distracted, and rather adorable. She smiled at him. "Hello, Dexter."

"Emma. Victoria."

"That's Lady Emma to you," Torie snapped.

He lifted an eyebrow at her. "I see your attitude hasn't changed. You might as well go ahead and order your wedding dress."

Emma expected Torie to leap all over that, but instead, she seemed to make an effort to pull herself together. She even managed to give Dexter a rather stiff smile. "I don't think that'll be necessary. If it's all right with Lady Emma, you can join us."

"Of course it's all right with me."

Dexter smiled and took a seat at the end of the table.

"You're not working today?" Torie said with forced politeness.

"I'm on my way. I've been staying late every night for weeks, and I decided to take some time off. What about you two?"

"I gave Lady Emma a driving lesson."

"You don't drive?" Dexter asked.

"She does now," Torie replied.

"Only a very charitable person would describe what I was doing as driving." Emma gave Dexter a lighthearted description of what had happened on the road, but instead of laughing, he encouraged her. Once again, she thought how nice he was, and, at the same time, she began to wonder if a match between Torie and Dexter was quite as outlandish as everyone seemed to think. They were both intelligent, attractive people, and each of them had something the other needed. Dexter's stability could easily turn to stodginess as he grew older. And Torie seemed to need an anchor in her life.

The conversation drifted to other topics, and gradually some of Torie's stiffness eased, until Emma began to believe she might even be enjoying Dexter's company. That changed when Emma made the mistake of mentioning that Torie had stopped smoking.

Torie glowered, then stuck her finger in Dexter's chest. "I've been planning to quit for months. It has nothing to do with you! Got it?"

He regarded her steadily. "I certainly do." Ignoring the French-manicured fingernail implanted in his shirtfront, he turned to Emma and asked about her plans for the day.

With one eye on Torie, Emma told him she'd hoped to go to Austin. "I wanted to spend a few hours at the University of Texas library, but Kenny seems to have disappeared."

"I'll be happy to take you," he said.

"Don't you have to work?"

"Our main office is in Austin, and there are some people I need to see. I can do that while you're at the library."

"Are you certain about this?"

"I wouldn't have offered if I hadn't wanted to."

"Well, then, I'd quite love to. You don't mind, do you, Torie?"

Torie frowned. "Why should I?"

Torie was obviously displeased, and Emma hesitated. Then she remembered her driving lesson and decided she wasn't the only person who needed to look the devil in the eye. It might be good for Kenny's sister to discover that not every woman found Dexter unappealing. "Excellent, then. I have my notebook in my purse, so I'm ready to go." She thanked Torie for the driving lesson, then let Dexter lead her from the diner.

Torie scowled as she watched the door close behind them. *Fine!* She hoped the two of them bored each other to death.

Through the plate-glass window, she caught sight of Ted Beaudine. He walked up to Dexter and Emma, and they all chatted for a few minutes. The next thing she knew, Ted was climbing into Dex's Audi, too, and all three of them were heading off to Austin. Without her.

"You want more coffee, Torie?" Mary Kate Pling called over from the counter.

"Uh, no. No, thanks." She leaned back in her chair and thought about how much she liked Lady Emma. Still, nobody would ever call her drop-dead gorgeous. So how had it happened that she had just managed to drive off with Dex and Ted, while Torie Traveler, unanimously regarded to be the most beautiful girl in town, had been left behind?

She scowled, gazed down into her empty mug, and chalked her bad mood up to nicotine withdrawal.

Kenny was furious. "What do you *mean*, Emma went off to Austin with Dex?"

Torie climbed out of his pool and wrapped a towel around the three scraps of amethyst nylon that were passing for her bathing suit. "Ted went along, too."

"Is that supposed to make it all right?"

"Why are you making such a big deal out of this? They're all adults."

"I can't believe you didn't stop her. At the very least, you should have gone along to chaperone. Why didn't you do that?"

"Because I wasn't invited! Besides, Lady Emma hardly needs a chaperone."

"That's what you think." Kenny stalked over to the table and snatched up one of the glasses of iced tea Patrick had brought out for them.

His housekeeper regarded him with a speculative eye. "It's flavored with passion fruit, Kenneth. Maybe you'd better drink something else. You don't want to OD."

Kenny ignored him. He knew exactly why Emma hadn't invited Torie. She didn't want any competition. Not that she'd try anything with

Ted, since she knew whose son he was, but she'd been attracted to Dexter from the start. He rounded on his sister. "You listen to me. Dexter is your responsibility, and I want you to keep him away from Emma!"

"Mine!" Beads of water flew from her hair as she whirled around. "Damn, Kenny, are you jealous?"

That really made him mad. "Jealous! Of course not. It's just that Emma's sort of a—a sexual predator right now, and she's got Dexter in her sights. The way she looks and everything—I mean, her mouth—well, the point is, if she sets her mind to it, it won't take her long to get him in bed with her, and that wouldn't be good . . . for him."

"A sexual predator?" Torie stared at him.

"Since you're a woman, you might have a hard time understanding, but you'll have to trust me."

"I'm not a woman," Patrick drawled, "and I think you've lost your freaking mind."

Kenny didn't lower himself to pointing out the obvious. "Both of you'll just have to believe me. Emma's one of those women who was born with . . . The thing is, the minute a *heterosexual* man looks at her, all he can think about is—well, her mouth, and—"

"*Emma?*" Torie's own mouth gaped in astonishment.

Patrick crossed his legs. "Maybe we're not talking about the same person. British accent? Good appetite? Hums songs from *The Lion King* when she doesn't think anybody's listening?"

Kenny clenched his jaw in frustration. "I knew the two of you wouldn't understand. I don't know why I even tried to explain." He glared at his sister. "You just keep Dexter the hell away from her!"

With that, he headed for his car. He wasn't sure where he was going; he only knew he wasn't hanging around so Torie and Patrick could laugh at him.

Torie watched his car peel down the driveway, then looked over at Patrick. "What was that all about?"

Patrick looked glum as he pushed his sunglasses on top of his head. "It seems I have a serious rival for Kenneth's affections."

"Ten minutes ago I would have said you're crazy, but I don't now. I like Emma a lot, but Kenny's way out of her league. It's like matching up Snow White with, well, Kenny Traveler."

"I like her, too. As a matter of fact, I adore her. But, you're right. She's hardly his type. Still, I must admit Kenny's little hissy fit has thrown me for a loop." He gave a deep, tragic sigh. "You have no idea what it's like being a victim of hopeless passion."

Torie regarded him sympathetically. Everybody but Kenny knew that

Patrick had been in love with her brother from the moment he'd started swinging his fists in that roadhouse fight. Torie used to feel sorry for Patrick, but, as she'd grown to know him better, she'd realized he loved the drama of unrequited love as much as he loved Kenny.

Still, Kenny lusting after Lady Emma? She'd known his suspension had thrown him into an internal tailspin. Maybe he needed an emotional resting place right now, and that was why he'd chosen Lady Emma. She was stable, available, and completely temporary. Thanks to their crazy mother, he didn't know how to relate to women as friends, and he'd confused his emotional needs with sexual ones.

Torie frowned, already worried about Emma. No woman could resist Kenny once he had his sights set, and Lady Emma, for all her intelligence, lacked experience, which made her more vulnerable than other women. If Kenny didn't come to his senses, she was going to end up with a broken heart.

Unless Dexter got to her first.

Torie shoved a stick of gum in her mouth and tried to tell herself that a mutual attraction between Emma and Dexter would solve a lot of problems. Torie'd be off the hook as far as marrying him, and Emma would be safe from all the heartbreak Kenny was going to bring her. Anyone could see that Dexter and Lady Emma were perfect for each other. He was a dweeb, but—All right! He was a sexy dweeb. And Lady Emma was a cute dweeb. The two of them were made for each other. So why didn't Torie feel happier about it?

Maybe because she'd just this moment realized something completely crazy. She'd been looking forward to getting to know Dexter a little better. But that wouldn't happen if Lady Emma'd already caught his attention.

Kenny sat on the chaise staring at the pool lights and having a serious love affair with a very expensive pinot noir. It was after midnight, but Emma still wasn't back from Austin.

Although Kenny wasn't drunk, he wasn't stone sober, either, which was okay by him because he was a lot more pleasant when he was sober, and he didn't want to be pleasant right now. He'd come out here after he'd made himself miserable watching a video of last year's final round of the Masters, but he'd only watched the video because he'd been trying to distract himself from images of Emma getting naked for Dexter.

If it weren't for Dallie, he'd be preparing for Augusta now instead of thinking about Emma naked. His short game had never been better, he'd cleared up the problem he'd been having with his driving, and something inside him had been telling him for months that this was his year to wear the green jacket. But instead of doing that, he was baby-sitting a domineering thirty-year-old virgin.

Above him, the lights went on in her bedroom. So, she'd finally returned. His eyes narrowed just as they did when he was lining up a lightning-fast downhill putt.

He took his time finishing his wine, then carried the bottle inside. Usually this place seemed to welcome him, but tonight it didn't feel so friendly. Maybe the house knew what he had in mind.

Carpet muffled the sound of his shoes on the stairs. He heard water running in the guest bathroom and, without bothering to knock, pushed open the door of the bedroom where she was staying.

She'd already put her mark on the place. Her straw hat decorated with cherries hung over one poster of the bed, and, although the flower-filled vase on the chest of drawers bore Patrick's artistic touch, the bright yellow teapot containing the same kind of wildflowers that grew near the pasture fence could only have been arranged by Emma. She had books open everywhere, along with a folder of her research notes, a pink lotion jar, and an enormous bar of Cadbury dark chocolate, with the wrapper peeled back to expose the jagged edge where she'd nibbled at it.

The clothes she'd discarded lay on the bed, along with a lavender bra printed with little white daisies. A matching pair of bikini panties lay on the carpet next to her sandals. He stared at them for a moment, then wandered around the room before picking up her jar of lotion. He un-screwed it and took a sniff.

Baby powder, flowers, and spice. Even in his not-quite-sober state, the symbolism wasn't lost on him.

He carried the jar to an overstuffed chair, sat down, and stretched out his legs. He dipped a finger inside and pulled out a fat pink curl of lotion, then rubbed it against his thumb. It was silky and utterly femi-nine. He brought it to his nose and thought about how women's things could lull men's senses. But not his—never entirely—because mixed with all that soft and silky femininity was a female's need to reshape a man to fit her image of what she thought he should be.

His own manhood had been so hard won that he'd never been tempted to put it at risk by letting another woman get a stranglehold on him, especially an opinionated one. There was a private place inside him that made up who he was, and nobody ever touched that. Yet somehow today Emma had done it. Not knowingly. But it had happened, and now it was going to end.

As he rubbed the lotion into his palm and replaced the lid of the jar, he thought that women weren't the only ones who could manipulate. His need to survive as a man had made him a master at the subtle art of getting what he wanted without giving up a thing.

The bathroom door swung open. She gave a hiss of surprise as she saw him and fumbled with the bath towel. He glimpsed breasts rosy from her shower, soft nipples, and damp ringlets of pubic hair a darker shade of butterscotch than the curls sticking to her cheeks. Blood surged to his groin.

"Bugger!" She finally managed to secure the towel. "You scared the life out of me! What are you doing in here?"

"Back a little late, aren't you?"

Emma felt her heart kick an extra few beats from fright. He looked dangerous—sensuous lips thinned, violet eyes hooded. Something had happened to set him off. "I had no idea you'd be waiting up."

"You must have forgotten that I'm responsible for you."

"Rubbish. I'm responsible for myself. Now you'd better leave."

He uncoiled from the chair and studied her for a long, hard moment. "Did you manage to give it away tonight?"

It took her a moment to absorb what he was saying, and then an indignant reply leaped to her lips. At the very last minute, however, she discovered that her curiosity was stronger than her displeasure. What was bothering him enough to make him look like a Cold War interrogator? "Are you asking if I had sex with Dexter tonight? Is that what this is about?"

Unfortunately, her directness didn't make him back down an inch. "It might have been tough with Ted looking on. But maybe the two of you managed to get rid of him."

Which to do first? Put on her robe or dump a pitcher of flower water on his head? She decided to stick with this a bit longer. "We dropped him off at his house about three hours ago."

"So you and Dexter have been alone since then? Just the two of you."

The flower water was too far away. She marched to the closet and pulled out her robe. "And I enjoyed every minute I spent with him." She shoved her arms into her robe, yanked the towel out from beneath, and secured the sash. "If you have anything else to say about this—and I strongly advise against it—we can talk in the morning."

"Nothing happened between you and Dex, did it?" A strange expression had come over his face. Almost . . . relief?

"The passion of his lovemaking was exceeded only by my screams of ecstasy."

He came toward her, but he seemed to be speaking to himself. "Of course nothing happened. I knew that all along." One of his hands curled over the bedpost. "But something could have happened, which is why I'm telling you right now that I don't want you alone with him again."

"If you'd been around this morning," she pointed out, "I wouldn't have been."

"I wasn't planning to be gone for long."

"I didn't know that, did I?" She dumped her clothes on a chair.

"From now on, you will. First thing tomorrow, we're heading for the range. Then the rest of the day is yours."

"Thank you. Now good night."

He didn't budge. "It's still early. Let's go for a swim."

"I just took a shower."

"So what? You can take another one. Matter of fact, I'll take one with you. Or—you know what?" He paused and his eyes dipped to her mouth. "How about we just skip the swimming part and go right to the shower?"

She no longer felt quite as much in control as she had earlier. "What are you getting at?"

"I guess it's obvious I've been worried about you."

"Whatever for?"

He dropped his hand from the bedpost. "Because I don't believe you realize how vulnerable you are. I guess I didn't realize it, either, or I'd never have said what I did about how nothing was ever going to happen between us."

She blinked her eyes. What exactly did he mean by that? "I'm not vulnerable."

"You sure are. You're hell bent on sleeping with somebody, and both of us know it. Unfortunately—and this is where I'm starting to lose sleep myself—you don't have the foggiest idea what you're doing."

She bristled. "Considering the fact that you're in my bedroom right now, and I'm nearly naked, I suppose I can't argue."

"I'm the safest man in the world for you to be nearly naked with."

"You? Safe?"

"Sure I am." Her incredulity seemed to irritate him. "Just think about it. You saw right through me the moment we met. You know I'm only out for sex, and you don't have a single illusion about me. I guess that makes me about perfect for what you need."

She swallowed. "That's true." Except it wasn't entirely true. Kenny liked to paint the worst possible picture of himself, but he wasn't the villain he pretended to be.

He gave her a satisfied nod. "Tonight I made up my mind not to take any more chances that you're going to hook up with someone completely unsuitable."

"Somebody like Dexter O'Conner, for example?"

His eyes narrowed. "He's your worst nightmare. In the first place, a man like Dexter's not going to know much more than the bare minimum about sex, so you're guaranteed to have a rocky initiation. And in the second place, he's likely to get distracted somewhere along the line and forget about birth control. The next thing you know, you'll be pregnant with a little nerd baby, but old Dexter will have forgotten your name."

She laughed. Obviously, he didn't know Dexter nearly as well as he thought. She wondered how he was going to react when he figured out that his sister, despite her protests, was attracted to the "nerd." For that matter, she wondered what Torie would do.

Emma considered the irony of knowing that Dexter was exactly the kind of man she'd always wanted to fall in love with, but not once today had she caught herself fantasizing about how he'd look naked. He'd been a marvelous guide, a great conversationalist, and they'd had a wonderful time, but she hadn't looked at his lips and imagined what they'd feel like touching her own.

She tore her eyes away from Kenny's lips. "So you're saying you've changed your mind?"

"I have to, don't I?"

His air of self-sacrifice got her hackles up. "Don't put yourself out."

"You didn't answer my question. Do you want to swim first, or just go right to that shower?"

"Forgive me for not being overwhelmed by your intensely romantic offer."

"Not interested, huh?"

"Not a bit."

He took a slow step forward. "Does this mean you aren't attracted to me?"

"Sorry." She noticed her panties on the floor, snatched them up, and thrust them into the pocket of her robe.

He sighed. "All right, then. I guess I'm a big enough man to handle honest rejection. It is honest, isn't it?"

"Of course it's honest."

"I'm not doubting your word or anything . . ." He came toward her in a lazy, sensuous movement that reminded her of oil sliding over water. "But just to be sure . . ." His slacks brushed her robe as he stopped in front of her.

"Kenny . . ."

He smothered her protest with his kiss.

She wouldn't do it! She wasn't going to give in to this blatant power struggle he'd mistaken for seduction.

And then his tongue glided over the seam of her lips, leaving heat in its path.

Her annoyance began to fade as he took his time, not rushing her but content to dabble. Oh, but there was something splendid about being kissed by a lazy man.

Her spine bumped the bedpost at the same time that his hips flattened against her own. He was already aroused. Huge. His body's response entranced her, and she deepened the kiss.

His hand flattened against the base of her throat, ready to dip lower and cup her breast. She arched toward him, craving his touch, but he played in her mouth instead, dallying here and there in intimate tongue play that went on until only the bedpost and his body were holding her upright.

Her breasts ached for his hands, but he still hadn't touched them. She rubbed against his chest to urge him on, letting the silk of her robe and the fabric of his shirt abrade her nipples. He didn't take the hint.

No longer so content with his laziness, she dropped her hands to his hips and cupped his buttocks. They were as hard as the rest of him, so different from her own body, which was plump and pliant.

Their kiss went wild. She loved it—loved kissing him—had never imagined kissing could be like this. But she wanted more, and she pushed her hand between their bodies to open the knot of her robe.

He drew her down to the bed without missing a beat. But instead of going on from there, he kept kissing her.

She throbbed. She purred. She moaned her need into his mouth. "Kenny . . . please . . ."

He moved his lips to thé tender spot just beneath her ear and dabbled there for a while. Her skin prickled, her toes curled. She realized she might very well melt all over the bedspread before he got to the good part. *Lower!*

Oh, why wouldn't he hurry? Obviously, he needed a little prodding on her part, so she mustered her concentration and reached between them for the snap on his slacks.

He immediately rolled over on top of her and used his mouth to investigate the throbbing pulse at the base of her throat.

Her breasts! Why wouldn't he touch her breasts? She wanted to plead with him, then realized she was too weak to speak.

He found an unbelievably sensitive spot on her collarbone, and she moaned against the top of his head. His hand moved lower. *Finally!*

But her relief was short-lived as his thumb slipped beneath the sleeve of her robe, only to stop and dawdle at her wrist. Her *wrist*! It was maddening! He was supposed to be an experienced lover, but he didn't seem to have even the vaguest notion how to find the sensitive parts of the female anatomy.

The skin along the underside of her arm quivered at his stroking, and tiny shock waves shot through her middle. But instead of taking advantage of her all-too-obvious arousal, he kept dawdling! How could she overcome his natural laziness? How could she point him in the proper direction?

She would simply have to be more forthright.

Chapter 13

"**K**enny . . ." *Emma's blurred senses made it difficult to talk, but she* concentrated on forming the words because honest communication between sex partners was vitally important, and he had to understand that *she had needs*!

"My robe . . ." She swallowed. "Take it off. Pull it off my . . ."

The tip of his tongue discovered a pulse point at the side of her neck, and she groaned. Long moments ticked by before she could once again collect her thoughts.

"No . . . not just there." She moaned. "Touch me . . . my . . . Take off your clothes and touch my . . ."

He drew back and frowned at her. His mouth was as swollen as her own, and his passion-silvered eyes reminded her of sugar-glazed violets. "Is something wrong?"

She cupped his jaw, caught her breath, and smiled so he'd understand she wasn't criticizing, merely providing some much-needed direction. "Could we move it along a bit?"

"Move . . . it . . . *along*?" Each word came out like a bullet.

"Uhm."

"You want to *move* . . . *it* . . . *along*?"

"If you don't mind."

"Are you in a hurry or something?"

"Something."

"Don't tell me you've got a shed-yule for this, too?"

"Not a schedule. No, of course not. It's just that I'm . . . well . . . I'm sure you'll be pleased to know that I'm thoroughly aroused, and I believe we can move on to—well, to the next part. The *good* part."

He arched one eyebrow. "This part isn't good?"

She realized she'd offended, and she hurried to appease him. "Of course it's good. It's wonderful. Really, Kenny, you're the most extraordinary kisser, but you're a little slow and . . ." His expression was beginning to grow ominous. "I'm having a super time. Truly. But we're done with that part now." Her voice grew smaller. "Aren't we?"

He rolled over onto his back and muttered, "I should have expected this. I don't know why I'm even surprised."

To her dismay, he pushed himself off the bed, only to stand right next to it pointing one finger in the general direction of her face. "Now you listen to me, Emma, because I'm only going to say this once. From now until both of us are wrung dry, *I'm* in charge. Do you hear me?"

"But—"

"And do you know why? Because *I'm* the expert, not you!"

Rebellion stirred in her heart. "I never said I was."

"Then why are you giving orders?" He asked with exaggerated patience.

"I merely thought—"

"No more thinking!" His jaw set in a stubborn line, and he rested the heel of his hand against the bedpost. "Now, here's the way it'll be. The two of us are going to practice a little sexual kinkiness called domination and submission. I'm dominating and you're submitting! Now, what that means, in case I'm not being clear, is that you can't issue a single order. Not one. You can moan. Moaning's fine. You can sigh. Sighing's okay, too. But no orders. And only when *I* say we're done can you talk. Then, just two words. *Thank* and *you*."

She should have been insulted—she was insulted—but at the same time, an urge to laugh had come over her. He was so blissfully arrogant. And he was also right. Sometimes she was too bossy.

He continued to scowl. "Now, have I made myself clear, or do I need to find that clothesline you picked up at the drugstore last night?"

Just to be saucy, she waved one lazy hand toward the corner of the room where she'd set down the sack containing her purchases.

His eyes narrowed.

She regarded him primly. "I might as well get some use out of what I bought, and I'm certainly not going to need that moisturizer."

"Damned right you're not."

Just as she was beginning to feel a bit smug for not crumbling in the face of his chest-pounding, he alarmed her by calling her bluff. As he headed for the corner of the room where she'd left the sack, she shot up in bed. "Kenny, I was teasing! About the clothesline."

"Uh-huh."

"I really don't think I could tolerate being—being tied up."

"Later. After you've had more experience."

He turned and she saw that he held two boxes of condoms in his hand. His expression dared her to question him as he came toward her, then set them side by side on the bedside table with two hard thuds.

She swallowed.

An ominous glint shone in his eyes. "Did you have something to say?"

She shook her head. While she was theoretically opposed to any sort of male domination, in this case it was definitely arousing.

"Good." He kicked off his shoes, then raked her body from head to toe with a gaze she could only interpret as smoldering. "Now, where was I? You've gotten me so darned upset, I forgot what I was doing." He sat on the edge of the bed and began toying with the hem of her robe while he thought it over. His fingers brushed her ankle, then slowly slid the hem upward until he came to her knee.

She caught her breath and realized he'd gotten the point after all.

He made a leisurely circle in the soft skin behind her knee, then another, then a slow figure eight with the very tip of his fingernail, then a comma.

Oh, my . . . She let her knees separate, silently encouraging him to go on with his tactile hieroglyphics by giving him a larger writing surface.

Abruptly, he withdrew and sighed. "This isn't where I was. I know how much you like everything in order, so I guess I'd better start all over again."

She whimpered. She couldn't help it.

The corners of his mouth curled with satisfaction.

And then he started all over. . . . More deep, lazy kisses; slow strokes with his tongue; feather touches on pulse points she hadn't known she possessed. Even her awful tattoo wasn't spared his attentions.

It felt as if decades passed before he finally nudged her robe open and touched the very tip of one nipple with the point of his tongue. His chest heaved and his shirt was damp beneath her hands, but he still hadn't undressed. She heard his hot breath, felt his fragile hold on self-control, wondered when he would break. Hoped . . .

He dabbled with his tongue at the needy peak. Her head thrashed to the side and her body arched on the bed. She was dewy and wet, silken and throbbing. She wanted more. Her thoughts were disembodied as she clung to the edges of an enormous cataclysm.

His mouth settled around the hard pebble of her nipple. Sucked hard. Twice. Three times. More.

With a cry, she dissolved.

He stiffened. Drew her into his arms. Held her against his chest until she stopped trembling.

Gently, he lay her back on the pillow and brushed away a lock of hair that had fallen over her face. "Did you just come?" he whispered.

She gulped. Nodded. Tears sprang to her eyes. "I tried to tell you, but you wouldn't pay attention!"

Instead of being properly chastised, his mouth curved in a smile that was filled with pleasure. "My sweet Lady E. You are really something special."

"I hope you're satisfied," she mumbled, no longer quite so upset.

"Not yet."

Without any warning, he pushed away the front of her robe and slid his hand between her parted thighs. She gasped as he opened the swollen folds, then gently inserted one finger deeply inside her.

"Not yet," he whispered again.

Her breath caught on a tiny hiss. Watching her intently, he slid his finger out, then back in. Dimly, she saw how flushed he was, noted the cords of strain at the side of his neck. Felt the clenching deep inside.

She gave a strangled scream and convulsed.

Once more he held her, then drew her to his chest and brushed her cheek with his lips. "I must be the luckiest man in the world."

As she caught her breath, he rose to shed his clothes, and by the time she found her voice again, he was naked. Lord, but he was beautiful, every part of him taut flesh and steely muscle. She dropped her gaze. Every single part of him.

She rose and sank back on her heels. He moved closer to her. She leaned forward, tilted her head, and licked his belly.

This time he was the one who groaned. She took a tender nip at the hard muscle that ran in a diagonal across one side of his abdomen, let her fingers trail up his inner thigh, nuzzled into a hollow by his groin. She was ready to play all day.

His strangled words let her know that wouldn't happen. "Tell me I'm not going to have to tie you down."

She hesitated only for a moment before she lay back, raised her arms until her hands touched the headboard, and smiled. "No need."

She couldn't imagine why she trusted him so much or why she was willing to put up with his ridiculous rules. She only knew that she felt safe. Safe and—despite two orgasms—unbelievably aroused.

He sat on the bed, covered her knees with the palms of his hands, and pushed them apart. Then he knelt between them and looked down at her, open and glistening, swollen. "You're so beautiful," he said.

As he observed her, she drank in the sight of his body. Now, that she'd experienced during the night, but she'd lost track. "I couldn't help it. I was crazed."

"Yeah?"

"You were, too, so you don't have to look so pleased with yourself."

"I sure was. I finally got all that energy of yours channeled in the right direction."

He pushed back the sheet and stepped out, oblivious to the fact that he was naked. As she withdrew a set of frilly underwear from the drawer, she watched the morning light play across the slopes and planes of his body. His crisp, dark hair was mussed, and she spotted a red mark on his back, as well as the beginnings of a bruise on the side of his neck. She rather liked the fact that she'd put those messy marks on such extravagant male gorgeousness.

He began retrieving his clothes from the floor. "Shelby called while you were in the bathroom. She's got a meeting, and Luisa has a doctor's appointment, so she asked me to take Petie for a few hours later on this morning. I know I told you the day was yours, but do you mind putting off going back to Austin until this afternoon?"

"Not at all."

"I'd like to hit the driving range first. Maybe you can read or something while I practice. Can you be ready in half an hour?"

When she nodded, he draped his clothes over his arm and, still naked, left her bedroom.

Seconds later, Patrick shrieked in the hallway. "Warn me next time, will you, Kenneth? I don't have my smelling salts."

Kenny laughed and then she heard the sound of his door closing.

She sighed as she walked over to the closet. It would have been nice if he'd kissed her before he'd left.

He really was an exceptional kisser. And a wonderful lover. Considerate, unselfish, thrillingly kinky, and so beautiful naked that she wanted to cry. As a matter of fact, she thought she just might. But not because he was beautiful naked.

She sank down into the overstuffed chair and bit her bottom lip. She had only a little over a week left and she needed to remember that Kenny Traveler was for thrills, for scandal, even for memories, but not forever. Regardless of what last night had meant to her, it was merely the tiniest detour on the great golf course of his life. He'd shared his body, but nothing of what he was, and, in the future, if he remembered her at all, it would only be because she was different from his other sexual conquests.

But she would never forget. She'd carry the memory of this night to her grave, and she knew it wasn't the orgasms she'd remember, but the

was beauty. Marble and steel. She yearned to touch him—h
touch—reached out her hand.

He shook his head. "Not this time, baby. Please. I only have so n
self-control. And this has to be perfect for you." He pulled off her n
and renewed his sensual dallying.

Deep, lazy touches.

The tip of a finger.   A dabble.

Nibble. Nibble. Nibble. Nibble.   Nibble.

And then . . . A long sloooow lapppp . . .   with his tongue.

It was too much!

He smiled as she cried out again. "The luckiest man in the world,"
he repeated.

He snatched up the box on the bedside table and was soon settled
over her, nipping at her kiss-swollen bottom lip and beginning to ease
inside her.

Despite everything, it didn't happen comfortably.

"Take it slow, sweetheart."

Glorying in the press of his weight upon her, she clung to his damp
shoulders and arched her hips.

He groaned. "Please . . . baby . . . don't try to take charge now."

"It's—I need . . ."

"I know. I know."

She only had part of him. She wanted more.

"Easy . . . easy . . ." He crooned to her or himself, she didn't know
which. Didn't care. Only knew that she was flying higher and higher.
. . . She sobbed as she split apart.

And then she had him all, and it wasn't over, but just beginning.

Deep heavy thrusts. Violet eyes darkened to midnight. Hands pinion-
ing hers to the pillow. Weight upon her. Inside her. Stretching. Pumping.
The feel and scent of this man.

Another climb. Another spiral. Years . . . decades . . . aeons . . .

Thick hot rush.

And . . . much later . . . return.

Thank. You.

Emma came out of the bathroom in her robe with her skin still damp
from the shower. She winced as she moved a bit too quickly toward
the dresser to fetch her underwear. Kenny squinted against the morning
light and grinned from her sadly rumpled bed. "I told you that last time
was too much, but would you listen? No, you wouldn't. You always
think you know best."

She tried to calculate how many of those blissfully explosive orgasms intimacy, the feeling of connection. Sleeping with someone, being held so tenderly in his arms, and hearing his heart beat. Letting herself pretend, if only for a few moments, that she was joined to another.

She gazed out the window and thought how easily attachments came to most of the people she knew. But not to her. For as long as she could recall, her life had been a series of broken attachments. She remembered being six years old and standing in the doorway of Orchard House watching her parents drive away to spend eight months in Africa. They'd loved her, but not as much as they'd loved their work.

She'd tried attaching herself to teachers and house mothers. Some of them had been fond of her, but they had children of their own, or they found other jobs and moved away. Only St. Gert's never changed. Solid, comforting, always there.

The grand old lady had been with her through both her parents' deaths, through long holidays when she had been the only child left at the school, and then later as a teacher when she'd grown to care so much about other people's children. St. Gert's was the single unbroken attachment in her life.

But not for long. Soon she'd be forced to leave the beloved old pile of bricks and stone. With that tie severed, there would be no place left in the world that she could call home.

It was tempting to allow herself a few moments of self-pity, but she wouldn't do it. No matter where her new life took her, she'd always have the satisfaction of knowing that the school lived on, that it would provide a place of shelter for other lonely girls. And, for now, she wasn't going to think beyond the present. For a few more days, she would simply cherish every moment of this brief, physical attachment to a man who didn't love her.

Chapter 14

Emma stood just outside the barrier around the petting zoo and watched Kenny carry Peter toward the center of the miniature barnyard. "It's all right, Petie. That old goat's not going to hurt you."

Petie wasn't buying it and he clung more tightly to Kenny's neck.

Emma smiled. The petting zoo had been set up in the parking lot attached to a small strip mall that was celebrating its first anniversary. The buildings' pastel-painted Wild West exteriors formed a background to a carousel, an assortment of clowns giving away balloons, and various family-friendly companies promoting their products with free food and games.

"This goat looks mighty hungry to me." Kenny stooped down and held out a handful of feed. As the goat nudged Kenny's legs to get to the food, Petie climbed higher on his brother's chest. Kenny laughed and dropped the pellets. "Maybe we'd better go see the rabbits. I think they're more your speed."

Emma tried not to let the image of the two of them together etch itself into her heart. Spending one night with a man didn't give her the right to start imagining that it was her child he held in his arms. Silly, desperate Emma. So hungry for love she wanted to imagine herself having a baby with a man who was completely unsuitable. Had she forgotten that she'd never fancied rogues? Her own pitifulness disgusted her. Still, truth was truth, and she couldn't deny the obvious. She had fallen deeply into infatuation with Kenny Traveler.

Infatuation, not love, she reminded herself. They didn't have enough in common for her to love him. But, oh, she was infatuated. She was infatuated by his humor, his easy charm, the love he displayed for his baby brother, as well as the way his quick intelligence forced her own brain to full alertness.

But she wouldn't pretend that there wasn't also a dangerous element to her infatuation. To the rest of the world, Kenny might appear to be nothing more than a sublimely handsome athlete with an overabundance of charm, but she knew better. He had a whole world of psychological demons haunting him.

She saw Peter's forehead wrinkle at the baaing of the lambs, and he drew up his knees to protect himself from their nosy exploration. Kenny kissed his head and carried him out of the petting zoo toward Emma.

"I think it's safe to say you're not going to have a big career as a farmer, Petie boy."

She tickled the baby's belly. "You're still young, aren't you, luv? Lots of time to get used to savage animals."

"Yeah, I swear that baby lamb looked a little bit like Hannibal Lecter around the eyes."

"Easy for a big man like him to make fun, isn't it?"

Peter gave her a drooly grin and poked a wet finger at her mouth. They began wandering toward a clown holding balloons. On the way, a young woman holding a clipboard approached them and smiled at Emma. "The next round of the Diaper Derby's starting soon if you and your husband would like to enter your baby."

A pang of embarrassment mixed uncomfortably with longing. "He's not my—"

"What's a Diaper Derby?" Kenny asked.

"A crawling race for babies."

"A race?" His face split in a grin. "Now we're talking." He tossed Petie up in his arms, tucked him like a potato sack in the crook of his elbow, and turned toward the Diaper Derby arena. "Greatness moves on to the next generation of Travelers."

"Kenny, maybe we'd better think about this." But, for once, she was talking to his back.

The race was being held behind a waist-high barricade on a padded red mat that was about thirty feet long and twenty feet wide with six narrow lanes divided by white lines. One parent positioned the baby at the starting line, while the other parent sat at the finishing line urging the child forward. The first of the six babies to make it was the winner.

"Now, here's the way we're going to do this," Kenny said after he'd studied the layout. "Petie'll crawl to me faster than you, so you start him off, and I'll wait for him at the finish line."

She looked over at the spectators who'd gathered to watch. "I don't know. Peter wasn't overjoyed with the petting zoo, and it's quite noisy here.''

"Petie's not afraid of a little gallery noise, are you, bro?''

Peter gave a baby chortle and smacked his fist against the Top Flite logo on Kenny's shirt. Kenny laughed, tossed him up again, and handed him over to Emma.

He went to her easily. Her heart ached as she looked into those bright violet eyes with their tiny fringe of spiky lashes. Despite her years of experience with children, she hadn't spent much time with babies. Now she felt a pang of longing so intense it surprised her. She pushed the emotion away and watched Kenny head for the opposite end of the mat. She realized he was actually studying the competition, and she hugged Peter a bit tighter. "I'm afraid you're in for it, luv.''

She could see Kenny dismissing a fairy-sprite of a little girl dressed in a yellow romper with layers of lace across her bottom. Then he passed over a blond-haired baby of indeterminate sex who was desperately clinging to his or her mother. For a moment, his attention lingered on a set of lively chocolate-colored twins, but they seemed more interested in each other than the event.

Suddenly he stiffened. His eyes narrowed, and she could almost hear the theme from *Rocky* playing in his brain. He'd found the one man who stood between a Traveler and athletic glory.

The challenger had a single spike of red hair shooting up from a nearly bald head. His body was strong and brawny, clad in plaid overalls and a Tigger T-shirt. His feet were encased in a pair of miniature Nikes that pumped as he struggled to get down. Twenty-five pounds of raw dynamite. This was the man to beat.

The young woman in charge gave the instructions. As Emma sat behind the starting line with Peter on her lap, she cast a wary eye at Kenny. He seemed to be taking this a little too seriously.

After one last look at the spike-haired bruiser in the lane next to Peter, Kenny crouched at the finish line and called down to his baby brother. "You've got to stay focused. Make them play your game, Petie. A hundred and ten percent. You've got to give it a hundred and ten percent.''

The mother of the little girl in the lacy romper looked at Kenny as if he'd escaped from a lunatic asylum.

Emma sighed and stroked the baby's soft arm, while she tried to catch Kenny's eye. But his entire focus, all one hundred and ten percent of it, was on the game.

"Ready. Set. *Go*.'' At the command from the starter, Emma set Peter on the starting line and released him.

With a superb display of finely honed Traveler crawling skills, he shot toward his brother.

Kenny slapped the mat. "That's right! Faster."

Peter slowed.

"Pick it up, Petie. Let's go!"

The baby came to a dead stop. Wrinkled his forehead. Plopped back on his bottom.

Kenny held out his arms. "Come on, Petie! Don't stop now. You've got the lead."

Peter stuck his fingers in his mouth and looked up at the cheering spectators. Kenny's knee inched forward across the finish line.

Two lanes over, the baby in the androgynous clothes dropped to the mat and began a lazy sideways scoot.

"Let's go, Petie! Let's go!" Kenny slapped the mat again as his other knee crept over the finish line.

Peter's bottom lip sagged in a pathetic quiver.

The red-haired bruiser let out a howl and darted back to the starting line.

Kenny's brows shot together. "You've got it now, Petie! The big man's DQed!"

Peter's eyes filled with tears.

"No, no! Don't do that!"

The chocolate-colored twins moved into the same lane and rolled on top of each other.

"They're dropping like flies! You can take it, Petie! Only a little farther."

Peter's small chest shook with a sob.

"Shake it off! Shake it off and come to Kenny." He crept farther into the lane.

Peter let out an earsplitting howl.

"No crying, buddy! Don't ever let 'em see you cry. Come on! I'm right here."

Frozen, Peter sat on the mat and sobbed.

The little girl in the lacy yellow romper shot across the finish line to win the race, but Kenny was too busy inching forward on his own hands and knees to notice.

"Don't quit! Nobody remembers a loser. Come on, Petie! You can't quit!"

Emma couldn't take any more. She hurried forward onto the mat and snatched the sobbing little boy up into her arms. "It's all right, luv. I won't let that crazy man get you."

Kenny came out of a trance and looked up. For the first time he seemed to realize where he was.

On his hands and knees.

A third of the way down the lane.

In the middle of a baby race.

Quiet fell over the small crowd. Kenny turned red and shot to his feet. The quiet intensified. Then a grizzled man in a John Deere cap gave Kenny an admiring salute.

"Now, *that's* the way you turn a kid into a champion."

Chapter 15

*K*enny couldn't breathe as the ghosts of his past crashed on top of him. Emma was clutching Petie to her breast. She gazed across the mat and gave Kenny a look that seemed tinged with pity. He couldn't tolerate it, and he rushed forward.

"Let me have him."

Petie screamed and gripped Emma's neck more tightly. "Just give him a minute," she said.

But he didn't have a minute. He jerked his wallet from his pocket, thrust it toward her, and grabbed Peter. "Buy yourself something. I'll be back."

He quickly left her behind and carried the screaming baby to his car. He could never let her witness this.

Accompanied by the sound of Petie's earsplitting shrieks coming from the car seat, he jumped behind the wheel and peeled out of the parking lot. "It's okay, buddy. It's okay."

He blinked his eyes and raced toward the edge of town. The baby's screams didn't subside. Finally, he found the privacy he needed, a narrow lane that led toward a patch of trees. He parked his car in the exact place he'd hidden his bike when he was a kid coming apart inside.

"Why'd you beat me up, Kenny? I didn't do anything to you."

As he retrieved the hysterical baby, Petie arched his spine, trying to get away. His shrieks hurt Kenny's ears, but the look of betrayal in the baby's eyes broke Kenny's heart.

"I'm sorry, fella. I'm so sorry." Pressing his lips to his brother's hot, damp temple, he carried him into the trees toward the rushing sound of the river. "Shhh . . . don't cry. Don't cry, scout. It's all over."

As he rocked and crooned, the baby's sobs gradually subsided. He walked him along the riverbank, stroking his little back, humming and talking nonsense, letting the rush of the river soothe the baby as it used to soothe him when he came here to recover from some piece of nastiness he'd unleashed on Torie or one of his schoolmates. Finally, Petie quieted enough for Kenny to settle down in the shade of a bigtooth maple. He leaned against the trunk and propped the baby on his lap.

"I know, Petie. I know. . . ."

The little boy reared back his head, and Kenny saw a whole world of hurt in his eyes.

"I won't ever do that to you again. I promise. The old man's going to be bad enough. You don't need it from me, too."

Petie stuck out a trembly lip. He'd been betrayed, and he wasn't going to forgive too easily.

Kenny used the bottom of the baby's bright blue T-shirt to wipe his small, drooly chin. "You don't have to win a race for me to love you, buddy. Do you understand? Despite what happened back there, I'm not like the old man. I don't care if you're last every time, if you stink at team sports. Even if the worst happens and you hate golf, it doesn't matter. You understand me? We're brothers forever." He drew the baby up to his face and kissed his slobbery cheek. "You might have to win the old man's love, scout, but I promise you won't ever have to win mine."

Emma stood in the middle of the crowd staring down at the wallet Kenny had thrust in her hand. After last night, she felt as if she'd been slapped.

Just as she was looking around for some privacy, she saw Ted Beaudine approaching. He gave her his shy smile. "I heard you were here, Lady Emma. Where'd Kenny go?"

"He left with Peter."

"You look a little upset."

Those old man's eyes of his saw too much. "A little." She opened her purse to slip in the wallet only to have him take it from her hand. "Is this Kenny's?"

"He shoved it at me right before he ran off." She couldn't stop herself from adding, "He told me I should *buy* something for myself."

"No kidding." Ted's mouth curled in a slow smile. "My daddy's rich, my ma's good-looking, and this is my lucky day."

Emma frowned as he tucked the wallet in his back pocket. "Your mother's rich, too; I've heard your father looks like a movie star. And give that back to me."

His hazel eyes crinkled at the corners. "Come on, Lady Emma. I'm a semi-impoverished twenty-two-year-old who just graduated from college and doesn't have a job. Kenny, on the other hand's, got more money than he has the energy to count. Let's go enjoy ourselves."

"Ted, I really don't think—"

But he was already moving. Catching her arm, he led her toward the parking lot and a rather battered open-topped red Jeep with black roll bars. "If any of you see Kenny," he called out to a group of teenagers, "tell him Lady Emma's at the Roustabout."

Emma found herself being driven away in a car with a set of golf clubs rattling in the back and a graduation tassel swinging from the rearview mirror. "Maybe you should let me have that wallet," she said as the Roustabout came into view.

"I will. Later. After we use what's in it."

"We're not spending Kenny's money, no matter how much of it he has. It isn't right."

"Texas women wouldn't see it that way. Women down here like their revenge. Do you know my parents once had a fight in this very parking lot? People still talk about it."

"I suppose public arguments can get a little nasty."

"Oh, this wasn't an argument. It was a fight. Physical." He chuckled. "I'd of loved to have seen that."

"Bloodthirsty boy. And I don't believe a word of it. Your parents have a wonderful marriage."

"Now they do, but it took them a while to get there. My dad didn't even know I existed till I was nine. They both had a lot of growing up to do."

Coming from any other twenty-two-year-old, the comment would have been humorous, but there was something about Ted Beaudine that made her a believer.

As they got out of the car and walked toward the Roustabout, she said, "I'm surprised you don't have a job yet. From what Torie and Kenny said, you have an excellent academic record."

"Oh, I've had lots of offers, but I want to stay near Wynette."

"You grew up here, didn't you?"

"I grew up all over, but this is the place my family calls home, and I'm pretty attached to it." He held the door open for her. "That limits me to two companies."

"TCS and Dexter's father's company."

"Both of them have done everything they could to hire me. Unfortunately, that's turned me into the prize in another one of their range wars. The situation's gotten a little ugly, so I'm stalling until I see whether Torie's ever going to figure out what a great guy Dexter is."

"If the merger happens, you don't have a problem anymore, is that it?"

"Exactly. In the meantime, though, I'm just about flat broke. And neither of my parents, being self-made people, is sympathetic." He slipped Kenny's wallet from his back pocket. "Which is why this is a gift from the gods."

Before she could stop him, he'd taken out one of Kenny's credit cards and turned to the crowd of businesspeople, ranchers, and housewives who'd gathered for lunch. Although he barely raised his voice, the crowd quieted to hear him.

"I've got an announcement to make. You'll all be happy to know that lunch is on Kenny. And he wants you to order whatever you like, so don't hurt his feelings by being chintzy."

As he passed the credit card over to the bartender, one of the ranchers called out, "Lions Club's meeting in the back room."

"Kenny's always been a real big supporter of the Lions," Ted said.

"You can't do this!" she hissed under her breath.

He gave her that dim-witted look the gorgeous men of Wynette must have perfected in the cradle just to drive women crazy. "Why not?"

"Because it isn't right."

"Was it right for Kenny to leave you stranded?"

"No."

"Then we don't have a problem, do we?"

For a quiet young man, he was surprisingly assertive, and she found herself being led to a booth. As she slid into the padded seat, she decided he had a point, and a few minutes later when the waitress approached, she defiantly ordered extra cheese on her turkey sandwich.

The day wasn't turning out anything like she'd hoped. She'd imagined herself and Kenny together, perhaps holding hands and smiling at each other. Her fantasies were silly. She decided to fight them off with food.

Just as she was trying to decide between chocolate fudge cake and a brownie sundae, she saw the burly man walk into the Roustabout. He glanced around the room, then stopped as he spotted her. When he realized she'd noticed, he looked away.

She was so confused. Was he Beddington's spy or not? If he was the spy, why hadn't he told Hugh about everything she'd bought at the drugstore? Just yesterday she'd concluded that she'd made a mistake and had the wrong person, but she was no longer so certain. This man definitely had more than a casual interest in her.

While Ted conducted a friendly flirtation with a cute redhead who'd come up to their table, Emma tried to puzzle it out. She noticed that the burly man was watching her in a mirror advertising beer, and her indecision fled. Beddington's man. Definitely.

She picked up her purse, opened it in her lap, and reached for the salt and pepper shakers. With a curl of her arm, she swept them inside. She turned to make certain he'd noticed and saw by his appalled expression that he had. She suppressed the urge to jump from her seat, march over to him, and order him to write down exactly what he'd seen so he wouldn't forget to report it.

Unfortunately, the burly man wasn't the only one who'd witnessed her thievery.

"What in Sam Hill do you think you're doing?"

She'd been so caught up that she hadn't noticed Kenny approaching. He was by himself, so he must have dropped Peter off. As he drew closer, the Roustabout's patrons began calling out to him.

"Hey, there, Kenny. Thanks for lunch."

"Much appreciate it, Kenny. The sirloin was real good."

She couldn't believe it. Once again, he'd caught her at a disadvantage. And this was *his* day to be in the wrong. He'd terrorized his baby brother and deserted her without warning. He was the sinner. Why did all the black marks keep showing up on her side of the ledger?

"Kenny, the Lions Club said to tell you thanks," a middle-aged waitress called out.

"Me and Deever, too," added a florid-faced heart attack in the making. "You should try some of that pecan pie yourself."

Kenny frowned. "What are they talking about?"

"You treated everybody to lunch," Ted explained. "And we all appreciate it. Joe's got your credit card."

Kenny shrugged, slid into the booth next to her, and reached for her purse. She tried to hold on to it, but he took it away. "I swear you get stranger by the day," he growled.

As Ted watched with interest, Kenny pulled out the salt and pepper shakers and set them back on the table. "Let me guess. You decided to put on another show for the duke."

"His investigator's here again." She jerked her head toward the burly man. "I had to do something."

He stared in the direction she'd indicated. One eyebrow shot up. Then he shook his head and handed the purse back to her. "I've never known a woman who could embarrass herself as much as you."

She couldn't tolerate his condescension after last night. "Let me out!"

"No."

"I was going to give them back!" She caught herself. "What am I doing? Why am I explaining? I don't have to tell you anything after what you've done today."

"I sure didn't lift any salt shakers."

Ted leaned back, enjoying their argument.

"That man told Beddington all I bought at the drugstore was a *tabloid*!"

"Nasty stuff. Full of lies. Do you know they printed a story about me once? How I was supposed to be having this big love affair with my former junior high teacher."

"That was actually true," Ted pointed out.

Kenny ignored him. "I can't imagine why you'd want to read one of those things."

"That's not the point!" she exclaimed. "But of course you know that. You think it's clever to act as if you're an idiot."

"So you decided to give him something else not to report?"

She wanted to scratch the smugness right off his face! How long was she going to let other people dictate the course of her life? Beddington? Kenny? That incompetent fool standing by the bar? It was long past time she took control of her own destiny.

"Let me out! I mean it, Kenny. I'm going to settle this with him for once and for all."

"I don't advise it."

"Either let me out or I'm going to crawl under the table."

"A perfect example of why you people lost this country in the first place."

"Are you moving?"

"Damn right I am!" He vaulted to his feet.

Several of the other onlookers poked each other. Kenny was going to give them something new to talk about.

She shot past him and headed straight toward the burly man. "I need to speak with you."

He blinked. "All right."

"In the first place, you were hired to do a job. But you haven't done it very well, now, have you?"

He looked embarrassed, but Emma couldn't afford to weaken. "For one thing, you haven't been giving Beddington complete information. And isn't that why he pays you? For example, you didn't bother to tell him everything I bought at the drugstore two nights ago, did you?"

He turned red from his neck all the way to his thinning, straw-colored hair.

She crossed her arms. "And please tell me why not."

"Well—"

"Did you just now see me stealing those salt and pepper shakers?"
He nodded.

"I was *stealing* them, you understand. I'm a thief! Now, are you going to tell him about it or not?"

"I—"

He looked so flustered that a little of her anger abated, and she began to feel a bit sorry for him. "Let me give you some advice, if I may. Beddington is a demanding employer. If he finds out you've been withholding information from him, he'll be enormously displeased. And I can tell you from personal experience that he's horrid when he's displeased."

If anything, he looked even more distressed. She felt like a bully, and her anger faded. "Everyone makes mistakes. It's how we recover from them that counts, isn't it? I suggest you make some careful notes before you call him. Tell him everything about the drugstore. And don't forget to be very specific about the salt and pepper shakers. How does that sound to you?"

He swallowed.

She waited, giving him time to consider his options.

"Who's Beddington?" he finally asked.

She stared at him. He looked so baffled, so embarrassed . . .

Heat began to crawl from her chest to her neck. She felt it creeping over her jaw and pooling in two bright circles on her cheeks.

And then she heard a familiar drawl coming from just behind her left shoulder. "Is this insane woman harassing you, Father Joseph?"

Father Joseph?

Emma whimpered. Kenny took her arm before she could turn and run. "Lady Emma, I don't believe you've been properly introduced to Father Joseph Antelli. He's been head priest at St. Gabriel's for—How long's it been, Father? Twenty years?"

"Nineteen."

"That's right. I was still raising hell when you came here."

The priest nodded.

She whimpered again. "But . . . you—you can't be a priest. You hang out in bars and wear orange T-shirts, and—"

"Now, Lady Emma, it's hardly polite to criticize a man of God for his lack of fashion sense. And the Roustabout happens to have the best food in town. If I'm not mistaken, the local clergy holds their interdenominational meetings here, isn't that right, Father?"

"The first Wednesday of every month."

"But . . . you were watching me."

"I'm very sorry about that, Lady Emma," he said earnestly. "I've always been a bit of an anglophile, and I wanted to chat with you about England. Father Emmett and I are planning a trip there in the fall. I should have simply introduced myself, but when I realized how . . . complicated your personal life was, I decided not to intrude on your privacy."

"Oh, dear. I can explain. All those things you saw—I mean, the other night . . . and the way I was sitting on Kenny's lap . . . and the salt and pepper shakers—It's—"

"Her friends are going to make sure she gets treatment real soon," Kenny said.

Father Joseph regarded her with kind eyes. "Psychological problems are nothing to be ashamed of. I'll pray for you, Lady Emma."

As Kenny drew her away, all she could do was moan.

"You made me look like a fool!"

Kenny followed her as she rushed from the Roustabout. "Excuse me for pointing this out, but you did that all by yourself."

"You should have told me who he was."

"How did I know you were going to charge over there and light into him like Xena Warrior Goddess? Besides, nobody can tell you anything. You know it all."

"I do not!" She realized some very nosy people had followed them outside to witness their argument, but she was beyond being embarrassed.

He shot ahead of her. "You're bossy and pigheaded. And you get strange ideas. This whole plan of yours, for instance. It's strange."

"I'm sick of listening to you criticize me. Especially after what I saw today! You might think about looking at your own lunatic behavior instead of being so concerned with mine."

Behind her, the door swung open and more of the Roustabout's patrons began to emerge.

"My lunatic behavior doesn't have anything to do with you!"

He annoyed her so much that she forgot about the crowd. "It does when you run away and leave me stranded next to a petting zoo!"

"I didn't run away."

"Ha!"

More patrons were gathering to watch. Kenny finally noticed and shot his finger toward the Cadillac. "Get in the car."

"Stop ordering me! Just because I let you get away with it in the bedroom doesn't mean I'll put up with it now."

"You tell him!" One of the women called out.

Kenny tensed as he realized they'd turned into a sideshow. "Get in that car!" he said under his breath.

"Go to bloody hell!" She snatched the keys from him and dashed around the front of the car. She expected him to yank her to a stop at any second, but what she heard instead was the sound of boots sliding, then a curse and a thud. Some of the men in the crowd groaned as Kenny slipped on the asphalt. She took advantage of his tumble and jumped in the car.

By some miracle, the key she shoved in the ignition was the proper one. In the mirror, she saw him spring back to his feet. She turned the key and stepped on the accelerator. The engine roared, but the car didn't move. She maneuvered the gearshift and the car lurched forward, but not before she heard his angry bellow.

"You can't drive!"

She barely avoided hitting a black pickup truck on her way across the parking lot. Her skin was damp, her mouth dry. What was she *doing*?

A glance in the rearview mirror showed Ted Beaudine standing in the center of the crowd, a huge grin plastered over his face. She remembered him telling her that his parents had once fought in this same parking lot. Then she glimpsed Kenny running, actually *running*, toward her, and she forgot about everything else.

Taking a hurried glance up and down the highway, she saw that it was blessedly free of traffic. *Right side. Right side. Right side.* With a jerk on the wheel, she turned out onto the road.

Her palms were so sweaty they slipped on the steering wheel. Never had she imagined she had such a terrible temper. And look where it had landed her—behind the wheel of a car she didn't know how to drive, being chased down a Texas highway by a multimillionaire golf pro.

As she concentrated on keeping the big Cadillac between the lane markers, she kept darting glances in the side mirror and saw that he was gaining on her. Biting the inside of her lip, she pressed a bit harder on the accelerator.

The needle edged to twelve miles an hour.

Cars began to stack up behind her.

She hated driving! Why had she done this?

The door on the passenger side flew open. Kenny ducked his head inside and shouted, "Pull over!"

She yearned to slam her foot on the accelerator, but as much as she wanted to murder him, she didn't actually want to *kill* him, so she hesitated, which proved to be a mistake because he jumped in the car. "Pull off the road!"

She kept going, eyes straight ahead, fingers rigor-mortized around the wheel.

He yanked his door shut. "If you're not going to pull off, then for God's sake speed up before you get rear-ended."

"I know what I'm doing! Torie taught me to drive."

"Then *drive!*"

She bit her bottom lip and pressed the accelerator. "There! I'm going thirty. I hope you're satisfied."

"The speed limit's sixty."

"You think I'm afraid to go sixty? I'm not!" She died a thousand deaths, but she got the speedometer to forty-five. The cars continued to stack up behind her.

She heard teeth grinding. His words had a tight sound to them. "Pull off up there on the right. Put on your turn signal."

Because she wanted to pull off, she did what he said.

"By that crooked tree. Turn there."

Horns blared behind her as she took the corner too fast and ended up in the sandy soil next to the narrow dirt road.

"You were supposed to slow down first!" he yelled.

"You didn't tell me that. You told me to go faster."

"Not when you're turning!" Once again she heard that awful tooth-grinding, then a deeply inhaled breath. "Never mind. Just keep going till you're behind those trees."

When she finally stopped the car, she was so relieved she felt limp. She propped her arm on top of the steering wheel, rested her forehead, and closed her eyes.

She sensed movement and heard him turn off the ignition. The leather creaked as he settled into the seat. Time ticked by. The unsteady sound of her breathing rasped in her ears.

Finally, something warm curled around the back of her neck. Rubbed. "You crying, Lady Emma?"

"No," she answered as firmly as she could. "Just thinking about it."

"Why don't you come over here and think about it?" He drew her close, and the next thing she knew, she was curled against his chest.

It was cozy. Comforting. He smelled nice. Clean shirt faintly overlaid with baby.

She refused to cry. Still, it felt good being where she was.

His breath tickled her ear as he spoke in a husky voice. "Would you think I was an insensitive jerk if I slipped my hands inside your blouse?"

She thought about it, then shook her head.

His fingers tickled her skin as he reached between them to unfastened the buttons, then opened the catch of her bra. He traced the shape of her breast with his thumb and kissed her. Then he said softly, "I enjoyed last night."

"I did, too."

"You make nice sounds in bed."

"I do?"

"Uh-huh." He touched her nipple.

She gave a hum of pleasure.

"Like that." He shifted her position and his mouth settled over the sensitive tip. He tugged. She arched and gave in to the delicious sensations. When she could no longer hold still, she pulled his shirt from the waistband of his jeans and slipped her hand inside to feel that warm, taut skin beneath her palms.

It seemed to be all the encouragement he needed. Within seconds, her blouse hung from her shoulders, her shorts lay in a heap, and her panties draped from one calf. She wasn't idle, either, and his shirt soon joined her shorts. Through the open zipper of his jeans, she saw navy silk boxers.

"I . . . need to do this." He shifted her so that she leaned back against the opposite side. Then he spread her legs and lowered his head.

Crisp, dark hair brushed the insides of her thighs, trailed over the soft skin, moved higher until she felt his mouth on her. There . . .

She gasped. Breathed his name. Lost her breath.

He took his time with this, as he did with everything else. She forgot her uncomfortable position, forgot that they were in a car, forgot everything except the touch of his fingers and the deep, wet stroking. Her orgasm came in a noisy sob that shook her entire body.

He stayed. Dallied more. Sent her flying again.

Oh . . . this was too splendid. She wasn't even aware of her own hands moving against him until he stilled them. She could feel his thick shape through the silk of his boxers and knew it wasn't lack of desire that made him stop her. She lifted her head and gazed questioningly into the smoky violet eyes.

He looked anguished, and he barely seemed to be able to get out the words. "I need my wallet. I don't have anything with me."

She smiled. "I'm on the pill."

"The pill? But—why didn't you tell me last night?"

"You ordered me not to talk." She brushed her lips over his. "And I didn't want to explain anyway. I've been on the pill for a while. Just in case."

"Just in case you—"

His words broke off as she straddled him. Smiling, she pressed her mouth to his ear. "With your permission . . ."

He groaned and reached beneath her.

This time she wanted to be in control, but he had other ideas, and as she tried to settle down on him, he restrained her hips. "Careful, sweetheart." He made a deep, indecipherable sound and took charge, only letting her absorb a little bit of him at a time.

"Me . . ." she murmured. "I want to . . ."

He distracted her with a kiss that couldn't get enough of itself, and, as he explored her mouth with his tongue, he eased inside her.

But even when she had accepted all of him, he still wouldn't let her take over. Instead, he established the rhythm, knowing instinctively what she needed and giving her everything she wanted except control.

The tips of her breasts rubbed against the light mat of hair on his chest. The insides of her thighs abraded the jeans he'd never completely removed. With her mouth above his, this kiss was different, and she reveled in the novelty. But she wanted more. She wanted him to trust her enough to let her lead the way.

His hands curled around her buttocks and his thumbs performed a trick she'd never imagined at the exact place where they were joined. "Don't stop . . ." she managed. "Whatever you do, don't . . ."

He didn't. And the sweet, hot flood swept them away.

Chapter 16

Afterward, Emma was glad of the activity, all the tissue-fumbling and clothes-sorting. Kenny seemed glad, too. Maybe he felt the same way she did, that there was something dangerous about so much urgency, something distinctly threatening about two incompatible adults being so wild to get their hands all over each other that they couldn't wait to find a bed.

She wondered if every woman had to be attracted to a bad boy once in her life. Apparently she did. Maybe she needed to get Kenny Traveler out of her system so that someday there would be space for the right relationship, one that was healthy and appropriate. Maybe she needed Kenny Traveler, just as she'd needed her immunity shots. One dose would protect her from playboys like him for the rest of her life. She began buttoning her blouse as she thought it over.

Kenny stepped out of the car. As he pushed his shirt back in his jeans, he noticed that Emma was fastening her buttons wrong, but he knew if he pointed it out, she'd just get all huffy again and say he was criticizing her.

As she looked up at him with those puffy, swollen lips and rumpled butterscotch curls that reminded him of ice-cream sauce, something weird happened to his middle. Last night had been so good he didn't even like to think about it, except it was just about all he'd been able to think about, which was probably why he'd gone so crazy during the baby race. And today . . . one minute they'd been arguing, and the next thing he knew, they were skin-to-skin in his car.

He couldn't remember the last time he'd done it in a car. Hardly ever. Rich kids didn't have to. Rich kids had cabanas, or if that wasn't private enough, plenty of cash to pay for a motel up in Llano County.

God, he'd loved making love with her. All that enthusiasm. She didn't know how to hold anything back. She gave it one hundred and ten percent, just the way he liked.

Because of the mismatched buttons, her blouse clung to one breast, which made him remember how it had filled his hand. As he gazed at her, he felt this traitorous tenderness. It made him nervous. She was too controlling, too demanding. Since he knew how badly he needed to get both of them back to the safe company of other people, he couldn't believe the words that came out of his mouth.

"Do you want to take a walk down to the river?"

She blinked those pretty honey-brown eyes. "I'd quite like that."

Just as if he'd asked her to join him for tea and crumpets.

She slid across the seat. He helped her out, then held on to her hand. It was small, but strong. He rubbed the callous on the side of his index finger over her palm. The sound of rushing water kept them company as they walked toward the river. He heard the chatter of a squirrel, the call of a mockingbird, everything but Emma giving orders. For someone who liked to talk so much, why did she have to choose now to get quiet? Her silence unnerved him, and he spoke without thinking. "I brought Petie here earlier."

"Did he settle, then?"

"Yes." He cleared his throat. "The two of us needed to talk."

She bristled. "You certainly did. I suppose we can only be grateful that something positive came out of that ugly incident. You'll never do that to him again."

Her prickly response should have set him off, but instead it felt good, almost relaxing. She knew exactly what that baby boy meant to him and how much he regretted what he'd done. Still, he didn't want her to get too full of herself.

"You've got to toughen them up when they're young or they'll turn into pansies."

She had the gall to laugh. "Give it up, Kenny. When it comes to Peter, you're putty."

"Yeah, well, he's pretty special." He smiled and started to change the subject, then realized he wanted to talk it over with her. Not exactly on a personal basis, more a professional one. She was an expert in child development, wasn't she?

"See, the thing is . . . the old man can be tough, and . . . I just worry about Petie, that's all."

Those honey-sweet eyes of hers zeroed in on him like high-tech weapons. "You're afraid your father will be as bad a parent to Peter as he was to you?"

He immediately bristled. "My father did what he needed to. After the way my mother behaved, he sure couldn't fawn all over me, too."

"No, but I suspect he went too far in the other direction. I've seen this happen with several of my students. From what you've said, your father doesn't seem to have been around much when you needed him, and when he was around, I can only imagine that he was highly critical of you."

"Mrs. Sneed called me at work. She said you ripped the head off Mary Beth's Barbie doll and then threw it down the sewer. Only a coward does something like that to a girl. A nasty little coward."

"I was a brat."

"Yes, well, quite a bit of that was his fault. I'm certain you were desperate for his attention, and misbehavior must have been the only way you could get it. You were a healthy little boy being suffocated by a highly neurotic mother, and your father didn't seem to have interceded when he should have. Really, Kenny, you received such appalling parenting that it's a wonder you didn't end up mutilating small animals. It's not surprising that you still resent him."

"I never said that."

Nothing stopped Lady E once she got going, and she went on as if he hadn't spoken. "You really need to forgive him, you know. For both your sakes."

He shrugged, acting real casual. "I don't have the slightest idea what you're talking about."

"And then there's the problem of Peter. You're afraid your father is going to neglect him the same way he once neglected you. That Peter is going to have to win his love as you did, instead of simply being given it as a birthright."

He forced his stiff jaws to open in a yawn. "You're so full of it you should be fertilizer."

Instead of getting huffy, she actually squeezed his hand, which, until that moment, he'd forgotten was tightly clasped around hers.

"Don't worry so much about Peter. Shelby isn't like your mother, and I'm certain she'll prove to be a staunch defender of his rights. I also suspect your father has learned from his mistakes. The way he looks at you when you're not watching is quite heart-wrenching. And even if I'm wrong, Peter has something in his favor you didn't have."

He scratched his arm and looked bored. "Yeah? What's that?"

"You, of course."

He felt as if he'd taken a sucker punch, which made it hard for him to respond as casually as he wanted. "Not a hell of a lot to take to the bank."

"Quite a lot, actually. Unconditional love is very powerful."

"I guess."

"When you think back on your childhood, Kenny, I hope you give yourself credit for having survived so well. It's hard to imagine anyone getting much worse parenting than you."

"What about Torie?"

"At least Torie had unconditional love from one parent. You didn't have it from either one."

"What are you talking about? My mother worshiped the ground I walked on. That was the whole problem."

"That wasn't real love. There must have been a thousand strings attached to her feelings for you."

She was right. He'd been expected to dote on his mother as if she were the only person in his life.

"Kenny, punkin', you don't want to go play with those white-trash boys. Stay with me. I'll buy you that new radio-controlled airplane we saw on television. They'll all want it, and you'll be the most popular boy in the school."

Instead, he'd been the most despised.

He tried to act nonchalant. "Yeah, I guess you might be right."

"I'm something of an expert on the subject."

He heard the slight edge to her voice. "I gather you're not just speaking professionally."

She shrugged. "Not entirely. My parents loved me, I suppose, but they loved their work more. I was quite lonely." She pulled away from him and walked down to the riverbank. As he followed her, he was glad the shoe was finally on the other foot.

She smiled at him when he reached her side. "There's nothing more boring than listening to successful adults whine about how mistreated they were as children, is there?"

"You're sure right about that." He picked up a flat stone and skipped it across the river toward the limestone bluff that rose on the other side. It hopped four times before it sank. "I guess I can understand why you might be a little peculiar when it comes to St. Gert's. Just like I might be a little peculiar about Petie." He skipped another stone, then looked down at her, feeling tense, although he wasn't sure why. "So, once you tell the duke what's happened between us, I guess you're off the hook."

She didn't reply immediately. "I don't know. He seems to believe what he wants to believe, doesn't he?" Her forehead crumpled, and this "off with his head" look flashed in her eyes. "I don't want to tell him what happened between the two of us! That was private, and it's none of his bloody business!"

He smiled, selfishly pleased by her response. "You do seem to have yourself in a fix."

She muttered something he couldn't quite make out, but he thought he heard another *bloody*.

"I'll bet I can hit that." He pointed toward a boulder rising out of the water on the far side of the river and picked up another stone. He threw, but he was short. "Two out of three."

"The water's so clear here. This is the most beautiful place."

"I've always liked it. I used to come here when I was a kid, right after I beat up somebody or bullied them until they cried." He hooked his second shot.

"I'm sure you believed that, if you were bad enough, someone would eventually put a stop to it."

"I guess." He missed again. "One more." The stone glanced off the boulder.

"Excellent." She smiled. "And that's what Dallie did, isn't it? He put a stop to it."

"Who told you that?"

"I put two and two together."

"I guess I've had about as much psychotherapy as I can handle in one day. Besides, you're the crazy one, not me. Just ask Father Joseph."

She winced. "It's a good thing I'll be leaving soon. I'll never be able to look that man in the eye again."

He didn't like to think about her leaving, even though, in some ways, he couldn't wait to get her off his hands. "I'll explain what happened. At least I'll explain most of it." He curled his hand around the back of her neck and rubbed. "If we still intend to get to Austin today, we'd better take off. We can stop at the house first if you want to change."

"I'd like that."

They drove back to the house, but the bedroom was too inviting, and they never did make it to Austin.

Torie had penned her emus at the back of her father's property. At least her folly was out of sight here, if not out of mind. Before her divorce, when she'd lived in Dallas, she'd boarded them at a ranch south of the city, but that had gotten too expensive, and she'd talked her father into letting her move them here. There were eighteen of the ugly ostrich look-alikes now, with their long necks, dark sooty feathers, and spindly legs. Sometimes she tried to convince herself they were pretty, but generally she didn't waste effort. She looked away from a nest with three more huge emerald eggs.

"That's Elmer by the fence," she said. "He's one of the original breeding pair. And his lady Polly's in the middle of the group over there.''

"You named them?''

She was already regretting the impulse that had led her to invite Dexter to see her animals. "What's wrong with that?''

He gazed down at her, and the green-flecked eyes behind the lenses of his wire-rimmed glasses reflected a depth of curiosity she found unnerving. "I'm not a rancher,'' he said, "but I understand it's generally considered harder to slaughter animals you've named.''

The evening breeze blew a lock of hair across her cheek. "Even without names, I probably wouldn't have been able to have them—Oh, never mind.'' She impatiently hooked a lock of hair behind her ear. "Investing in the emus was stupid, but my marriage to Tommy was falling apart and it seemed like a good idea at the time.''

"You wanted to be able to support yourself. That's understandable.''

"It was stupid.''

He pushed his hands into the pockets of another of what seemed to be an endless supply of khaki slacks. "You're a risk-taker. These things happen. At least you're trying to live up to your responsibilities. I understand lots of people just let their emus loose so they won't have to feed them.''

"I'm irresponsible, but even I wouldn't do anything like that.''

"I don't think you're irresponsible.''

He spoke so sincerely that she felt flattered. It was nice to have the approval of someone as serious-minded as Dexter O'Conner. That pleasant feeling vanished at his next words.

"Have you thought about what you want to do with your life, in the event we do get married?''

"We're not getting married!''

"Probably not. But if we do, you'll need to find a better way to spend your time than shopping and worrying about your emus.''

"You've got a ton of money. I could shop for years without putting a dent in it.'' She realized he'd once again sucked her into a discussion of the unthinkable.

"That's not the point. When I come home in the evenings, you'll probably want to ask me about my day, and I'll tell you the parts of it that you might find interesting. Then I'll ask you about your day, and all you'll be able to tell me is that there was a sportswear sale at Nieman's. That would be humiliating for you.''

"You're so weird.''

"I'm not necessarily talking about a full-time job. But it's time you contributed something more to the world than a beautiful face. You'll never be happy if you don't have a higher purpose than shopping.''

"You have no idea what makes me happy!''

He ignored that. "If you could do anything with your life, what would it be? And I'm not talking about raising children because we both already know how we feel about that, and only time will tell.''

She waited for the stab of pain that the subject always brought to her, but, for once, it didn't come. She couldn't understand why. What was there about this goofy, brainy man that she found comforting? She thought about the confrontation she'd had with her father after she'd learned he'd been behind the scheme to marry her off to Dexter. He hadn't tried to deny it, hadn't even apologized. He'd just told her he loved her and said that enough was enough. Afterward, she'd felt completely worthless.

"All I know how to do is cuss, play golf, and look good in clothes.''

"And?'' He waited patiently.

"And nothing.''

"That might be enough for other women, but not for you. You're much too intelligent.''

His expression was so earnest that she couldn't resist. "All right. Maybe I've harbored a secret fantasy of doing something with . . .'' She hesitated, then thought, *Why not?* "Maybe doing something with photography.''

"Photography? How interesting.''

He really did seem interested, and she realized she wanted to tell him more. She began hesitantly, but quickly warmed to the subject. "I've learned a lot from Patrick in the past year. He's lent me one of his cameras, and we spend a lot of time together in the darkroom. Lately he's even let me do some developing for him. He says I have an eye.'' She was embarrassed by her own enthusiasm. "He's probably just being nice.''

"I'm sure that's not true.'' He sounded so sincere that she found herself wanting to tell him more.

"I love it, Dex. Once I start working, I lose track of time. And I've been haunting playgrounds. I swear, the police are going to arrest me for being a suspicious character, but I love photographing kids. They're so—'' She broke off.

"It's all right, Torie. I'm not going to make fun of you.''

She heard the understanding in his voice, and she hated it. "I don't even know why we're going through with this charade. You admitted that having children was important to you, and you know I'm barren. Why don't you just leave me alone?''

"The doctors haven't conceded that you're barren, so why should I? But if it does prove to be true, we could adopt."

She felt this peculiar thump in her chest, as if her heart had skipped a beat. "You'd do that?"

"Of course. I told you I wanted children."

"Tommy wouldn't even discuss adoption."

"You displayed sounder judgment buying the emus than when you married Tommy."

She laughed. "You're right about that. But Tommy sure was better-looking."

"Looks aren't everything." For the first time he sounded defensive.

"You're not bad-looking, Dex. As a matter of fact—now, don't let this go to your head, but of all the geeks I know, you're the best-looking. Except for Ted, but then Kenny's about the only one who's got Ted beat, so you can't get all bent out about that."

"Exactly how many geeks do you know?"

"Hey, you're talking to the microchip princess here. Don't forget that I was raised around geeks. When I was little, Daddy used to take me to work with him."

"And you really think I'm the best-looking?"

She struggled to keep from smiling. He really was sweet in a doofus sort of way. "Absolutely."

"Normally, I wouldn't care, you understand, but I know that physical appearance is important to you."

Something about the way he had gone all stiff and starchy, but at the same time seemed worried, went right to her heart. Not to mention a few other places. She couldn't remember ever being so mixed up, and there was only one thing she could think of to do about it.

"Okay, Dex, I've made up my mind. I'm going to take you out for a test spin."

"What do you mean?"

"We're going to do the dirty, Dex. You, me, and a mattress. I think it's time I put you through your paces."

His starchiness vanished, and amusement took its place. There was something about the way his eyes crinkled at the corners that made those curls of heat that had been unfurling inside her burst into flames. "Oh, you do, do you? Well, what if I told you that I'm holding myself back as your wedding night prize?"

"You're kidding. You don't want to sleep with me?"

"I can hardly think about anything else. But, crudely put, why should you buy the steer if I let you have the beef for free?"

"You think you're some kind of *prize*?"

"Definitely." His eyes sparkled. "I don't want to be arrogant about this, and I certainly wouldn't have said anything if you hadn't brought up the topic, but I'm quite an excellent lover."

"Brother . . ." She rolled her eyes.

He laughed, pulled her into his arms, and kissed the breath right out of her. In the dimmest recesses of her mind, she noted that he wasn't too indifferent to cop a feel, but his hand felt good curled around her breast, so she wasn't in any hurry to push it away.

Dex put a lot into his kisses. As his tongue delved into her mouth, she tried to tell herself that there was something pathetic about being so desperate for a man's affection that she'd descended to kissing Dexter O'Conner, but his kiss didn't seem pathetic. It was sweet and erotic, and it left her wanting more.

They separated, and as soon as she'd stopped seeing stars, she realized Mr. Sober Sides was just as shaken as she. "All right," he said unsteadily. "I'll marry you."

She curled into that strong, warm chest, felt his breath against her forehead, and for a fraction of a moment, she wanted to say yes. "Oh, Dex . . . you'd regret it within a month."

"No, I wouldn't. And neither would you."

She should have simply walked away, but some devil inside wouldn't let her do that. "Bed first. Then I'll make up my mind. I'm not buying a pig in a poke."

He gazed down at her and a vaguely dangerous smile caught the corner of his mouth. "For now, we're both keeping our clothes on. But if I change my mind, you'll be the first to know."

Chapter 17

As Emma walked next to Kenny along the less populated part of San Antonio's beautiful Riverwalk, it occurred to her that Lady Sarah Thornton might have been foolish for having returned to England when she'd so clearly loved Texas. There was something special about this state that she couldn't help but respond to: its energy, its people, and its sheer, raw size. She found herself taking a long, deep breath for no reason, almost as if her lungs had developed a larger capacity. Somehow she felt bolder here, and, in a way she couldn't explain, less limited.

The last five days had been magical. Kenny had shown her two of Texas's most colorful cities: Austin, then San Antonio. In Austin, he'd regaled her with anecdotes from his college days as he'd shown her the University of Texas campus. When she finished her work at the library, he'd taken her through the state capitol building and given her tours of the city's parks and shops. At night, they'd visited wonderful restaurants and listened to Austin's best music.

San Antonio had been even more wonderful. In the mornings, while Kenny practiced at the range, she finished up the last of her research at the Daughters of the Republic of Texas Library at the Alamo. Then they spent their afternoons together. She'd never laughed so much, or argued so much either. Her body felt warm and languid from Kenny's love-making, and she couldn't imagine how she would ever live without it or without him.

A cloud of depression settled over her. Her time in Texas was nearly over. These last few days had been enchanted, but it was Friday and she would be flying home on Sunday evening.

She turned her face into the breeze, unwilling to spoil what little time she had left with introspection. Instead, she considered the guided tour of the Alamo Kenny had given her that afternoon. As he'd led her through Texas's most famous shrine, she'd realized all those volumes of history and biography she'd seen scattered around the house hadn't been put there by Patrick as decorative accents.

His hand felt large and comforting curled around hers. She admired a lovely old building on the other side of the river, then smiled up at him. "You're a real history buff, aren't you?"

"Why do you say that?"

"For one thing, you know a lot more about Texas history than most people."

"I wanted to major in history in college, but my high school grades were so crummy that my counselor recommended against it."

"That's unfortunate."

"Not really. He was probably right. Even taking easy subjects at UT, I pretty much made straight C's. And then I dropped out my senior year to turn pro."

"Yes, well, I should imagine it's difficult to do much better than C's when you hardly ever went to class."

He darted her a curious glance. "How'd you know that?"

"By spending five minutes in your company. Really, Kenny, I've never known anyone so afraid to challenge himself."

He dropped her hand and looked aggravated. "You happen to be standing here with a man who's won two majors in the past three years. I know everything there is to know about challenge."

"But winning tournaments is different, isn't it?" She took his hand back and gave it a comforting squeeze. She knew this weekend was especially hard on him with the Masters being played at Augusta, but he'd maintained a stoic silence on the topic. "The golf course is probably the only place in the world where you're not afraid to let people see you working hard."

"That's because it's the only place in the world where I *do* work hard."

She smiled at him and pressed her cheek against the side of his arm for just a moment. "Give it up, Kenny. You work hard at lots of things. Your exercise program, for example. It's only because you make everything seem so easy that you don't look like you're doing anything."

"You are so full of it that—"

"I should be fertilizer, I know. You *want* people to believe you're lazy. It's almost as if you think you don't deserve anyone's good opinion."

"Bull." Tension ticked at the corner of his mouth, and she knew she'd hit a nerve.

There were so many topics neither of them wanted to talk about, including his suspension and her problems with the Duke of Beddington. For the past five days, she'd been drifting along in a sensual haze, acting as if tomorrow would never come. She'd seen no signs of anyone following them, and now, with her return only two days away, she had to face the fact that she'd been behaving irresponsibly. She hadn't tried to contact Hugh or done a single thing to upset him. It was as if she'd been lulled into a sensual world where the future didn't exist.

A flutter of panic ruffled her stomach, stealing away some of her pleasure in the day. "Are you certain you can't remember the names of anyone who was in the drugstore that night?"

"I told you the last time you brought this up that I was concentrating on finding the right shoelaces, so I wasn't paying attention."

"But surely you spoke to someone."

"Not that I remember."

Her spirits plummeted. She was no better off now than she'd been when she'd stepped off the plane. "Beddington knew I bought a tabloid, so his spy had to have been right there in the drugstore. But why didn't he report anything else?"

A shapely female jogger approached, her ponytail swinging, but Kenny didn't seem to notice. She appreciated the fact that he didn't look at other women when he was with her. He really was a wonderful man, despite his foibles. Intelligent and entertaining. He also had a surprisingly old-fashioned sense of courtesy. Already today he'd been interrupted at least a dozen times by fans, and he'd responded to all of them politely while, at the same time, making it evident that his first obligation was to her.

They had reached the end of the accessible part of the Riverwalk, and they turned around. It was quiet here, tucked down below the city streets, with only the occasional interruption of a passing river taxi or a stray tourist. The feeling of privacy reminded her of St. Gert's in the late afternoon. Even with the girls racing about, there were wonderfully secluded spots tucked away here and there.

"I should never have assumed the spy was a man," she said. "It could just as easily have been a woman."

"Now I recall I do believe I saw Old Mrs. Cooligan over by the Fannie Mae display. She's eighty if she's a day, but she's real spry."

"Go on and make fun. It's creepy knowing that I was being followed, but not being able to figure out who was doing it. And why have they stopped?"

"I understand, sweetheart. And you know how I feel about your attachment to that pile of stones on the other side of the pond, so I'm not going to say anything more about it.''

"I know what you're thinking." She regarded him peevishly. "You're thinking I'm going to turn into one of those dotty, dear things. That I'll start talking to myself and collecting cats and wearing ratty old jerseys that smell like mothballs."

"I have to confess those things didn't enter my mind. Now, seeing you in a black garter belt with—''

"Just because I'm British and unmarried, and because I have a respect for tradition, doesn't mean I'm eccentric."

"I believe your freeway just sprouted a strange exit ramp. Where exactly are you headed with this?''

"Oh, I don't know. Forget it."

"You know, Lady E, instead of accusing me of psychological abnormalities, you might try looking inside your own muddled brain."

"Me? I'm as clear as a glass of water."

"If that's so, why do you keep seeing yourself as some dried-up old maid?"

"I don't. But I know I'm not exactly a sexpot."

"Now, there's a lie."

"It isn't a—" She looked up at him. "What are you saying?"

"That you're a sexpot."

"You're only being nice."

"I'm only being male. See, I've got this thing about your mouth—''

"There you go again! It's so unfair. If I were a man, I'd be considered a strong leader. But because I'm female, I'm bossy."

"We're not talking about bossy—although you are. We're talking about the fact that you've got about the sexiest mouth I've ever seen on a woman."

"My mouth is sexy?"

"Uh-huh."

She swallowed. Stared at him. "Now I know you're lying."

"I only lie about things that aren't important. Do I have to remind you of what you were doing with that mouth around eight o'clock this morning?"

She didn't see how he could still make her blush, but it happened. "Yes, well, thank you."

He laughed and drew her close. "Thank *you*."

Instead of trying to contact Hugh, Emma spent the next morning in bed at the ranch making long, lazy love with Kenny. She couldn't imagine any woman having a more thrilling, more considerate lover, but she wished it weren't so important for him to stay in control. Not that she wanted to take over all the time—it was lovely having someone so blissfully competent in charge—but occasionally she'd like to have the upper hand, if only so she could experiment on that lovely body of his. It was a problem she was certain they could have worked out over time, but there was so little left.

After a leisurely breakfast, they headed for the stable, and, for the next few hours, rode through the woods, then along the Pedernales. Kenny, mounted on Shadow, slouched comfortably into a western saddle, while she rode China on an English one.

"Kenny, have you noticed . . . ? It's probably just wishful thinking on my part, but my tattoo seems to be fading a little."

"Just settling deeper into your skin, is all."

"I suppose you're right." She heard a rustling in the woods and saw an armadillo rooting near a fallen tree trunk. Imagine being so close to such a curious animal. Her thighs ached pleasantly from being on horseback, or maybe she was still experiencing the aftereffects of their lovemaking.

He tilted his Stetson lower over his eyes. "I've been thinking . . . your next term doesn't start for another week, and the Antichrist doesn't seem to be in any rush to lift my suspension, so there's no need for you to hurry back. Why not stay a little longer?"

She straightened, then shot him a quick glance. "I have nonrefundable airline tickets."

"I'll take care of the tickets. Don't you worry about it."

At least he was no longer in a hurry to get rid of her. The idea should have made her happy, but she felt depressed instead. If they hadn't been sleeping together, Kenny wouldn't have wanted her to stay. "I'm an administrator. Classes might not start right away, but my job does. Two weeks is the longest holiday I can take."

"I don't get it. You already told me the duke's going to fire you. What difference does it make if you don't show up?"

"He hasn't fired me yet, and until he does, I'm responsible for St. Gert's." She worried her bottom lip. "I still have another twenty-four hours or so. Maybe something will come to me."

They rounded a bend, and, as she saw the house in the distance, she thought how much she loved it. She loved this ranch, this state. She felt like a different person here, one who wasn't so lonely.

He frowned. "It just doesn't seem like you need to rush off right now when we're having such a good time."

They were having a good time—the best time of her life—and she couldn't repress a certain wistfulness. "Better to end it on a positive note, don't you think?"

It took a moment for him to respond. "Yeah, I guess you're right."

"Of course I'm right," she said briskly, concealing the ache she felt.

Anything else he might have wanted to add was lost as the stable came into view. He straightened in the saddle and uttered a particularly foul obscenity, the same one that sent St. Gert's girls to Emma's office for a pointed discussion of appropriate language.

She followed the direction of his gaze and saw a group of men standing next to a paneled white van. One held a professional-quality video camera on his shoulder and was filming them as they approached. Another stood slightly off to the side looking down at the notebook in his hand. He was shorter than the others and more formally dressed in a dark brown sports coat, tan slacks, and a pale green sport shirt. As they drew nearer, she spotted gold snaffles glimmering on the vamps of an expensive pair of loafers.

"Keep your mouth shut," Kenny growled. "I mean it."

"Who are they?"

"Trouble, that's who."

As they rode closer, Emma noted that it was the man with the notebook who held Kenny's attention. Of medium build, he had a square-jawed face, small nose, and a brush haircut. A pair of high-fashion sunglasses hung by a cord around a muscular neck.

The cameraman moved closer, pointing his lens directly at Kenny as he reined in his horse. "This is private property, Sturgis."

"I've never seen your ranch, Kenny. I heard it was nice. How about taking me on a tour?" The man had the deep, well-modulated tones of a professional broadcaster. His smile was oily, and Emma detested him immediately.

"I don't think so." Kenny dismounted, passed the reins over to his stable boy, then helped Emma down.

"This is business, Kenny, and I want an interview."

"You're the last reporter I'd give an interview to. By the way, how's that eye healing up? Who'd have figured you'd turn out to be a bleeder?"

The man shot Kenny a look of undiluted hostility, then turned to Emma. "Sturgis Randall. I'm with *World Sports Today* on the International Sports Channel."

"This is Emma," Kenny said before she could respond.

That was all—no last name and no title from the man who loved telling everyone they met, from store clerks to busboys, that she was royalty, even though she wasn't.

Sturgis nodded, then dismissed her. He was far more interested in his mission than in Kenny's companion. "While you've been out playing cowboy, Tiger's ten under at Augusta. The fact that you're not there to challenge him is big news, and I'm going to report it."

"And here I thought you'd already done enough for me."

Sturgis bristled. "You attacked me in front of a few million golf fans."

Emma had heard the story from Torie, and she knew Sturgis had thrown the first punch, but, as usual, Kenny didn't defend himself.

"Both of us are professionals," Sturgis went on. "We can put it behind us. Let's see the ranch."

"Some other time."

"The folks at Global National think an interview is a good idea. And since they're one of your sponsors and a big advertiser on my show, they seem to be calling the shots on this one. But maybe you don't mind losing a sponsor. . . ."

A sense of outrage came over Emma at this invasion of Kenny's privacy. The fact that he was a public figure didn't give anyone the right to barge in on him like this.

Kenny's face was set in stone. "No interview. I already told your boss that."

"And every other reporter in the country." His tone grew unctuous. "I understand, Kenny. So I'll tell you what . . . we'll just film your ass as you run away."

His expression grew smug, while Kenny's complexion darkened with anger. It took her a moment to understand, and then she realized he'd made it impossible for Kenny to refuse without looking churlish. Randall must know that Kenny wouldn't be able to stomach the idea of every golf fan in American seeing footage of his backside as he walked away from the camera.

And then her skin prickled as she realized that she'd been presented with a golden opportunity. A reporter! A television camera! Just when she'd been about to give up, she'd been handed a chance to disgrace herself in a more public manner than she'd ever imagined. She caught her breath. Even Beddington couldn't ignore this!

Kenny heard Emma's quick inhalation and then saw the calculation in her expression. Her eyes darted from Sturgis to the cameraman, and every hair on the back of his neck stood up. Lady E had just realized she had a national audience right at her fingertips ready to witness whatever shenanigans she came up with.

He braced himself. Emma was quick, and any second now she was

nto his arms, or strip naked, or start

sink his career, he had to get her out of
tting to an interview. "All right." He shrugg
good chance to set the record straight." He turn
is going to be boring. Wait for me inside, wil.
you

He brace   lf for the worst and tried not to think about the fact
that she was about to turn him into the biggest joke in professional golf.
Lee Trevino's pranks, Ben Wright's comments about lesbian golfers,
even Fuzzy Zoeller's remarks about fried chicken and collard greens
after the '97 Masters, would be nothing compared to whatever Emma
was getting ready to bring down on his head.

And then . . . nothing. He watched with astonishment as she took a
deep breath, nodded, and turned away. He felt like pinching himself.
Was she really going to walk away?

Without giving the cameras a second glance, she walked straight toward the house, leaving behind what might be her last chance to cause
a public scandal. And he knew exactly why she wasn't kicking up.
Because she didn't want to hurt him.

"We're ready to go," the cameraman called out. "Over there."

He tore his thoughts away from Emma and headed toward the fence,
trying not to think about what she'd just sacrificed. Distracting pictures
started floating through his mind of the way she'd looked that morning
as she'd slept next to him with her forehead puckered as if she were
trying to conjure up scandalous schemes in her sleep. He remembered
butterscotch curls spilled across the light blue pillowcase like ribbons
of honey trailing over the sky.

"Kenny?"

He tensed. Since when did an ol' boy like him start thinking about
ribbons of honey? He sure didn't need that kind of distraction right now,
and he resolutely turned his attention back to Sturgis.

"Let's get this sonovabitch over with."

Fool! Emma yanked open a drawer looking for a corkscrew. She'd
let the opportunity of a lifetime slip by! And why? Because she was an
idiot, that's why! A complete *id-jut*!

The door banged as he stalked into the kitchen. He looked tense and
irritable. Good! She wanted an argument right now. She craved one!
Anything to release this awful frustration.

He stopped next to the counter, took off his hat, looked at her, and
smiled. As he gazed at her, all the tension seemed to melt from his

going to throw herself into his arms, or strip naked, or start doing a hula.

If he didn't want to sink his career, he had to get her out of here, even if it meant submitting to an interview. "All right." He shrugged. "Why not? It'll be a good chance to set the record straight." He turned to her. "Emma, this is going to be boring. Wait for me inside, will you?"

He braced himself for the worst and tried not to think about the fact that she was about to turn him into the biggest joke in professional golf. Lee Trevino's pranks, Ben Wright's comments about lesbian golfers, even Fuzzy Zoeller's remarks about fried chicken and collard greens after the '97 Masters, would be nothing compared to whatever Emma was getting ready to bring down on his head.

And then . . . nothing. He watched with astonishment as she took a deep breath, nodded, and turned away. He felt like pinching himself. Was she really going to walk away?

Without giving the cameras a second glance, she walked straight toward the house, leaving behind what might be her last chance to cause a public scandal. And he knew exactly why she wasn't kicking up. Because she didn't want to hurt him.

"We're ready to go," the cameraman called out. "Over there."

He tore his thoughts away from Emma and headed toward the fence, trying not to think about what she'd just sacrificed. Distracting pictures started floating through his mind of the way she'd looked that morning as she'd slept next to him with her forehead puckered as if she were trying to conjure up scandalous schemes in her sleep. He remembered butterscotch curls spilled across the light blue pillowcase like ribbons of honey trailing over the sky.

"Kenny?"

He tensed. Since when did an ol' boy like him start thinking about *ribbons of honey*? He sure didn't need that kind of distraction right now, and he resolutely turned his attention back to Sturgis.

"Let's get this sonovabitch over with."

Fool! Emma yanked open a drawer looking for a corkscrew. She'd let the opportunity of a lifetime slip by! And why? Because she was an idiot, that's why! A complete *id-jut*!

The door banged as he stalked into the kitchen. He looked tense and irritable. Good! She wanted an argument right now. She craved one! Anything to release this awful frustration.

He stopped next to the counter, took off his hat, looked at her, and smiled. As he gazed at her, all the tension seemed to melt from his body, and the transformation was so astounding that she couldn't quite absorb it. It was as if a great thundercloud had been dispersed by a single shaft of light.

His smile was so warm she felt as if she were being bathed in it. His eyes . . . those astonishing eyes . . . Her skin prickled, her heart pounded, blood surged through her veins. Her ears rang, her sight blurred, her bones quivered. She gripped the edge of the counter.

After days of being so sexually aware of him that her body seemed to exist in a constant state of arousal, this was entirely different. This reaction had come from someplace so deep inside her that she hadn't known it existed.

Every self-protective instinct she possessed began to scream. *Not this! Please! Anything but this. Not with this man. Please, God, not . . . love.*

She loved him. It wasn't infatuation at all. And the knowledge of her love hadn't come as a gentle unfolding, the way she'd always imagined it, but as a life-shattering cataclysm. It was so inappropriate. So impractical. So horribly, exceedingly painful.

"Something wrong?"

"Wrong? N-no. No, not at all. Of course not. How did your interview go?" She hoped he didn't noticed her hands tremble as she finally found the corkscrew and tried to insert it into the bottle of wine he'd chosen earlier.

He took it from her. "I got through it without punching him, so I guess it went okay." He turned the corkscrew and once again cursed her with that bone-melting smile. "Thanks for not taking advantage of the camera."

She snatched up a salt shaker just to busy herself. Patrick was out for the day taking photographs. Earlier, she'd been glad of the privacy, but now she wished he'd return. "What do you mean?"

"You know exactly what I mean."

She bit her bottom lip and ran her thumb over the ceramic top.

"You're a pretty terrific person, you know that, Lady E? And I don't just mean in the bedroom."

She turned back to him, and her voice sounded small and uncertain, completely unlike herself. "You think I'm terrific in the bedroom?"

"Don't you?"

"Well, yes, but that's because of you, isn't it?"

He gave a sharp nod. "Absolutely it's because of me, so prepare yourself for a major letdown when you start trying it with somebody else." He began to smile, but then his mouth seemed to suffer some sort of cave-in.

She realized she couldn't imagine making love with anyone else. She couldn't imagine being that uninhibited and vulnerable. Why had she allowed herself to have sex with him? She never did anything casually, so why had she thought sex would be the exception? When she'd given him her body, she'd been unconsciously giving him every part of herself, including all those parts he hadn't asked for and didn't want.

She moaned.

"What's wrong? You look like you've just eaten bad shrimp."

"Worse than that."

"Emma?"

"I can't talk about it."

"Sure you can. Tell me."

Tell him that she loved him? Not bloody likely! She could just imagine his reaction. First he'd look stunned, then horrified. There'd be no more talk of extending her stay, no more ease between them, none of those flashing smiles that made her feel as if she were drowning in an ocean of sunlight.

Then the most astonishing thought came to her. Why not be honest? It had always been her nature to take the bull by the horns, and this would be the perfect way to save herself. If she told him the truth, it would be like an amputation. Quick and brutal. His horrified reaction would put an end to any silly daydreams she might have about little violet-eyed children and happily-ever-after.

Without letting herself ponder the matter for a moment longer, she found her mouth opening, heard herself speaking, "The most ridiculous thing has happened." She cleared her throat. "I just realized I—It's most annoying, completely foolish, but—" Her tongue felt clumsy in her mouth. "You're going to be absolutely stunned. Probably angry. And I quite understand."

He waited patiently.

"Oh, never mind. Forget I—" But even as she began to retreat, she stopped herself. She possessed many faults, but cowardice had never been one of them. And who made the rule that a woman could only protect her pride by hiding her deepest feelings? She was made of sterner stuff, and she blurted out the words.

"You see, I've fallen in love with you."

He stared at her as if snakes had started to sprout from her ears.

She snapped up her head. "Do not say a word! I'm so furious with myself I could scream. Can you imagine? It is so bloody ridiculous! You! Of all people!" She snatched up a meat fork from the counter. "Why don't I just stick this right through my heart instead? Or decide I'm in love with Tom Cruise? Or—or Daniel Day Lewis? Or some silly rock star? It would be just as irrational." She slammed down the meat fork, crossed her arms over her chest, and began tapping her foot to keep from falling apart. "Yes, well, I'm not going to put up with this, am I? There are some things that simply cannot be endured. I'm putting an immediate stop to it."

His mouth opened and shut, then opened again. "How—how are you going to do that?"

She shot up her chin. "I just did, didn't I?"

She was afraid she was going to cry, and there was only so much humiliation she was willing to undergo. The telephone rang, and she ignored it. "I know it's not your fault, but I'm quite furious with both of us right now, so please excuse me."

The phone rang again. She began to move away, then bumped into a barstool and nearly knocked it over. Furious, she snatched up the receiver. "Hello!"

"It's Torie. Grab Kenny and get over to the house!"

"What's wrong?"

"You'll see when you get here. Hurry!" Offering no more information, Torie hung up.

Emma slammed down the receiver. "Your sister is having some kind of crisis."

"What's wrong now?"

All she wanted to do was flee to the privacy of her bedroom, which apparently was no longer possible. "I don't know, but she wants us both over at the house right away."

"We'd better go, then. She prob'ly murdered Dex and wants us to bury his body."

The trip to the Traveler estate was agonizing. She couldn't bear being trapped with his pity or his embarrassment, and she immediately turned up the radio just loud enough to make conversation impossible. He didn't turn it down, so she knew he didn't want to talk either.

Shelby appeared as soon as they entered the house. Her eyes were shining, her cheeks flushed with pleasure.

"Oh, Lady Emma, we've had the most unexpected visitor. A business acquaintance of Warren's—a big investor—but I don't think he's here because of Warren. I think it's because of you! Just wait until everybody in town hears I'm entertaining a real, live *duke*!"

Chapter 18

Emma froze.

"A *duke*?" Kenny said.

"The Duke of Beddington!" Shelby chirped. "He's in the living room! Warren calls him Hugh." She dropped her voice to something approaching a stage whisper. "Apparently they've known each other for years—the duke's been an investor in the company since the early eighties—but this is the first time they've met. Go on in and introduce yourself. I have to get another tray of hors d'oeuvres. He has quite an appetite."

Emma felt as if she'd been turned upside down. First realizing she was in love with Kenny, and now this. She'd known that Hugh had made a fortune through investments in high-technology companies, but there were so many. How could she have known that TCS would be one of them? And she was going home tomorrow. Why had he decided to come all this way to see her now?

Kenny clasped Emma's arm. "You're going back to the ranch. You don't have to put up with this."

His protectiveness comforted her. How tempting it would be to go along with him, but she knew she couldn't. She gave him a shaky smile. "Thank you, but I'll take care of it."

Gathering her determination, she headed for the living room.

"Emma, my dear." The chair creaked as Hugh got to his feet. He was impeccably dressed in a dark gray three-piece suit designed to minimize his stout figure. His thinning auburn hair was combed neatly back from his round face, and his shaggy eyebrows topped a pair of small, pale eyes. The air around him reeked of expensive cologne.

Behind her, she heard Kenny whisper, "Sonovabitch is a dead ringer for frigging Henry the—"

She quickly moved forward. "I'm stunned, Your Grace. What on earth are you doing in Texas?"

Hugh's fleshy fingers clamped around her own. "Wanted to surprise you. I have to be in the States on business for the next few weeks, so I wasn't going to be able to see you when you got back. And your descriptions of Texas have been so tantalizing, I wanted to visit the place for myself."

It was a blatant lie. He was the least curious traveler she knew. He had come all this way to make certain she was still under his thumb.

She couldn't imagine why he cared. There were thousands of women in England who were prettier than she, and a lot more willing. With his title and his money, he could have his pick. Why had he locked in on her?

Sonovabitch! Kenny watched Hugh Holroyd's eyes settle on Emma's mouth, and he understood exactly why the Duke of Beddington was so obsessed with St. Gert's headmistress. The horny bastard.

Kenny's fingers clenched at his side. Emma was so naive she thought all Holroyd cared about was her title and her respectability, but Kenny was willing to bet the ranch it was her curvy body that had turned the duke into an upper class stalker. Hugh'd been having visions of Lady E's sexy little mouth doing to him exactly what it had been doing to Kenny.

Which wasn't ever going to happen. Kenny still hadn't adjusted to Emma's startling revelation in the kitchen. It wouldn't have been so surprising coming from another woman—he was used to fending off declarations of love—but Lady E was extremely smart about people, so how had she managed to convince herself she'd fallen in love with him?

He reminded himself that, for all her big talk, she was pretty much a prude. For her own peace of mind, she probably needed to convince herself that she was engaged in something more important than recreational sex. She had to believe she'd fallen in love. But it wasn't true, and he needed to explain that to her.

The idea depressed him, but he didn't have time to think about it because his father was speaking in that overly jovial manner he reserved for major investors. "Hugh, I'd like you to meet my son, Kenny. Hugh's had an open invitation to visit for years, Kenny. I'm just glad he finally took me up on it."

"Ah, yes." Hugh had a handshake like a wet golf towel. "Pleasure, indeed, Ken. Can't tell you how grateful I am that you've taken such good care of my Emma."

Kenny's jaw tightened. "No problem."

Torie stepped forward, and the protective way she looped her arm through Kenny's indicated she could read her brother's mind. "Hey, bubba. Hugh here's a golfer, and I was just tellin' him about my round at the club this morning. If I hadn't missed a four-footer, I'd have shot a seventy-nine."

Hugh gave her a patronizing smile. "Yes, well, I suggested to your sister that she might be moving her head when she's putting. I've been known to miss a few short ones on the links myself. Not often, you understand. Although I'm not in your league, Ken, I've made my share of pars."

"Is that so."

Shelby hurried back into the room with Peter propped on one hip and a tray of hors d'oeuvres in her opposite hand. The baby's cheek was creased, and he rubbed one eye with his fist. "Sorry I was gone so long. Peter just woke up."

Hugh stared at the baby as if Shelby had brought a rattlesnake into their midst, but Shelby didn't seem to notice. "Peter's nine months old and the apple of his daddy's eye."

Warren smiled. "There's something to be said for having a second family, Hugh. You get a chance to correct old mistakes."

Kenny recoiled from the faintly wistful note he heard in his father's voice. "Let me take Petie from you, Shelby, while you give Hugh some more of those hors d'oeuvres."

Hugh bristled with displeasure over the lack of formal address, but Kenny pretended not to notice.

Shelby passed over the baby and headed toward Beddington. "You have to try Luisa's stuffed mushrooms, Your Grace. They're delicious. And have some cheese straws. They're from a Martha Stewart recipe, but I overlook that." Hugh was soon resettled in a wing chair with a napkin full of hors d'oeuvres positioned neatly across his vast lap and a suspicious eye on Peter, who was rubbing his nose across the Cadillac logo on Kenny's shirtfront.

"You know what I've been thinking?" Torie's eyes gleamed with mischief. "We need to show Hugh some Texas nightlife. I was planning to meet Dex at the Roustabout later. Why don't we all go and take Hugh along? You ever tried line dancing, Hugh?"

He frowned at Torie's familiarity. "Emma and I have some catching up to do, so the two of us are going to have a quiet dinner at the hotel. Emma, it will be more convenient for me if you're staying there, too, so I had my secretary book a room for you. On a separate floor, of course."

Kenny opened his mouth to tell Hugh what he could do with his room, only to have Shelby interrupt.

"No way, Your Grace. Warren and I couldn't stand having you stay at that drafty old hotel. Luisa's getting a room all ready for you upstairs. You'll have your own bathroom and a pretty balcony."

Shelby enjoyed acting like a birdbrain, but she was sharp as a tack, and Kenny tried to figure out what was going on. Was she trying to help him out by keeping Hugh away from Emma, or did she only care about having bragging rights to housing an English duke?

The last of the hors d'oeuvres disappeared into Hugh's mouth. He blotted the corners with the napkin. "Awfully nice of you, but I really don't believe—"

"Nobody wants to admit it," Warren said, "but the hotel's been having a problem with cockroaches."

It was the first Kenny'd heard about it, and he studied his father more closely. What exactly did they have up their sleeves? It only took a moment for him to figure it out. His father wanted to keep Hugh nearby so he could leverage more money out of him and maybe put off the merger.

"Cockroaches? Oh, dear . . ."

Petie made a soft, muffled noise, and Kenny remembered that he'd just gotten up from his nap. He quickly moved forward. "You didn't get a good look at my baby brother, and I know from Emma how fond you British are of children. Here."

He gently, but purposefully, set Peter in Hugh's lap. Hugh stiffened. Peter looked up at him and crumpled his forehead.

Kenny shot him a pointed look. *Just do your thing, little bro.*

The baby settled, but he didn't look happy about it. Hugh looked even more unhappy. "See here . . ."

"Emma said you had some kids of your own." Kenny gave him a genial smile while keeping an eye on Petie, who was gradually getting red in the face. "Two little girls, isn't it?"

"Uh . . . yes . . . they're at school now."

Petie grunted.

"At school?" Kenny said. "They don't have a vacation like Emma?"

Petie's grunting grew louder and his face redder. Shelby was distracted by the maid coming into the room and didn't notice, but Warren saw what was going on, and, to Kenny's surprise, he didn't say a word.

"Well, yes, but I'm quite busy, and it's better for them to stay at their school. First-rate place. Not like St. Gertrude's. Not that there's anything wrong with St. Gert's—Emma's done an outstanding job there—but some of the girls aren't quite the thing. We have an active scholarship program, if you understand my meaning."

Oh, he understood plenty.

"Our scholarship students are our hardest workers," Emma said firmly.

The room began to fill with the smell of a loaded diaper.

Way to go, bro. Kenny gave Petie a proud smile. The little boy was as regular as clockwork.

Hugh wrinkled his nose and tried to shift Peter farther away from him.

"Now, how many scholarship students do you have there?" Kenny inquired politely.

"I—uh—" Hugh moved Petie to the very end of his knee. The baby, Kenny noted, was beginning to squirm, but he still looked real pleased with himself.

"We take in fifteen each year," Emma said.

"Well, now, isn't that something. Tell me, Hugh, what's it like being responsible for so many bright young people?"

Petie had dropped a good one, and the duke's ruddy color began to pale. But he was too full of himself to mention what was, after all, a perfectly natural occurrence. "One must do one's duty."

"You sure are right about that." Kenny began a long, cornpone monologue on the values of education and the joys of philanthropy. Everything was going just the way he wanted until Shelby finished talking to the maid and caught a whiff.

"Peter Traveler, what did you do, you little scamp?" Laughing, she swept up the baby. "We'll be back in a few minutes. Kenny, Emma, there's plenty of food, so the two of you stay for dinner, and afterward we'll head over to the Roustabout and show His Grace just what Texas is all about."

Hugh looked as if he'd rather eat worms.

Torie beamed at him. "What a great idea. I can't hardly wait to teach you the two-step, Hugh. I'll even let you wear my Stetson."

Kenny promised himself right then that he'd buy his sister a whole truckload of emu feed whether she wanted it or not.

All through dinner, Kenny kept waiting for Emma to start cuddling up next to him and calling him *lover*, but, instead, she treated him as little more than a casual acquaintance. Unbelievable! When they hadn't been having sex, she wanted everybody to think they were. But now that they were, she didn't want anybody to know about it.

He tried to get annoyed, but what he felt instead was this crazy kind of warmth. There'd been a lot of women who'd exploited him over the years, but Emma sure wasn't one of them.

He remembered what she'd said down by the river, about not wanting to tell Hugh that she and Kenny were lovers. *I want this to be private. Just between us.*

Still, she had to know that the only way she was ever going to get rid of the pompous bastard was to let him know she'd found herself a lover, and Kenny didn't really mind. But in the meantime it was nice watching her try to stick to her principles. Nice to know that she thought she loved him, even though he knew she was just confused.

The Roustabout was busier than normal that night, and as they led the duke inside, he looked as if he'd just stepped into the contents of Petie's diaper. Shelby chatted away with him as Torie led them all to a large table in the back. They'd no sooner gotten there than Emma excused herself and made a beeline for Ted Beaudine, who was sitting at the bar reading Plato's *The Last Days of Socrates* and sipping a big mug of something that looked suspiciously liked Mountain Dew.

Kenny watched as she talked to him earnestly. Ted immediately accompanied her to the dance floor, then snuggled right up as she led them into the steps of a cozy little ballad. Kenny had a pretty good idea where this was headed, and he wasn't surprised when Ted's hand began to ease toward Emma's bottom.

Ted shot him a slow grin over the top of her head. *What am I supposed to do? She's forcing me.* Kenny glowered and made a silent vow to whip the kid's ass good the next time he got him on the course.

Hugh was talking to Warren, so he wasn't watching the dances, but Torie and Shelby were. They exchanged glances; then, in what was obviously a misguided attempt to protect Lady E's reputation, Torie shot up and insisted Hugh trade seats with her right that minute, so he could have a better view of the bar, as if that were some big privilege. She managed to reposition him with his back to the dance floor so he couldn't see Emma flirting with Ted. Poor Lady E. Try as she might, she couldn't seem to ruin her reputation.

And it all went downhill for her from there. Hugh was so busy being condescending, he didn't notice the way Emma held Ted's hand as she brought him over to the table for introductions, nor did he seem to find anything wrong with her ordering tequila shooters. Kenny was the only one who noticed her turning green around the gills after the first two. She ordered the third, then the fourth. But before she could drink it, she made a quick exit to the ladies' room.

When she returned ten minutes later, she was pale, but no longer green, so he knew where the shooters had ended up. He gave her hand a comforting squeeze under the table and wished he could help her out, but this was something she had to do for herself. He simply didn't have it inside him to ruin her reputation.

The evening dragged on. After a few shots of the Roustabout's best single-malt scotch, Hugh treated them to such a detailed description of his family lineage that even Shelby grew bored.

And then Sturgis and his film crew arrived.

Sturgis had mentioned he'd be hanging around until tomorrow so he could shoot some local color, and that obviously included getting footage of Kenny loafing around the Roustabout while Tiger rested up for the final round of the Masters tomorrow. Kenny's anger simmered as he watched Sturgis move around the room to conduct a series of interviews with Kenny's old school chums, who were dredging up every story they could recall about what a little prick he'd been. Sturgis had already nearly ruined his reputation with the golfing public, and his friends were going to finish him off.

Hugh kept trying to get Emma alone, but Torie wouldn't let that happen, and Kenny knew his sister had taken as big a dislike to the Englishman as he had. Out of desperation, Hugh asked Emma to dance, but Torie shot up and said Emma didn't know squat about dancing, and Torie herself was going to show Hugh how it was done.

Club soda seemed to have helped settle Emma's stomach, and before long she decided to take another stab at upsetting Hugh by talking to Torie and Shelby about how wonderful Ted was. Didn't they think he was the best-looking young man they'd ever seen, and didn't his jeans look good on him, and that kind of stuff, all of which went right over Hugh's puffed-up head.

Then Dex appeared, and Kenny went on full alert. It was one thing for Emma to flirt with Ted, but there was no way in hell he was going to sit here and watch her try it with Dex.

To his surprise, Torie intervened again. Before Emma could make a single move, Torie forced Dex to the dance floor. As Kenny watched her cuddle up to him, acting for all the world as if she enjoyed having a man she detested as her dance partner, he realized how much he owed his sister. They returned to the table, and she kept Dex so occupied with conversation that, if he hadn't known she was just trying to keep him away from Emma, he would almost have thought she was enjoying his company. Kenny gave him a dirty look that sent a real strong message— Warren Traveler might have turned his back on his daughter, but her big brother was still on the job.

Lady E started looking so depressed he couldn't stand it any longer, and he stood up. "Come on, sweetheart. Let's dance." He emphasized the endearment and made sure his voice was loud enough to penetrate even the duke's self-absorption.

His Royal Pain in the Ass frowned.

Kenny felt Emma's resistance as he pulled her from her chair. She was still holding firm to her principles. What was happening between them was to remain private. "I don't—That is . . ." An edge of desperation crept into her voice. "Ted, are you sure it won't upset you if I dance with Kenny?"

Kenny gave the little punk a glare that promised the balls he'd be missing come next week wouldn't have Titleist stamped on them if he opened his mouth. Ted got the message and shrugged. Kenny pulled Emma to the dance floor and, ignoring the news team that was probably going to film them, slammed her right against his chest. "Shut your mouth and put both arms around my neck. Let's get this over with."

She drew herself as far away from him as she could manage and looked up with desperate eyes. Seeing his tough, feisty little head mistress falling apart just about broke his heart. "I'm trying to help you out," he said softly.

"I can't do it, Kenny. I just can't. He's tarnishing every other part of my life, and I won't let him tarnish this." She drew a deep, shaky breath. "I—I have another plan."

It was as clear to him as the nose on her face that she didn't have a plan at all, but was still hoping she could come up with one.

"The guy's a jerk, honey. Just tell him so, and you're off the hook."

"You've met him. You can see how huge his ego is. He has to be the one to break it off, or he'll get even with me. And we both know how he's going to do that."

If Kenny heard one more word about that damned school, he was going to break something.

She started working away at her bottom lip, scheming to beat the band. "When we get ready to leave, I'm going to give Ted a passionate kiss. He already said it was all right."

"I'll just bet he did."

"Then, as soon as I get Hugh alone, I'm going to tell him how Ted and I've fallen in love."

"No, you're not."

She regarded him with pleading eyes. "Please, Kenny, don't make a fuss. There isn't any other way. I'll make it up to Ted."

Ted? She was going to make it up to *Ted*?

She gave him one of those dead-on looks that she did better than anybody else. "I'm not telling Hugh about us. I know that was my original plan, but . . . what happened is too special." She shot him a

w what was coming, but he had a good idea that he
e it. He hesitated just as Emma thrust herself forward
alms to her chest.

lie any longer!''

trying to keep this to myself, but it's no use!''
actly like a bystander watching a car accident about to
being helpless to stop it.

ith will set me free!'' Emma sucked in a great big gulp of
the truth is . . .'' She sucked in another gulp. ''I'm in love
ie!''

u're what?'' Torie's eyebrows shot halfway up her forehead, and
ok an automatic step backward.

t Lady Emma was on a roll, and nothing was going to stop her
. With a great lunge, she threw open her arms and planted a pas-
nate kiss right on his sister's lips.

challenging look, as if he couldn't
a dozen books before the end o'

Something happened insid
A warm sensation. But the
over and only jumping i

She sighed and pu'
her by not telling her
didn't want to talk about
felt crummy—mad at himself

Right away, Lady E saw that
began to crumple. "Wh-where did
Warren nodded toward the back. '
with his long irons, and Ted's giving him
to tell you he'd be right back."

Hugh stood up. "The trip was quite exhaus
enough for the evening."

"Me, too." Shelby rose along with him. "I'm sta
need to feed Peter."

Hugh blanched.

Shelby's mouth widened in a huge smile. "Just wait till you
comfy that guest room mattress is. Isn't it, Warren?"

His father smiled and gave her a look that made the old man se
about eighteen.

"But—I really—I need to—" Emma looked desperately around,
hoping Ted would magically reappear so she could lay a big one on
him. Kenny had to practically drag her to the door, and, as they reached
the parking lot, he felt her growing more agitated. Since he'd already
witnessed the havoc she could wreck when she got desperate, he knew
he had to get her away quickly.

"My car's over there," Dex said to Torie. "I'll drive you home."

Instead of making up an excuse, his sister nodded.

Shelby waved. "We'll see y'all in the morning."

"Good night, Emma." Hugh gave her a frosty nod, as if this were
all her fault, and Kenny knew he was storing up some big sonova-
bitchin' lecture to slam her with as soon as he got her alone. Which
wasn't going to happen. The only person allowed to criticize Lady E
was himself.

Hugh began to follow Warren and Shelby toward their car. Emma
was vibrating with tension, and a prickle of uneasiness came over
Kenny.

"Wait!" Emma's screech was so loud that everybody in the parking
lot heard.

Chapter 19

Emma's cheeks flamed. But she locked one arm around Torie's waist and faced them all down. His sister had boots on, so she stood a good six inches taller than Emma, and she looked like someone who'd been cybernetically frozen. Dex's expression was faintly bemused, Shelby's lips had grown slack, Warren's ruddy complexion had paled.

A wheezing sound came from Hugh's mouth, and his eyeballs protruded so that he looked like a giant guppy gulping for air.

"I was afraid to tell you," Emma said lamely.

Torie was beginning to come out of her stupor. She gazed down at Emma. "I didn't know you cared."

Kenny was so furious he could barely contain himself. That hardheaded, know-it-all, blindsided stubborn female had just thrown her lifetime career of teaching little girls right out the window.

Emma worked away at her bottom lip as she finally let go of Torie. Hugh's face had taken on a purplish hue. "You *degenerate!*"

And then everything happened at once.

Hugh shot forward, drew back his arm, and cracked Emma hard across her cheek with his open palm.

The camera crew emerged from the Roustabout too late to see Hugh's attack, but just in time to watch Kenny throw himself through the air and catch the duke in the midsection.

Hugh was more solid than he looked, but he was no match for Kenny, and he stumbled backward. Before he could hit the blacktop, Kenny grabbed him and slammed a fist into his gut.

The camera whirred away, brutally recording the sight of a tall, muscular athlete cravenly attacking a short, plump, middle-aged man.

Hugh crumpled, made another wheezing sound, and tried to butt his head into Kenny's stomach. Kenny brought up his knee and caught him in the chin. Hugh gave a grunt of pain and collapsed onto the asphalt.

Hugh was still conscious, but his face was a mask of fear as he gazed up at Kenny. Kenny bent down to jerk him back to his feet only to have his father catch one of his arms and Dex catch the other. The two men held him back.

Through the red haze of his anger, Kenny saw the camera crew and realized they were recording everything. Hugh stumbled back to his feet, gasping for air as blood dripped from the corner of his mouth.

Kenny watched the red mark on Emma's cheek grow livid, and he didn't give a damn about the camera crew. All he cared about was destroying the man who had struck her.

"I'm okay now," he said to his father and Dex. "You can let me go."

They let him go.

He slammed his fist into Hugh's jaw.

"Oh, Kenny . . ." Emma tried to hurl herself at him, but Torie, who understood justice when she saw it, grabbed her away.

"Come here, my little passionflower. I'll comfort you." She curled Emma to her bosom by throwing a hammerlock around her neck.

"I'm trying very hard," Dex murmured as he watched the females embrace, "not to get turned on."

Kenny's chest heaved as he stared down at Hugh crumpled on the pavement.

"Kenny!" He turned toward the commanding sound of Emma's voice. Her plump little mouth was set in a determined line and she looked every inch the schoolteacher putting an end to a playground fight—a schoolteacher with an ugly red smear on her cheek. "Don't do it. Please."

Torie released Emma, and he walked toward her to touch the mark on her cheek. "Are you all right?"

She gave a brisk nod, but he could feel how shaken she was, and it made him want to take Hugh Holroyd apart all over again.

In his peripheral vision, he saw the camera crew circling like vampires. They'd caught everything on tape—everything except the moment Hugh had slapped Emma. Right then, he knew exactly how it would be. The camera would show bad boy Kenny Traveler throwing himself at a defenseless man.

Never apologize. Never explain.

Sturgis Randall rushed forward and thrust a microphone in Kenny's face. "Tell us what happened. Why did you start the fight?"

"Get out of here," he growled.

"No!" Emma clutched his arm. "Tell him exactly what happened."

But Kenny'd swallowed his pride once today by talking to Sturgis, and he wasn't going to do it again. Besides, there was no point. Sturgis had film, and he wasn't interested in the truth.

Acid boiled in his stomach. Without another word, he pulled away from Emma and walked to his car. Randall shouted out a question, but he ignored it. He'd just thrown his life away, and he had to be alone.

Dismay washed over Emma as she watched him go. What had she done? As the Cadillac sped away, she faced the terrible knowledge that the events she had set in motion could destroy what was left of Kenny's career.

Warren shot forward. She was accustomed to seeing his neediness as he gazed at his son, but now she saw a hardheaded businessman. "Dex, get Hugh to the hotel. The more I think about it, the more I realize he'll do just fine there. Cockroaches need to stick together."

Dex grabbed Hugh and led him toward his Audi, but at the last minute, Hugh wrenched free and turned on Emma. "Don't think I'll ever let you near that school again! Or any school, for that matter. Twisted, perverted women like you shouldn't be allowed near innocent children."

Emma felt a cool, moist wind blow across the parking lot, and in her mind it smelled of neat English lawns, sun-splashed flower beds, and old brick buildings that sheltered lonely little girls. The only home she'd ever known.

Sturgis rushed toward Hugh. "Tell us what happened. Why did Kenny Traveler subject you to that brutal assault?"

Dex put the car into gear and raced out of the parking lot before Hugh could denounce Kenny. Furious, Sturgis turned back to his cameraman. "Let's get this film to the airport."

"No!" Emma rushed toward the camera. "Interview me. I'll tell you everything. I was attacked by Hugh Holroyd. Kenny was only acting in my defense."

Her heart sank as she saw the skeptical look on Randall's face "Anybody else see this?" he asked the onlookers.

"We all did," Warren said.

Shelby hurried forward, and the parking lot lights showed two damp milk-circles on the front of her sweater. "That English lizard slapped Lady Emma, and Kenny defended her."

Randall, still looking skeptical, turned to the crowd. "Is this true? Did anybody else see it?"

"If Shelby says it's true, then it is," one of the men called out.

"You're damned right it is," Torie said. "And you'd better tell the whole story."

Randall gave her a long look, and once again turned to the crowd. "Did anybody who's not part of the Traveler family see what happened?"

There was silence.

"Dex did!" Torie exclaimed. "Dexter O'Conner. He just drove the lizard to the hotel. You can talk to him."

"O'Conner? Isn't he the man you're going to marry? Not exactly an unbiased source."

"Who said I was marrying him?"

Sturgis passed his microphone over to a crew member and closed the notebook he was holding. "The bartender and about six other people."

The self-satisfied look on his face told it all, and Warren shook his head. "You don't want to know the truth. But then, you've got a long history of ignoring the facts. You're the reason Kenny got suspended, and now you want to string him up all over again."

Randall regarded him pompously. "I don't make the news. I just report it."

"Don't you mean *dis*tort?" Shelby said.

But Sturgis Randall had his story exactly the way he liked, and he wasn't interested in hearing any more. "Pack up, boys. Let's get out of here."

Emma's stomach sank. She'd desperately wanted to get rid of Hugh, but she'd never intended to destroy Kenny in the process.

Emma waited up for Kenny until nearly four in the morning, then fell asleep in the chair she'd pulled to her bedroom window. When she awakened at six, he still hadn't come home.

Still wearing her clothes from the night before, she stumbled into the bathroom. The mirror showed dark circles under her eyes and the faint shadow of a bruise on her cheek where Hugh had hit her. She brushed her knuckles against it, but it didn't hurt nearly as much as her heart.

Today was the day she was flying home. She thought of the way Kenny had rushed to her defense, an act of pure chivalry that had not only ruined his chance to get back on the tour for a very long time, but would permanently scar his reputation with the public. If only he'd let her handle it. But gallantry was as much a part of his makeup as his offbeat sense of humor. She'd known their affair had to end, but she'd never dreamed it would end like this, with her having so clearly wronged him.

She was going to need transport to Dallas today so she could get to the airport. She also needed a shower and fresh clothes, but there was something she had to do first.

Ten minutes later she was behind the wheel of Patrick's car and creeping down a blessedly empty highway toward town. As she concentrated on staying on the proper side of the road, she told herself that her days as a nondriver were over. She might never be comfortable at it, but she wouldn't give in to her phobia any longer. As soon as she returned to England, she was going to get a license.

The morning desk clerk at the hotel turned out to be the attractive redhead Ted had been flirting with at the Roustabout. She recognized Emma, and it didn't take long for her to turn over Hugh's room number.

After knocking at his door, Emma stepped far enough to the side so she wouldn't be visible through the peephole. Then she approximated a Texas drawl. "Room service."

Seconds ticked by. She heard the sound of movement, then the click of locks. The door opened. "I didn't order—" Hugh froze as he saw her.

He'd thrown a silk robe over his pudgy body, and the legs of his royal purple pajamas stuck out beneath. His feet were bare and ugly, with a gnarled big toe. She was gratified to notice that the bruise on the side of his jaw was a lot nastier than hers.

"Get out of here!" His small eyes darted past her into the hall, and she realized he was afraid Kenny had come along.

She pushed past him into the room. "I'm alone."

He slammed the door behind her, as if he still expected Kenny to wedge himself inside at any moment. "He's a madman! If I'd known he was insane when I spoke with him that first time, I'd never have—" He broke off and his fleshy lips curled. "Do you have any idea the extent of the humiliation you've made me suffer?"

As he took a threatening step toward her, common sense told her to retreat, but she stood her ground. "If you touch me, I shall scream so loudly everyone in the hotel will hear. Is that what you want?"

He glared down his nose at her but didn't come any closer. "You're wasting your time. You don't really believe I'll still marry you now that I know about your *perversion,* do you?"

His lip curled as if he'd just spit out poison. If she *were* a lesbian, she would find his attitude highly offensive. He thrust his hand through his oily auburn hair, but instead of straightening it, he forced it into a pair of spikes that reminded her of devil horns.

"Don't plan on ever returning to St. Gert's because I'm dismissing you. If you set foot on the property again, I'll have you arrested for trespassing."

"Of course I intend to go back. Everything I own is there."

"It'll be packed up and sent to you."

She wouldn't even get a chance to say good bye, but she knew she had to pick her battles, and she couldn't afford to think about that. Instead, she had to concentrate on all the girls who depended on her.

"Very well, Hugh. But if you don't want chaos reigning at St. Gert's, I suggest you replace me with Penelope Briggs. She's highly competent, and she'll do an excellent job."

"That ruddy-faced woman? The one with the awful braying laugh?"

Penelope might be loud, but she was also wonderfully cheerful and extremely intelligent. Hearing her dismissed that way made Emma bristle, but she did her best to hide it. "She gets on well with the staff and the girls. She's also extremely well-organized. You couldn't find anyone better." *Except me,* she wanted to say. *I was the best headmistress St. Gert's ever had.*

He shrugged. "Since she won't have the job long, I suppose it won't make any difference."

"What do you mean?"

He regarded her with a self-satisfied smirk. "I'm going to sell the school to a developer, Emma. I believe I mentioned that possibility."

Her breath came out in a slow hiss. He wanted his revenge, and he knew exactly how to take it. "You miserable worm."

"I don't think you have room to call anyone names, you pathetic excuse for a woman. And I'm warning you right now that you'd better keep quiet about your perversion. I won't have anyone knowing that a lesbian ever served as the headmistress of St. Gert's."

She couldn't do this any longer. She'd lost everything that counted, and at least she would accept defeat as herself and not someone else. "I'm not a lesbian," she said quietly. "I kissed Torie because I was desperate to get rid of you."

"You're lying."

She took a deep, steadying breath. "If I were a lesbian, I wouldn't be ashamed of it, but I'm not. I told you from the beginning that I didn't want to marry you. Not only did you refuse to listen, you blackmailed me."

"I did no such thing."

"I don't know what else you'd call it. You threatened to sell St. Gert's if I didn't comply with your wishes. I love that school. You didn't leave me any other option."

He drew himself up, and his chest expanded pompously. "You're deluded! As if I would have to force any woman to marry me. My name is one of the oldest in England."

Once again she was reminded of how useless it was to argue with him. When it came to his own self-importance, Hugh Holroyd had no match. She fired her final salvo, knowing how flimsy it was even as she spoke. "I'm warning you right now that, if you close St. Gert's, I'll do my best to destroy you."

Her threat hardly brought him to his knees. Instead, he sneered at her. "What could a nobody like you do to destroy someone like me?"

"I could tell the truth."

He looked bored.

"That's really all I have to do, you know. Oh, I don't possess your lofty media contacts, but I'm well-acquainted with Colin Gutteridge at the *Lower Tilbey Standard*, and I taught Evelyn Lumley's daughter. Evelyn is the home and garden reporter for Lower Tilbey's radio station. She's a magician with roses, so she has a very loyal group of listeners. I admit my contacts are humble ones, but even a small stone causes ripples, and both of them are quite loyal to me. They'll be more than happy to report my side of the story."

"No one will believe them," he scoffed. "You can't prove a thing."

"Perhaps not. But the speculation will be messy."

"Do you really think your unimportant little friends could hurt someone in my position?"

"I fight with what I have," she said simply.

She had the satisfaction of seeing that she had his attention. Perhaps her small threat would make him think twice.

He shot his hand toward the door. "Get out of my sight. And don't expect any decent schools in England to hire you because I'll make certain that doesn't happen."

Did he really have so much power? She doubted it, but she also knew he could make it impossible for her to secure the type of position she was qualified to hold.

She realized she was trembling, and she knew she had to get away. But she couldn't leave until she said what she needed to. "You are a small-minded, pompous man, Hugh. But even worse, you have a wicked heart. St. Gert's deserves better."

Francesca stared through the living room window at the gleaming stretch of Florida beach. It was beautiful, but she missed Wynette. She returned her attention to the disagreeable telephone conversation she was having with her husband. "Yes, darling, I've heard what they're saying on the news. But I'm sure Kenny has a rational explanation."

She wasn't sure of any such thing, and she winced as her normally soft-spoken husband adamantly voiced his displeasure.

Finally, he quieted enough for her to speak. "I'll admit the news clip is a bit damning, but the Duke of Beddington's such a rotter. Really,

Dallie, if you knew him, you'd simply detest him. I'm certain he had it coming.''

She lifted the receiver a few inches from her ear as he erupted again. He was calling her from Augusta, where the final round of the Masters was being played even as they spoke. Reporters had been stalking him all morning, and guilt nipped at her. This was her fault for sending Emma to Kenny. Beddington had obviously gone to Wynette because of her, and something, just as obviously, had gone drastically wrong.

Ever since Francesca had seen the footage of the fight in the Roustabout parking lot on the morning news, she'd been trying to reach Kenny, but she kept getting a busy signal. She'd hoped Emma would have a positive influence on him, but, instead, she seemed to have landed him in deeper trouble. None of this would have happened if Francesca hadn't decided to try a little offbeat matchmaking, as her husband was now reminding her.

The other line buzzed. Dallie was still raving, and she slipped him on hold.

"Hi, Mom, it's me."

"Teddy, darling! Thank goodness you called. I have your father on the other line, and he's being completely disagreeable. Hold on."

She clicked back to Dallie, who seemed to be threatening her with a rather interesting sexual variation if she ever tried matchmaking again. "Sweetheart, I'm sorry to interrupt, but Teddy's calling."

Dallie immediately quieted, as she'd known he would. Of the many blessings in her life, witnessing the love between Dallie and his son was surely the greatest.

She took advantage of his brief silence to end the conversation. "Hurry home tonight, my darling." And then, to punish him for being so cranky, she dropped her voice into the husky purr she'd perfected before her sixteenth birthday. "I bought the most exquisite massage oil yesterday. Almond with a faint overlay of sandalwood. Imported, of course, and outrageously expensive. But I insist on using only the very best . . . on every part of you . . . that will touch . . . certain parts of me."

There was a long, eloquent pause, and when he finally spoke, his voice sounded just the slightest bit hoarse. "Francie, I do believe I'm going to catch an earlier flight."

Francesca smiled as she gently disconnected him. *As if there'd ever been any doubt.*

"I'm going to kill him!" Torie exclaimed, over the voice announcing final boarding of Flight 2842 to London's Heathrow. "I really will, Lady

E. The minute Kenny resurfaces, I'll do it. Tell her, Dex. Tell her I always mean what I say.''

Instead of replying, Dex slipped his arm around Emma's shoulders and gave her a hug. "I'm sure once Kenny's had a chance to think things over, he'll be in touch.''

Emma thought how difficult that would be since she was getting ready to fly across the ocean. She was also homeless and jobless. "It's all right. After what happened last night, I don't expect him to speak to me again. Really.'' But she'd hoped he would. She'd hoped he'd forgive her.

She fumbled in her purse for her boarding pass. She'd postponed getting on the plane as long as she could, just as she'd postponed leaving the ranch when it finally became evident that Kenny wasn't going to return, but she couldn't stall any longer.

At least she'd be getting away from Torie, who'd been nagging Dexter all day. No matter what he did or said, Torie found fault with it. He'd been bearing her insults with admirable restraint, but Emma'd been forced to bite her tongue to keep from calling her to task.

To make the trip even more uncomfortable, Emma had told them the truth about Hugh and his threats. After what they'd seen last night, they deserved the whole story, and, although they were both sympathetic, her confession made her feel like a dotty, dear thing, completely incompetent and out of touch with the world. The only secret she'd kept was the fact that she'd fallen in love with Kenny, but she was afraid both of them already knew that.

Torie's worried expression only reinforced the feeling. "Kenny's got a slow fuse, but, unfortunately, once it gets lit, it takes a while for him to cool down. And the fact that Tiger just won another Masters won't help.''

"Yes, well, I seem to have run out of cooling down time.'' She kissed Dex's cheek, then gave Torie a fierce hug. "You've been wonderful to me. I'll miss you dreadfully. You'll never know how sorry I am for what I put you through last night.''

"Are you kidding? I was glad to help out.'' She shot Dexter a peeved look. "Besides, it's nice to be around someone who's spontaneous instead of a person who has to think every damn thing through from top to bottom.''

Dexter smiled.

Torie squeezed Emma's shoulders. "And don't think you've seen the last of me, Lady E. We'll keep in touch.''

"I hope so.''

"You can count on it. Our love affair might have been brief, but it sure was memorable."

Emma laughed, then felt her throat close tight. She was going to miss this wacky band of Texans. "Be good to Dexter, Torie," she whispered. "He's a wonderful man."

Torie hugged her back and looked unhappy. Emma gave them both a shaky smile, then hoisted her tote and turned toward the jetway.

"Emma!"

Her heart lurched, and she spun around to see Kenny racing toward the gate. He looked terrible. His slacks were wrinkled, he was unshaven, and he'd stuck a navy Dean Witter baseball cap over rumpled hair.

"Hold on!" Kenny rushed forward, nearly knocking over an elderly woman in the process, and came to a stop in front of Emma. His chest heaved, and he took a deep breath.

Now what? As Kenny gazed at Emma silhouetted in front of the jetway, he couldn't seem to get his air back. He'd run all the way from the parking garage, but that wasn't why he couldn't breathe. It had something to do with the way his lungs were crushed in his chest.

Last night, after he'd left the Roustabout, he'd driven around for a few hours, then found himself headed for Dallas. When he arrived, he'd gone straight to the golf course instead of to bed. He'd played thirty-six murderous holes; then, when he'd heard what Tiger was doing at Augusta, he'd hit the driving range for another hour. Bleary-eyed with exhaustion, he'd been about to make his way to his condo when he'd realized what day it was. That was when he'd turned around and headed for DFW.

"Ma'am, you'll have to board now," the gate attendant said with determined politeness.

Kenny saw Emma's forehead wrinkle, and then her mouth crumpled. She banged her tote bag against his hip as she curled her hand around his arm. "Oh, Kenny, I'm so sorry about what happened. I never meant to involve you. I wasn't thinking. I just reacted, and . . . I'll never forgive myself. Everything happened so fast, and—"

He could see that, if he didn't stop her, she'd spend the rest of their time together apologizing, but now that he was facing her, he couldn't think of any of the dozen things he needed to say, especially not with Torie and Dex looking on. He just knew he couldn't let Emma leave until he'd told her how she'd screwed up his entire life. And also . . . he had to say good-bye.

He whirled on his sister. "Will you get out of here?"

"Not until I'm good and ready."

"You're ready!"

Dex stepped forward, took her by the wrist, and drew her far enough away so Kenny could have a little privacy.

"Ma'am, we're getting ready to close the doors. You have to board." He glared at the gate attendant. "Just tell them to wait a minute!"

"I'm sorry, sir, we can't do that."

Emma gave the attendant her boarding pass and shot Kenny a pleading look. "I have to go."

Kenny gritted his teeth. "You're not going anywhere until you tell me what you intend to do about the mess you've made of my life."

Her eyes clouded. "I tried to reason with that awful television reporter—all of us did—but he refused to listen." She began walking backward into the jetway. "I promise, Kenny, I'm going to talk to Dallie and set things right. I left several messages, but he hadn't returned them by the time I left. I'll call again as soon as I get on the plane."

"You did what?" He dashed into the jetway and pulled her back out.

The attendant hissed, "Sir!"

He gave Emma a little shake to get her attention. "By damn, if you say a single word to Dallie about this, you'll be sorry."

The attendant stepped closer. "Ma'am, do you want me to call security?"

"No, no." Emma shook her head. "Everything's fine." Once again, she grabbed his arm. "Of course I have to talk to Dallie. I'm the one who's responsible. I have to explain how this is all my fault."

"You're damn right it is, and you've got a lot of making up to do, starting right now. Don't get on that plane."

"I have to. I have to go back."

"And leave me to face the mess you created? Not hardly."

"I won't. I already told you I'd explain to Dallie, and—"

"And I already told you to mind your own business."

"But . . ."

"Ma'am, are you getting on this plane or not?"

"Yes!"

"No, you're not!"

Without any warning, Emma's eyes filled with tears. Why did she have to tear his heart out by crying? "You stop that right now!" he exclaimed. "You're not getting your way just by turning into a damn crybaby!"

"I'm not trying to get my way. I'm trying to straighten this out."

"Fine! That's exactly what I wanted to hear." He glanced over at the gate attendant. "Don't wait for her any longer. She's not going with you."

"Kenny! Stop it this instant! I've already apologized, and I told you

I'd call Dallie and explain, but you don't want that. I can't think of anything else to say. What am I missing? Tell me exactly what it is you *do* want from me."

She had him there.

"That's what I thought." Her schoolmarm's look told him he didn't have a chance of changing her mind. "Good-bye, Kenny."

She pulled away from him and turned into the jetway.

"You get back here right this minute!" he called out. "We're—" Something was burning a hole right through the middle of his brain. "We're going straight to Vegas."

That stopped her—stopped him, too. She glanced back at him, and her expression was completely baffled, which made him even more irritable. "Vegas? What do you mean?"

The hole in his brain was getting bigger by the second. "Las Vegas. It's in Nevada."

"I know where it is. Why do you want to go there?"

"To elope." The words came out like a croak. "It's where people go to elope."

"Elope?" She was walking back toward him now, not as though she wanted to do it, but more like a zombie. "Do you mean get married?"

No! No, that's not what he meant at all—he didn't want to get married!—but he couldn't back down now, not with that damned gate attendant staring at him as if he were a nutcase, and Emma looking like the walking dead, and Tiger wearing the green jacket again.

His eavesdropping sister started shrieking in the background and jumping up and down just like the sorority girl she'd been in her not-so-distant past. "You're getting married!"

He thrust out his jaw at Emma. "You've got a problem with that?"

Those amber brown eyes looked as if they were going to swim right out of her face, and her throat muscles contracted as she swallowed. "This is—is foolish. You don't want to marry me."

She'd never spoken truer words, but he wasn't going to admit it now. "Don't you try to tell me what I want and what I don't want. Just because we're getting married doesn't mean I'm going to put up with you bossing me around."

"Ma'am, I'm afraid you'll have to get this sorted out on your own time. Good luck."

As the gate attendant shut the door, Kenny went light-headed with relief. He didn't try to examine his reaction. He only knew that he'd just survived a sudden-death playoff.

Behind him, Torie continued to squeal. "Married! Oh, Kenny, this is perfect! You and Lady E! Shelby's gonna die. Oh, my God! Does this mean you get a title, too? Does it, Lady E? Is he going to be Lord Kenny now?''

Kenny shot Dex an imploring look. "If you've got an ounce of compassion, get her out of here.''

Dexter slipped his hand around Torie's waist. "I don't think we're needed.''

"I have to call Shelby. And Ted! Wait till I tell Teddy Beaudine about this.'' As she fumbled in her purse for her cell phone, she grinned at her brother. "I can see why you like her so much, Kenny. She's a real good kisser.''

Every person still standing in the gate area turned to stare at Emma. Torie regarded them haughtily. "Well, she *is*.''

Chapter 20

*I*t didn't take Kenny long to collar one of the airline employees, establish who he was, and get VIP treatment. Ignoring Emma's protests, he made arrangements for their flight to Las Vegas.

She should have simply dug in her heels and refused to move, but instead, she trotted along at his side, barely keeping up with Mr. Speedy, as she tried to talk to him. He refused to listen, refused to wait for her luggage to be retrieved, and before she knew it, she was headed to Las Vegas for an elopement.

She wouldn't marry him, of course. She couldn't. It was unthinkable.

But so tempting.

And so wrong.

"Kenny, we have to talk about this!"

"Nothing to talk about." He pulled his baseball cap down over his eyes and leaned back into his first-class seat next to her. "You ruined my reputation. Now you're going to save it."

"Rubbish! We don't have to get married for that."

"You already told me Hugh fired you, then kicked you out of your house. What else are you going to do?"

"I'll find another job and a place to stay. I'm not helpless, and I'm not in need of rescue!"

"If you don't mind, I'd like to catch up on my sleep."

"I do mind. I mind very much. I—Oh, what's the use? Until you decide to talk, I'm wasting my breath."

She turned to gaze out the window of the plane and wonder how her life had slipped so far out of her control in such a short time. What an awful day. She'd barely slept last night, and then there'd been that horrid meeting with Hugh.

Something nagged at her, something Hugh had said, but she couldn't quite put her finger on what it was. She tried to reconstruct their interview, but that only depressed her.

At her side, Kenny stirred in his sleep. She had to make him listen to her, and, as soon as he woke up, that was exactly what she would do. No matter how difficult it might be, she had to right the terrible wrong she'd done to him. But first she needed to talk him out of this silly notion that they were going to elope.

The woman in the seat behind her had been arguing with her male companion ever since the plane had taken off, and, once again, she raised her voice. Emma thought of Torie. She'd been awful to Dexter all day. Why had he put up with it? Emma knew Torie was going through a lot of emotional pain, but it really wasn't fair to take it out on him.

Fair. As if anything about life was fair.

As Emma pondered life's unfairness, Torie led Dexter through the front door of Kenny's Dallas condo. She'd told him she needed to pick something up here, but the truth was, she wanted to settle things between them, and she'd rather do it here than back in Wynette.

The condo was stuffy, so she made her way over to the air conditioner and flipped the control. Then she stalked into the kitchen. Maybe something cold to drink would improve her mood.

Dex headed for Kenny's stereo, but instead of looking through the CDs like any normal person, he pulled out one of the components and inspected it from behind. Damn him. He'd been stiff and starchy all day. At least he had been with her. With Emma, he'd been all friendly and chatty. And he'd gotten worse after they'd left the airport. Torie might as well have been invisible because nothing she did got a reaction from him. She'd criticized his driving, made fun of his vocabulary, and told him he could have gotten a better haircut from a dog groomer, but he hadn't paid any attention. Instead, he'd merely gotten quieter, as if she no longer interested him.

She grabbed a can of Sprite from the refrigerator, tossed her purse on the counter, then kicked off her chunky-heeled leather sandals. She was wearing them with a long black knit tank dress that set off her figure and should have made him drool, but didn't seem to be having any effect. She'd never felt as insecure around a man as she did around Dexter. "If you want something to drink, get it yourself," she snapped.

"Nothing, thank you."

His quiet manner enraged her. "You could be a little more supportive, you know. This hasn't been an easy day for me."

"Why is that?"

"Isn't it obvious? My only brother's getting married."

"You're happy about that," he pointed out with a patience that made her want to scream. "Remember?"

"I hate it when you're sarcastic."

"I'm never sarcastic."

"Well, aren't you Mr. Perfect."

He sighed. "Suppose you just tell me exactly what's bothering you."

Everything was bothering her! He was bored with her. He hadn't given her a single compliment, or noticed that she wasn't smoking, or even defended himself when she'd attacked. She knew exactly what was going on. He'd grown bored with her because she wasn't smart like Emma, and she wasn't kind like Emma, and she wasn't as interesting as Emma. Now all he wanted to do was get away from her. Well, she wasn't going to let him go. Not until *she* kicked him out!

"We'll have to spend the night here." She sprawled down on the couch, letting her dress slide up as she settled back into the cushions. "I'm too tired to drive back to Wynette tonight."

He spoke in a low, tight voice that was unlike his normal thoughtful tones. "I don't think that's a good idea."

"Of course you don't! Because you're a tight ass who wouldn't know a good time if it bit you."

"Torie . . ."

Furious, she leaped to her feet. "Can't you stand the truth? You're stuffy and boring and—"

"I suggest you be quiet."

"What's the matter? Are you afraid I'll jump you and find out that you're missing a pair of balls?"

"That does it!"

The next thing she knew, she was dangling upside down over his shoulder. "Let me down! What in the hell are you doing?" She punched him in the back.

"I'm taking you upstairs to spank you."

"What!" She was so shocked that she stopped punching him. And then her mood soared. She finally had his attention. "You're kidding."

He wrapped his arm tighter around the thin knit fabric that covered her thighs and began hauling her up the stairs. "How could I be kidding? I have no sense of humor. Remember?"

"Oh, yeah." The upside-down jolting made her dizzy, but, at the same time, she was beginning to feel better than she had all day.

The jolting stopped as he reached the top of the stairs. He hesitated for a moment, then made his way into the nearest bedroom, which happened to be Kenny's. He dropped her in the middle of the bed.

"I'm afraid you've pushed me too far, Victoria."

Finally! She set her teeth in what she hoped looked like a snarl. "You go to hell."

He grabbed her, jerked her toward him, and turned her over his knees. "I realize this will be painful," he said in that stodgy way that he knew pissed her off, "not to mention politically incorrect, but it has to be done."

She snorted. Not in a million years would he go through with this.

"I mean it, Victoria. You'd better brace yourself."

She cocked her head, looked up at him, and said dryly, "Maybe you'd better give me a piece of wood to bite down on for the pain."

He chuckled.

She smiled to herself.

Then he smacked the flat of his hand down on her butt.

She was so surprised that she nearly spoiled the whole thing by rolling off his lap. "Ow! That hurt."

"I apologize." He smacked her again.

She winced, then thought about biting him in the calf or simply pushing herself away, but she was too curious to see what was going to happen next. And she also felt this warm little wriggle of . . . something . . . that wasn't entirely unpleasant. Imagine Dexter O'Conner, the biggest dweeb in Wynette, Texas, having the nerve to do something like this.

Another smack.

It didn't feel good, but it didn't exactly hurt either, and, in a perverse way, it was nice to have finally riled him so much. "You brute," she managed.

"Believe me, this is hurting you a lot more than it's hurting me."

She grimaced, then braced herself for his next smack. Instead, his open hand came to rest on her butt, and she had the distinct impression he was copping a feel.

"Whatcha doin' back there, Dex?"

He snatched his hand away and cleared his throat, but he still sounded a little hoarse. "Have you learned your lesson?"

"Uhmm."

"Well? Have you?"

"I wonder if Kenny knows he's got a dust bunny under his bed."

He smacked her, then sighed. "*Now* have you learned your lesson?"

"I can't believe you're wearing brown socks with blue pants."

A long silence. Finally, "This isn't working, is it?"

"Maybe we should try it naked and see if that improves things."

She tensed, waiting for him to get all stodgy and let her go. But he surprised her again by giving a resigned sigh. "An excellent idea."

A thrill shot through her as he tugged up her long skirt and flipped it over her head. His palm settled over her bare bottom, and she shivered.

She waited in anticipation, but his hand didn't move.

"Torie . . . your panties . . ."

"Yes?"

"Where are they?"

"Look for a tiny little strap of flesh-colored silk."

"I don't see any—Oh, there it is." His voice had developed a rasp. "Kind of wedged down between . . ."

"I'm sure a more experienced man would have found it right away."

"I have plenty of experience. I'm just used to seeing panties from the front." He paused. "This is nice, though."

"Glad you approve." She smiled to herself. "Dex?"

"Uh-huh?"

"The blood's starting to pool in my head. Do you think you could get on with it?" She shifted her elbow on the carpet to make her position more comfortable, and, as she moved, discovered she was resting on a lumpy surface. One very large lump in particular.

Once again, he cleared his throat. "Get on with it? Oh, uh—yes. Sure."

His open palm connected with her bottom, but his heart wasn't in it, and it didn't even sting. Then he began stroking. As if he were caressing silk.

It felt good—wonderful, in fact—but her awkward position kept her from enjoying it as much as she wished. "I think I'm pretty sure I've learned my lesson now. Do you suppose I could get up?"

"Well . . . yes, I—I don't see any reason to embarrass you further." He traced another delicious curve over her bottom.

She let her eyes drift shut as he doodled. It felt so good that it took her a while to remember she had an agenda. Mustering herself, she straightened, then turned and sank back on the bed, not making the slightest effort to push her dress down. The strap of flesh-colored lace that covered her in the front wasn't wide enough to be really significant. She slipped the very tips of her fingers beneath it and gazed up at him. Then she licked her lips like a cheap porno queen.

He paled. Was that a film of perspiration on his forehead? Poor baby. She stroked herself again. Her antics might be a little skanky, but they sure were effective. Still, as she looked up at him with half-lidded eyes, she tried to prepare herself for disappointment. Dex was an egghead, not a stallion, and he was bound to be a dud. Even so, she'd come here to settle things with him, and nothing would do that more effectively than bad sex.

He stood, and his hands went to the buttons on the cuffs of his oxford shirt. A thrill of victory shot through her as he began unfastening them.

He, however, looked displeased. "You do understand that I'm philosophically opposed to the two of us having premarital intercourse."

His eyes were glued on her fingers as she toyed with her lacy thong. She shifted one knee a bit to improve his view. "You've made your opinion on the subject real clear."

He began opening the front of his shirt. "Unfortunately, a weakness in my character is making it impossible for me to continue standing by my principles."

"That must be real painful for you."

"You have no idea."

She couldn't repress a grin.

His shirt dropped to the floor, and then one eyebrow arched in amusement. "You're having the time of your life, aren't you?"

She grinned, let a hand drift to her breast, and, like a male sexual fantasy come to life, caressed herself through the dress.

His earlobes turned red. Then he set his jaw in a stubborn line and crossed his arms over a lean, but nicely formed, chest. "If we have intercourse, we're getting married."

"Will you stop calling it intercourse! It's f—"

"Torie . . ." His voice sounded a low, warning note. "Until we're both naked, you'll watch your language."

Abandoning her porn queen routine, she threw her arms over her head and groaned. "You are such a geek!"

"Exactly. And don't you forget it." He set his knee on the bed, cupped her inner thigh, and then stretched out beside her. For the first time, she noticed little golden lights dancing in his eyes, as if he possessed some secret knowledge that had escaped her. She began to feel uneasy. His fingertips brushed the soft skin of her thigh.

"If, at any time, my size bothers you, please say something at once."

Her eyes popped open.

He smiled.

She swallowed. "When you say *size*, Dex, you're talking about your height, right? I mean, you're a tall man, and . . ."

"No, Victoria. That's not what I'm talking about."

"Oh." Just like that, she lost the upper hand. She tried to think how to get it back, but his gentle caresses were screwing up her brain waves.

"I'm going to kiss you now."

She glowered at him. "Jeez, are you going to announce every damn thing you're—"

"I want to avoid miscommunication."

She thought about slugging him, but then his lips settled over her own.

Mmm . . . Dex did kiss nice. Her days of nicotine deprivation no longer felt like such a sacrifice as he managed to find that perfect point between dry and sloppy, with his tongue giving a delicious hint of things to come. She decided she could kiss Dexter O'Conner for hours.

And then she realized that he'd let her. Unlike her ex-husbands, Dex was a man who appreciated process, not just results, and he didn't appear to be in any hurry to get to the main event. He stroked the inside of her mouth and let their tongues play. It was soft, sweet, and thrilling. She ran her hands over his back, his hips, appreciating the textures of him, the clean, honest scent. For the first time in her life, she felt as if she were making love with a man instead of a series of boys. Her eyes teared.

He sensed the change in her mood and drew back slightly. But instead of asking her a lot of stupid Dex-questions, he simply kissed her eyelids, then returned to her mouth.

That made the tears pour in earnest.

He drew back again. Through a haze, she saw the concern reflected in his serious, thoughtful face. "Do you need some time?"

She shook her head.

He took her at her word. He kissed her eyelids again, sipping up the moisture, then returned to her mouth. Her arms wrapped themselves around him, and she no longer felt like crying. This was too sweet to spoil with tears.

Once again, he seemed to sense her change of mood, and once again, he drew back and whispered to her. "I'm going to touch you now. Not inside your panties. Just outside."

She felt herself nod.

He traced the little strap of moist lace between her legs. Up and down. Rubbing. Stroking. Thrilling her beyond belief.

It went on and on until she could barely stand it. Then his lips met her earlobe. "I have to take off your dress. I need to see you."

And she wanted to show him. Oh, yes . . .

He removed her dress with an uncharacteristic clumsiness. Then he touched the clasp on her bra. "After I take this off, I'm kissing your breasts."

Was he going to broadcast every move? "You don't have to ask for permission."

"Oh, I'm not." He pushed aside the cups of her bra and gazed down at her. "Just giving you a chance to prepare yourself."

Then he set about making her feel as if her breasts were the most precious objects on earth. He studied them, kissed, tweaked, suckled, and studied them again. "I think," he said, "it's time for me to take off your panties."

"I think," she said, "it's time for me to take off yours."

He gazed down at her, took another nibble. "All right."

She shot to her knees, and her fingers flew to the fastener at his fly. But before she could open it, he stilled her hand with his own. "Just remember what I said about getting married."

"Yeah, yeah." She brushed his fingers away and pulled on the tab. A moment later, she was nearly speechless.

"Don't worry," he said. "We'll take our time."

Her mouth felt dry as she stared down at him. "I'm not exactly worried. Astonished is more like it."

He chuckled, then shed the rest of his clothes. She tossed aside her dress and bra until the only thing left between them was a flesh-colored thong. He slipped his thumb beneath it and pulled it off. "Lay back in the pillows, sweetheart. I'm going to love you."

A sigh slipped through her lips. She couldn't ever remember feeling so safe.

As the minutes ticked by, she discovered new things about Dex. He liked to inspect everything. Thoroughly. To evaluate, measure, and caress. And his curiosity seemed just about insatiable.

She also discovered he had amazing powers of concentration, that he wasn't the slightest bit fastidious, and that he didn't grow bored easily. A less pleasant discovery was the pleasure he took in making a woman beg.

"Please, Dex . . . no more. Oh, please . . ."

"Soon, sweetheart. Soon."

When he finally worked himself inside her—announcing his intentions first in language that was thrillingly graphic—she discovered that they fit together just fine. His last announcement, however, was the one that sent her over the moon.

"I'm going to come inside you."

Moments later, she discovered that Dex was a man of his word.

Chapter 21

Kenny couldn't believe he'd fallen asleep, but one minute Emma was yapping at him, and the next thing he knew, the wheels were bouncing against the tarmac as the plane set down in Vegas. The fact that he hadn't made it into bed the night before must be why he'd slept so peacefully.

And then he remembered. He was on his way to get married to the bossiest woman he'd ever met. He groaned.

Her forehead scrunched as she looked over at him, and he watched her mouth begin to open.

"Not one word." He closed his eyes.

She made this huffy sound, but she didn't say anything.

As soon as they were off the plane, he steered her past all the slot machines that were a staple at the Vegas airport and toward the Avis counter. It was nearly midnight, but it didn't take long before he had a car and they were on their way into town.

That's when she started talking again, and nothing he said would hold her off.

"... certain we can work this out. ... And once Dallie learns the truth. ... then I can catch a morning flight to London ... no reason on earth for us to get ..." On and on she went, and, as she spoke, gusts from the car's air conditioner sent wisps of butterscotch curl flying around her head. A tendril came to rest on the tip of that small, sweet nose. She brushed it aside, her mouth still moving. "... the whole idea is absurd ... difficult for me to understand ... and the notion you have about rescuing me ..."

He'd been heading for a hotel along the Strip, but, instead, he whipped into the driveway of a pink-and-white-stucco wedding chapel where a red neon bell flickered back and forth in the front window. He pulled into one of four parking places, then turned off the ignition. There was a small flower garden near the walk, guarded by a chipped plaster elf.

"Kenny!"

He couldn't stand to listen to any more talking about things he had no answers for, so he dragged her into his arms and smothered her mouth with his own. As their kiss caught fire, it occurred to him that this whole situation might turn out all right if they spent most of their time like this, but, try as he might, he couldn't convince himself it would be that easy.

A bony, middle-aged woman with spiked blond hair and red glasses met them at the door. Not long after, they were standing inside a white lattice arbor covered with dusty silk roses and getting ready to speak their vows. He hadn't thought about Emma's wedding ring, but it was a full-service chapel and, for an additional fee, he was provided with one.

Lady E looked like she was going to cry again. "Kenny, I really don't think—"

He kissed the rest of what she wanted to say right out of her, and the ceremony began. As the woman in the red glasses started in on the Dearly Beloveds, he began to feel as if he were standing outside himself looking on—horrified at what he was doing, but helpless to stop it. And Emma's small, uncertain responses didn't sound anything like her normal storm-the-barricades speech. He squeezed her hand to give her confidence, or maybe to steal some for himself. *What in the hell did he think he was doing?*

By the time they got back in the car, they were both shaking. "That was awful." Emma shuddered.

"It's over. We don't ever have to think about it again."

"We can get a divorce. If it's this easy to get married, it has to be just as easy to get a divorce."

"We'd need to fly to Mexico, and I'm too tired." He started the car.

"This can't be a legal marriage. It was too tawdry."

"The state of Nevada doesn't care about good taste. Just out of curiosity—That thing Torie mentioned . . . do I get to be Lord Kenny now?"

"You do not! Of all the absurd notions—" She stopped as she realized he was teasing.

He went on because, if he didn't, he knew she'd start in again. "The way I see it, you've got two choices. You can either keep your last name or you can use mine, but you're damn well not going to string them all together. Nobody will ever take you seriously if you go around calling yourself Lady Emma Wells-Finch Traveler. At least not in Texas. Am I making myself clear about that?'' He watched her glance down at her new gold wedding band.

"Perfectly.'' As Emma twisted the ring, she wondered if her finger would turn green by tomorrow. She looked over at Kenny's hand and wished she'd thought to buy him a ring, but it hadn't occurred to her.

She'd spoken those vows of her own free will—he hadn't forced them out of her—so why had she done it? Because she owed him, and restoring his reputation was the least she could do. But she couldn't see how getting married was going to accomplish that. It would have been much more effective to simply have called Dallie and explained, except that every time she'd mentioned it, Kenny exploded.

She was lying to herself. The truth was, she hadn't wanted to say no, even though she knew it was wrong. The garish lights of the Strip splashed over the car, and shame at her own weakness overwhelmed her. She tried to distract herself by thinking of other things—how a stranger would be going through her possessions in the cottage and packing them up, Penelope's reaction when she learned she was St. Gert's new headmistress, Hugh's spitefulness.

As she thought about Hugh, she once again experienced the sense that she'd missed something in his hotel room this morning. What was it he'd said? It had slipped by her at the time, but . . .

She shrugged off her uneasiness. She had enough real problems to worry about without creating imaginary ones. For example, what were the odds of ever seeing her luggage again? "I don't have any clothes.''

"That's not exactly a disadvantage from my point of view.''

"You don't have any either.''

"That's why God invented credit cards.''

"I'm not taking your money.''

"Our money. It's all going into one big pool now, so get ready to open up your bank accounts and turn over all those pounds you've got tucked away.''

"There aren't that many,'' she said glumly.

The corner of his mouth curled. "We'll work it out.''

Half an hour later she was standing under the shower in the spacious marbled bathroom of their hotel suite. The door slid open behind her and two suntanned arms encircled her waist. She leaned her head back against his chest. "Oh, Kenny, we should never have done this.''

"I don't see what the big damn deal is, especially since you already told me you loved me.''

"Marriage bloody well is a big damn deal!''

"Don't cuss. Profanity just isn't effective with a British accent.'' He nuzzled her ear. "Even if you all of a sudden let loose with the Big One, it'd still sound like something you could say from the pulpit."

She sighed. What was she going to do with him?

"Wash my back, will you?"

She soaped the washcloth, slipped behind him, and began stroking it over his shoulders. Slowly, she moved lower, to his waist, his buttocks, his thighs. "You have to be faithful," she said. "As long as we're married, you have to be faithful."

He took the soap from her and replied softly, "I'm not the one who tried to buy herself a gigolo."

"Still . . ."

He dipped his head and kissed her. She kissed him back—loved the feel of his mouth, loved the slide of his tongue, the scratch of his whiskers—but, even so, her kiss turned into a yawn.

He drew back. "I think this'd better wait until you've had a good night's sleep."

"Rubbish." She could see what his consideration was costing him, and she mustered herself. "The only reason I yawned was that I didn't sleep much last night either, and it's late, and—Go ahead. Really. It's fine."

He lifted one eyebrow, turned her around, and began washing her in an impersonal fashion, as if he were taking care not to arouse either one of them. But it definitely wasn't working for him, and as his finger accidentally brushed one of her nipples, she realized it wasn't working for her either. She rubbed her soapy back against his front.

"Emma . . ." His voice held a husky, warning note.

She pulled his head under the shower and kissed him.

He took her right there in the shower, holding her against the wall, her thighs locked around his waist. Afterward, as they lay in bed together, their bodies were so closely entwined it was hard to decide where one of them began and the other left off. But as exhausted as she was, she didn't fall asleep immediately.

As she listened to the deep sound of his breathing, she tried to absorb the fact that this man was her husband. She knew she loved him, and she certainly desired him, but that travesty of a marriage ceremony had given her no real connection to him. Where was the feeling of attachment she'd been searching for all her life? Despite Kenny's ardent lovemaking and apparent fondness for her, he didn't truly love her, and pretending anything else was too self-indulgent to even contemplate. Her relationship with him felt as transitory as those temporary bonds she'd had with teachers and friends, as fragile as her relationship with parents who were all too eager to forget they had a daughter.

If only she had some idea what he was truly feeling, it might be easier, but he remained as closed off from her as a locked door.

The next morning she awakened to the sound of him speaking quietly on the telephone in the suite's adjoining living room. "I'm not going to talk about it, Shelby. And I'm not telling you where we're staying, either. Now come on. Just put him on the phone."

There was a pause before Kenny spoke again. This time his voice was pitched higher. "Hey, Petie. It's Kenny. Listen, buddy, I didn't mean to disappear on you. I'll be back soon, and we'll go swimming, okay? Swimming. You and me."

Emma smiled to herself. This was the side of Kenny she loved the most.

Another pause, then his pitch deepened, so she knew Shelby had come back on. "If you know which hotel we're in, you'll somehow let it slip, and then the press'll be all over me." Another pause, then he said dryly, "Yeah, it was a real romantic ceremony. Uh-huh. I'll tell her."

He appeared in the doorway, his hair still rumpled and his stubble approaching the pirate stage. "Shelby says hi."

Knowing Shelby, Emma imagined the message was much longer than that, but she didn't question him.

They spent the next few hours in bed with Kenny directing the action, as always, but being so sublimely attentive to her needs that she couldn't complain. Finally, they wrapped themselves in hotel bathrobes and ate a room service breakfast. Several times she tried to get him to talk about the enormity of what they'd done, but he shrugged it off as if they'd committed themselves to nothing more complex than a Saturday night date. Sex seemed to be the only connection he wanted to have with her, and the knot in her stomach grew tighter.

After they'd finished eating, they went out to buy a change of clothes for each of them. Kenny tried to disguise himself in a pair of trendy sunglasses and his Dean Witter cap, but several people in the store still recognized him and wanted to talk about what had happened. He dismissed their questions by acting as if he didn't understand them.

Eventually, they found some anonymity by mingling with the tourists walking along the Strip. Although Emma'd seen photographs of Las Vegas, the reality of this resort built in the desert was far different. She found it fascinating from an anthropological standpoint, but not exactly to her taste, and Kenny seemed to read her mind. "Come on. I'll show you a place I know you'll like."

"Where?"

"You'll see."

Less than an hour later, they were looking out over Hoover Dam. The sheer size of the structure took her breath away.

"I know you have lots of cool castles and awesome cathedrals and things like that back in England," he said. "Not to mention some great golf courses. But you've got to admit this really kicks ass."

His boyish enthusiasm made her laugh. "It certainly does."

He gave her a squeeze, then gently brushed a tendril from her cheek. She wondered if the tender expression on his face was a trick of the light.

"Sweetheart, I know you're itching to sit down and analyze this thing to death. Make a big list, fill out a whole bunch of *Cosmo* compatability quizzes, discuss short-term objectives and long-term goals, and who knows what else. But could you just let it go for now? Could we take it easy? Have a good time and see how things work out?"

As she gazed up into those marsh violet eyes with their fringe of spiky black lashes, she reminded herself that this was a man who'd made laziness his life's goal. Or at least the appearance of laziness. Kenny didn't want anyone ever to know he worked hard at anything. And apparently he had no intention of working hard at this. Or did he? In so many ways, he was still a mystery to her. She didn't believe life's important issues could simply be ignored, but she also knew she couldn't make him talk about it. What he was asking was wrong, but this might be the only way he knew to cope.

And maybe she didn't want to talk about it, either. The notion startled her. She was a person who'd always confronted problems head-on, but did she really want to hear him spell out the fact that he liked her, but didn't love her? Did she really want to hear him say that he had no intention of taking this marriage seriously, that he'd been upset and sleep-deprived when he'd gone into it, and that he regretted the whole thing?

She was ashamed of her cowardice, and she gazed across Lake Mead toward a pair of sailboats. "All right, Kenny. Just for now."

He smiled down at her. "Have I ever told you that you're one terrific lady?"

"No. Just that I'm bossy."

"One thing doesn't necessarily cancel out the other."

"You're mad, do you know that? A complete madman." As she smiled at him, her own words triggered a fragment of memory from the morning before, and she heard Hugh's voice exactly the way it had sounded when she'd marched into his hotel room.

He's a madman! If I'd known he was insane when I spoke with him that first time . . .

A funny prickling ran along her arms. This was what had been bothering her yesterday. What had Hugh meant when he'd said that? The *first time* implied there had been other times. But as far Emma knew, the men had only met once, in Shelby and Warren Traveler's living room. Still, why would Hugh have said something like that if they'd only met once? Why would he have—

She let out an audible gasp as it all became clear to her.

"You bastard!"

"Wh—"

She slammed her purse into his thigh. Anger swirled around her and she found herself running. But there was nowhere to go, and this time she couldn't commandeer his car since the keys were tucked safely in his pocket.

She raced blindly toward a Gray Line tour bus and pounded on the door to awaken the driver who snoozed at the wheel. "Let me in!"

"Emma! For Pete's sake, what—"

The driver swung open the door, and she rushed up the steps. "Shut the door immediately. And whatever you do, don't let that man in—"

Kenny stepped into the bus. "We've been having trouble getting my wife's medication adjusted ever since her brain transplant. I'll take care of her."

"Stay away from me!"

"Honey . . ."

She rounded on him in the aisle. "Liar!"

"Now, Emma . . ."

"You weasel!"

"I'm not a—"

"*Blackguard!*"

He blinked. "Now, there's a new one."

"Don't try to be clever! Driver, throw this man off the bus!"

The driver—short, balding, sixty if he was a day—blanched. Emma was so furious she could barely contain herself. Why hadn't she been born tall and muscular and male?

"Don't you think we should talk about this?" He advanced on her down the aisle. "Whatever it is?"

"Now you want to talk." Suddenly, her knees would no longer support her, and she sank into one of the cushioned seats. "How could you have done it? How could you have betrayed me like this?"

His face grew stony as he stopped beside her. "I don't betray my friends."

Not only was that blatantly untrue, but hurtful as well. Was that how he regarded her? As just another one of his friends? "I know what you did. The moment Hugh said it, I should have realized what he meant, but I was too distracted by everything that had happened to pay attention.'' As she gazed up at him, she was filled with outrage. ''You were Hugh's spy.''

He took a deep breath, then sat in the seat across the aisle. She waited for him to deny it—wanted him to—but he didn't. ''Somebody had to watch out for you.''

She felt as if she'd been ripped open. ''*I* was watching out for me! I didn't need you to do it.''

''Now, there's a lie!'' He sprang back up again. ''Of course I fed him information. I sure wasn't going to let him find out that you were buying lice shampoo and kissing your escort in the middle of town, not to mention getting tattooed.''

''I *wanted* him to find that out.'' She jumped to her feet, too.

''Well, now, that just goes to prove my point.''

A new thought struck her. ''My tattoo! Of course it's fading. It's not permanent, is it?'' She shoved up the sleeve of her T-shirt and looked at the tattoo with fresh eyes. Sure enough, it was fading. ''You—God!'' She jerked down her sleeve. ''You must have put something in my margarita. I wasn't drunk! I was drugged! And the tattoo wasn't done with needles. It's some kind of dye.''

He splayed one hand on the back of the seat in front of him and leaned in to her. ''Don't you dare tell me you're upset that you won't have to spend the rest of your life with my name tattooed across your arm! If I don't hear a thank-you in the next thirty seconds, we're going to have a serious argument.''

Her skin was burning. ''You drugged me!''

''Some knockout drops I got from one of my acquaintances in the medical profession. And the wife of an old friend did the artwork. She has a background in textile design.'' He acted as if that made it all right, as if the details somehow mitigated the depth of his duplicity.

''What else have you done that I don't know about?''

''Not enough, that's for damned sure, or we wouldn't have been forced to get married!''

She froze.

His voice softened. ''Your plan was crazy from the start; you know that. And since I was supposed to be looking out for you, I felt responsible. All I wanted to do was make sure you still had a job when you got home.''

''Well, that didn't work out, did it?'' she managed.

''I'm not the one who French kissed Torie in the middle of the damn parking lot!''

"I didn't French kiss her!"

"Close enough." He took a deep breath. "Will you just let your brain work here for a minute instead of your emotions?" He pushed her back down, then once again took the seat across from her, sitting on the edge, so his long legs blocked the aisle. She felt the full voltage of those violet eyes. "I tried to get you to listen to reason from the very beginning, but you wouldn't do it, and I couldn't just stand by and watch you throw your whole career away over some idiot who wouldn't take *no* for an answer."

"It wasn't your decision."

He ignored her. "The day you told me about Hugh, something clicked in my mind. I remembered my father mentioning to Shelby that he was a big investor in TCS. After that, it was easy to get his phone number. I called and told him somebody needed to watch out for you, and after he huffed and puffed for a while, he let it slip that he'd already hired a Dallas PI to do the job. I told him that his PI wasn't watching you nearly close enough, but that I'd volunteer for the job out of respect for his long relationship with TCS. He took me up on my offer, and that was pretty much it."

She regarded him stonily. "Hugh acted as if he didn't know you when you were introduced."

"He's arrogant, not stupid. I'm sure he realized you wouldn't be too happy to learn that he'd set a spy on you. And it's not like we were old school chums. We only talked once. After that, I gave my reports to his flunky."

"Now I know why you rushed me into getting married," she said bitterly. "You did it out of guilt."

"How do you figure that? I don't have a damn thing to feel guilty about."

Once again, she sprang to her feet. "You lied to me!"

He shot up, too. "I never lied. I just didn't tell you everything."

"Are you people about done back there?" the bus driver called out. "My tour group's on its way."

"We're done," she said firmly. And then she looked Kenny straight in the eye, so he wouldn't mistake her meaning. "We're absolutely done."

"Don't you say that!" To her astonishment, he grabbed her arm and pulled her tight against him. "I never figured you for a quitter. Where's all that British stiff upper lip bull? First little bit of trouble on the horizon, and you're ready to give up."

"This is more than a little bit of trouble. I don't know you at all."

"You're going to give up, aren't you? You're going to walk away."

"I just need some time to think."

"There's a guarantee of trouble."

"Don't you dare be condescending. I can't play by your rules, Kenny. I'm not made that way. I can't take things as they come and see what happens. I need time to adjust and think things through."

It was a long, silent drive back to the hotel.

Chapter 22

On the plane, Kenny buried himself in a book he'd bought at the airport gift shop, and Emma pretended to read a magazine. They barely spoke, but this time she didn't challenge his silence because she had nothing more to say to him.

She was so ashamed of herself. How could she have agreed to this travesty of a marriage when she'd known there was nothing between them except sex? There was no honesty, no understanding, no real commitment. Yet she'd married him anyway, just like a dotty, dear thing making a desperate, last-minute lunge for the brass ring.

As they arrived in Dallas and made their way down the concourse, Kenny had never moved more slowly nor looked more unapproachable. Not even the fans who recognized him seemed to want to come any closer. It wasn't until they'd reclaimed her luggage that he finally looked fully at her.

"What's it going to be?" he said stonily. "Are you running back to England like a scared rabbit, or are you going to stay here and fight?"

She'd been thinking of nothing else since they'd left Hoover Dam, and she'd already made up her mind what she was going to do. "This isn't a war."

His eyes were as cold as frozen amethysts. "Let's just say it's a test of character, then. Who has it and who doesn't."

"Are you implying that I'm lacking in character?"

"I don't know yet. Are you running or are you staying?"

His attitude infuriated her. "Oh, I'm going back to Wynette, all right. I've already made up my mind about that."

A flicker of satisfaction passed over his features. "You're finally making sense."

"Unlike you, I know this isn't a game, and I'm going back so we can sort this out. But I'm not staying at the ranch."

"What do you mean?"

"I mean that I'm not running, but I'm not moving back in with you either."

"That doesn't even half make sense! You were living at the ranch before we got married, so why would you move out now?"

"Stop looking so outraged. This isn't a real marriage, and you know it."

"It's as real as it gets, and I've got the license to prove it."

"Stop it, Kenny. Just stop. You know exactly what I mean, so don't try to hide behind that righteous indignation."

"I don't have a clue what you mean." He picked up her suitcases and stalked toward the parking garage.

She didn't even try to keep up with him. She was going to attempt to live up to her responsibility because that was the way she was made, but she wouldn't go scurrying after him.

When she finally got into the car, the radio was blasting. He glared at her and began pulling out of the parking space. As she fastened her seat belt, the sports report came on.

No official word yet from PGA commissioner Dallas Beaudine concerning golfer Kenny Traveler's latest brush with—

He punched another button and turned the volume up. He needn't have bothered because she had no intention of bringing up the subject of their marriage right now. The next move was his.

The trip to Wynette seemed to take forever. Although they'd both ignored the airline food, neither of them felt like eating, so they only stopped for gas. Just before dusk, Torie called from Wynette to find out what time they'd be getting in. She also told Kenny that she'd spent the night at his condo, and Emma found herself wondering whether Dexter had been with her, although that possibility didn't seem to occur to Kenny.

The miles crawled by, and finally they reached the northern edge of Wynette. "Would you drop me off at the hotel, please?" Even as she was saying it, she wondered why she'd wasted her breath because she knew exactly how he'd respond.

"If you're going to run away from home, you'll have to do it on your own. I'm not going to help you."

She was too tired to argue with him. Tomorrow was soon enough. She leaned back in the seat, closed her eyes, and didn't open them again until they reached the ranch.

They entered the house from the garage. Kenny moved ahead with her suitcases, then set them down to unlock the door. He held it open for her and she stepped inside.

One moment the kitchen was dark, and the next it blazed with light.

"Surprise!"

"Surprise! Surprise!"

"Here comes the bride . . ."

Emma gazed at all the bright, cheery faces that filled the kitchen and realized that her miserable day had just taken a turn for the worse.

"Time to cut the cake!" Patrick called out after the toasts had been delivered and guests introduced.

Kenny and Emma moved from opposite sides of the room toward the confection Patrick had created, a creamy vanilla tower with two of Peter's Fisher-Price figures perched on top, along with paper flags of the bride's and groom's respective countries. Emma wondered if anyone had noticed that the bride and groom in question had been talking to everyone except each other.

Her head ached, and she wanted nothing so much as to curl up and go to sleep. She gazed enviously at Peter, who had fallen asleep on Kenny's shoulder, leaving a drool mark on the collar of his golf shirt.

In addition to the Traveler family and Dexter, Ted Beaudine was present, along with Father Joseph, a few executives from TCS, and a score of Kenny's friends from the Roustabout who'd been entertaining each other with more stories of Kenny's misbegotten childhood: how he'd stolen one woman's science project, thrown someone's best pair of sneakers onto a power line, lost someone else's little brother.

She pushed aside the protective instincts that their gleeful stories of Kenny's headlong rush toward self-destruction always aroused in her. He was a grown man, and if he didn't choose to defend himself, it was no concern of hers.

She moved toward the cake from one side of the room, while Kenny approached from the other. As Warren came forward and took Peter, he smiled fondly at Emma. "If I haven't said it before, welcome to the family, Lady Emma. I couldn't have found a better woman for Kenny if I'd picked her out myself." He regarded his son with that overly eager look that broke her heart. "Congratulations, son. I'm proud of you."

Kenny barely acknowledged his words as he positioned himself in front of the cake. Her heart ached for both of them: the father who wanted to make up for old sins, and the son who couldn't forgive a childhood of neglect.

Patrick handed Emma the cake cutter, which he'd decorated with red, white, and blue ribbons. "More patriotic than bridal," he sniffed, "but I didn't have much warning."

She smiled at him, then looked down as Kenny's hand settled over hers, that broad, tan palm sheltering her own smaller, whiter one, those strong, elegant fingers curling around hers. The sight of their joined hands made her eyes sting. If only their hearts were as tightly linked.

Kenny took a sip of wine, then moved across the kitchen to turn off a light that had been left burning on the sunporch. Lady E had fled upstairs the minute the last of the guests had left, and he knew it wasn't because she was in a hurry to hop into his bed. No, Lady E was holed up by herself tonight. He wondered if she'd go so far as to lock her door, but then he knew she wouldn't. She'd rely on his honor instead to keep him away.

His honor. To the public, it was badly tattered, but nothing could make him regret what he'd done to Hugh Holroyd.

He stepped out onto the sunporch, then saw too late that he wasn't alone. His father sat on the couch with Petie curled up asleep in his arms. He felt himself stiffen as he always did when he was with his father. "I thought you'd left."

"I sent Shelby back with Torie. I wanted to talk to you alone."

Warren was the last person Kenny wanted to talk to tonight, or any night for that matter. "In case you haven't notice, I'm on my honeymoon."

"From what I saw tonight, it doesn't look like much of a honeymoon. Lady Emma was barely speaking to you." Petie made a little mewing sound in his sleep, and Warren cuddled him closer.

Had his father ever held him like that? He was startled to feel a stab of jealousy. It made him ashamed, and then something inside him relaxed. Emma was right. Warren had learned from the past, and all the worries Kenny'd been having about his little brother were groundless. Petie wasn't going to have to earn their father's love.

"Petie should be in bed," he said gruffly.

"He will be soon." Warren pressed a kiss to the top of the baby's head. "He was so comfortable, I didn't want to disturb him."

Once again, that queer, painful stab. Petie was being given his father's love as a birthright. Torie had received the same thing. Only Kenny'd had to earn it—one tournament at a time.

Now his father wanted to pretend that everything was fine between them. But it wasn't fine. Kenny had needed a father when he was a kid; he sure as hell didn't need one now.

"I'm concerned about you and Lady Emma."

"Her name's Emma. She doesn't use her title. And there's nothing to be concerned about."

Warren stroked Petie's back and gazed out the sunporch windows toward the dark pecan grove. "I'm not much of a praying man. I can't do it right—just doesn't come naturally to me—so I leave it up to other people. Like Shelby. Now, she's a real good prayer, and she says Emma's the answer to her prayers for you."

"I didn't ask Shelby to pray for me."

"No, you didn't. I asked her."

"If she's so good at praying, put her to work getting me back on the tour." Kenny tossed back the remaining contents of his wine glass and turned toward the kitchen, but his father's voice stopped him.

"Come back here and sit down."

"It's late. I'm tired."

"I said, *sit down.*"

It was the nightmare voice from his childhood: "*Set your butt right down on that chair. You're a damn disgrace! You know that, don't you? A spoiled little brat . . .*"

But Kenny wasn't a kid anymore, and if Warren wanted a showdown, then by damn they were going to have one. He set his wine glass on the table, leaned against the doorjamb, and stared insolently across the sunporch at his father. "You got something on your mind, just come out and say it."

"All right." Warren had to look up at him, but it didn't seem to bother him as much as Kenny wanted it to. "I know you don't think much of me, and it's no mystery why. I wasn't there for you when you needed me, and you're not going to forgive that. But you're still my son, and I can't stand by and watch you screw up the most important thing in your life because you're still fighting all those things that happened to you when you were too young to defend yourself."

Kenny's lips felt stiff. "I don't have any idea what you're talking about."

"I'm talking about the way your past keeps affecting your future. I like Lady Emma. We all do. And when the two of you are in a room together, you don't seem to be able to take your eyes off each other. You've never been like that with any other woman."

He wasn't going to explain that his marriage to Emma was more an accident than a lifelong commitment. Instead, he stared belligerently at his father. "I married her, didn't I?"

"Yeah, you married her. But it's plain that the two of you still have a lot of problems to work out."

"Whether we do or not isn't any of your damn business."

"Listen to me, Kenny. For just once in your life, listen. I've never been happier about anything than I am with the way you've made something of yourself, even though I know Dallie Beaudine deserves the credit rather than me. More than anybody on the face of this earth, including your sister, I understand exactly what you've had to overcome to get where you are. And I'll tell you this: There aren't many people who could have done it."

For a moment a flash of gratitude shot through him, but the praise had come too late. "Get to the point," he snapped.

"What I'm trying to say is . . . as I get older, all the things I've done to make money have become less important in my life. I'm proud of the company. I built it up from nothing, and I'm sure as hell not going to stand by and watch it get eaten up. But when I'm sitting out on the patio on a Sunday afternoon, and I start counting my blessings, it's the people I love that come to my mind, not the company."

Kenny didn't want to hear this. "You sound like a fucking Hallmark card."

But his father refused to retreat. "You've got a chance to have a real life for yourself, one that doesn't start and end on the golf course. You've got a chance to build a relationship with a good woman, to have children, and ride your horses, and enjoy this ranch. Don't screw it up."

Fury at Warren's hypocrisy boiled inside him. "Maybe you'd better think twice about that advice you're handing out. If I start taking time to smell the roses, I won't be able to win so many golf tournaments. And then you won't have anything to brag about at all your corporate cocktail parties."

Warren didn't flinch from the attack, which made Kenny feel small and mean. Instead, he nestled his palm around Petie's head and rose to his feet. "It's all right, son. I understand. I've gotten used to feeling guilty where you're concerned, and you don't have to forgive me."

Petie stirred and tried to drag his eyes open. They drooped shut again as Warren snuggled him closer. "You're a good man, Kenny. And that's thanks to Dallie, not to me. You're decent and smart as a whip; you care about other people. I guess what I'm trying to say is that it's time you accepted what the rest of the world's already figured out—there's a lot more to you than just another rich boy who can play some golf."

He began to move to the door, but Kenny couldn't let him go like that. It felt too much as if his father'd had the last word. "You'd better not pull any bullshit with Petie," he snarled, "or you're going to answer to me."

His father's expression grew so sad he could barely stand to witness it. "I like to believe I learn from my mistakes, and I plan to do my best with him. Even so, I'm not perfect. But I guess you know that."

He shifted the baby in his arms and disappeared, leaving Kenny with the feeling that he'd left something important undone.

Emma spent a lonely, unhappy night in the guest room. She missed the solid feel of Kenny's body next to hers, the way he hogged the covers when he turned over, and reached out in his sleep for her. As she made her way to the bathroom the next morning, she glanced out the window and saw him swimming laps, but instead of his customary slow crawl, he was churning through the water as if he wanted to conquer it.

She rested her cheek against the window frame and watched him reach one end of the pool and immediately race back toward the other. As he attacked the water, she considered the way everyone would react when they learned this marriage wasn't going to last.

Kenny screwed up again. I always knew it wouldn't work. The only thing he's ever been good at is playing golf.

The legend of lazy, spoiled Kenny Traveler would only grow larger.

She told herself that wasn't her problem, but she felt dismal. She showered and dressed, then headed down to the kitchen. Patrick had left a note on the counter directing her toward a bowl of fresh fruit in the refrigerator. He also suggested she not answer the phone. As she retrieved the fruit, she heard the front door open, then the sound of Torie's voice, with Dexter's quieter response.

Torie sailed in wearing a cropped blue and purple batik-print top and shorts, along with chunky leather sandals. "I guess I should ring the bell now that this isn't bachelor's quarters anymore. Sorry, Lady E."

"That's all right." Emma smiled at Dexter. "Have some coffee."

"Thank you." He moved toward the kitchen, then looked up as Kenny came in from outside. A gray T-shirt clung to his damp chest, and water dripped from the curly ends of his hair, while his bare feet left damp tracks on the terra-cotta floor.

"Hey, bubba."

Kenny managed a smile for his sister, then spotted Dexter and glowered. "What are you doing here?"

"I invited him."

Kenny gave his sister a dark look. "Why'd you do that? I thought you wanted to get rid of him."

"Yeah, well, it's a lot harder than I figured."

He frowned, then looked at her more closely. In three strides, he crossed the room, shot out his hand, and cupped her chin to tilt it toward the light. "Did he do that? Did he put that sucker bite on you?"

"He might have." She shrugged off his hand. "By the way, you must have had about fifty messages yesterday on the answering machine at your condo. Everybody in the world is trying to get hold of you. Your fight with Hugh's got you on the front page of the sports section all over again."

Kenny whipped off the towel draped around his neck and spun on Dex. "You got her drunk, didn't you? Last night. You weren't having any luck seducing her when she was sober, so you got her drunk."

Torie sank back on a counter stool and smiled. "He did worse than that. A lot worse. Didn't you, Dex?"

Emma felt a prickle of alarm as Kenny grew very still. He dropped the towel, and the muscles beneath his damp gray T-shirt tensed. "What are you talking about? What did he do?"

Her eyes sparkled. "He beat me."

"He what?"

Emma immediately stepped between the two men and rested her hand on Kenny's chest. "Your sister is deliberately baiting you. Torie, stop it at once."

Torie tried to look cowed. "Yes, ma'am."

Kenny turned to Dex, his expression threatening. "Maybe you'd better tell me exactly what you did."

Dexter filled the mug Emma had given him with coffee. "Torie's a much bigger threat to herself than I am."

But Torie wasn't done having her fun. She hooked one heel of her sandal over the rung of the stool and looked injured. "He spanked me, Kenny. He overpowered me, threw me right over his knees, and spanked me. Bare butt. Or closest thing to."

Kenny went completely still. He stared at Dexter. "Is that true?"

Dex stirred a teaspoon of sugar into his coffee and gave an absent-minded nod.

To Emma's astonishment, all the tension seemed to trickle out of Kenny, and, for the first time, he regarded Dexter with interest instead of suspicion. "No kidding. Even I wouldn't have the nerve to do something like that."

His reaction upset Torie. "You should beat him up, Kenny! Although maybe I'd better warn you that he's stronger than he looks. Still, he's not exactly Hercules, and you'll be able to take him without too much trouble."

Dexter sipped from his mug and nodded at Emma. "Excellent coffee."

Emma suppressed a smile. "I'll pass on your compliments to Patrick."

Kenny looked from his sister to Dexter, then walked over to pour a mug for himself. He leaned back against the counter and studied the other man. "So, Dex, how's come you're still alive to tell the tale?"

Dexter wiped up a small coffee spill, then sat on the stool next to Torie. "All I'm prepared to say is that your sister and I slept together, and, since I compromised her, I intend to marry her."

Torie dropped her forehead and banged it three times against the countertop. "You are such a geek."

"Doesn't sound like she's too enthusiastic about it," Kenny said.

"She's enthusiastic." He reached over and stroked her shoulder. "But she has her pride. She's also frightened, which is understandable, although it doesn't make any difference. She and I made a deal, and we're getting married."

"What kind of deal?"

"That's private," Dex said as Torie opened her mouth to respond. He regarded her with amusement. "Victoria, has it occurred to you that you really don't need to reveal our private life to everyone?"

"Kenny's not everyone."

Dex lifted an eyebrow and caressed the corner of her mouth with his thumb.

"Oh, all right," she grumbled. Then, trying to regain lost ground, she turned the conversation. "I couldn't help but notice last night that the two of you weren't exactly acting like a couple of lovebirds. What happened, Lady E? Has Kenny started beating you, too?"

Emma grabbed the sponge from the sink and dabbed at the clean counter. "It's complicated, that's all."

"Not that complicated," Kenny said. "Some people just want to make it seem that way."

Torie looked back and forth between Emma and her brother. "I don't know why, but I'm siding with Lady E on this one."

Kenny slammed down his mug, sloshing coffee all over the counter. "You don't even know what's happening."

"I know that Emma's levelheaded, and you're notoriously screwed up when it comes to women."

"Levelheaded? She let the whole world believe that you're her lesbian lover!"

Torie grinned at Emma. "That was sooo cool."

Kenny grabbed his mug and headed for the door. "I'm taking a shower." Then he stopped to regard Emma with chilly eyes. "Maybe you'd better make your big announcement before I leave. I don't want to deprive Torie of the chance to blame me for this, too."

He was giving her the opening she needed to tell them that she wasn't staying at the ranch but moving to a hotel.

Kenny Traveler screwed up again. I always knew it wouldn't work. The only thing he's ever been good at is swinging a golf club.

She realized she couldn't do it. Her plan to stay at the hotel had seemed sound yesterday on the plane, but now she was in Wynette, where news carried quickly, and she simply couldn't tolerate having Kenny once again held up to public ridicule, especially when she knew he wouldn't defend himself. "Well, the truth is that I've decided to get serious about learning to drive." She turned to Torie. "And since Kenny yelled the only time he rode with me, I'm wondering if you'll give me another lesson."

He leaned against the doorframe and watched her, a wary expression in his eyes as if he were waiting for the other shoe to drop.

"I don't know why you think I'd blame you because Lady E wants to learn to drive, Kenny. Sometimes I believe you have a persecution complex." Torie smiled back at Emma. "How about driving me over to see Father Joseph this afternoon?"

Kenny's attention shifted from Emma to his sister. "Why do you want to see Father Joseph?"

"I don't *want* to see Father Joseph," she replied, clearly exasperated. "I *have* to see him. Haven't you been listening?"

"Apparently not well enough."

"This thing with Dex, is all." She fidgeted.

"The spanking?"

"No, not that! Weren't you paying any attention? Or didn't you hear what he said?" Her chest expanded as she drew a deep breath. "The sonovabitch is making me marry him."

Dex regarded Kenny steadily. "I believe I did mention that."

Torie gazed at her brother, an expression of entreaty on her face that made Emma want to hug her. Torie couldn't quite swallow her pride enough to admit that she'd made a mistake about Dexter. She simply wanted Kenny to understand.

Long seconds ticked by. Torie's hand crept toward Dexter's. He covered it with his palm.

Kenny finally spoke. "Well, I guess you'll have to go along with it, then."

Emma smiled. Kenny wasn't nearly as obtuse about other people's hang-ups as he was about his own.

Torie snuggled a bit closer to Dex, whose serious eyes held a decidedly dreamy expression. She, on the other hand, gave a long-suffering sigh. "I don't know why Dex had to fall in love with me. And I don't know how I'll ever hold up my head in this town again. He's got something like a thirty-two handicap."

"I've already apologized for that, Victoria. If you're willing to work with me, I'm sure we can shave off a few strokes."

"I s'pose. But even then, you'll prob'ly never be much more than a hacker."

"That's true." His lips curved. "And I'm sure I'll spend the rest of my days listening to you complain about sacrificing your reputation to marry me."

"Damn right I will." She gave him a melty, unTorielike smile. Then she seemed to remember her brother was watching and reddened in embarrassment.

Kenny was too much the older brother to let her off scot-free. "So what brought about this change of heart? Other than the spanking."

"Nothing. Nothing, really. It's just—Never mind."

"You might as well tell me," he said. "You know I'll worm it out of you sooner or later."

"Oh, all right. Dex is—he—well, he wants a kid of his own and everything, but he's still . . . he's still willing to take a chance on me." Her voice began to soften. "And if things don't work out—which I already warned him they wouldn't—he said we could adopt."

"I see." Kenny wasn't done needling her. "That's why you're marrying him, then? Because you'll finally get to be a mother?"

Emma watched Torie struggle between her pride and the truth. "Can you blame me? You know how much I want a baby. And he's—I mean, for all his faults, any fool can see that he'll be a good father. Except when it comes to sports, but I figure between you and me, we can make up for his shortcomings in that department. And then there's . . . there's just something about him." She gave an uncomfortable shrug, clearly wanting to put an end to the conversation. "Something sweet and . . . Oh, I don't know."

"Your sister's fallen in love with me," Dex said, in case Kenny had missed the point.

Torie looked up at her brother and scrunched her face in embarrassment. "He's just so damn good. And understanding. And he's funny. Not funny like you and me, but funny in his own strange way. And he likes my emus. I don't know how it happened—God knows I'm embarrassed about it—but I guess there's no figuring the human heart."

Kenny looked thoughtful. "Tell you what, Dex. Why don't just the two of us work on your game by ourselves. Torie's a terrible golf coach. She cusses too much."

Emma knew Dex had been prepared to fight Kenny to the bitter end, but it was obvious by his slow smile that he was glad he didn't have to.

"I'd appreciate that."

As the front door closed behind the two lovebirds, Emma turned to Kenny. He hadn't shaved, and his hair stood up in short tufts on one side where it was beginning to dry. Even so, he was the most beautiful man she'd ever seen, and she had to struggle to conceal the weakness that came over her.

"That was very nice," she said briskly. "You could have made it much more difficult for Torie, but you didn't."

"What did you expect me to do? Lock her in the attic?" He regarded her searchingly. "Changed your mind about moving to a hotel, did you?"

"I simply decided to keep our private business private."

"Good. I'll help you carry your stuff into my room." He turned to the stairs.

"No, thank you," she told his back. "I'm staying where I am while we sort this out."

He stopped on the second step, looked down at her, and sneered a spoiled brat sneer. "Like hell."

It didn't surprise her that he was being difficult about this, since he was difficult about everything that had to do with her. "It's for the best. I don't have any illusion that you'll understand, but I've discovered that I don't seem to possess the proper temperament for uncommitted sex."

"We're *married*."

She fiddled with her wedding band. "Yes, well, that's only a bit of paper. We're not married in our hearts, are we?"

He descended one step and studied her. "I see where this is going. You want to tie me up, don't you, in some needy little slobbering package you can take out and play with when it suits you, then tuck away when it doesn't."

Looking into those bleak, hard features, it was hard to believe this was the same lazy fool she'd met two weeks earlier. She spoke quietly, "You've just described your own motivations, not mine."

"Yeah, right," he scoffed.

"Oh, Kenny . . ." She sighed, threw up a hand, then let it fall to her side. "I can't do this all by myself. You have to help a little."

"I'm not the one locking the bedroom door."

"But sex is all you want from me. Don't you see how that hurts?"

"Even if that were true—which it's not—I don't see what would be so terrible about it. Since we didn't go about this marriage in the regular way, we have to build on our strengths."

"That kind of havey-cavey thinking might work with your old girlfriends, but not with me. Our sexual activities allow us to pretend everything is fine, but we both know it's not."

"Now, see, that's where you're wrong. Everything *is* fine if you just stop and let it be fine. You spend so much time worrying about what's wrong with us that you never stop to consider what's right."

"Sex."

"Is sex all you can think about? How about the fact that we enjoy each other's company, that we like history, and Texas, and riding horses. We enjoy good wine, we both see right through Torie, Petie likes you, and you seem to be able to tolerate my father and Shelby. Neither of us is a snob, and we don't have much patience with hypocrites. I happen to think there's a lot that's right between us."

She'd always focused on their differences instead of their similarities, and she was so taken aback that she didn't realize he'd been edging closer until he touched her elbow with his fingertips. Just like that, her insides turned to pudding.

His fingers skimmed her arm and brushed the outer slope of her breast. Her skin prickled, her limbs felt heavy, and her body urged her to give in to him. Would it be so bad to do it his way? Would it be so bad to go through the outward motions of having a real marriage, even though there was no lasting connection between them? What difference would it make? She reminded herself that she was accustomed to spending her life with emotional leftovers, but she didn't want that from Kenny. More important, she didn't deserve it, and she stepped back.

His arm dropped to his side, and his eyes darkened. She watched his lips thin and knew he was furious, just as she knew he would walk away without saying a word.

Not long after, he left for the practice range, and she forced herself to go to work on the laptop computer she found in his office—an office that, as far as she could tell, only Patrick used. For the rest of the morning and into the early afternoon, she alternated between working on her article about Lady Sarah Thornton and making notes for Penelope Briggs detailing the information she would need to get the spring term off to a smooth start. She stopped when Torie arrived for her driving lesson.

Emma made it into town and back to the ranch without hitting anything. As she carried the laptop out onto the sunporch to resume work, she decided that Torie's happiness was the single bright spot in an otherwise depressing day. Patrick emerged from the kitchen with two glasses of iced tea topped with orange slices.

"The word's out. The International Sports Channel just broadcast your wedding announcement."

She could see that he was worried as he set her glass on the table, then carried his own over to the couch. "What's wrong?"

"Nothing, exactly. I'm probably just being paranoid." He took a sip of tea, then straightened the lamp on the table next to the couch. "The announcement was short, no comment on the fight at the Roustabout, just a brief statement that Kenneth had married a member of the British aristocracy, Lady Emma Wells-Finch, daughter of the fifth Earl of Woodbourne."

"The press was bound to find out sooner or later."

"That's not what worries me." Patrick slid his finger around the rim of his glass. "There wasn't any mention of your occupation, no sense of the type of person you are. The announcement made it sound as though he'd married a flighty piece of Eurotrash."

Emma finally understood why he was upset. "And so the legend of the spoiled playboy golf pro only grows bigger."

"Exactly." Ice tea sloshed over the rim of his glass as he set it down with a thud. "His image has already taken a beating, and this doesn't help. By not making the announcement on his own, it's almost as if he's deliberately shooting himself in the foot. I can just imagine what that bitchy Sturgis Randall is going to say during his show this evening. I'm not even watching."

But neither he nor Emma could resist, and after a dinner at which Kenny remained notably absent, Emma carried their coffee mugs over to the couch while Patrick turned on the television.

Sturgis Randall waited until the end of his program to pounce. *"The fact that his career is on the skids doesn't seem to be bothering golfer Kenny Traveler. Instead, the troubled champion has taken a bride. And no ordinary American girl for our Kenny. Instead, the Texas millionaire, who also happens to be the heir to giant Traveler Computer Systems..."*

"That's not true!" Patrick exclaimed. "He made Warren disinherit him years ago."

"... has chosen a British blueblood, Lady Emma Wells-Finch. That's Wells-Finch, with a hyphen. It seems the beautiful noblewoman is the daughter of the fifth Earl of Woodbourne."

"Beautiful!" Emma was outraged. "I most certainly am not beautiful!"

"In the meantime, Traveler's troubles with the PGA have gotten worse since he was involved in a brutal barroom brawl with an elderly international businessman."

Emma shot up out of her seat. "He's not elderly! And it wasn't a barroom brawl!"

"No official statement yet from acting commissioner Dallas Beaudine." Sturgis gave the cameras a smarmy smile. *"A word of advice, Kenny . . . Since your golfing career doesn't seem to be going anywhere, maybe you and your socialite bride can take up fox hunting."*

Emma couldn't bear it. "How can he get away with that?"

"His ratings are good. In America, that's all that counts." Patrick jabbed at the remote to turn off the television. "Let's go to a movie. We need a diversion."

It was a little after eleven and the lights were still on when Kenny returned to the ranch. He'd practiced all day, then stopped at his father's house to play with Petie for a while. Afterward, he'd parked down by the river so he could nurse his various grudges against Emma for making something difficult out of something simple, but the river wasn't a good place for him. He kept remembering that they'd made love there.

As he let himself into the kitchen, he felt a stab of guilt for leaving her by herself all day. Then he reminded himself that he wasn't the one causing all the commotion in this marriage.

He headed to the refrigerator to see if Patrick had left him anything. As he pulled out a plate of cold chicken, the door that led from the backyard to the sunporch squeaked. He looked up and felt a catch in his throat as Emma walked in.

Her hair was tousled and her cheeks flushed from the breeze that had picked up outside. She looked so pretty, and he wanted her so much. He didn't like the feeling. He didn't like wanting things he couldn't win with big drives, solid irons, and steady nerves.

She started as she saw him. "Oh, I didn't know you were back."

Guilt hit him again, but he determined not to let it get the best of him. "I do happen to live here."

"I'm aware of that."

Her calm response made him feel like a prick. "You want some chicken? There's plenty here."

"I ate earlier."

"Some wine, then. We could take a bottle upstairs."

"No, thank you."

He moved around the counter toward her. He'd hit golf balls until his muscles ached, but he hadn't been able to get her out of his mind.

Now he knew he couldn't keep his hands off her a moment longer. Somehow he had to talk her out of her stubbornness. Or seduce her out of it.

Maybe it was her steady gaze or that inherent sense of dignity she seemed to carry around with her whether she was buying lice shampoo or stealing salt shakers, but he suddenly wasn't so sure he could seduce her.

Patrick came into the kitchen. "Well, well, look who finally remembered where he lives." He waved the piece of paper he held in his hand. "This fax came in earlier. Looks like it's showdown time in Dodge City."

"What are you talking about?"

"It seems that a certain Dallas Fremont Beaudine is requesting the pleasure of your company on the first tee at Windmill Creek Country Club at seven o'clock tomorrow morning."

"Great," Kenny muttered in disgust. "This is just great."

Patrick turned to Emma. "Francesca scribbled a note on the bottom. She'd like you to call her as soon as you get up in the morning."

Kenny slapped down the drumstick he'd just picked up. "So he's back in town. Now, doesn't that just put the icing on the cake."

Patrick folded the fax neatly in half. "If I were you, Kenneth, I'd be very nice to Lady Emma. Who knows what tales she might tell Francesca."

But as Kenny looked across the counter into Emma's solemn eyes, he knew she wouldn't say one bad thing about him to Dallie's wife. And somehow that bothered him more than anything else.

Chapter 23

*T*he morning sun formed a corona behind him, this man whose legend was as big as the Texas sky. Although age had dabbed the temples of his dark blond hair with silver and deepened the brackets around his mouth, it hadn't whittled away at the strength in his tall, lean body or dulled the gleam in those Newman-blue eyes.

A decade earlier, this man and the great Jack Nicklaus had met each other on a course people called the Old Testament and played one of the greatest golf matches in history. On that fateful day Jack Nicklaus had played for the glory of sport, but Dallas Beaudine had played for the heart of the woman he loved . . . and he'd won.

A shoulder injury had temporarily sidelined Dallie, forcing him into the role of acting commissioner, but he was nearly recovered now, his term as commissioner would soon be over, and the senior tour lay ahead of him like a juicy bone waiting to be devoured. First, however, he had some loose ends to tie up. One loose end, in particular.

Morning dew glistened on the toes of Kenny's golf shoes as he stepped off the path and walked toward the first tee at Windmill Creek. His stomach gave a nervous twist as he saw Dallie standing there, even though he told himself he had no reason to be nervous. The two of them had played hundreds of rounds of golf over the years, beginning when Kenny was a teenager with the most expensive equipment money could buy and no idea how to use it. Dallie had taught him everything. No, Kenny shouldn't be nervous, but a film of sweat had broken out on his chest.

He hadn't seen Dallie since the day he'd been suspended, and he hid his sense of betrayal behind a cool nod as he stepped up onto the tee. "Dallie."

"Kenny."

Kenny turned to acknowledge the grizzled Jack Palance look-alike sprawled down on the bench with a red bandanna tied around his forehead and a rubber band holding back his thin salt and pepper ponytail. He was Skeet Cooper, the most famous caddy in golf. Skeet and Dallie had hooked up several decades earlier after a brawl at a Texaco station outside Caddo, Texas, when Dallie'd been a fifteen-year-old runaway and Skeet an ex-con with no future. They'd been together ever since.

"You got a caddy?" Dallie asked.

"He's on his way." Kenny's regular caddy, a wizard named Loomis Crebbs, was carrying Mark Calcavecchia's bag while Kenny was on suspension, and Kenny'd never missed Loomis more than he did right now. Still, he'd found a good substitute.

Clubs rattled behind them. Skeet Cooper rubbed the corner of his mouth with his thumb and rose from the bench. "Looks like Kenny's caddy's here."

Dallie lifted an eyebrow as his son stepped up on the tee carrying Kenny's bag.

Ted smiled. "Sorry I'm late. Mom made me eat breakfast. Then she started fussing with my hair, don't ask me why."

Dallie took the driver Skeet handed him. "Funny you didn't mention that you were going to caddy for Kenny today."

"Must have forgot." Ted smiled and shifted the bag. "I told Skeet."

Dallie shot Skeet an annoyed look that didn't bother Skeet one bit. Kenny gestured toward the tee. "Be my guest. I believe in showing respect for the elderly and the infirm."

Dallie just smiled. Then he walked over to the tee, swung a couple of times to loosen up, and striped a beautiful drive down the center of the fairway. It was the kind of golf shot Dallie'd cut his teeth on.

Kenny tried to quiet his nerves as he approached the tee, but that film of sweat on his chest wasn't drying up. He told himself there was no reason to get all agitated about today's round. Not only did he know every nuance of Dallie's game, but the residual effects of the older man's shoulder injury were going to give Kenny a distinct advantage. Even so, his jitters wouldn't go away because today's match was about something bigger than a round of golf, and both of them knew it.

Kenny stepped up to the tee, adjusted his stance, and hit a nasty duck hook into the left trees.

Dallie shook his head. "I thought we fixed that when you were eighteen."

Kenny couldn't remember the last time he'd hit a shot like that. *A fluke*, he told himself as they walked off the tee and down the fairway, with their caddies following.

"I hear from Francie that you got married," Dallie said.

Kenny nodded.

"Simplest thing for you to do, I s'pose." Dallie chewed the words as if they had a bad taste to them. "Hard for the press to get too riled up about a man defending his bride. Easiest way out."

Kenny had to struggle to keep his voice even. "Only a person who doesn't know Emma could say something like that."

Ted piped up from behind Kenny's shoulder, "That's what I tried to tell him, but he wouldn't listen." He stepped between them. "The thing is, Dad, Lady Emma's a lot like Mom once she gets an idea in her head."

"I doubt that. Your mother refused to marry me until I got my life straightened out. Seems Lady Emma's not that particular."

Kenny didn't like the implied criticism of Emma, and he was getting ready to say so when Ted stumbled over nothing and bumped him hard with his bag. "Sorry. Hey, Dad, how's your shoulder feeling?"

"The shoulder's fine. It's my game that's rusty."

Not all that rusty. Kenny ignored the sight of Dallie's ball lying in the middle of the fairway and concentrated on his slight of Emma. "Maybe I should give you a couple of strokes," he said. "Doesn't seem fair taking advantage of a handicapped senior citizen."

Dallie pointed off to the stand of trees on the left where Kenny's ball rested. "I figure your handicap's going to even out mine."

"What handicap are you talking about?"

"The fact that you're scared shitless."

A chill slithered right down Kenny's spine. He should have known better than to bait a master strategist like Dallie. Still, he couldn't let Dallie intimidate him, and he started to respond only to have Ted bump him with the bag again.

"Will you watch where you're going?"

"Sorry."

And sorry was the word for the way Kenny played for the next nine holes. He missed half the greens and left himself miles from the pin on the ones he hit. Fortunately, Dallie's driving distance and long iron play weren't back to normal, so after nine holes, Kenny was only down by two.

Just as they made the turn for the back nine, a golf cart came clattering up. "Kenny, darling!"

The British accent was less noticeable than the one he'd recently grown used to, but just as familiar. He turned and began to smile, then saw that Francesca Serritella Day Beaudine wasn't alone.

Next to the gorgeous television star sat his very own wife. She was wearing his favorite hat, the straw one with cherries on the brim. They bobbed as the golf cart hit a bump. Both women wore sunglasses. Emma's were her no-nonsense pair with the tortoiseshell frames, while Francesca's were trendy oval wire-rims.

She waved with one hand, while she drove the golf cart with the other. Francesca was one of his favorite people—not only beautiful, but smart, funny, and kind, in her own peculiar fashion. Still, he wished she were anywhere but here. "Emma and I decided to ride along and give the two of you moral support."

As the cart drew closer, he saw that Francesca was wearing some kind of pricey designer outfit, but it was Emma's simple, flower-strewn T-shirt that caught his attention. As he observed the gentle rise and fall of her breasts beneath the bright yellow cotton, he remembered that he hadn't been able to curl his hands around those breasts last night because his new wife insisted on sleeping alone.

He frowned. The last thing he needed while he was struggling through one of the most stressful rounds of golf he'd ever played was to be distracted by Emma's breasts. And he couldn't give Dallie an even bigger psychological advantage by letting him see that the women's appearance had unsettled him, so he forced a smile as he approached their cart.

"Hey, Francie."

"My darling Kenny!" He was enveloped in a cloud of chestnut hair and expensive perfume. "You eloped, you naughty boy. I'll never forgive you." She beamed at him, and then her green cat's eyes flew to her son. "Teddy, you're not wearing a visor. Did you put your sunblock on?"

Kenny had to give Ted credit for only rolling his eyes once. "Yes, ma'am."

She turned her attention to her husband. "Dallie, how's your shoulder? You're not pushing yourself too hard, are you?"

"My shoulder's doin' just fine. I seem to be two holes up on your darlin' Kenny."

"Oh, dear. And I'm certain you're both being quite beastly about it. They are, aren't they, Teddy?"

"Oh, no, ma'am. They're acting like perfect gentlemen. That's the kind of game golf is."

Dallie grinned at his son, and even Kenny had to smile at that one.

Francesca introduced Emma—who seemed to be ignoring Kenny—

to Dallie. He chatted with her for a few moments, then, apparently satisfied with their conversation, turned back to the tee. "Ladies, you're in for a treat today. You're about to see how age and experience can overcome youth and laziness. I believe I'm up."

As Dallie stepped onto the tee, Kenny wanted to wrap his driver right around the sonovabitch's neck. It was one thing for other people to tease him in front of Emma, but he didn't want Dallie doing it.

For the next seven holes, Kenny played as hard as he'd ever played, but his long game wasn't there, and he hit the ball all over the course. Luckily, his putter kept him alive, and, going into seventeen, the match was finally even. His nerves, however, were as jagged as his long game. And the women weren't making it any easier.

After a dozen years of marriage, Francesca still hadn't gotten the hang of even the most rudimentary golf etiquette. Kenny didn't mind the talking so much, although that aggravated him. What really bothered him was that Francesca kept deciding to move her golf cart just as he was getting ready to hit. In all fairness, she moved it when Dallie was getting ready to hit, too, but it didn't seem to bother Dallie. It sure did bother Kenny, though. And the one time he'd politely asked her if she had her cart parked right where she wanted it before he teed up, she'd looked hurt, Emma had given him a glare that could have frozen a swamp, and Dallie'd snapped at him as they walked down the fairway. "You haven't learned a damned thing this past month, have you?"

"I don't know what you're talking about."

"I'm beginning to believe it." He turned away to walk with Skeet, and Kenny rounded on Ted.

"What the hell's he talking about?"

Ted gave him a pitying look, as if he were thirty-three and Kenny twenty-two. "Just what he's been saying for years, is all. That some things are more important than golf."

What kind of answer was that? Kenny was so frustrated he wanted to scream, but he couldn't do that, so he gritted his teeth, grabbed his seven iron, and proceeded to hit his ball five yards over the green.

Emma, in the meantime, continued to ignore him. She smiled at Ted, laughed at one of Dallie's jokes, regarded Skeet warily, and chatted away with Francesca. The few times she looked at Kenny, she had this closed-up expression on her face, as if she'd sealed herself away from him. It made Kenny feel guilty, which made him even madder.

He sweated through another glove, and his shirt was soaked as he pulled his second shot on number eighteen and ended up in heavy rough. He couldn't let Dallie beat him. If that happened, it would be as if everything Dallie believed about him was right, as if, somehow, the suspension could be justified. In all his life, Kenny'd only done one thing really well, and now even that had deserted him.

Dallie's second shot was a perfect lay-up in the middle of the fairway. Kenny wiped the sweat from his eyes with his sleeve and tried to ignore the cattle stampede that had started in his stomach. He had to dig this one out of the rough to get it close to the pin. One great shot. That's what he needed to wipe the smug expression off Dallie's face. One great shot.

Ted handed him his wedge. Kenny took his stance and drew back the club, but as he was about to connect, Emma sneezed. It distracted him just enough that he got too far under the ball, which caught the front of the green and came to a stop a good thirty feet below the pin.

He slammed the club head into the ground, an act of temper he hadn't displayed on the golf course since he was seventeen. Then, Dallie had taken away the abused club, snapped it in half, and shoved it into Kenny's bag. *Guess you won't be needing that club anymore.*

"You got it a little fat," Ted pointed out unnecessarily.

Dallie didn't say a thing.

Francesca asked Emma if she'd steal Patrick's recipe for lemon pound cake. Why wouldn't they go away! Why wouldn't those women take that damn, noisy, rattling golf cart and, even more important, the straw hat with its bobbing cherries, and get out of here!

Kenny threw the wedge back at Ted and marched toward the green. This was Emma's fault! If she hadn't shown up, he'd have been able to pull himself back together. But here she was sucking everything right out of him. Just like his mother used to do.

And then the miracle happened. Dallie's approach shot, which was dead on line, caught a gust of wind that blew it long. The ball ended up nearly as far above the pin as Kenny was below it.

"Well, now, weren't those two sorry excuses for golf shots," Dallie said, as if it didn't matter all that much.

It mattered to Kenny. Each of them had long putts, but Dallie's was tougher, and Kenny had one of the steadiest putting strokes on tour. For the first time since the round had begun, Kenny began to feel some confidence. He was going to make this putt.

Dallie pointed to the small wooden bridge that led to the eighteenth green and reminded Francesca that she couldn't take her cart across. "That's all right," she replied. "Emma and I need to stretch our legs anyway, don't we?"

Emma said nothing, and he wondered if she had any idea what was at stake right now. As she got out of the cart, the gold wedding band he'd slipped on her finger caught the sun. He remembered the expression on her face when they'd spoken their vows, an endearing combination of earnestness and apprehension that had made him want to wrap her in his arms and tell her he wouldn't ever let anything hurt her.

Behind him, the women's sandals tapped on the wooden bridge as they crossed to the green. Kenny heard Francesca explain that it was the last hole, and the men were tied, and after all this time the entire match was coming down to a putting contest, and wasn't golf the most ridiculous game.

He couldn't argue with that. He whipped off his sodden glove and shoved it in his pocket, but even though his shirt was sticking like glue to his skin, he felt his old confidence surge back as he took his putter from Ted and approached the green. Over the years he'd played in more high-pressure rounds than he could count, and he wasn't going to let Dallie psych him out like this.

He glanced at Emma, and when he saw the way she was watching him, a rush of adrenaline shot through his veins. This was the first time she'd seen him play, and, by damn, she wasn't going to watch him lose to a man nearly twenty years his senior.

He finally felt as if he were in control. His stomach quieted, his mind settled, and, right then, he knew he had it. Nothing on earth was going to stop him from making this putt. Dallie Beaudine was about to learn that suspending Kenny Traveler had been the biggest mistake of his life.

He smiled to himself and looked over at Dallie, who had folded his arms over his chest and was studying the position of the two balls, one at the top of the green, one at the bottom, the pin in the center.

Then Dallie grinned. "Let's have ourselves some real fun, Kenny, and leave this match up to the ladies."

Kenny stared at him. "What?"

"Our wives. Let's let them finish up for us."

If Dallie had been speaking Greek, Kenny would have understood him better. "Our wives?"

"Sure." Dallie turned and smiled down at the women, who were standing near a live oak tree. "Francie! Lady Emma! Kenny and I are tied up here. Just to make it interesting, we've decided we're going to let the two of you putt out for us. Nobody's playing behind us, so you can take all the time you need."

Emma's eyes widened, and Kenny exploded. "Bull! We're not doing any such thing!"

The acting PGA commissioner turned to stare at him, his Newman-blue eyes icy. "*I've* decided that we are."

Kenny felt a hitch in his spine, and his stomach, which only moments before had been calm, twisted into another agonizing knot. "You son of a bitch!" he hissed.

Dallie smiled at him pleasantly, then spoke so softly only Kenny could hear. "It might not be a good idea to let your wife see you're upset. Might make her tense, and a sensitive woman can't putt worth a damn if she's nervous. I'm only mentioning this because I've decided we're going to let the two of them settle this whole thing between you and me."

A feeling of dread crept through him. "You can't mean it."

"Oh, I mean it." Dallie's soft words fell over him like a poisonous vapor. "If Emma wins for you, you're back on the tour. But if Francie wins for me, then your vacation just got extended."

"You can't do this!"

"I'm the PGA commissioner. I can do any damn fool thing I please. And you'd better keep your voice down because, if you let Lady Emma find out what's really at stake here, you're not going to have a chance in hell of finishing out the season."

A roaring went through his head like a demonic train. Dimly, he heard Francesca chatter on about a new shampoo, and Emma say something about a conditioner.

"You're crazy! This isn't legal, and it sure as hell's not ethical! I'm going to have my lawyers all over this."

"You do that. Considering how fast our legal system works, it should only take four or five years for you to win your case." Dallie glanced toward the women, smiled, then looked back at Kenny. "You're the one who turned this golf round into a life-and-death match. Isn't that why you sweated through that pretty shirt of yours before we even got to the second tee? I'm just playing your game now, Kenny, except I'm making it interesting enough to keep myself from dying of boredom."

Dallie turned his back to him and, oozing charm with every step, walked over to Emma. "I don't know how familiar you are with golf, Lady Emma, but the object right now is for you to get Kenny's ball into the cup with fewer strokes than it takes Francie to get mine there. I'm sure if you just do your best, Kenny'll be happy."

Kenny's voice was coldly furious as he stepped around Dallie, then turned himself so Emma couldn't hear. "It's not even close to a fair contest. Emma's never held a golf club in her life. Francesca's been around it for years."

Dallie raised one eyebrow. "You've seen Francie play. Everybody in Texas knows she's the worst golfer that ever picked up a club. Seems to me I'm the one at a disadvantage here."

Kenny's fists clenched at his sides. "You're crazy, you know that? The craziest son of a bitch I ever knew."

"That's the way most people make their lives enjoyable, champ. Being a little crazy. I keep waiting for you to try it for yourself."

There it was again! That insistence that he was missing something everyone else understood.

Dallie walked over to Francesca, kissed her nose, and handed her his putter. "I know putting isn't your strong suit, honey, any more than using a driver or hitting an iron, but if you concentrate a little bit, I'm sure you can put that ball right in the cup."

Kenny spun toward Emma. Ted was handing his putter to her—the same putter Kenny'd used to win last year's Players Championship. As she took it, she started nibbling away at her bottom lip with that worried expression on her face that always managed to twist around his heart. Now, however, it just made him feel violent. He forced himself to go over to her. "Just relax, will you?" The words didn't come out in the reassuring way he'd intended, but like a drill sergeant's barked orders.

Emma's teeth sank into her bottom lip. "Kenny, what's going on here?"

She'd gotten real quick on the pickup when it came to his personal business, and he wasn't surprised that she'd figured out something was up. He managed to shrug. "Sonovabitch finished me off when he suspended me. I guess now he's just spitting out the bones."

"You don't want me to do this, do you?"

"I don't have much choice."

"Remember what I told you about female psychology and golf," Dallie called out from the other side of the green.

Kenny tried to take a deep breath, but the air was too thick to penetrate his lungs. "You ever putted a golf ball?" he asked Emma as calmly as he could manage.

"Of course I have."

Relief shot through him. "You have?"

"I played miniature golf several times when I was a teenager."

He winced. A long-ago experience on some two-bit miniature golf course was worse than useless. "That's good, then," he managed. "You know what to do."

On the other side of the green, Dallie was coaching Francesca. "I know it looks far, sweetheart, but it's all downhill, so if you hit the ball too hard, it's going to fly right by the cup."

"I know that," she sniffed. "Really, Dallie, it's a simple matter of physics."

Francesca sidled up to the ball, and Kenny was relieved to see that

she was lined up so crooked she wouldn't come within six feet of th
cup.

Unfortunately, Skeet Cooper had to open his big damn mouth. "Aim
a little more to the left, Francie, or that ball's gonna end up in Tulsa."

Francesca gave him her thousand-watt television star smile, adjusted
her stance, drew back the putter and hit the ball so hard it flew down
the green, past the cup, and nearly hit Kenny's ball on the opposite
fringe.

Teddy groaned. "Mommm . . ."

"Beastly game."

Dallie lifted one eyebrow. "I thought you said it was a simple matter
of physics."

She stood on her tiptoes and planted a kiss on his jaw. "I've never
been good with science."

Francesca's wild putt had given Kenny a reprieve, but, as his gaze
flew back to Emma, he knew the match was far from over. She had
such a death grip on his putter that her knuckles had turned white.
Somehow he had to relax her, but he was so rigid with rage and re-
sentment, he couldn't speak.

Ted moved up next to her. "Let me show you how to hold the club,
Lady Emma." He peeled the putter from her fingers, then repositioned
it in her hand. "You need a firm grip, but not that tight. And the important thing is to stay completely still over the ball. That's the reason
Mom can't putt; she's always moving around. Mainly talking." He
stepped back.

Emma needed a hell of a lot more instruction than that! Kenny strode
toward her. "Since Francesca missed, you don't have to get it in the
cup on your first putt, but you have to get it close. Aim right for the
cup. And hold the club a little lower. Keep your head still. Just do
everything Ted said."

He'd meant to reassure her, but her knuckles grew pale again as she
resumed her death grip on his putter.

Ted shot him an annoyed look, but Kenny had too much at stake to
stand idly back and allow her to screw this up for him. "Move your
arms, but keep everything else completely still. The motion comes from
your shoulders, do you understand? Take the club back and then move
it right through the ball in one smooth motion. Got it?"

Instead of listening to him, her grip grew even tighter as she moved
behind the ball. He realized he'd been thrust into his worst nightmare.
He'd been forced to hand control of his life over to someone else. And
not just anyone, but a domineering woman who professed to love him.
It was his childhood all over again.

His eyes felt gritty as she drew back the club and tapped the ball. It barely rolled four feet before it came to a stop.

"The cup's up there!" he exclaimed. "You're not even close!"

"I didn't want to hit it too hard like Francesca."

He ground his teeth. "Francesca had a downhill putt. Yours is uphill. You *need* to hit an uphill harder."

"Well, you might have told me that first instead of bombarding me with all that other twaddle."

Twaddle!

He realized Dallie was staring at him, and his gaze was even more censorious than before. "Francie, you're away. This time it's uphill. Just try to get it close, okay?"

"Of course, darling."

She lined up all crooked again, and Kenny shot Skeet a lethal look, daring him to intercede. Unfortunately, he'd picked the wrong person to intimidate because it was his own turncoat caddy who betrayed him.

"Move your right foot back, Mom, or you're going to hit it way to the left."

Francesca did as he suggested, then stopped to push a lock of hair back from her face. "If I'd known I was going to play, I'd have brought barrettes. You don't happen to have a barrette, do you, Emma?"

"I don't think so. Let me check my purse."

These women were going to kill him! "Emma doesn't have a barrette!" Kenny snagged Emma's arm as she started to head back to the cart. "I took her last one this morning."

Francesca gave him a snooty look, held back her hair with one hand, grasped the putter with the other, and sent the ball flying up the green.

Kenny caught his breath. She'd hit it way too hard, but by some miracle her line was straight. If the ball caught the back of the cup, it was going to drop. It was going to . . .

The ball clipped the right edge of the cup, and Kenny's heart stopped as he waited for it to fall.

It wobbled, held the edge, then rolled past.

Francesca let out a whoop. "I almost made it! Did you see that? Did you see it, Dallie?"

"I sure did!" Dallie beamed at her. "What do you think, Kenny? About the best putt this woman ever hit. A little strong, but she had the right idea."

Kenny felt sick. Francesca's ball had stopped barely ten inches above the cup. Even she could tap it in from there. If Emma didn't put the ball close on her next putt, she wouldn't have a chance at a tie. And he no longer believed she had it in her to put it close. Her behavior had grown too erratic. He had to do something.

His heart raced. He moved toward Dallie. "I've got an idea for a new contest, Dallie. Francesca and me. I only get one putt, she gets two. What do you say, Francie? You're not even a foot away, and I'm over twenty-five feet. If I don't make my putt, you win."

Francesca shaped her lips into a little girl's pout that was at complete odds with her barracuda brain. "Absolutely not! Emma and I are having fun, aren't we, Emma?"

Emma's complexion had turned green beneath her sunglasses, and he knew she'd figured out that more was at stake here than a simple game of golf. "As a matter of fact, it might be a good idea if Kenny—"

"Oh, no, you don't!" Francesca settled a hand on her slim hip. "Kenny's one of the best putters on the tour. Even from that far away, he'll probably put it in, and then I'll lose. At least I have a chance with you." She pointed one manicured fingernail toward Kenny's ball. "Hit it, Emma."

Kenny squeezed his eyes shut. Francesca was going to sink her putt. But could Emma put hers in in two? Not a chance if she didn't get it close. "Hit it smooth." His jaw was so tightly clenched it ached. "All you have to do is put it up there."

She lined up properly, but the club head wobbled as she took it back. He closed his eyes . . . heard Ted groan . . . opened his eyes . . .

She'd left it short by two and a half feet.

His ball now rested nearly three feet below the cup, while Dallie's was less than a foot above. If both women sank their putts, it would be a tie. But Emma's putt was farther.

"My turn!" Francesca said.

His ball was away, and it wasn't her turn. He waited for someone to correct her, and, when nobody did, started to say something himself only to hold back at the last second. If he said anything, they'd all stare at him as if he'd twisted the head off a kitten. His blood boiled, and he could feel himself beginning to lose what remained of his self-control.

Francesca stepped up. "Do you think I should putt with my sunglasses on or off?" she asked her husband.

Of all the idiotic questions! His entire future was at stake, and Francesca was worried about her sunglasses!

Dallie, however, acted as if her question was perfectly reasonable. "I guess that's up to you. However you feel comfortable."

"Are you going to keep your sunglasses on?" Francesca called across the green to Emma.

Emma turned to him and Kenny felt himself losing it.

"I don't know," she said. "What should I do, Kenny?"

"Don't worry about the fucking sunglasses!"

Francesca frowned at his explosion. "Little pitchers," she said with a pointed look at Ted.

Ted sighed.

Dallie grinned.

Kenny felt as if the top of his head had blown off.

Francesca moved into position. "This is so exciting. I've never won before, and even I can make this. You won't be upset if I win, will you, Emma? I'm not actually very good, but—Oops."

Yes! Kenny could barely contain a whoop of victory as Francesca's putt caught the lip of the cup and rolled past six inches.

"Bloody stupid game!"

Oh, yes! Yes! Now that the pressure was off, even Emma could do this. She had two chances to win this thing for him and only a two-and-a-half-foot putt. His sexy, determined, Emma!

He slipped in front of her, turning his back to the rest of them so no one else could hear. Every one of his senses was fully alert as he willed her to concentrate. "Now listen to me, sweetheart. Pay attention to every word I'm saying. You've only got a two-and-a-half-foot putt, and you have two chances to get it in. You can do this. I want you to line up nice and straight and take that club head back smooth, not like you did last time. I don't want to see any wobble. And hold yourself completely still. Nothing moves except your arms, you understand? Take the putter straight back, then bring it through the ball right toward the hole. Now do you have any questions? Any questions at all?"

She bit her lip and peered up at him from beneath the brim of her straw hat. "Do you love me even a little bit?"

Oh, God. . . . Not now! Not this! Shit! Wasn't this just like a woman! He bit back a stream of expletives and tried to speak reasonably. "We'll talk about it after we're done, all right?"

She shook her head. The cherries bobbed. "I need to talk about it now."

"No, Emma. It doesn't have to be now." His own eyes stared back at him from the reflection in the lenses of her sunglasses, and they looked wild.

She lifted her chin an inch. "Yes. It does."

Blood churned like acid through his veins. "Don't do this to me. Why? Why does it have to be now?"

"I don't know. I only know that it does." Her chin trembled, she slipped off her sunglasses, and he saw that her eyes were dark with pain. His unruly stomach cramped as he watched her try to pull herself together. "Never mind. I'm being foolish. Besides, I already know the answer." She slid her sunglasses into her pocket. "What a goose I've been about all this. I'm in way over my head with you. Of course, you've known that all along. Well, it has to stop." She managed a brisk little smile. "I'll do my best to hit your putt, Kenny. And then I'm getting out of your life."

His stomach . . . it wasn't ever going to be the same. "You're talking stupid. I don't want to hear this."

"Nevertheless, it has to be said. And you of all people should understand. Don't you remember, Kenny?" Once again that heartbreak of a smile, full of strong intent, but wobbly at the corners. The saddest thing he'd ever seen. "Love that has to be earned on the golf course, or anyplace else, for that matter, isn't worth it. Love has to be a free gift or it doesn't have any value at all."

Just like that, she pulled the world out from under his feet.

She stepped around him to line up, and as she gripped the putter, he remembered his father, and Petie, and the Diaper Derby, and the way Emma'd looked when she'd jumped on that Gray Line tour bus. He shivered. All morning he'd been sweating, but now he was chilled right down to his bones. And somehow he knew that, if he let her hit this putt, he would have lost her forever.

The knowledge came to him from someplace deep inside, a small, constricted place where he'd kept so many feelings locked away. Now that place spilled open and he saw that he loved this woman with every breath in his body.

She'd already drawn back the putter, her line was perfect, and his heart shot right up into his throat. *"Emma!"*

The putter wobbled. Stalled. She looked up.

He smiled at her. Or at least he tried. His vision blurred as his life settled into place around him. "The game's over, sweetheart," he said huskily. "We're going home now."

"What?" Dallie shot forward, his eyes glittering. "You can't do that! You heard what I told you. If you walk away, you know exactly what you'll be giving up."

Kenny nodded. "I know. But this is upsetting Emma, and I'm not going to have it." He snatched the putter from her hand and shoved it at Dallie. "I forfeit the match. It's all yours, and you can damn well do whatever you want with it."

Then he wrapped his arm around Emma's shoulders and began to lead her off the green.

"But your putt . . ." she said. "I told you I'd make your putt."

"Shhh . . . it's all right. You don't have to earn my love on any damn golf course, Lady E. It's yours for the asking."

She stopped walking and stared up at him.

He'd just thrown his career out the window, but as he gazed down into that heart-stopper of a face, he knew this woman was worth a thousand careers. And with that knowledge, he finally understood everything that had eluded him for so long. He understood that, each time he'd played eighteen holes, he'd been trying to justify his life, and that he wasn't going to do it anymore. He saw that he was more than a man who knew how to swing a club, that he had a brain, ambition, and some dreams for the future he hadn't even known existed. As he stood there next to the eighteenth green, he finally understood what had been eluding him—that there were a lot of things more important in his life than golf, and the way he loved this woman was at the top of his list.

He ducked beneath the brim of her hat and brushed her lips with a kiss.

Dallie's soft chuckle drifted his way across the green. "Congratulations, champ. I knew you'd get the idea sooner or later. And welcome back to the pro tour."

Kenny barely heard. He was too worried about the fact that Emma wasn't kissing him back.

Chapter 24

As Kenny saw the stricken expression on her face, he realized he was going to have to do some fast taking, but he couldn't do it here, not with the Beaudine family right on his heels. They were too unpredictable, and he had no idea who they'd side with. Besides, the self-satisfied expression on Francesca's face was distracting him. It made him wonder if she was quite as bad with that putter as she'd seemed to be.

"We're getting out of here." He began half pulling, half dragging Emma toward the clubhouse, gripped by a sense of urgency he didn't even try to understand. Normally, he would have gone to the locker room to shower and change. But not today. Today she was going to have to take him sweat and all because he wasn't letting her out of his sight, not until she understood that he loved her, and that they were married for now and forever. Not until she figured out they had a life together that included filling up their ranch house with a whole passel of kids.

The thought of Emma pregnant with his babies was so sweet his damn eyes started filling up with tears. He had to get her out of here right now before he embarrassed himself in front of everybody. Except . . . he'd left his car keys in his locker.

"Listen here, Emma. You stand right there—right by those golf carts, while I get my keys. Don't you move! You understand me?"

She regarded him stonily. "I haven't understood you since the day we met."

It wasn't the most encouraging response, but he risked brushing another kiss over those stiff lips. "Yes, you have, sweetheart. You understand me better than anybody I've ever known." He began backing toward the door. "Please, just stay right there."

He whipped around, rushed into the pro shop without bothering to knock the dirt off his shoes, and raced for the locker room, moving faster than anybody at Windmill Creek, or the entire town of Wynette for that matter, had ever seen him move.

His hands were shaking, and he had trouble with the lock on his locker, but even so he didn't leave her alone more than two minutes. By the time he got back, however, she'd disappeared.

There was only one explanation. The Beaudines had her. Those rotten, perverse Beaudines! The same Beaudines who were coming toward the clubhouse right now from the eighteenth green, with Ted driving the cart, and Dallie and Francesca strolling behind, their arms around each other.

"What did you do with her!" he shouted, even as he realized that she wasn't with them, so they couldn't have done anything with her.

Dallie looked amused, Francesca distressed. "Oh, Kenny, you can't have lost her already."

He spun around and ran toward the parking lot. Emma didn't have a car, and she was in a snit, so she'd decided to walk, that was all. She'd be right out there on the highway, marching along the white line like a drill sergeant, probably picking up litter on the way and God help anybody who spit out the window of his pickup.

He raced down a row of cars toward the entrance, his worry mounting because she was too mad at him to pay one bit of attention where she was going. And he didn't even know why she was mad. Except he did know. He'd been so slippery with her right from the beginning that she didn't trust his feelings for her.

He stopped running when he reached the entrance to the parking lot and looked up and down the highway, but he didn't see anything except an old blue Dodge heading in one direction and a Park Avenue heading the other. Maybe he was wrong, maybe she hadn't come this direction at all. Maybe she'd gone inside the clubhouse and headed for the Wagon Wheel Room to get something cold to drink.

He spun on his heel and ran back across the parking lot, past the Beaudines, and into the club house. But she wasn't in the Wagon Wheel Room. She wasn't anywhere.

Emma leaned against the fence and stared at Torie's emus pecking away at the ground. She was no longer furious; she was simply numb. Once again, Kenny had used her emotions against her. But this would be the last time.

She had no idea what had motivated his display on the eighteenth green; she only knew that she had once again been manipulated. Somehow Kenny had decided to use her as a pawn in his get-even scheme against Dallie Beaudine. Well, she'd finally had enough. She couldn't bear having her emotions spun about in the whirlwind that made up Kenny Traveler's life any longer.

What an idiot she'd been! Like every other woman in history who'd fallen in love with the wrong man, she'd imagined that she could change him, but that wasn't going to happen. And today, with his false declaration of love, he'd finally and forever broken her heart.

One of the larger emus lifted his head to study her. Nothing had ever been more welcome to her than the sight of Shelby and Torie rounding the corner of the clubhouse just as Kenny had disappeared inside. They'd taken one look at her face, thrust her into Torie's BMW, and brought her here.

On the way, they'd picked and prodded at her in their typically American way, demanding that she give up her secrets and tell them everything. She'd evaded them, but when they'd gotten to the Traveler house, they'd started questioning her all over again.

She knew their probing was well-intentioned. In their minds, they couldn't help her if they didn't know what was wrong, but she couldn't tell them. The truth made her seem too pitiful—the dotty, dear thing who'd unwisely fallen in love with a gorgeous, violet-eyed rogue who couldn't commit.

Besides, she understood something about them that Kenny couldn't seem to comprehend. Despite all their protests that they'd never speak to him again because he'd upset her, he was theirs, and they'd do anything for him.

It was Torie who finally seemed to realize how much she needed to be alone, and she'd suggested Emma wander down to the emu pen to see her "critters." Now, as Emma propped her hands on the wooden fence post and gazed at the ungainly birds, she knew it was time to do what she should have done on Sunday. It was time to get on a plane and go home.

Kenny charged through the front door and nearly ran into his father, who was coming down the stairs into the foyer. "Where is she?"

"Where's who?"

"Don't you dare try to hide her! Torie already called and told me she's here."

"I just walked in the door," Warren replied. "I don't know what you're talking about."

"I do." Shelby came into the foyer from the back of the house. As she spotted Warren, she smiled at him like a high school cheerleader looking at the hero of the football team. "I didn't hear you come in."

Even through his distress, Kenny noticed the way the old man's eyes lit up as he gave Shelby a light kiss. "I was just coming out to find you. Where's Petie?"

"On the patio."

Kenny interrupted the love fest. "Somebody'd better tell me where Emma is."

"Let's talk about it on the patio," Shelby said.

"I don't want to go out to the patio. I want—"

"We're your family, Kenny. The only family you have."

The quiet intensity behind her words stopped him in his tracks. He looked back and forth between them and felt rattled. He'd seen those stubborn, worried expressions on their faces before, but he hadn't taken them in, not like he did now. He saw concern there, and caring . . . even from Shelby, his father's too-young bride, who, despite everything, was starting to seem like another sister. And maybe having another sister wasn't the worst thing that could happen to him. He loved Torie and, in his own way, he guessed he was starting to feel the same about Shelby. She sure was a good mother. And she'd made his dad happy.

His father slipped his arm around Shelby's waist, and Kenny felt as if he were staring into a mirror. All his life he'd heard how much he and his old man looked alike, but now he could see it for himself. And as he gazed into that older, but still familiar face, he finally understood exactly how a man could screw things up for somebody he loved, not meaning to, just being stupid.

He drew a deep, shaky breath. He couldn't explain any of this to his father right now, although he'd have to find a way to do it later, so he just nodded and headed for the patio. But when he got there, he discovered he was in for one more shock in a day full of surprises.

"Boys they wanna have fun. Oh, yeah! Boys, they wanna have fun." Torie stood in the middle of the patio swinging Petie around in her arms and singing to him with this smile spread all over her face. Petie was laughing to beat the band while Dex sat on one of the banquettes with a beer in his hand and a grin that stretched from one ear to the other. As Kenny absorbed the change in his sister—the same sister who'd barely been able to look at that little baby boy—he had this crazy urge to kiss Dex smack on the lips, just as Emma'd kissed Torie.

His sister saw him in the doorway and stopped swinging Petie. Petie let out a deep baby-chuckle as he spotted him. Warren and Shelby came out to the patio. His father walked over to the tray of drinks that had been set up, while Shelby sat on the banquette, pulled her knees up to her chest, and watched Kenny with anxious eyes. They were all gathering around to help him straighten out his life. Just yesterday the idea would have driven him insane, but now it was almost comforting.

Petie extended his chubby arms toward his brother and let out a demanding squeal. Torie came forward, her expression as worried as Shelby's. Kenny took the baby, but his eyes remained riveted on his sister. "Where is she?"

"You screwed up bad this time, Kenny. She's really leaving."

"No, she's not," he said stonily.

"She's made her plane reservations. Shelby and I tried to talk her out of it, but you know how she is. What took you so damn long to get here?"

"I was looking all over the place for her, and I didn't get your message until a few minutes ago." He dodged the wet fist the baby was trying to shove in his mouth. "Tell me where she is."

"Inside calling Patrick and asking him to pack up her things," Shelby said from the banquette. "We told her she needed to go back to the ranch first and discuss this with you, but she said there wasn't any need, that even if she tried to talk to you, you'd refuse to talk back."

That stung because he understood exactly what Emma meant. He spun toward the door to go and find her, only to come to a dead halt as he saw that she was already here.

She stared at him without saying a word, and the chill in her eyes went straight to his bloodstream. She was giving him her schoolteacher's stare, a stare that told him, plain as anything, he might not be suspended from the tour any longer, but he'd been suspended from her life.

He realized he'd started to sweat through his golf shirt again. This was one hard-eyed woman. A woman who'd been done wrong by her man a time too many. And all because it had taken him too long to say the words he'd refused to let out of his heart.

"Sweetheart?" His tentative tone made him sound like a wimp, but he was no fool, and he knew she needed to be approached cautiously.

She blinked her eyes, drew back her shoulders, and shot up her chin. "Ah, Kenny." Then she barreled forward, all full of dangerous business, and even though she wasn't carrying her umbrella, he could feel the tip plunging straight into his groin. "I'm delighted you showed up. It saves me having to write a note."

A note? She'd planned to leave him a *note*? He started to fume all over again.

"Patrick's bringing over my things, and I've spoken with Ted. He agreed to drive me to San Antonio,"

That little prick.

"Of course, since you seem to own this town and everybody in it, neither of them will do what I asked, so I've also called a car service. Once I get packed and arrive in San Antonio, I'm catching a short flight to Dallas, and I'll be out of your hair in no time." She brushed her hands together . . . brushing him right out of her life. "That should do it. Sorry things didn't work out. As soon as I get settled, I'll send you my address so we can straighten out any annoying legal business."

And then she stuck out her hand, actually *stuck out her hand* for him to shake.

"Uh-oh."

Emma heard Torie's muttered warning, saw fireworks go off in Kenny's eyes, and realized she'd pushed him too far with the handshake. But she'd been determined to go out with her dignity waving like a Union Jack in the wind.

He thrust Peter into Torie's arms, then his fingers manacled her wrist. "If y'all don't mind excusing us, my wife and I have some business to conduct in private."

He spoke in a menacing drawl, with an extra bite on the word *wife*. She started to dig in her heels, but he was already dragging her toward a gate in the middle of the back wall. Her former friend, the traitorous Dexter O'Conner, rushed ahead of him to open it.

Kenny pulled her into a small, shady garden with a wedge of lawn to one side and a swimming pool just beyond. Then he backed her right against a tree.

"You're not doing this, Emma. I swear to God, I'm not letting you throw away a good solid marriage just because you've got yourself in a snit over the way I've screwed up."

A good, solid marriage? His audacity nearly took her breath away.

"You should know me well enough by now to know I always screw up when it comes to you. And exactly what kind of marriage are we going to have if you decide to run home to England every time that happens? You'd be gone most of the month."

The whirlpool that made up Kenny Traveler was once again trying to suck her into its hazardous depths. But this time she wouldn't go, and instead of attempting to reason with him, she gazed at him stonily. "This discussion is over. We have nothing more to say to each other."

"I know I didn't pick a good time to tell you I loved you," he went on, just as if she hadn't spoken, "but it didn't hit me until today."

That hurt so much she couldn't let it pass. "How bloody convenient! Especially since this sudden revelation managed to get you back on the tour again, didn't it?"

His eyes narrowed, as if he were the wronged party. "Is that what you think? You think I somehow figured out that, if I told you I loved you in front of Dallie, it was going to magically get me back on the tour?"

She regarded him steadily. "That's what happened, isn't it?"

For a moment he simply stared at her, then he erupted. "That's not what happened! I can't read his mind! I didn't know that was all he was waiting to hear from me."

"All!"

"I didn't mean it like that! I only mean—"

With a violent shove, she pushed herself away from him and rushed blindly forward, not thinking about where she was going, just knowing that she'd lost the dignity she'd been trying so hard to maintain, and hating him for it.

"Emma!"

Tears were clouding her vision, tears she couldn't let him see. When had she turned into such a crier? Her weakness made her furious all over, especially when she heard him coming up behind her. "Don't you dare touch me! Don't you ever touch me again!"

He pulled her to a stop and swept her into his arms, up against his sweaty golf shirt. "Listen to me! I love you, Emma! I don't know how to say it any plainer."

She drew strength from her fury and looked him straight in the eye. "Save your breath because I don't love you! I never did! It was all sex."

Something devastating came over his features, something that made her feel ashamed. But she wasn't the guilty party, and her anger, combined with a strong sense of self-preservation, rescued her. She spun away from him.

As she began to march toward the house, she saw that they were all gathering by the gate to watch, these nosy, impossible Texans. And not just Kenny's family. The Beaudines had shown up, too! All of them were—

She was suddenly flying through the air as Kenny picked her up and grabbed her beneath the knees. He began to run. Run! With a full-grown woman in his arms!

The soles of his shoes struck concrete. She felt the muscles in his arms bunch, and then she was flying. Flying through the air as he threw her into the deep end of the Traveler family swimming pool.

The water closed over her head. She sank . . . rose . . . sputtered . . . and blinked her eyes until she could see through the strands of wet hair.

Kenny stared down at her from the side of the pool with the most tragic, stricken look on his face she'd ever seen. As she tried to make sense of it, his body straightened and he dove in after her, shoes and all.

Her own sandals slipped from her toes as she began to tread water, waiting for him to surface.

He came up sputtering and desperate. "I love you!" he cried. "And it doesn't have anything to do with golf, or the tour, or anything except what's inside me! And you love me! It's not just sex. You've got too much integrity for that."

She stared at the inky hair plastered to his head, the water streaming down his gorgeous, tanned face, his dark, spiked lashes, and eyes that smoldered with intensity. "I'm sorry I figured it out at an inconvenient time, but when have I ever done anything conveniently? And I finally do have it figured out. I have all kinds of things figured out." He regarded her searchingly. "I know I'm asking for a lot. The idea of spending the rest of your life with somebody who's been as unstable as me has to be scary, but you've got a lot of grit, and you can do it if you set your mind to it." He paused. "Can't you?"

She was too stunned to speak.

Despite her lack of response, he wasn't giving up, and he continued treading water as he tried to convince her. "I know I might never mean as much to you as that school of yours, but a school can't give you what I can. A school can't give you kids, and a school can't walk along the Pedernales with you in the evening, and a school can't make you laugh." His voice softened, then grew husky. "I can do all those things, Emma, and a lot more. Just give me a chance."

Despite the chill of the pool water, warmth was beginning to spread through her. Why hadn't she remembered that Kenny never did things like other people? That was what made him so infuriating and so wonderful.

The weight of his heavy golf shoes had pulled him lower in the water than she was, but he continued speaking in those urgent, desperate tones. "We're married, sweetheart. The ceremony might have happened in a seedy Vegas chapel, but I didn't take those vows lightly when I was saying them, and I'm not taking them lightly now. If you don't feel married, we'll do it all over again, right here in Wynette, or we can go back to England and get married there, whatever will make you understand that this is real. We're attached to each other now, and that's the way it has to be."

Attached. This man was attached to her.

"I know how much that school means to you. Maybe I can—I don't know—buy it or something. I could take out some loans, pick up more endorsements. We'd have to sell the ranch, but I'm willing to do that if it'll make you happy."

He'd knocked the breath right out of her. He was willing to sell his ranch to buy St. Gert's? She couldn't imagine—couldn't think—but her spirits had begun to fly. At the same time, seeing that desperation in his eyes had become intolerable, and she managed to speak.

"That's the second time you've thrown me in a pool."

He looked devastated. "You were getting ready to walk away for good, and it was the only thing I could think of to do."

"Throw me in the pool?"

He nodded, his expression an endearing combination of anxiety and stubbornness. "I had to."

Only Kenny Traveler, the terror of Wynette, Texas, could try to convince a woman that he loved her by throwing her, fully dressed, into a swimming pool. "Yes, well, you've managed to ruin my very favorite pair of sandals."

He grew still, then said softly, "I'll buy you a hundred more."

Oh, no, he wasn't going to get around her that easily! Not after what he'd put her through. "That's not the point. The point is, I liked those sandals. They were Italian. And you're sinking."

His eyes were still wary. "You got something to say?"

"I certainly do. But I prefer to say it on dry land."

He thought for a moment, then shook his head unhappily. "I'll do anything for you, but I can't let you out of the water until we get this settled. You're still too mad at me, and you might decide to run away again."

"You're sinking," she pointed out again. "It's your shoes," she added.

"Don't you worry about it."

She was getting tired, but she continued to tread. "Very well. In the first place, you will not be selling the ranch. The very idea. And in the second place—"

"What about St. Gert's?"

Even though his gaze hadn't lost any of its seriousness, she thought she detected a spark of hope there. "I have to put St. Gert's behind me."

"You love that old school, sweetheart. Maybe I can find another way to come up with the money. The season's just heating up, and there are some fat purses out there. If I get lucky, I might be able to pull off a couple of big wins."

She could feel herself succumbing to his sweetness, but she wouldn't surrender yet, not until she'd finished stating her position. "I have no intention of letting you buy St. Gert's for me, although I appreciate the offer. I know if I think hard enough I'll come up with another plan."

He immediately looked wary.

"I finally understand that I can't dedicate my entire life to an institution, although I still have to think about the girls." She pushed the wet hair from her eyes. "Moving on to my next point . . . point number two. You'll need to put aside any aversion you might have to a working wife because I love teaching, and I won't give up my profession."

He studied her closely. "Will you give it up long enough to have my babies?"

She could barely resist throwing herself in his arms. "Certainly."

"Then I don't have any objection."

She knew she was making this too easy for him, but the vision of little violet-eyed children so thoroughly entranced her that she could barely pull herself back together. "Point number three . . ." She cleared her throat. "This one's important, so pay attention, please. If at any time—any time!—I feel the need to publicly defend you, I will do so, do you understand?"

He blinked. "Just please don't kill anybody."

She needed something difficult. Something that would be nearly impossible for him to agree to. Just one small something to repay this rogue of a husband for all the upheaval he'd put her through.

And then she knew exactly what it would be.

"Come along, Kenny. We have somewhere to go." As she set out for the side of the pool, she was delighted with how officious she'd made herself sound, but when he caught her ankle and turned her back around, she was disappointed to see that he was smiling instead of gritting his teeth.

"You're determined to have your pound of flesh, aren't you?"

She could no longer repress her own smile. "They were my very favorite sandals."

His grin spread until it seemed to envelop her, too. And his eyes were so full of love that she felt as if she were floating. Then he sobered. "I love you, my sweet Lady E. You know that now, don't you? Please tell me you know it." She heard the urgency behind his words, and she nodded. "And please tell me you still love me."

She nodded again, and he curled her body against him. Groaning, he cupped her chin in one hand. "I've been so damned stupid." He rubbed his thumb over her cheek as if he were memorizing her face, then sealed his mouth over hers.

His kiss was a promise from a man who didn't make promises lightly. It was also a covenant that joined them forever, and she understood that he was giving himself to her in every way he knew how. In his kiss, she tasted all their tomorrows, saw their children, felt his passion and tenderness. She was being offered everything she'd dreamed of having but had given up believing could be hers.

They finally separated, if only to breathe.

"First he half drowns her," Shelby drawled, "then he kisses her. You've got strange ways with women, Kenny."

They both looked up to see that the entire family as well as the Beaudines had gathered around the pool to watch them.

"At least he didn't spank her," Torie said.

Dex wrapped his arm around her shoulders and smiled.

Kenny gazed up at them with a mixture of annoyance and affection, and Emma realized she felt that same blend of emotions herself. They were so nosy, and so caring. Well, she'd always wanted a family, and it seemed she'd finally been given one.

"Would it be asking too much to have a little privacy?" Kenny growled.

"Not a good idea," Torie said. "If we leave you alone with her for much longer, you'll just screw everything up again."

Emma decided it was time to take her stand. "That's quite enough, Torie." With a great deal of reluctance, she detached herself from her husband and headed for the ladder.

"I'm just trying to look out for your best interests, Lady E," Torie said as Emma climbed out onto the deck.

"No, you're not. You're baiting your brother."

Kenny had climbed out behind her, and she shot him a warning glance, reminding him of their agreement. Then she returned her attention to his family.

"I want everyone to listen to me because I only plan to say this once. Kenny is a highly intelligent, extremely talented man. And contrary to public opinion, he is neither spoiled, lazy, nor incompetent. Am I making myself understood?"

They all stared at her. All of them except Dallie Beaudine, who tucked one hand in his pocket and smiled.

"Let me be even clearer," Emma went on. "Kenny and I plan to have children, and I've no intention of allowing them to grow up listening to stories of their father's youthful misdeeds. I am counting on every one of you to make that extremely clear to the good citizens of Wynette. To be more specific, if I hear another story from anyone in this family . . . or in this town . . . about Minnie Mouse cookies, stolen lunch money, school suspensions, miscellaneous property damage, or any other escapade I've yet to learn about, I will make certain that all of those dollars Kenny is pumping into local charities instantly dry up.'' She lifted her hand and snapped her fingers. "Just like that.'' She turned to Kenny, hoping he'd understand that enough was enough, and this simply had to be done. "So I don't recommend any of you testing me on this because I have a great deal of influence with my husband. Isn't that right, Kenny? And he will go along with my judgment on this matter.''

Was she the only one who saw the crinkles of amusement forming around his eyes before he gave his family an apologetic shrug? "I'm sorry. She made me promise that she could defend me whenever she wanted. Who knew it'd go this far?''

Torie's nostrils flared with indignation. "How could you agree to something so lamebrained?''

Emma shot her a warning look.

"She was holding all the cards,'' Kenny replied.

Torie frowned, then sighed. "I'm sorry, Lady E, but this is going to spoil all kinds of fun.''

"That's too bad,'' Emma replied. "You'll simply have to find someone else to be the butt of your jokes because from now on Kenny Traveler is to be treated with respect, both inside and outside this family. *Is that crystal clear?*''

"Yes, ma'am.''

"Yes, ma'am.''

"Yes, ma'am.''

When the chorus finally stopped, she condescended to give them a satisfied nod. "Excellent.''

Shelby leaned toward Torie and whispered, "Just tell me she's not going to make us call him Lord Kenny.''

"Not,'' Emma replied, "as long as you don't upset me.''

They regarded her warily. She turned to Dallie and smiled. "Thank you for looking out for him. We're very much in your debt.''

Behind her, Kenny started to choke.

"My pleasure.'' Dallie's answering smile was as warm as the Texas sun.

She continued addressing him as she pounded Kenny on the back. "I assume you'll be issuing a press release announcing Kenny's return to the tour.''

"First thing tomorrow.''

"Would it be too much to ask if I could have some input into its content?''

Dallie looked at Kenny, who finally had his breath back. "Your wife seems to want to start writing your press releases.''

Kenny looked a little embarrassed, but not too much. "I'll talk to her."

For a moment, she allowed her cheek to rest on his sodden golf shirt. "It won't do you any good. You'll defend everyone in the world except yourself." She turned to the group. "In case the rest of you still don't understand this, Kenny doesn't believe he deserves to be defended. It's because he's still doing penance for his misguided youth." She gazed up at him. "But no longer. Promise me."

"Point number four?" he said.

She nodded.

He smiled. "I'd already made up my mind about that."

As Dallie's gaze returned to Emma, his eyes were filled with respect. "I'll have one of our PR people call you first thing tomorrow. The two of you can work it out on the phone."

"The three of us will work on it," Kenny said. "I have our future children to think about."

Emma smiled up at her husband. "Now," she said softly, "it's time for point number five."

"You're making me nervous."

"That's too bad." Emma locked the door behind her. "Where's that clothesline I bought?"

"Clothesline!" he croaked.

"I may not have to use it. Not if you follow instructions."

He regarded her warily. The first thing she'd done when they got back to the ranch was order him into the shower—by himself!—and announce that she'd meet him when he was done. Now here she was, wrapped in a frilly little white piece of nothing with violets scattered all over it.

He'd pulled on a pair of jeans, but, feeling optimistic, he hadn't bothered with anything else.

She gave him a brilliant smile, happy right down to the tips of her toes. He understood the feeling. This woman was the love of his life, and he wasn't ever going to let her go. That didn't mean, however, he'd allow things to get boring.

"Maybe it's about time you tell me exactly what point number five involves."

"Let me see. . . . How to explain in a way you'll understand. . . ." She tapped her index finger against her front tooth, then smiled brightly. "Nothing to do, I suppose, but come right out with it. I'm dominating, you're submitting."

"You're kidding."

"Oh, no." She walked over to the nightstand, picked up *his* wallet, pulled out some bills, and dangled the money in front of him. "I believe this will take care of your fee for the night." She took her time stuffing the bills into the front pocket of his jeans. Damn, but he was going to enjoy being married to this woman.

"My fee?"

"For following orders. Being my submissive sex object. My hired *escort* for the night." She studied his body, making him feel as if he were being scrutinized for purchase by a very cute wolf. It was a nice feeling. But he didn't want to spoil her fun by giving in too easily, and he managed to glower at her. "Exactly what do you think you're doing?"

"Uhmm . . ." She actually licked her lips. "Deciding which part of you I'm going to feast on first."

Hot blood surged through his body, and his skin got clammy all over again. She knelt on the bed, looped a finger through one of the belt loops of his painfully tight jeans, and tugged. "I pick . . . here." Clasping his hips in her palms, she nuzzled the skin right above his zipper, and, before he knew what was happening, she had him naked and flat on his back, where she began subjecting him to the most exquisite torture he'd ever experienced.

As he fought for sanity, he tried to remember why he'd been so adamant about not letting her take the lead in bed. Just one more way he'd allowed his past to screw up his life. Well, no more. . . .

"I think . . ." he managed, "you're missing a spot."

"It's a lot more than a spot," she said saucily, "and I want to hear you beg."

As it turned out, a whole lot of begging went on in that bed for the rest of the night, and not all of it came from him. Most of it did, though, and he had the time of his life. Point number five, he decided, had a lot going for it.

Toward dawn, they found themselves awake again. "Did you ever imagine it could be like this?" she whispered against his inner arm.

"Not in a million years." He trailed one of her silky curls through his fingers. "I love you so much, baby. More than you can imagine."

"I can imagine," she said. "Because I know how much I love you."

They lay there for a while, petting each other and feeling happy.

"I've been thinking . . ." He smiled against her hair. "With your leadership skills and my talent for rescuing you from embarrassing situations, I do believe we're going to have ourselves a fine life."

"A very fine life." She kissed him. "I insist upon it."

Epilogue

*E*mma opened one of the buttons on the light blue dress shirt Kenny had just finished fastening. "I'm in the mood for point number six."

His hand was warm as it curled around her hip. "Absolutely not. The last time you insisted on point number six I pulled a hamstring."

"Stop exaggerating. You didn't pull a hamstring."

"Just about." He bathed her with the smile he kept in reserve just for her. "Besides, pregnant women have no business messing around with point number six."

One of the very best things about seeing so much of Francesca was having the opportunity to learn from a master, and Emma actually managed a pout. "But I have my heart set on it."

He nibbled at her bottom lip . . . which was one of the very best things about pouting. "You sure?"

"Uhmm . . ."

"All right, then. I s'pose we can let Patrick entertain our guests till we get downstairs."

"Our guests! I forgot!" She leaped away from him and scrambled toward her closet, where she grabbed a loose-fitting coffee-colored sheath. "Goodness, Kenny, they'll be here any minute. This is all your fault. If you hadn't started kissing me . . ."

"Can't seem to avoid it. You and your big belly are about the cutest things I've ever seen."

She grinned at him. She was only three months pregnant, and her belly wasn't big at all. They hadn't even told anyone yet, although they planned to do exactly that during today's Thanksgiving dinner.

She and Kenny had loved keeping this secret to themselves, whispering over it just before they fell asleep at night, discussing names, exchanging secret smiles. Who could have imagined that a handsome rogue like Kenny Traveler could get so much enjoyment from having a pregnant wife?

Her condition had made her emotional, and her eyes misted. She loved being married to him, loved him so much that just watching him walk into a room filled her with pleasure. He was proving to be the very best sort of husband—passionate, loving, and utterly steadfast.

And she was rather proud of herself for being the best sort of wife—at least for him. She knew she was partially responsible for the fact that he had stopped letting the past shape his identity. Now he was the man he should have been all along—someone who was comfortable in his own skin and no longer doing penance for his childhood.

Although he still loved playing the lazy doofus within the family, no one seemed to be fooled. And since their marriage, his popularity with the public had blossomed, thanks in large part to Francesca Beaudine, who'd overlooked her long-standing policy of not interviewing golfers—"the most boring athletes in the world"—on her monthly *Francesca Today* television special.

The interview had taken place on the sunporch at the ranch, with Kenny and Emma sitting on the couch and Francesca elegantly perched in a nearby chair. During the course of the interview, Emma had, among other things, reduced Sturgis Randall to toast. She'd also defended her husband with a humor and vigor that had convinced the American public that Kenny Traveler couldn't be quite as pampered as they thought, not if he'd chosen to marry a down-to-earth scrapper like Emma. It hadn't hurt that Francesca, who at no time during her career had ever pretended at journalistic detachment, also joined in Kenny's defense.

"The most embarrassing interview I ever went through in my life." Kenny'd shuddered afterward to Warren and Dallie. "With the way those two women were going at it, I could hardly get a word in edge-wise. Promise me something, both of you. If Emma ever decides to drag me in front of the cameras like that again, one of you'll just shoot me."

While Dallie had laughed, Warren had pretended sympathy, but Emma knew he was delighted to have his son publicly vindicated.

Unlike Sturgis Randall, Hugh Holroyd had escaped her public censure, but only because Emma had been afraid he'd use St. Gert's to retaliate. At the time of the interview, her continuing worry about the school's future had been the only mark on her happiness. Not long afterward, however, she'd hit upon a new plan of action. After dozens of phone calls, she and Penelope Briggs had managed to put together a consortium of parents, alums, local businesspeople, and miscellaneous Travelers who wanted to buy St. Gert's. Unfortunately, Hugh had discovered Emma was behind the deal and had perversely refused to accept.

Until Kenny had intervened.

Emma fastened her latest gift from her husband around her neck, a breathtaking necklace of delicate gold vines. She smiled to herself as she remembered what had happened at Royal Lytham and St. Annes three months earlier during the British Open.

Playing spectacular golf, plus having an English wife, had made Kenny the most popular of the American players with the British public and press, and just before he'd gone into the final round, he'd asked Warren to put a phone call through to Hugh. Acting on Kenny's instructions, Warren had advised the Duke of Beddington that Kenny would be using his press conference that day to entertain the press with some fascinating stories of his wife's conflict with her former employer. Unless, of course, Hugh decided to behave reasonably.

It had been one thing for Emma to threaten exposure to Lower Tilbey's garden columnist, but CNN was quite another matter. Hugh had agreed to accept the consortium's offer and wash his hands of St. Gert's.

Now, in addition to Emma and Kenny, Shelby Traveler was also a part owner of the old school, a surprise birthday present from Warren for his Anglophile wife. Shelby had become a fierce watchdog for St. Gert's, and, at Emma's suggestion, had ably represented the consortium at the last Founder's Day celebration.

In the months since their marriage, Emma had grown increasingly fond, not only of Shelby, but also of Warren Traveler. In the way of men, he and Kenny didn't talk much about the fact that their relationship had finally healed. Instead, they simply spent time together: on the golf course, riding horses, playing with Peter, or just enjoying Kenny's victories. He was currently one of the leading money winners on the tour, despite the fact that he'd grown increasingly selective about which tournaments he played in because he didn't want to be separated from her.

And that was one of the best things about her substitute teaching job. She had the pleasure of being back in the classroom, but she could also travel with Kenny whenever she wanted. She planned to continue her scholarly writing when she was home with the baby, and she was also developing a series of teacher training workshops to introduce some exciting new methodology in social studies instruction. She'd presented the first workshop last week, and it had been a huge success with Wynette's middle school teachers.

"Come on, sweetheart." He brushed his thumb across the tip of her nose. "The reigning British Open champion needs to be fed."

An hour later, eight of them were gathered around the dining room table to celebrate Emma's first American Thanksgiving and enjoy the platters of food they'd all pitched in to prepare according to Patrick's orders. Peter perched in a high chair between Warren and Shelby, while Torie fed Dexter particularly juicy morsels of turkey breast from her own plate. Patrick refilled serving bowls and fretted about an overly brown crust on one of the pumpkin pies he would be serving when the Beaudine family and Skeet Cooper joined them for dessert.

"She kicked me!" Torie shrieked in midbite. "Dex! Feel!"

Dexter immediately put his hand on Torie's seven-months-pregnant belly, while Shelby rolled her eyes. "Honestly, Torie, you'd think you were the only woman on earth who ever had a baby. That's the fourth time you've made Dex feel your belly since Patrick passed the turkey."

"I don't mind." Dexter leaned close and kissed his beautiful wife's cheek.

Torie kissed him back, then turned to Shelby. "You'd better stop complaining or I'll describe everything I'm doing to get ready for breastfeeding."

They all groaned except Dexter, who looked like a man well-pleased with himself.

Kenny smiled as he remembered his sister's wedding dinner toast to her brand-new husband.

"Here's to you, Dex. My third and final husband, along with being the love of my life. Do you remember that I told you I had a surprise for you today? Well, guess what, you gorgeous geek? You knocked me up!"

There'd been no living with her since then. She strutted when she walked, shoving out her pregnant belly for all the world to see and insisting that everyone, from the truckers who ate at the Roustabout to Patrick's special new friend, Raymond, feel its contours. At the dinner table, she loved nothing more than to share the intimate workings of both her digestive and excretory systems until all of them, even Emma, had begged Dexter to spank her again.

Kenny's eyes drifted to the other end of the table where his wife sat. His own pregnant wife. Her love had made him a better person than he'd ever dreamed he could be. And she finally had all those attachments she'd wanted after years of being alone.

They exchanged one of the secret smiles that stroked his soul. He'd never imagined he could love a woman the way he loved this one. She tilted her head in Torie's direction and lifted one eyebrow.

He understood immediately. They'd planned to share the news about their own baby with the family today, but Torie was having such a wonderful time strutting her stuff that Emma thought they should postpone their announcement and let her hold on to the limelight just a little longer.

He lifted his eyebrow back. *Torie doesn't know how lucky she is to have a sister-in-law like you.*

Her forehead creased. *Will you be awfully disappointed if we wait another week or so?*

He brushed the corner of his mouth. *Maybe we should negotiate with point number six.*

She laughed.

"They're doing it again," Shelby grumbled. "That silent talking."

"I don't know why you're complaining," Torie said. "You and Dad do it, too."

Shelby set down her wine glass. "Which reminds me . . . everybody can see how much you and Dex love each other. Why don't you two do it?"

"I try, but Dex is too literal, and he doesn't understand all the nuances."

Dex was unruffled by her criticism. "I understand the nuances. I just prefer direct communication."

Torie patted her belly and gave a cat-and-canary smile. "Yeah, well, your direct communication is pretty damn good."

All of them laughed, and Kenny thought how lucky he was.

Not long after dinner ended, the Beaudines and Skeet arrived. Ted, who was now gainfully employed in the new company that had formed since the merger, had brought along his girlfriend, an enchanting and sublimely intelligent social worker nearly five years older than he was, which seemed about right.

Everyone insisted they were too full to eat more than a sliver of dessert, then proceeded to devour Patrick's delicious assortment of pecan and pumpkin pies. Torie got out her newest camera and shot an entire roll of film just of Peter. Then they all sprawled around the fireplace, too stuffed to do anything more than enjoy each other's company.

"Guess what the hot new rumor in town is," Patrick said.

Everyone turned to look at him.

"Well . . ." He prolonged the suspense by readjusting a throw pillow. "According to Paulette Cot, who's apparently been the head secretary at Wynette High School for years . . ."

"Since the early sixties," Dallie said.

"Anyway . . ." Patrick fussed with the pillow fringe. "According to Ms. Cot, a certain Kenneth Traveler's permanent record seems to have permanently disappeared."

"No kidding?"

"How'd that happen?"

"Is she sure?"

"That's weird."

There was a long silence. And then every one of them turned toward Emma.

Kenny nearly laughed aloud as she made a great business out of adjusting her necklace. His own public defender. It was embarrassing . . . but wonderful, too.

"I don't know why you're all looking at me." She actually managed to purse her lips, the very picture of offended dignity. "As if I'd do such a thing."

"You'd do it, all right." Torie laughed. "And I've got twenty bucks says you'll figure out how to get your hands on Kenny's checkered college records by this time next year."

Not a single person at the table would take her bet.

Much later, when the guests had left and the house was once again theirs alone, they headed for bed, arms around each other. But they weren't even halfway up the stairs when Kenny stopped to gaze down at his wife. "I want something from you, Lady E. No questions. No arguments."

"Oh, dear . . . that sounds dangerous."

"It's definitely dangerous, but I want you to agree anyway."

She regarded him warily.

He smiled. "I just want you to love me. Like you do right now. But for the rest of our lives."

Her eyes shone. And he knew right then—straight to the bottom of his heart—that his bossy little head mistress would do exactly as he asked.